Husk a novel **Corey Redekop**
ecw press

Published by ECW Press
2120 Queen Street East, Suite 200, Toronto, Ontario, Canada M4E 1E2
416-694-3348 / info@ecwpress.com

LIBRARY AND ARCHIVES CANADA CATALOGUING IN PUBLICATION

Redekop, Corey
Husk : a novel / Corey Redekop.

ISBN: 978-1-77041-032-9
ALSO ISSUED AS: 978-1-77090-265-7 (PDF); 978-1-77090-266-4 (EPUB)

1. Title.

PS8635.E338H88 2012   C813'.6   C2012-902682-4

Editor for the press: Jennifer Hale
Cover design: Dave Gee
Author image: Judd Dowhy
Printing: Trigraphik | LBF   5   4   3   2   1

The publication of *Husk* has been generously supported by the Canada Council for the Arts
which last year invested $20.1 million in writing and publishing throughout Canada, and by
the Ontario Arts Council, an agency of the Government of Ontario. We also acknowledge
the financial support of the Government of Canada through the Canada Book Fund for
our publishing activities, and the contribution of the Government of Ontario through the
Ontario Book Publishing Tax Credit. The marketing of this book was made possible with the
support of the Ontario Media Development Corporation.

PRINTED AND BOUND IN CANADA

For Cathy,
for reasons that should be obvious.

&

For Elda,
who asked me to write a book she would like.

Grandma, please close the book now.

Acknowledgements

My undying gratitude to:

Cathy, the love of my life, the sweetener in my granola, my muse, my amusement, who can make me laugh with a look, and with whom I am more in love every day. Except Thursdays. Those days are just for "me time."

Jen, the greatest editor anyone could wish for, one so fearless and sure she could honestly tell me I had spelled "fuckadeedoo" wrong.

Mom and Dad, for being there time and time again (and again, and once more after that).

Anthonie, for keeping me honest on my word count. Damn you to hell.

Judd, for his photographer's eye.

James Morrow, one of the finest novelists out there, who coined the phrase "tattered ambulatory cadaver" in his wonderful novel *Shambling Towards Hiroshima*, and was kind enough to let me steal it. If you haven't read his Godhead Trilogy, you've missed out on some of the greatest satire of the twentieth century. I feel sorry for you.

Everyone at ECW Press who worked so diligently to get this book into print, a fine troupe of publishing artistes who put up with my rage-saturated demands and nightly bouts of weeping over the phone, and were decent enough to never mention in public that certain incident I'm sure they all remember with great horror and shame. You guys are the best. Hugs!

Mocha, the strangest, spazziest feline on the planet. What kind of cat is afraid to jump?

Every author, actor, and director who brought zombies to life. You filled my head with horrors innumerable, with blood and viscera and unspeakable filth. Weird that I should thank you for that, but there you have it.

Every person who liked *Shelf Monkey* and suggested I keep at this writing thing.

The following is a work of fiction.

Any errors discovered within are purely the result of your fevered imagination.

You really should get that checked out.

I miss breathing.

Sounds stupid, yes. Autonomic system was always there for me. Did the work whether I remembered to inhale or not. Took breaths in and out unfailingly. Never let me down.

Except that one time.

Chug-chug-chugged along no matter where I was, what I was doing. At sporting events (there were a few I recall) my breathing always clicked into overdrive without my having to shift first, supplying copious molecules of oxygen to the blood, organs, muscles, brain.

Something that was always there.

Like sunsets.

Rainbows.

Complex if I ever thought about it, but why would I? Taking things for granted is a core component of the human experience.

Nevertheless, I miss it.

There *are* other things to miss. I know this. Doubtless, people will criticize me for miserably pining for the overrated sensation of thickly carbon-dioxided atmosphere rushing down into my lungs, then up and out again. In and out.

Back and forth.

Lather, rinse, repeat.

So many other things out there to miss. Bodywise, anyway.

Getting a good scratch going? Scraping your keratin against that pesky chigger bite? That's a good one, I give you. Although the itch preceding it is rarely as fun.

Come to think of it, I miss the itch, too.

Blowing my nose. I always enjoyed that. Getting a solid three seconds of blow into a tissue, feeling my insides — for that is what it is, the mucous, the snot, it's all you, tiny chunklets of moist soul, part and parcel of the whole — feeling effluvium flee my sinuses and escape into the warm, dampened confines of an eager two-ply.

Good feeling, that.

Nice sound, too, very unique. People praise the low baritone of a lengthy belch; where's the love for a high tenor nasal evacuation?

Now, no need exists. I tried blowing my nose, once, near the end, just for old-time's sake. Just to feel *something* again. A jellied chunk of matter loosened itself from its perch, clogged the passageway until I had to go in after it.

I didn't try again after that. I can't prove it, but I'm positive I knew how the theory of relativity worked until that happened. Einstein's theorem, vanished forever in a snort, blow, and excuse me.

Sex. They all get to that eventually. The number two question from every interviewer, after the obvious. What about sex. What about erections. What about fucking. What about waking up from a sex dream with a throbbing birddog so engorged it throws off your center of gravity as you bumble your way toward the toilet. Do I miss it? Is my existence even worth the trouble of unbridled continuance without the possibility of bumping very uglies once in a while?

Not really. I can't claim to have ever been a Casanova, but I did okay for myself. A boner is only as good as the blood pressure behind it. That's hardly an issue anymore.

Arousal is an impossibility anyway. I don't see people as objects of desire. It's impossible to.

I can recall a time when the mere glimpse of a bare muscular leg could instill in me bouts of gleeful dizziness. When that velvet cleft of skin between the buttock and the thigh was all I ever wanted. I would bury my face there and know true happiness. I hunted for that spot in every person I met, every actor who walked across a screen, every glistening hunk of pumpflesh that teased me from the glossy safety of the stroke mags I kept in the backyard shed, rolled up in an old paint can, hidden away from the prying eyes of the all-knowing mater Funk.

What did I know.

Men, women, all the same to me now — curves, mounds, arms, legs, aureoles, scrotums, breasts, cunts, pricks. All meat. We are nothing but bone and shit and offal encased in bags of rotting meat. When you make peace with this conclusion, arousal ceases to be an issue.

No, it's breathing that I spend the most time contemplating. I miss breathing in. I miss inhaling particulates of grass and dandelion after I mow my lawn. I miss becoming overwhelmed by second-hand smoke as I enter a bar.

I miss yawning. Good Christ do I miss yawning. Taking an enormous gulp of air, throwing my entire body into the act in a writhing spasm of glorious inhalation. Feeling bones shift and crack as my ribcage expands under the pressure. Getting light-headed as oxygen reserves deplete into the red zone.

I would give anything to experience that sensation just one more time.

Just one tiny yawn.

Lord, but I do miss it.

Shock

"Jesus Christ!"

If I had been more self-aware at the time, more in possession of my faculties, I would have remarked that 'Jesus Christ,' as epithets went, was a touch on the nose.

That's a resurrection joke, by the way.

I was not yet in that frame of mind, however, my ready wit as limp and wilted as fast food lettuce while flash grenades exploded behind my eyelids.

But I will admit that later, upon reflection, I got quite a shame-faced giggle out of it.

I was everything.

I was the vacuum. Eternity. I floated free, one with the macroverse.

No sense of self.

No awareness beyond the ink.

No up.

No down.

No time.

I was all. There was no I. There was only all.

All was all.

Then.

Disruption.

Noise.

Sounds. Far away.

Somewhere, deep in the gray goo, an impulse gathered itself together out of surplus atoms and hurtled over the vast chasm between two thought-deceased neurotransmitters.

A spark formed, gaily glittering in the all.

Starting a process.

Completing a chain.

Commencing a reaction.

Ruining everything.

It was not noise.

There were voices.

Peaceful nonsense syllables in the dark. Easy to ignore. Aural detritus caught in the back eddy of the cosmos, I told myself. I returned to the void, attempted to once more rejoice in absence.

But the damage was done. The veil had been pierced, threads began to snap.

I fell through the big empty.

I became aware.

I did not float. Weight pressed in around me.

I lay on something.

Something hard.

My shoulders were cold. My back was cold.

Accompanying this was simple knowledge.

I have shoulders. I have a back.

Time materialized.

There were events occurring around me. A logical flow of connecting intervals moving forward through the ages.

Three seconds went by. I already had a past. The recollection of chill on my skin from moments before. My birth already a memory.

Here, then gone.

Another sound, closer. The clank of metal. A sense of movement, the blackness sliding away as I drifted forward.

Light. Everywhere, such magnificent light. Rods and cones protested at the intrusion of their slumber, vowed mutiny at this cruelty.

I was grabbed and lifted, my back hauled up off the surface, air rushing to fill the space.

Too much light to focus. Could only stare.

Voices. Indistinct, muddled, a language outside my experience.

The speakers drew closer.

I became cognizant of myself as an entity distinct and individual from the all. Alone, abandoned.

Loneliness washed over me, grotesque, fathomless.

The voices continued, louder now. Words became burdened with purpose. Layers of context draped over vowels and consonants as my synapses slowly organized themselves into battalions, began firing in sequence.

Comprehension.

"*mjkm grimhly slttygh dftll*are we recording?"

"Check."

Light.

"Ho-kay, we have here a Caucasian male, age approximately, what would you say, Jamal?"

"Fortyish? Mid-thirties?"

"Split the diff, approximately thirty-seven years of age, 170 pounds, thereabouts."

Sharp explosions behind the voices, curses, mechanical screams.

"Shit, hold on, forgot to turn off the teevee."

"What's on?"

"Dunno. Van Damme, I think. *Bloodsport*? There, that's better. So, again, thirty-seven, 170."

"What's with his face?"

"Huh. Maybe he's with that group, you know, the bald guys."

"Blue Man?"

"That's the one. What's his name?"

"Uh . . ." Rustling paper, flapping under the dance of fingers. "Unknown."

"Where was he found?"

Bright, bright white light.

5

"Bus washroom."

"Bus station washroom?"

"No, bus. Poor guy collapsed with his pants down while the bus was on the road. Driver only found him when a passenger complained she couldn't get in to take a leak. He was slumped against the door, pants around his ankles."

"Explains why his knees are bent like that. Give me a hand?"

"Sure. Make a wish?"

"Funny. Just push down on his knees, straighten him out."

Wonderful, all-encompassing light.

Crunching. Like footsteps on dried leaves.

"Hard."

"Rigor completely set in. I'd put time of death at between, oh, one and three yesterday morning."

"Why are we getting to him now?"

"Backed up. That pile-up yesterday, took time to sort them all out. So, no name?"

"Nope. No wallet, no bag, nada ID. Says here cops think another passenger may have skipped off with his stuff from his seat, they're checking it out. Coronary you think?"

"Maybe. Could be overdose."

"In a bus john?"

"Why not? I ever tell you, once we got this junkie? Died in a heating vent in a bakery."

"No shit."

"Snuck in from an alley to get warm, we think. Took the time to shoot up, got stuck, and died. Or shot up and died. Hard to tell. He was in there for weeks, the heat baked him hard. Like, gingerbread hard."

"Harsh."

"You want to make the first incision?"

"Sure. Scalp?"

"Do the torso first, you need the practice. Besides, I dibbed skull last time."

A pinprick above my right nipple, followed by smooth tugging across and down my chest. Cutting, slicing, dicing.

An infinitesimal portion of me now devoted itself to pain and its consequences, very aware of a knife edge entering, slicing down, through, but it couldn't define where the sensation originated. Pain in the abstract, far preferable to pain in the actual. Most of my attention was concentrated on the fluorescent wattage that hovered above me. There was only that radiance, glorious, shining down upon me. The voices, they were white noise, easily forgotten in the majesty that was the light.

"Nice cuts."

"Not my first time."

"Grab that."

"Here?"

Sensation. Strong hands on my chest. Nice. Soothing.

"Yeah. Okay, pull up and away."

My skin, suddenly chilled on both sides. Struck me as unusual somehow.

"Ew. Augh."

"Knock it off, it's nothing you haven't seen before. Cut away the fat there, clean it off."

"Everything there?"

"Looks like. Ribs are strong, nothing visibly broken. So, through or under?"

"Listen to your heart."

"Ha. Okay, through. Hand me the Stryker."

"I hate this part."

"What, this?"

Whirring noise. A tendril of smoke floated up and away from below my eyeline. My peripheral vision strengthened, noticed hairlines, hands, arms, moving just outside my focus.

"Yes, that."

"It's just like deboning a chicken."

"When do you think I've ever deboned a chicken?"

"City boy."

The hands pulled back. My chest suddenly felt lighter. A sound, just next to me, like sticks rattling inside a steel drum.

"Well, now I'm off chicken, thanks, Craig. You want a coffee or something? I'm bushed already."

Coffee? I like coffee. Do I like coffee? What's coffee?

"Lightweight. We got a full backlog here."

"They're not going anywhere. And I'd like to be awake for most of the shift. So?"

"No. Yes, yeah, that'd be good. Black."

7

"I'll be back."

"No rush. Turn on the teevee, will you? I like Jean-Claude."

"No accounting for taste." A click, more explosions. Hinges squeaked. Footsteps faded away.

"Let's have that out there, pal."

Hands on my chest again, then gone. Then, snipping, shifting something deep within me. A sucking sound, a boot extracting itself from mud.

Not important.

The light was significant. It fascinated me. Cold light, harsh, unforgiving. I was supposed to move toward it. Full consciousness had not yet returned, but whispers of my past were hissing within my subconscious. A lifetime's worth of televangelists squirmed their way through my medulla, telling me that, when the end came, it was imperative that I run toward the glory of that light. Rush toward it, arms pumping, eyes bulging, heart bursting with the love of the Lord.

Or something.

I was hazy on the details, but forward momentum toward the light was essential for full release to the ethereal plane, I was sure.

Wasn't there supposed to be a choir of angels or something, chanting hallelujahs at my arrival?

"There we go, big boy."

I became determined to get there. I didn't have time to consider my surroundings, or the fact of my lying down, or why I was all of a sudden certain that I was stark nude, my clothing having deserted my body. The *light*, that was the important thing. All other considerations were secondary.

Inner peace, just within reach.

I sat up and took it.

The light was decidedly closer than I had realized. And solid. My forehead smacked against the glass of the bulb, the impact shifting the entire apparatus, the spotlight swinging out on its arm and rudely nudging the man standing next to it.

The man, Craig — full name Craig Neal, medical student and night shift morgue attendant for Toronto General — had his back to me, oblivious, murmuring into a tape recorder while a brightly lit screen sat on the counter, blaring images of carnage. He was a young man for his position, thirtyish, clad in a white lab coat, and was prodding something on the tabletop before him with a pencil.

"Weight is eleven one-half ounces, no immediate signs of stress," he said. The lampshade struck his upper arm and he turned, annoyed. "Fuck, Jamal, don't mess—"

He stopped.

Stared at me.

I stared back. He was lit from behind and above, the glare of the overhead lights combining with my still-adjusting eyes to lend him a facial halo. *Angel?* I thought, and lifted my arms toward him so that he might gather me in his heavenly embrace and absolve me.

Then, "Jesus Christ!" He dropped the recorder, scrambled his hands over the tabletop next to him, yelling vowels, found something shiny, and came at me with a bone saw, hacking at my upraised arms, screaming with unalloyed panic.

There wasn't much choice in the matter. Whatever had just happened, I knew that I was as far from Heaven as I could reasonably expect to be. I tried to yell, but there was no sound. I fought back, grabbing his forearm and wrenching his wrist back, shattering the bone, sending shards of radius and ulna on an outward jaunt through the epidermis. And then he *really* screamed, his voice blending into the chorus of men being struck by the flying feet of a hugely muscular man on the television screen. He jabbed frantically at me with his other hand. His fist thwacked against my side, my face, pawed at my ears, eyes, mouth. His palm slid briefly overtop my teeth, my incisor gouging a crescent trench. My vision clouded over red and I bit down, pulling pork from the meat of his thumb.

Even in his already weakened state, his blows should have caused me some discomfort. The sensation of pain was there yet not there, near enough to notice but far enough away to easily ignore.

But the slapping was annoying, and I pulled my head back from his reach. I took hold of his other arm and snapped it like a bundle of wet sticks, furnishing Craig with a matching pair of splintered appendages. There was no malice in this; it only seemed like the most obvious and natural course to removing an irritant. He shrieked once, brief and wild, and sagged in my arms. I let him go and he dropped, bouncing his skull off the edge of the tabletop on the way down and knocking over a tray, scattering its contents.

Looking at the man, splayed out, blood pooling beneath his head and seeping forth in a festively red, bulbous shape, I confirmed to myself that Heaven was nowhere nearby. Aside from the manic attacks of unidentified assailants, the afterlife wouldn't look so shiny. I expected clouds or white hallways. Here was only metal, everywhere metal. Metal doors in the wall, small ones, three feet square, one stacked atop the other, one open and empty behind me — my previous abode before this one, I realized, but why I should have lived in such a cramped space remained a fuzzy puzzle. Metal light fixtures. Metal tools on the metal side table next to me. Metal under my ass.

Interesting.

This is what I thought.

Interesting. An unexpected turn of events. I took a small dose of pride in myself for behaving so rationally in a situation that clearly called for lunacy. I stroked at my chin, rubbed my scalp.

Time to take stock.

I looked for a mirror. Metal everywhere, but all burnished and dully reflective.

I'd like to point out that I can only ascribe my calmness to some form of shock. What had happened was not yet clear, but my emotions, like my sense of touch, were blunted to such an extent I could only react to stimuli with clinical detachment. I had no memory of anything beyond the room, and only niggles about the strangeness of my place in the cosmos kept me from lying back down and waiting for someone to come in and explain it all to me. I had no past to draw inferences from. All I could function on was instinct. I'd feel bad about Craig later, but I contend that any newborn child, if forcibly ripped from the womb possessing greater mental wherewithal and a sizably stronger physical prowess, would tear the arms off the obstetrician like they were fly's wings after such a sudden and nightmarish transference of self from one reality to another.

I was naked and sitting atop a slab of silver. An electric fan slowly rotated in the corner, sending gusts of sterile air over my face, my shoulders, my ribcage. I thought this odd. There was a sensation of movement around my midsection, a vague yet not entirely unpleasant impression of something flapping in the breeze. I couldn't remember how the human body was put together exactly, but I did intuit that the torso was naturally a more solid object, not prone to fluttering.

A quick glance downward.

Followed by a prolonged stare.

Shouldn't there be more down there? I thought.

Two deep incisions had been made, one from each shoulder. They descended toward my sternum, meeting up above my ribcage and merging into a single slice that continued downward, splitting horizontal just past the navel. The musculature of my chest and torso had been peeled back and away, exposing all points beneath. My hide hung loosely open in two ragged wings, shivering whenever the fan oscillated in their direction.

I expected ribs, muscles, connecting beams of bone and sinew, *something*, but where once there had been situated a bloody xylophone there was only empty space. The bones had been cut clean through, I noted, and the majority of my ribcage had been removed.

I was inside out. I was being autopsied. I had woken during my own dissection, rudely interrupting the accepted procedure for a postmortem.

This is when panic set in, raw and volatile. I tried to scream, to tear the walls down with my fear. My jaw cracked as the full force of horror unimaginable issued forth.

Nothing.

Not a peep.

I sat there, straining, my mouth yawning wide. The panic abated, replaced by vexation.

I tried again, baring my teeth, thrashing my tongue about, whipping my head to and fro.

I should be able to do this. This shouldn't be hard.

Nothing.

It was hopeless. I gave up for the time being, reminding myself to fully collapse in abject terror when I could better do so.

I gave my chest hole a closer survey, maneuvering myself on the table so that more light could flood the area. I experimentally poked a finger into the cavity, craning my head forward. Two brownish sacks dangled limply inside like distended plums hanging from a branch. Abnormally large plums. Lungs, I decided. By the looks of them, they were rather depleted of air, a piece of information that rankled me. I watched, but there was no movement. Behind them, the bumps and nodules of my spinal column protruded from the inner meat of my back. A few of my sweetmeats were directly beneath the lungs, tucked away within coils of sausage that threatened to unspool.

I straightened up, and the intestines sloshed back into the base of my new orifice. I pushed them back further, earning myself a sensation not many have experienced, the impression of being prodded from the inside. My bowels squished comfortably down toward my pelvis, and I gave them a little extra squeeze to keep them in place. A kidney threatened to slip out, but I forced it back between a few ropes of innards to keep it still. There were more important things to attend to than an errant refugee from a butcher's window.

My heart, for example. I was pretty sure it wasn't where it was supposed to be. I felt around my lungs at the area I approximated the heart should be, then widened the search to the entirety of the hollow, digging my hands into the morass of me. While the majority of my circulatory system seemed to still be in place — later research would prove this correct; if nothing else, my circumstances have forced me to become relatively conversant on human anatomy — the heart was most definitely absent.

I chewed this over, but a haze of perplexity clouded every thought. There was no how, or why, or where, or what that I could form a coherent thought around. There was only me, the room, and a body on the floor, to which I had contributed a large degree of mangling. The body was apparently still alive, as an occasional moan escaped from its lips. I took in a breath to clear my head. Correction: I tried to take in a breath. The mechanics of the task had become lost to me, and I sat, mouth open, awaiting the occurrence of a natural process that was plainly not going to occur. I tried to call to mind the actions required to inhale, trying to work the muscles. I pushed my chest out in imitation, hoping to jar a reflex memory, but gave it up when I remembered that there was barely half a chest left. I looked at the lungs, flattened and useless at the end of my trachea. I extended a finger and poked at the right sac. The side dented inward and moisture seeped out of the membrane, a sponge releasing its watery contents to the world. I pushed harder, and felt a tiny bubble of air rise slightly into my throat. I grabbed both lungs and gently gave them each a squeeze, taking care not to puncture the meat with my fingers. I noted the sensation of the muscles, the diaphragm, trying to gain back my control over it. Gradually, as I re-acclimatized myself to the exercise, a miniscule flow of air traveled slowly up my throat and out past my teeth. I let go, and worked at reversing the flow. Soon, I had the sacs working at capacity, inflating and deflating for all to see. When I shifted my attention to other matters (i.e., the missing heart), however, the bags deflated, refusing to continue the rhythm on their own. Nevertheless, I continued to function. I tabled the breathing versus not breathing conundrum for a later discussion, as I had finally laid eyes on my dismembered remains.

My heart — I thought it was my heart, anyway; I was fairly certain that the misshapen piece of meat was my ticker — lay on the floor, a few feet from Craig's legs. Nearby lay several mucous-soaked pieces of bone, which I surmised were my rib trimmings. Looking down, I noticed the slab I sat on was wheeled at the legs. It was a gurney. One of several placed about the room, two of which were topped by large black bags filled, no doubt, by other drowsing gentlemen of the naked sort. They didn't appear to be as mobile as I was, but perhaps in time they'd rise up and help me figure out my situation. Until then, my unwillingly segmented sections were of primary importance. The word *morgue* finally began to dance about in my mind, but I shoved it aside as needless ephemera to the task at hand. It was stupid, but I felt it was of vital importance that my heart be placed back within my body.

My blood pump, seeping slime, had slid across the floor and come to rest against the wall, leaving streaks of ocher in its wake. Craig had knocked it off the table in his mad scramble to defend his under-standing of the way the universe operated. I stared at it as comprehen-sion finally took a pickax to the wall of my mind and began hacking out a doorway. My heart, my engine, my valentine lay across the room from me, immobile, unloved, separate and apart from its warm housing, finally experiencing the world on its own.

It did not look happy. It looked . . . violated. Its ventricles had been sliced open, its aorta gaping open to the re-circulated air. It wasn't meant to be outside. It had been weighed and measured, raped, and tossed aside to fester in the cold, cruel world.

This would not stand.

I swung my legs over the side of the gurney and cautiously slid myself off, taking care to cross my arms over my hollow and keep its residents from joining their leader on the floor. I placed my gray feet firmly on the tile. My lungs swayed and bumped against the inside of my arm at the movement. Standing, I took a step, and my upper half swayed back as a willow in a breeze. My spine was intact, but the absence of ribs threw off the stability of the entire structure. I tee-tered wildly at the waist, leaning forward and feeling the remnants of my ribs reach forward, trying to reunite with their opposite fellows. I flailed my arms out for balance, releasing my internal cargo to the grip of gravity. I grabbed at another gurney, toppling it, flipping its black bag off. The zipper had been opened, and the recently breathing resident slipped out and collided with the linoleum with a *splorching* sound. I had a brief, abstract instance of regret; he was a companion to me now, a bosom compadre in the *hey what happened to my life* club. My floor buddy did not look peaceful in death. Whatever had happened had not been pleasant; there were jagged holes in his chest and his nose had been sheared almost clean off. Any peace death might have provided was now disguised under a pile of innards that had fallen atop him from my frantic attempts to regain balance.

I watched my intestines unreel themselves and drape the body in glop. My spleen drooped over the edge of the incision, trying to permanently depart my corpse and fulfill its organ donor obligations. One kidney made a break for it; there was a mildly pleasurable irritation as it stretched its tether, like picking a scab, before it snapped and flew free. It bounced off the man's chest and slid quickly to a stop near Craig's head. My spleen tugged at its imprisoning ligaments, and I enjoyed the unpleasant sensation of being torn in pieces from the inside out. The rest of my organ population deigned to stay where they were, but their connecting tissues were only so strong. Further defections were imminent without action.

I took handfuls of viscera and shoved them back inside, unheeding as to proper placement. It seemed important that they be inside me, whether they fulfilled any functions or not. The kidney I decided to leave, I had a spare somewhere. I pushed the entire mass deep inside me, packing it tight with a few good punches. I teetered my way over to my heart and scooped it up, placing it back where I approximated it usually resided. It rested there for a moment between the weight of my lungs, shifted, and thumped back to the floor.

The room was seriously losing its luster of hygienic sterility. I retrieved my heart a second time, forced it deep within my entrails. *Fix it later.* Folding the flaps of skin down across my chest, I crossed my arms to keep the entirety from spurting back out and looked for something to fix the mess in place. If this *was* a morgue, there had to be something around for patching a torso back together.

What kind of hospital doesn't have at least one roll of tape lying around? Duct tape, string, anything. A stapler? I rummaged through cabinets until I found a roll of tensor bandages and clumsily wound the elastic cloth tightly around my abdomen. Tying it firm, and feeling more in control of myself, I took a moment to weigh my options.

One: stay put. Jamal would undoubtedly be back soon, bringing coffee. I could explain that there had been some sort of horrible mistake, and I was plainly alive — mysteriously so, very strangely so, but alive all the same. Craig was an accident, an understandable reaction to an unprovoked attack. Yes, the man looked bad, but science could repair his limbs. What was important here was that a serious error had occurred, and luckily I was little worse for wear. I couldn't remember the particulars of my identity, but that was a nevermind, it would come back. I could already feel the inklings of personality swimming back toward my shore.

Flaws with option one: I had no voice with which to explain myself. The man in the white lab coat lying in his own personal bloodslick displayed external signs of forced trauma, and I was the only other mobile inhabitant of the room. And I was carved up like a Christmas turkey. A sure bet Jamal would react poorly, and I couldn't be sure I wouldn't behave in the same fashion as before.

Option two: flee. Head for the hills, or even better, home. Get myself in a controlled environment. Take the time to sort out everything.

Flaws: I was naked. Falling apart. And not sure where home was.

A whistling from outside. Footsteps. Not good. I looked around for some place to hide, but the room was in a shambles, and I had seconds at best.

The door began to push in.

I ripped my bandages off and collapsed to the floor.

"Craig, I got doughnuts, you want?" Jamal asked, pushing the door open with his back as he carried coffees and snacks inside. "Sorry it took so long, couldn't believe the lineup. It's three in the morning, you believe that?" He turned around slowly, balancing the coffees and asking about preference, chocolate or sprinkles, when the chaos of the room hit him.

"Holy jeez," he whispered, and stepped forward, stumbling over my outstretched arm. He looked down, and a squeak of fear popped from his lips. I kept still, staring at a spot on the far wall. "What the fuck . . ." He took another step and saw Craig on the floor, his arms bent at unusual angles. For a few moments Jamal spun slowly about, holding the Styrofoam cups and bag of pastries in front of him, his eyes bulging as he took note of the blood, the bodies, *my* body, open for inspection. Tiny puffs of air rushed from between his teeth.

"Heh . . . huh . . . heh . . . huh . . ."

Down on the linoleum, peripherally observing Jamal undergo mindfuck meltdown, I decided to speed this along. My foot was near a cart; I shot my leg out, catching the wheel and pushing it into Jamal's hip.

That got things moving.

Jamal screamed, coffee and pastries soaring into the air as he bolted, tripping over my arms and flying into the door. It swung open, depositing him into the hallway. He scrambled to his feet and ran, yelling for the guard, a nurse, police, anyone. I quickly lumbered upright, reinserted my gizzards, grabbed the bandages and tottered out the door, moving in the opposite direction of Jamal's wailings. My knees refused to rise, my gait a reeling lurch that sent me careening into walls as I fought for balance and tried to keep my folds shut.

I turned a corner into a corridor lined with doors. There was an exit sign at the end of the hall. I peeked into the first open doorway. Bins of soiled towels and hospital gowns. Laundry. I dug into the first container, finding a towel that I wrapped around my chest, binding it with the bandages for added containment. Then, real luck, clothing. Scrubs. Blotted with blood, but actual clothing. I pulled a lab coat on, then leaned against a wall and forced my knees to obey my will and bend appropriately as I struggled into a pair of light blue pants. No shoes, but there was a pile of used paper surgical booties near the door.

I slipped on a pair, and poked my head back out. No people in sight, but definite sounds of panic and dismay wafted down the hall.

For the briefest of instants, I contemplated staying put. Take off the clothes — or don't, add an extra blanket of mystery to the night's proceedings — and lie down in the hallway. Let them find me. Stay still. They'd never believe Craig, if indeed he lived. They'd attribute his ravings of a corpse attack to shock and medicate him for weeks. They'd finish up the examination, weigh my components, stuff me full to bursting with sawdust and formaldehyde.

Bury me, let me rot.

What was happening was clearly not of the norm. I shouldn't be. Couldn't be.

A brief impulse.

Maybe, given hindsight, the correct one.

But as freaked out as I was becoming, I still felt that there was a rational explanation for everything. We talk of the supernatural, we may want to believe in guiding forces outside our realms of perception, we may even pay fealty to the gods of our parents and purposefully seek salvation in the nebulous ether of the limbo beyond, but when we reach the nucleus of our being all we really want is someone to tell us in the soothing tones of a learned professor that everything that is happening is perfectly natural.

Unusual, oh yes, definitely, but not unheard of, and most certainly not incomprehensible. Just . . . odd.

That was my lifeline.

I could figure this out. This was solvable.

But not now, no. Not like this. Not with nurses and doctors and security guards and police officers aplenty rushing in with guns drawn to gawk at the charnel house I had created.

So flee it was, then. As calmly as I could, I left the room and trod stiffly down the hall toward the exit. Just another doctor, lurching his way outside for a smoke. Behind me, faint sounds of footsteps, drawing closer. Exclamations. The sounds of gagging.

And then I was outside, clad in thin cotton garments in subzero temperatures. Snow and wind battered me, pushing me across the ice rink of a parking lot. I fought to stay upright, crossing my arms tightly to keep my insides inside. My thin coat flapped behind me like a cape as I shambled past the parked cars and escaped the lot.

I had not a clue where to run, but wisps of memories were blowing through the corners of my mind. I had been in this location before. An attack of appendicitis had allowed me two full days of rest and relaxation in one of the upper rooms, accompanied the entire time by my roommate, a triple-coronary who wheezed constantly and told the most racist jokes I had ever heard. The brain of my new birth did not have this memory, not yet, but there was the familiarity of the building, accompanied by a sense of direction.

North. Thataways and parts beyond.

I stumbled forward into the blizzard, walking to the street. After hobble-sprinting across the lanes, I entered a carpark and blundered through to the streets beyond. If my internal GPS was working, some miles north was a copse of tenement buildings and low-rent housing complexes.

Somewhere in that labyrinth was home.

Safety.

The cold ate through the coat, freezing the water in my skin, but there was no pain, only discomfort most meager. I shushed through the rising white, my only witnesses the occasional passing car wafting plumes of snow over me. My booties fell apart in the drifts, and I could feel myself slowing. My joints began to seize, tighten, refuse. I stiff-walked the final two blocks.

Home.

My brain had been numbed to only the basest of primal urges, but it recognized shelter. The door was locked, sense memory leading my fingers to the flap of loose siding and the poorly hidden key that I had lodged behind for emergencies.

A few agonizing minutes later, my fingers stiff branches, barely able to keep the key steady and guiding it into the keyhole more by luck than skill, the door swung open and the warmth of the womb issued forth. I reeled inside, shoving the door shut with my shoulder, fell to the carpet, and slept.

Here's what I *am* sure of.

Whatever this is, whatever force has taken command over the natural process of life that I used to enjoy, it does not adhere to any logical permutation of the way life is supposed to subsist on this level of existence. Which could mean that my condition is extraterrestrial in nature.

Or supernatural.

Or ultradimensional.

Or something.

See the problem?

It's hard to define what something is when it's the only example of its kind. All I can do is compare myself to an existing standard of reality. No one realizes that, while I do indeed exist in physical form on this material plane, I cannot be expected to adhere to *all* the immutable laws that pertain to this reality.

For example, blood.

I have no need for it.

Which implies I have no need for oxygen. My body is able to function quite effectively without it. When I'm not paying attention, I can go days without a whisper of air entering my lungs.

Granted, similarities do exist. I need to eat to continue as a functional being. However, if a human, or any member of the animal kingdom, ceases to eat, that creature will invariably die, and fairly quickly. If I do not eat, I do not die.

If I forego food, I begin to rot.

I mean, rot more.

Rot faster.

There was no sleep.

I lay on the floor in a coat of hoar, melting in the warmth and soaking the carpet. I was a tangle of limbs and bafflement, prone on my back. Arms crushed underneath in a position, to the outside observer, of agonizing awkwardness. But there was no moving me, not yet. My limbs were dead, flash-frozen, freeze-dried. I had no inclination to revive them.

Slumber was what my rime-encrusted brain craved. Dreamless dark for hours, a break in the confusion of the past few lifetimes. It *was* dark, but the streetlamps lit up my foyer through the decorative glass bricking around the doorway. Distorted shadow puppets from the fir trees that lined the house played their monster fingers about the walls. I could make out the hall closet, the hanging photos of a person I recognized as myself in a tropical paradise, a trip with some high school buds I had taken years back.

Why was I seeing this? Was I dreaming, so weary my mind couldn't be bothered to come up with dreamscapes of a more fantastical nature?

No, my eyes were wide open. Very wide, I noted. Oddly rigid. Immobile. My eyelids rebuffed my best efforts to blink. My surroundings, déjà-vu familiar, were fogged and distorted. Silently groaning with the effort, I raised an arm and wiped the back of my hand across my face. A film of ice varnished my eyes, I realized, my lids now held forcibly ajar by chilled glazing. I prodded around the sockets and was not rewarded with the satisfying squish of optic fluids being forced against the walls of their confinement.

What I felt was irregular hardness.

I tapped my pupil with my fingernail and heard an icy *clink* that I felt in the hollow recesses of my skull.

My eyeballs had frozen solid.

My head was an ice tray.

I was a meat popsicle.

This can't be good.

I lay still, contemplating. Either I would thaw out or I wouldn't. Not yet willing to move — *What if more of me is frozen? Will my legs snap off if I stand?* — I waited for my head and body to soften, and set my mind to the situation at hand.

First, I was suffering from a bout of amnesia, one already showing signs of retreat. I remembered Jamaica, the Caribbean locale of the photos lining the walls above me. That was me, and . . . Raj and Boone, two chums I had not seen in years apart from occasional holiday emails and nonsensical Facebook updates.

I remembered Facebook. Weird that I could remember that and not my own name.

No matter. Soon, I was positive, the river of memories would crest the levies of my forgetfulness and come flooding back, destroying all fortifications in its path.

Second, let's admit the obvious: I was dead. Stiff, corpsified, worm meat. No aerial bombardment of scatterbrain-bombs could wipe that fact from my mind. Whether in command of one's wits or nay, one was never, *never* supposed to be able to remove his heart and have time afterward to contemplate said excavation. It simply wasn't done, and if it was, never more than once.

It was too much, too soon. If my heart had been attached and functional, it would have been thumping in near-panic mode. Better to concentrate on the immediate problems at hand, the whos and the whats, and worry about the whys and hows later on.

So. Who?

I had found my way home, so there was some positive indication of a retained cache of information within my presumably still-operating brain. It stood to reason that there would be things at hand that could crack the whole thing open like an egg, let the omega-3s of my past gush forth. Photo albums, journals, home movies. I prayed that I was a compulsive note-taker — it would make things much easier.

After a time of immobile self-scrutiny, my body had defrosted to a point where I could sense the heat of the room. And something more. There was an extra weight on my legs. I had been staring at the ceiling, watching as the ice melted and the room solidified into focus, taking in the flowery tiles that bordered the upper walls — whatever else I could remember, I was positive that I had never liked that pattern, a repeating rose-and-leaf motif that would have induced nausea if I still retained the ability to vomit — when I noted the mass draped over my thighs. I raised my legs slightly at the knees, just a tremor of movement. The weight shifted, rotated, and slowly made its way up toward the sternum.

Risking a snapped vertebra, I bent my neck and looked down toward my feet. Two yellow-green marbles stared back at me in the dark, regarding me with supreme indifference.

A cat.

An obscenely large calico cat, vastly overfed, placid, and very okay with my new state of non-being. It seemed to know me, as it casually trod up over my chest (sinking slightly as the bandages stretched inward under its tonnage) and began licking at my nose and forehead.

Its collar tag banged against my face as it stretched up to tongue the moisture from my hair. It then wandered back down and curled up in the depression of my chest, staring at me, awaiting . . . what? I cautiously wiggled my fingers, and hearing no cracks of frozen bone, I lifted my arm and stroked the cat across its back, earning a gratifying purr in response. I took the collar in my fingers. My eyes were able to shift and focus now, and I took a look at the metal tag. The inscription read *Sofa*.

Sofa. Sofa the cat.

A trapdoor sprung open and a few boxes thumped out. I had picked her out at the cat shelter with a boy. Zane something, Fabbrizio or Fazzio, Italian probably. He volunteered with the SPCA. Zane had this gorgeous vein in his neck that throbbed and bounced when he was excited. I wanted Zane in the worst way, yearned to suck that vein up to the surface and gorge on his skin until I was full. Eager to find common ground to build a tryst on, I had agreed to foster a cat when the shelter got too full. I picked out a bright and feisty kitten named Sofia, and the way Zane cooed and gasped at the fuzzy little bundle, I felt a bout of mutually satisfying fellatio was imminent. Sadly, there was no forthcoming fucking: Zane was uninterested in local strange, soon splitting to Edmonton with a rough trick named Jeffrey. The cat stayed with me. The city had misread her license application, and the tag had come back *Sofa*. By then, the cat had already begun to pack on the pounds, and somehow the name fit. So Sofa it was.

Sofa, I mouthed. I remember you, cat. And she, me, I thought, unless she was indiscriminate in her affections.

Sofa gave my neck a final sandpapering and gracefully galumphed her vast bulk off my torso. She waddled down the hallway and entered the room beyond.

I'd likely been gone for a while. The enormous feline must be hungry. I slowly rolled over and heaved myself to my feet. My joints cracked, and flakes of wet snow and ice fell about. Sofa poked her head back in and gave a contemptuous meow. Plainly, my absence had been noted, and dinner had best be served with utmost haste lest I risk her wrath that, from the size of her, could be deadly. To anyone bound by the corporeal definition of the term, of course.

I shuffled into the room and fumbled for a light switch. The sudden illumination blinded me, my eyes still slightly refrigerated, slowing dilation. As the glare receded, I could make out the aqua-blue Formica countertops and mechanical doodads that signaled a kitchen.

Sofa pawed at a door next to the refrigerator, loudly protesting my sluggishness. I walked over and opened it, finding a sparsely occupied pantry. I was apparently not much for cooking. I didn't suppose that would be much of a hindrance anymore. Did I even eat? An open bag of dry cat food was on the bottom shelf, and Sofa immediately plunged her head inside and began contentedly munching. I left her to it and looked for her dish, which lay empty near the doorway. I filled her water bowl at the sink and placed it back down. She was famished, but she'd get to the water when she wanted it.

Leaving the kitchen, I wandered through the house, turning on lights as I went, step by step re-opening my brain and topping up my remembrance depository.

Bedroom. Quite likely mine, blankets jumbled in heaps over the queen-size. Nothing triggered. I switched off the light and moved on.

Bathroom, messy. Toothpaste muddied the faucets, soap stains dulled the shower tiles.

Closet, disorganized. Medicine and towels fought for dominance.

Another bedroom, this one more ancient, not used for some time. Furniture older, all polished wood and curved legs. Thick white carpet. A faded photograph, framed, placed on the end table; two people, posed and artistically blurred, Sears quality. A room of absent parents.

My father was dead.

An impersonal memory, no emotional impact yet. Workplace accident when I was child. Fell off a ladder as he was replacing a light bulb. Quick concussion, coma, *pfft!* I didn't think he was in janitorial services, though. Something whiter in the collar, something that added just the right touch of crass humor to his mode of exit from this plane of existence. Something in government. A civil servant or something. Accountant, maybe.

24

A joke rang through my head, chanted by particularly intelligent children who knew how to craft cruelties for maximum devastation.

How many civil servants does it take to screw in a light bulb?

More than one, apparently.

I pawed through dresser drawers and closets, searching for clues. Socks brought me nothing. Shirts made me realize I had *way* too many flannel tops. Old receipts indicated I shopped at Sears and The Bay almost exclusively, with an occasional excursion to the sale racks of The Gap.

No triggers. No memories. The person who had slept in this room was a shadow to me, insubstantial, ether.

The next room was better by a trifle. A guest bedroom converted to an office space. Bookshelves offered proof of an interest in the arts. Books on acting by Stanislavsky and Uta Hagen. Monologues from famous movies. Was I an actor? Was I any good? A photo album displayed head shots, pictures from plays set in abandoned railway stations. Images of me in period costumes, helpfully labeled — Orlando in *As You Like It*, Tranio in *The Taming of the Shrew*, Biff in *Death of a Salesman*. A younger me standing in a group snapshot behind Harrison Ford and Liam Neeson. No name yet, but I was getting closer. I could remember plays, anyway. And the names of movie stars.

Strange that I should remember Arthur Miller and *Star Wars* better than my own name.

A laptop offered cyber-clues. I turned it on — no problems remembering anything tactile — and searched through the files. A file titled *Resumes* looked promising, and finally bequeathed me a name to hang my hopes on.

Gary.

Huh.

Gary Jackson. Nondescript sort of name. Unmemorable. So dull it activated nothing. Meant zip.

I was Gary Jackson, zombie. Whoopity-doo.

Disheartened — HA! — I wandered through the rest of the house, getting glimpses and shapes, no results. The basement was wood paneled, 1950s mod. A tiki bar lounged in a corner, and a matching pastel couch and loveseat faced an elderly cathode-ray television coated with dust, the whole set screaming future yard sale, two bucks OBO. The connecting laundry room showed signs of use, but cleanliness was obviously not high on my list of priorities. There were power tools on the shelves, but they were aged, worn, coated in dust. Hand-me-downs from my father, I suspected. Kept for remembrance's sake rather than practical use.

Disappointed, I doddered back upstairs and wandered into the kitchen. I opened the refrigerator, seeing that I must have a taste for sushi and vegan pizza, but if there was an epiphany to be had on the sagging white metal shelving, it escaped me completely.

I *was* hungry, though. Not hungry, not exactly that, but there was a hole in my stomach that needed filling. I opened a bottle of Diet Dr Pepper and took a tentative swig. After a moment of swishing it about my mouth, I spit the black fizz out into the kitchen sink. It's not that there was no taste; there was simply no *need* for it to be anywhere near my digestive tract. I tried again, this time a healthy gulp of Brita water. The impulse was to expectorate but I fought it, forcing my throat to expand and let the liquid sluice down my esophagus.

I waited. There was no burning, no nausea, no bodily signal that I had imbibed something unwanted. Emboldened, I took another few swallows, deeper. Again I waited. Then, the entire mass came roaring back up, hurtling out of my mouth like an enraged fire hose. I drenched my front, the sink, the window above, the curtains.

After that, I took it slower. My body craved *something*. I nibbled at a cookie and spat it out. An apple looked promising, but a few chews convinced me to let its juice and pulp dribble undigested down my chin.

I looked to the freezer and found an antique half-pound of raw hamburger wrapped in cellophane and Styrofoam. Freed of its wrapping, the iced meat looked — what can I say? It looked right, or rather, *righter*. I took a lick and felt a tingle. I gnawed through the ice and let the raw beef sit nakedly atop my tongue.

Definite tremors of the tastebuds, buzzing. There was excitement in the air. But not quite right.

I gnawed off another sizable chunk and held the ball in my mouth, savoring it. The buds were dancing, screaming as the beef slowly thawed and released thickly chilled blood over the budscape of my tongue. *So close*, I thought, so close to being *exactly* what I wanted. Like ordering a Coke and getting Pepsi; who really cares *that* much to return it for partial refund?

It would do, I decided, and swallowed the mass in one enormous gobble. I felt the ball tumble down my throat, snagging on nooks and crannies as it fell, and fancied I could hear a splash as it hit whatever juices remained in my stomach.

Nothing.

Check that.

Rumblings of unhappiness.

Murmurs of insurgency.

Uprising, and . . .

Spewage. The bread basket rebelled and tossed the intruder out. An asteroid of chuck rocketed up my throat and out, hitting the window and three-pointing a perfect rebound into the sink.

Damn. It just wasn't right.

I suppose that, amnesia or not, I knew what *was* right but didn't want to face that reality at the moment.

Discouraged, I left the kitchen and ambled about the living room for a few minutes, idly checking out my blu-rays. Some of the titles twigged familiar: *Casino Royale, Glengarry Glen Ross, Spaceballs.* The hunger, if that's what it was, wouldn't kill me. *Won't kill me more,* I corrected. I took a seat at the dining room table. I was surprised I had a dining room, frankly; the person who occupied this house, the pre-death me, gave every indication of being an individual who ate meals over the kitchen sink or balancing a plate on the arm of the recliner in the den as he watched TV. Sofa wandered in and leapt gracefully upon the table. She thoughtfully allowed me to minister to her various itches, purring and stretching out on her back as I absent-mindedly scratched her all over. *This cat is centered,* I thought. *She has life all figured out.*

I envied Sofa her contentment. I was glad I had come back, if only to make sure she didn't die from hunger. *Was there something to that?* I wondered. There had to be a purpose behind all this. Classically, people do not arise from the grave without there being an overarching theme behind it. I was flummoxed, but I was sure that becoming a supernatural pet-sitter was not a reason for reanimation. Still, whatever happened, I'd make sure Sofa was cared for somehow. She deserved better than a lonesome death in this house, curled up under the bed and mewling for an end to her pain.

A flickering light brought my thoughts back to the present. Red, blinking light. On the wall. *Phone,* I thought. A cordless phone, and a red, blinking, oddly insistent light. *Messages.* I reached over and pressed *Play.*

"Shelley? Are you there?" a female voice asked.

Shelley. Was that a name?

"Pick up, Shel, good news on this end."

Lightning flashed and leapt over the gulch between the hemispheres, connecting the neurons, repairing the holes, patching up knotholes, stuccoing the drywall of my past.

The key to the lock. Door ajar. Floodgates open. Alert the townspeople, the dam has burst. Everything coming out. I could hear the cubbyholes and inglenooks of my brain strain, flatten, and push out under the force of thirty-seven years of memories swarming in with unrestrained glee. My eardrums popped and fizzed. I felt a *pop!* and collapsed, my forehead smacking the dark oak of the table. Sofa leapt up, hissing at the sudden action, and ran for the next room.

Denial

There was shit on the seat.

Holy shit.

I blinked.

I rubbed my eyes.

I blinked again.

I looked away and looked quickly back.

The greasy log refused to vanish.

I took another look to make absolutely sure.

Yes.

Shit.

Shit.

This was a bus, for god's sake. How the hell do you bust out a growler on a public bus without people noticing? There had to be *someone* who would have observed the groaning creation of excrement occurring in such an enclosed area. Why would they let people on?

Nevertheless.

Shit.

On the seat.

By process of elimination, *my* seat.

I glanced at the man in the seat next to the window, a listless-looking twentysomething cursed with a sad fauxhawk and extended lobeholes so vast I could fist them, seeking acknowledgement of the absurdity of it all. Maybe he could offer up a solution my stress-addled self was unable to arrive at, but his eyes were closed, head slumped against the grease of the window and earbuds amped to max carnage, blaring classic Foghat for the enjoyment of the other passengers.

Foghat? Who the hell listens to Foghat anymore?

I scanned the bus for options. Nothing left, of course. I sighed and wrote the seventeenth mental note of the day reminding myself to quit Rowan as soon as I reached home. Or grew a sack. Whichever came second.

All my worries about leaving as tiny a carbon footprint as I could began to evaporate the longer I looked at the excreta claiming the last seat as its own. *It even has peanuts in it, for Jesus' sake*, I thought. *No deference to the faltering ecosystem is worth this*. No one would blame me for taking a plane now and then; even Al Gore flew to environmental conferences, right? *Fuck Mother Earth for once, we're talking human shit here. There's gotta be a limit.*

I cursed loudly as I stared at the log, daring it to offend me further. A woman across the aisle hissed out a sustained *shush!*, covering her daughter's ears as the girl sniggered at my f-bomb droppage. I stood back, allowing the woman an unobstructed view of the moist monstrosity that glimmered and pulsed (to my fevered mind) in the soft lighting. She formed an *O* with her mouth and looked quickly away, huffing out air and pushing her daughter back into her seat as the child craned forward to get a look at the fuss-causer. The woman then paused and took another gander.

"It's chocolate, shithead," she sniffed.

"What?"

"Chocolate. Snickers or Mars maybe. Look closer." She motioned for me to lean in. Hesitating, I slowly inched my head downward to the cushion. There *was* something rather manufactured about it. It was almost too perfect a specimen. I crouched down and leaned in closer, taking the briefest of sniffs.

Chocolate. Sweet, sweet product of the cocoa bean.

Never had I been so happy to contemplate such an unlikely event as sitting atop a softened bar of chocolate. Compared to the rest of the day, feeling my buttocks slide and smoosh over a sweetened mahogany snack would be an absolute relief. I gave the woman a wide grin of idiotic amusement, but she had already forgotten me and was busy fussing over her daughter's mp3, securing the earphones over the girl's thick mass of blonde curls while the daughter whined, unable to find her favorite tweener megastar of the micromoment in the menu. The woman, I couldn't help but notice, was uttering a string of masterly expletives as she pressed the music player in various spots. I guessed familial obscenity was okay with her. Better the girl learn that language in the safety of her own home.

"Bus is leaving, pal," the driver said from behind me. "Take your seat, I gotta do the head count."

I straightened up and took another look around for any open seats. "But there's a melted chocolate bar here," I said.

The bus driver looked at the seat. "I care? Sit. Leave. Same to me."

"Do you have anything I could use to clean it, or something to cover it?"

The driver scoffed. "Where do you think you are? This is a *bus*, you're lucky it has cushioning. Now sit, or I get security."

"And they'll clean it?" I shot back. Fuck if I'd take some abuse now, when I was so clearly in the right. It mattered not that the driver outweighed me by eighty pounds, nor that his forearms were wider than my head. If this was to be my Alamo, then so be it. It was the principle of the thing, the *thing* being that one hundred and twenty-odd Canadian dollars might not purchase luxury or speed or a properly functioning heating system, but they should at least purchase a seat on public transport that didn't stain your Dockers-clad bottom with creamy brown paste.

The driver crossed his arms (a spectacularly complicated maneuver given his proportions) and awaited my countermove. I took in his physical dimensions. The driver was a walking brick, a flesh cinder block, genetically perfect for his job. His dimensions completely filled the aisle, allowing for no squeezing past. If he was coming down the aisle, the only options were to sit, flee back to the lavatory in the rear, or be crushed underneath his treads.

Reluctantly, I asked the busbeast to *please wait one moment* and grabbed a couple of glossy headshots of myself from my valise. I wadded one up over the dewy bar, smearing bog-brown goo over my scrunched-up half-smile, and wiped up the chair as best I could, depositing the whole mess in the tiny-to-the-point-of-useless plastic garbage bag offered to each seat. I then put another picture facedown on the leftover smear. Grimacing, I lowered myself gingerly onto the paper, checking to make sure rogue caramel wasn't spurting out the side. All seemed dry, although the sensation of the photograph, lubricated, sliding forward under the weight of my ass made me squirm. The driver continued dawdling down the aisle, counting passengers in a loud grunt, my dilemma already a forgotten memory.

Before the bus could get moving, I whipped out my cell phone and checked my messages. Nada. Either Rowan had not yet received my recorded diatribe on just how humiliating this last audition had gone — the words "useless" and "new agent" and "planning on getting a" had been uttered several times, alone and in clusters — or she was employing her usual tact when dealing with an upset actor; ignore it, because he has no power whatsoever save the capacity to whine. Still, the venting had felt good, cleansing. There's something about tearing someone a new one by screaming into a cell phone while walking through Times Square that makes you feel alive.

I wasn't even the most manically upset person on the street — while I was forcefully reminding Rowan via wireless tantrum that my success paid a fraction of her salary, I stormed by a slickster in a three-piece tearing at his hair and throwing his battered briefcase under the wheels of a passing garbage truck. Papers blew outward under the pressure and he shrieked in tribal joy at the mayhem he had created. He then silenced, noticing me noticing him, and gave me a knowing nod/wink combo. I replied with a solemn thumbs-up. We were part of the same clan, the unendingly unappreciated. Then we parted, and my harangue on Rowan's ineffectualness continued unabated.

I snapped my phone shut and closed my eyes, ignoring the headache that had transferred its power to the rest of my body. I ached all over, nausea flitted about my insides. I half-listened as the busmonster clicked on the intercom and informed his passengers that tonight's ride from New York to Toronto was about to commence, would take approximately eleven-plus hours, please have our passports ready at the border, keep our arms inside the bus at all times, and smoking while on board was a definite no-no and punishable by ejection from the vehicle. Whether or not he'd actually slow the vehicle down before expulsion wasn't clear.

The bus jerked, and the lights fluttered, dimmed, then extinguished, plunging the riders into darkness. The city began to drift away, streetlights flickering through the grime of the windows. The driver droned on about how happy he was to be the chauffeur on our mystical trek to the unholy coldland of Canada, and that, again, smoking was not allowed on the bus, not even in the restroom. My seatmate had the right idea; I dug my iPod out of my briefcase and shoved the buds as far into my ear canals as I could, cranking the volume until the roar of the engine was only a throbbing sensation in my back. Early Fiona Apple filled my brain, warbling smoky notes of ennui that thrummed in my eardrums and caressed my medulla. I mentally flipped the city the bird and began to replay the day in my head, cursing my twelfth-grade acting teacher who had thoughtlessly encouraged me to follow my dreams.

The audition had not gone well, not even by standards set by earlier failures, a very high bar indeed. The previous winner for Most Debased Audition was for a brief role in a cheap slasher flick being lensed in Vancouver. You haven't honestly withstood career humiliation until you've been yelled at by an epithet-spewing German director on a low budget tax-dodge of a horror film for not bringing the necessary level of terror to your portrayal of scared victim number four.

It is one thing to be turned down for a role because of a bad line reading, or a height requirement, or an abundance of age lines, or a refusal to sleep with the casting director. All had happened to me. All were things I could deal with.

This had been different. This was an audition that made one seriously question an entire life's worth of vocational choices, an audition that showed me that, even at thirty-seven (the new twenty-five, I kept telling myself), the world was passing me by, and I did not understand its rules anymore.

Acting is a sucky way to make a living. It sucks eighty percent of the time, it sucks big-time another ten percent, it suckles at the nadir of your soul for a further eight percent, which leaves two percent for something tentatively approaching happiness and normalcy. A life of acting is a life devoted to the absence of pleasure. Every friend is a competitor. Every job temporary. Every compliment back-handed.

"Reality is where it's at, Shelley, and you know it." Rowan had finally worn me down. Despite my threats to let her go, thereby denying her the fabulous wealth she received by leeching a percentage off my increasingly rare paychecks, she wielded all the power in our relationship. I told myself as many times as necessary to keep from slicing my veins that I was an artist, I had a craft, I was in all improbability an unrecognized virtuoso, but it was all so much shit. I was product. I was synthetic material processed into a vaguely human shape and thrust into an indifferent marketplace. I was a PlayStation in a PlayStation 3 world. And people weren't buying. "There's nothing major filming right now, the recession is hitting everybody, studios and producers included. Reality is cheap and popular, and if you want a little bit of that easily earned money, you are going to have to get over yourself. Tell you what, consider it 'televised improvisational theater' if it helps you sleep at night. It's *commedia dell'arte* for the hillbilly and housewife set. Now suck it up and get going, they need someone in your age bracket to round out the housemates." 'They' being the producers of *House Bingo*, Fox Television's latest entry into the 'how low will someone sink for a chance to be on the teevee' sweepstakes.

"Oh, and sweetheart?" she said as I was about to hang up.

"Yes?" I dreaded what was inevitably next.

"Don't forget: do *not* act like yourself." Her motto for my entire career. I should have had the phrase crocheted into a decorative wall hanging to display at my front door, to read as I left the house for another day's worth of whoring my body: *Do not act like yourself.*

The concept behind *House Bingo* was simple, the execution ridiculously complex: a house — located in some atypical nether-world where no one questions where a house with twelve separate bedrooms, a pool, and a Starbucks in the basement could be located — was populated by a variety of personality types, all of whom were competing for the grand prize of a quarter of a million dollars (U.S.). Ideally, the roommates were to be stereotypes, a representative cross-section of the population:

a body-builder
an airheaded bimbo who probably votes Republican
a smart-yet-devastatingly-sexy brunette
a still fit septuagenarian
a nerd or two (both sexes)
a more mature professor type (either sex)
a rocker (either sex)
a religious fanatic (not Muslim)
someone clinically obese (either sex, female preferred)
a farmer
a nurse

an Asian

a homosexual, and finally,

cannon fodder: a few extra 'others' to fill out the cast, those rejects with no discernible skills or personality who would in all likelihood go down very early in the series unless they somehow beat the odds and became a fan favorite.

Guess into which slot I fit. If it helps narrow it down, I never had to come out as a professor.

At the beginning of the show, every contestant would be provided a card with a series of numbers, akin to a bingo card (ah, hence the title, I just got that). Over the course of twenty-three tri-weekly episodes — plus a surprise finale, broadcasted live! — numbers would fall from an enormous Plexiglas tumbler that hung from the ceiling in the main den. If the number was on your card, you had to perform a task or game, something essentially useless and superfluous to existence in the real world but which was of vital importance in the 'reality' of the program. Some tasks would involve physical acts, some would necessitate that the competitor have at least a few brain cells in good working order. Eating things not normally consumed by man was definitely one of the tasks. Survive, and you get to fill in the number on your card. Fail, and you get nothing but sore bones and a foul taste in your mouth. As you're expected to live with people, teamwork is allowed, and backstabbing is encouraged. Fundamentally, *Big Brother* crossed with the more vicious elements of *Survivor* and *Fear Factor*.

It was not an easy assignment, convincing myself that somehow, in some microscopic way, this was acting. Most watchers believe that reality television must be just that, reality, not realizing that the primary element in the phrase was *television*. You're putting out a manufactured article of entertainment, and you want to make sure that it will tickle a certain segment of the masses. This was a game show, and what people want in such series are attractive and relatable personalities that they can heap scorn upon like so much soil over your coffin. Everything is calculated to achieve this effect, nothing is left to chance. The producers know ahead of time, through a battery of personality tests, who will fold early, who will explode on cue, who will sleep around, who will betray, who will win.

But — and this is how I kept from swallowing my tongue on the lonely bus ride from T.O. to N.Y. — if I could approach it from the aspect of its own artificiality, subvert the paradigm from the inside, perhaps I could justify the whole experience as a prolonged experimental art piece à la Beckett.

Such was my wretched state of being that this made a modicum of sense.

And there *was* the money. The monthly fees for Mom's room at the nursing home were becoming insurmountable, and as much as I feared the blow this show could do to any future reputation as a serious actor — hey, Clooney was on *The Facts of Life*, Alec Baldwin did a few soaps, was this *really* any different? — I dreaded the thought of a future with increased mother contact far more. It was either this or sell the house.

"Not gay enough!"

Not fucking goddamned fucking gay enough.

I couldn't do it. Even under any delusion I could muster, the end result would be that it was *me* on the screen being *me*. No one watching would grasp the craft behind the portrayal, because no one watching had any conception of artistry. There was no curtain of artifice between the intended audience and myself. No one would watch and think, whoa, he's really putting himself into this role. No one could possibly watch Fox Reality and create analogies to the great method actors of the age.

"Not gay enough!" This was shouted into my face by the casting director. "Fag it up. We're all sisters here, don't be afraid to be yourself."

Did they ask the Asians to be more Asian? Farmers, more hick? Blacks, more street? Of course they did. The woman they ultimately chose to represent the Asian contingent was from fucking Arkansas — "born 'n' raised in Clinton's own little slice a' heaven," she told me in the hallway, accent thick as grits — but she understood the game, and auditioned with inflections jingly with the music of Korea. They had to eventually use subtitles, it was so offensively stereotypical.

"Could you repeat that?" I asked. I had heard the words clearly; I simply needed a moment to shore up my residual levels of self-loathing.

"Did I stutter?" the casting director said. "I said, gay it up. Mince. Sashay a bit. Lisp."

I sighed. I had no reserves of delusion left to tap. "Could you give me an example of 'gaying it up'?" I asked. "Just so I know exactly what you're expecting from me?"

"Well, aren't you the fuckin' prima donna." She put a hand on her hip, put her weight on the opposite foot, and hung her other hand out in the air, palm up, wrist limp. "Like thith, honey," she lisped.

"Vamp it up a bit. Let'th thee the woman come out of the clothet. Now, thtart again. Tell uth a bit about yourthelf."

I threw a wrench into the gears of my eyeball rotation mechanics to thwart their urge to roll up and expose my contempt. The ATM card in my wallet, my lifeline to the near-drained puddle of nickels and quarters that comprised the whole of my savings, applauded the effort.

I shifted my weight slightly, giving me a more relaxed appearance. "Hi there," I started, talking directly to the camera, lightening my voice by a good half-octave. "My name's Gary. I'm an actor by trade, but don't let that scare you, I'm really a good, good person."

"Faggier!"

A prancing wisp of lisp entered the dialogue. "You might notice that I'm a little older than the others, so I want to be upfront." I took a deep breath, as if this was a huge reveal or personal secrets. "I'm thirty*ouwth!*" A well-placed theatrical cough, just enough to bring a smile to the viewers. "So, yes, a *little* older, but well, that just means I've got more experience. I've been around the block multiple times, sister, and I know the neighborhood. And I'm good teevee, I put the show in show-mo-sexual."

"What, is this a meeting of the NRA? Christ fuck, *gayer!*"

Jesus. I thrust my hip out and leered past the camera at her, cocking an eyebrow. "Sweetheart, if you knew anything about being gay, you'd know there's nothing gayer than the NRA. All those big guns, polishing the shafts, stroking triggers, those aren't gun enthusiasts, that's a man-on-many-other-men orgy of repressed sexual desires, those are GLAAD conventions. Schlongapalooza."

"Finally, the inner shrew comes out," she said, turning off the camera. "Good stuff there. You're smart, you're sharp, and you're completely non-threatening."

"The homo you can't wait to bring home to mom and cornhole your brother."

"Exactly that, smart, with a friendly edge that'll keep people guessing. Adam Lambert, but not trying so hard. You keep that up, you're definitely in the running."

"Terrific," I said, smiling thanks as my bowels churned with bile. "You've got my info, I'll just get my agent to call you with my information."

That's what I should have said. That would have made sense.

But no.

"Wait, wait," I said, ignoring the dying screams of my bank account. "I just can't do this. I thought you wanted reality. This is who I am, the real me. You're layering an artificial construct over something you claim is the real thing."

"Well, duh. This is *television* reality, buddy. No one wants just *you*, they want you to the *eckthtreme*." She gave up her lisp and wiped down her chin, sighing. "It's been a long day, buddy, and I can't deal with another 'actor'" she air-quoted that one "with some oblique moral objection as to what the job requires. It's all the same. You think I wanted this? I want to direct dramas, not coach actors on how to better flutter their eyes. I spent all day yesterday yelling myself hoarse to get blondes to be blonder, nerds to be spazzier, and brunettes to be smarter. Ironically, the 'smart brunette' we've lined up is probably the dumbest person on the show, and that is saying something. I mean, this isn't MENSA, but wow, so dense she could run for Congress. You want this gig? I won't lie, you've got a good shot, you fit the age bracket we want, but you've got to play to get the pay. Your call. Tick-tock on this one, I got" another heavy sigh of self-animus "twelve other faggots outside, and then the old people. Oh, god, the old people."

I stood mutely for a few tension-suffused moments. "Would I have to wear eyeliner?" I asked after a spell of sufficient portentousness had passed.

"What do you think?"

I gathered up my belongings and left.

I watched the world speed past the head of my still-sleeping seatmate. He had dozed through every rest stop, as well as the half-hour we sat at the border as the bus slowly inched forward in the auto lineup until a border guard could be bothered to come aboard, share a tired laugh with the driver, give the riders a bored yet vaguely threatening once-over with his eyes, and waved us through. Homeland Security, protecting your interests with the best of the best. Guess he didn't see a turban.

I envied him his coma, my seatmate. My id would not accede to my demands of sleep, obsessively walking through the events of the day over and over. *Would it have killed me, a little bending? Two months' work, a steady paycheck even if I didn't win, and enough money* to cover the rest of mom's draining life if I did. But that was too much to ask. Too much. No one would have watched the thing. Barely anyone.

Enough people would, I argued. *Agents would. Directors. Actors. They'd know. I'd carry the taint always. Marked like Cain, or Snookie, doomed to walk the Earth until the end of days.*

A little melodramatic, even for you. Too bad you couldn't have been that queeny during the audition.

Oh, fuck you. And go take a piss, you've been holding it for hours.

Fine. But I'm only going because I've been sitting for a while and don't want to get thrombosis.

Whatever.

I stood up, my joints popping with the bus-bends, and prepared myself for the humiliating trek to the restroom. *Look, everyone, someone has to expel urine!* I wavered and wobbled my way toward the washroom, guided by the gloomy illumination emitted through its entranceway, its door open and swaying slightly with the constant motion of the bus. An old 'N Sync ballad chirped in my headphones, a cheesy ode that I saved from deletion in a bout of sentimentality. This was not helping my nausea. *Pizza was probably off*, I cursed, remembering the abundance of slices I had absconded with after the audition, picking off the meat and willing myself to ignore the lingering taste of processed pepperoni. *Cheapskate producers couldn't even spring for a decent spread for the applicants, had to get fucking Sbarro, worst pizza on the planet. Probably going to bring Ebola to Canada.*

Halfway to my destination, a set of legs bisected the aisle, their master a snoring pimple-jockey who had managed through a combination of teenage surliness and pubescent stank to procure a pair of seats all to himself. I fumed, the thought of returning to my chocolate cushion while this future frat boy had somehow finagled a whole two seats to himself on a crowded bus driving the impulse to knock the kid on his ass. His head and torso had contorted themselves into a precarious loop, his face pressed into the scratchy weave of the chair's back, the bulk of his torso balanced on the seat's outward edge. To prevent the upper-half from toppling to the floor (a scenario that appeared likely given the driver's penchant for targeting every pothole), the lower half was positioned as a counter-weight across the aisle. The feet were propped atop the armrest of the seat across, imprinting against the slack bicep of the octogenarian who sat there, also asleep. The whole effect was that of a mouth-breathing horizontal question mark.

I grabbed the luggage rails that lined the sides of the bus and hoisted myself feet-first over the denim vault, sticking the landing with no small amount of difficulty. Stabilizing myself, I glanced back, slightly impressed that my athletic prowess had managed to overcome the obstacle without awakening the teen.

I then placed my foot against his thigh and shoved with all my might.

I reached the lavatory before he could regain his senses and figure out what happened, pulling the door quickly shut behind me. I slid the locking mechanism over to turn the main light on, a light that wholly eclipsed the stand-by light by a good twenty watts. In the dim I could make out the seat of the toilet, spattered with liquid. The wall behind it was layered with shiny polished steel rather than mirror, preventing the likelihood of breakage, a likelihood all the more probable judging from the number of impressive dents that marred its surface. I could just discern my face in the murk, distorted to funhouse freakishness through the metallic depressions, hidden altogether in spots by magic marker graffiti advising that I should consider fucking both myself and my mother, should I be so inclined. The artist apparently hoped I was, although I presumed he would change his mind should he ever meet said matriarch. The self-fucking would have to suffice.

Taking a hold of the grab bar affixed to the wall for balance, I stood on my left foot and toed the seat open with my right, thanking whatever immortal being in charge of bodily functions that all I had to do was piss. The toilet was a square brick of identical metal, rising from the corrugated floor to just below my knees. A bottomless pit was placed in its middle, a smooth hole with walls that descended twelve inches into the belly of the bus. Beyond that, a roiling mixture of used toilet paper, cigarette butts, formless chunks of fecal matter, and an indigo chemical mixture sloshed about, propelled by the natural centrifugal force of the moving bus to rise up the sides of the well and daintily mist the rim. Holding fast to the bar with my left hand, I unzipped my trousers with the right, fumbled with the button until it finally slipped free, and slid my pants down, propping my legs wide and bending slightly at the knees to prevent the pants from slipping and coming into contact with the goodly amount of moisture which, I now saw, coated the entire floor. This accomplished, I slid my underpants down just enough to allow access to my understudy. Freed from the confines of its cotton prison, it flopped and shivered about as the wheels of the bus rumbled over the shoulder of the road. I took hold and aimed, using my fingers to push down the elastic of the boxer-briefs and my thumb to steady the shaft for release. Two streams of urine arched in the air, one splashing against the rim of the hole before hitting the liquid below, the other going rogue and spattering the wall. "Fuck," I shouted, instinctively letting go of the bar to allow both hands to reposition my fabric/penis arrangement and compensate for the errant flow. My right pulled my underwear down farther; my left pushed the head so that the streams hit alternating sides of the hole, but the angle was too wide, and both squirts straddled the target. Droplets sprinkled my bare legs.

I crouched and leaned forward, hamstrings shaking, trying to lessen the distance the water had to travel and decrease the area covered. Finally, both jets collided with the walls of the hole and sprinkled downward. I moaned with relief (*Heaven!*), clenching my pelvic muscles and forcing the stream out to finish faster.

A loud crunch resounded through the stall as the right rear wheel — the wheel I was almost directly above — entered and exited what felt like a pothole of satanic depths. My feet left the floor, slid back, up, and for a brief moment I was weightless, an astronaut of the loo. My hands released their fleshy tube to flail for a stable surface. Urine cascaded out of my now-undisciplined member, coating the toilet, the sink, my arms. A single thought popped into my head, barely registering in the onrush of adrenaline flooding into my system: *gross.* Gravity then resumed, and my knees slammed down on the sharp front ledge of the toilet. I gasped in torment, my mouth sucking in air, my body preparing for the great-grandmother of shrieks, when the recoil of the liquid in the urinal nether-pit discharged a perfect storm of disinfectant slurry directly into my face. And then I did scream, long and heartily, my eyes blind and roaring, swords thrust deep in my sockets and forcefully stabbing my brain, Justin Timberlake assaulting my ears, moaning about the girl he could never have. The taste of chunky bleach overwhelmed my senses, became my world. There was nothing to the universe but searing white torture, chemical death. My stomach rebelled, vomit flowed from my mouth. My body battered itself about the tiny room, insane with agony. My legs tangled in my pants, now down at my ankles and mopping up the liquid. My balance shifted as the bus took a hard turn and I fell into the door, my hands now operating as my eyes, grabbing for everything, anything. A flat surface, a knob, a depression. *The sink! Water!* I twisted the faucet, grasping at where water should pour forth but feeling nothing. I squinted an eye open, earning another knife-thrust. No water. Above the sink, a gray plastic device labeled Antibacterial Hand Scrub was affixed to the wall. I squeezed the dispenser's lever feverishly, filling my palm with clear gel. I rubbed it over my face, my mouth, my tongue, swishing it through my teeth, gargling, spitting, yelling with equal parts shame and revulsion all the while. Still frantically rubbing, I slid down to the floor and curled my legs to my chest, gagging as my tear ducts worked overtime.

An eternity later, my eyes smarting but clear, I rose unsteadily to my feet, leaving my pants down and doing my best to ignore the gruesome fluid saturating the fabric. I grabbed handfuls of tissue paper and rubbed at my face, applying more hand gel that went on clear but came back blue. I peeked at myself in the metal. Streaks of cobalt and sapphire ribboned down and across my face, giving me the look of a mercenary camouflaged for a *fabulous* night on the town. I must have popped a few blood vessels; my eyes bulged red. Globules of almost-digested cheese and dough spackled the front of my shirt and pretty much the entirety of the vehicular outhouse. I massaged my face with clean paper, lightening the hues, then applied more scrub to my arms, the urine smell lessening, my fingertips inked. How I was going to leave the room wasn't a thought to be crossed yet; the only thing important in the world was cleaning myself.

I scrubbed harder, almost frantic.

My head pulsed. The veins squirmed in protest to their forced compression. The skin around my skull felt too tight, constricting my braincase, as if it was a wool toque thrown heedlessly into the dryer. My arms felt anesthetized. It was difficult to hold on to the wads of paper. *Adrenaline crash*, I decided, forcing my hands to continue their rubdown. Bulbs of sweat loosened themselves from their perches and exited my pores.

My heart palpitated, anxious.

Too anxious.

The emergency was over, although public embarrassment was still pending. I should have calmed down. Even in the throes of my improvised ablutions, I thought: *That's kind of weird, that shouldn't do —*

A boa constrictor snaked its way under the door, undulated up my torso, and squeezed.

Pain seized my body, locking my joints. My brain melted from the stress.

A vengeful deity stomped down from on high and began punching me about the torso.

Strength fled my legs and I slumped, my chin hitting the edge of the sink.

I bet that'll leave a mark, I thought through the blur, but I couldn't bring myself to care.

My head cracked against the metal wall, and again when it collided with the floor.

That really should have hurt more.

A bricklayer took a quick job on spec and sealed up my windpipe good and proper.

I lay curled on the grating.

There's something I'm supposed to acknowledge when this happens, I thought. *All this seems like it should be important somehow. To someone.*

Lance Bass chirped out the last few notes of a ballad to someone's girl, somewhere, that he could not ever have for his own.

God, don't let that be the last thing I hear.

For a good time, call Brenda.

My vision faded, and the universe displaced itself.

All I could see was green.

Am I outside?

What's that smell?

Who's Brenda?

Shel. Sheldon Funk. Shelley to my mom. Shel to my friends, of which I had . . . none to call home about. Gary Jackson, stage name, an alias forced upon me by my agent, insisting *Sheldon* was not a name that inspired confidence, would not open doors. Not manly-sounding.

My head pressed into the varnish as the message continued.

I remembered everything.

I thought one's life was supposed to replay before death, not after.

It was unspeakable.

It was *everything*.

The warmth of the womb, then screaming light. Floating monsters in smocks grab my head, haul me forth from aqueous Eden into the gaseous atmosphere of nightmares.

A spider bites my eyelid while I coo and burble in my crib; my shrieks bring my mother running into the room. Her hands flail at my face, brushing the spider away, her nails wounding in her alarm, scratching my nose and forehead.

My first skinned knee, my mother hollers at the driver who brushed his Buick against me in the Safeway parking lot.

Fiona. First kiss in grade five. Clumsy, sloppy.

The death of my father. Roland Funk, the accountant. His face smooth and calm, the complete negation of everything he had been in life. My mother, emotionless, stares into the coffin, holds my hand tightly as a warning to keep my tears in check. It was a church, after all. All her friends are here, it wouldn't do to cause a scene.

Adam Garwood. First *real* kiss. Grade eleven, backstage during a high school production of *The Pirates of Penzance*, he the Frederic, I the Major-General. His breath, stale with cigarette smoke, harsh, the most marvelous air I had ever tasted. His hands paw at my ruffled shirt, ripping off buttons as I gasp around his tongue, my moustache falling loose from the friction.

My mother, Eileen, always religious, now fundamentally insane without the calming counterweight of Roland. Condemns me for becoming an actor. Asks me if I had prayed to God about my choice; she was worried deviant lifestyle choices were imminent. My response, "Yes mother," an agreement brought on by a lifetime's conditioning to obey at the cost of my happiness. My partners all introduced as "friends in the play," no possibility of truth within the walls of her house. Relief floods me as I watch her emotional character succumb to early senility, slowly draining her personality of everything her.

The whole of me, all at once.

Every film I ever watched.

Every book ever read.

Every shirt/pant combo worn.

Every dream, every daydream, every masturbatory fantasy brought to conclusion.

The combination to my seventh grade locker, twenty-four left, three right, eighteen left.

That missing peacoat I turned the house upside-down looking for, only twelve feet from where I sat, in the closet behind an old parka I never used anymore.

My demise. Cold and alone in a bus restroom. My head wedged against the door. The light dimming. My absolute last thought, repeating the phone number scrawled on the wall over and over as if it was of some importance. The smell of lawn after a heavy frost — then nothing but eternity.

No person should have to go through one's own death twice. It's once too often, and doubly unpleasant.

All my moments, everything *me*, my me-ness bludgeoned deep into the tender cushioning of my brain, the only fully functioning organ I had left now imploding from psychic pressure. I was an empty bucket suddenly filled, wet and heavy. A dried-up peapod husk mysteriously called back into service, brimming with vegetable matter and nonplussed at the odd turn of events.

"It's Rowan, babe," the voice from the speaker continued. Rowan. My agent, the one who set me up for that exercise in humiliation known as my last audition. She sounded distant, as if the phone was farther away than the three feet to the wall. I moved my head slightly, and realized I was now deaf on my right side. The eardrum had blown out under the physical power of the memory deluge.

"Listen," she continued, so far away. I rocked my head over onto its right side, bringing the operational ear closer. "I know you're down, and that's partially my fault. Clearly, reality is not your forte. But lest we forget, I *told* you not to be yourself.

"But listen up. I got you in to see Fern Davidson, she's casting for Platinum Dunes, so this is big, honey. They're doing a remake, something horror-ey, and they like your looks. She said to me, and I am not making this up, that you, my darling, have a look. A *look*, Shelley. That's as good as saying you're in. They want an unknown, someone fresh to play the older brother of a serial killer who haunts co-eds or something in a small town, I know, what bullshit, right? But this, I kid you not, has major money behind it, and they are, brace yourself, actually thinking the word *franchise*. A tentpole film with an option for three more films *at least* if the first one makes money, which it will, because these things always do. And I know what you're thinking, Shelley, you're thinking *I am an artist*. You know that, I know that, but no one else knows, and this is a real foot in the door opportunity for you.

"Call me when you get this, don't worry about the time."

A clicking noise, the phone hanging up.

Under any other circumstance, I would have been spurting joy in all directions. I had been toiling in the trenches for the better part of fifteen years; I was a prostitute in every way except the most obvious (and sometimes even that), selling my body to any bidder desperate enough to consider me. Visions of glory on the Broadway stage and rave reviews in the *New York Times* rapidly rotted to sludge under a crush of bills, debt, and a mother in the final stages of dementia. The highlight of my professional acting career thus far was a four-line role as Confused Car Buyer #1 in a national Saturn commercial, an utter rending of the only withering moral fiber I had left in my body, which nevertheless earned me enough to set Eileen up in a second-tier care facility.

As it was, it was all I could do to muster a silent retch of exuberance. All my crap about being an artist vanished in a puff of ego. Every sacrifice I had made suddenly meant something.

I jerked myself up, my spine crackling loudly. I was in no shape for acting. I had been up all night, for one thing. I was dead on my feet. Somehow in my excitement I had managed to pave over that pressing issue. In times of distress and uncertainty, go with what you know, and what I knew was how to prepare for an audition. Sure, yes, I was dead, but I was an actor. Dying was easy, people did it every day. Comedy, now, that was hard.

It was high time I had a better examination of myself.

My joints popped as I forced myself back into a sitting position.

I pushed against the table to right myself and bumbled toward the washroom, home of a mirror, water, and clean bandages.

The reflection was not kind.

First off, my face was blue. Not with cold, not with death, but with bus-grade chemical disinfectant. I soaped up a loofa and gently scrubbed until my natural hues were all that remained. Not that my efforts made me much more presentable.

My face exuded the unhealthy pallor of a drowning victim after a lengthy stay in a lake. The flesh covering my face seemed overly loose, leathery. More so than usual. My face had always looked a little slack and un-elastic, prone to wrinkles, with a perpetual resemblance to Droopy Dog that was only going to get worse as I aged. I was not ugly, exactly, but neither was I a Brad Pitt–esque example of human perfection. I had played up my features as a plus to casting agents, trying to gain attention through the less-showy character roles that could benefit from a uniquely memorable visage. Worked for Giamatti and Buscemi, anyway. But now, the face that was going to launch a career of "best friend" and "business partner" roles — maybe even going so far as to afford me acting employment as a violence-prone henchman or a wacky next-door neighbor in a syndicated dramedy — that face was magnified and extended well past its best-before date.

This face was . . . the face was dead. The lips hung loose in a slack howl of apathy. The bags under my eyes had gained weight, pulling the skin down and showing a tad more of my eyeballs than I was comfortable with. The complexion was a mixture of pink and gray, battling for supremacy, and gray was winning. What I looked like was what I was, a recently reanimated corpse, shambling and lurching about.

Fucking depressing.

Ignore it, I told myself. *You're a professional. You once auditioned for a Renée Zellweger flick while suffering from a flu virus, high on Nyquil and Advil. You didn't get the part, but the point is, you showed up, gave it your all, and so what that you threw up on the stand-in, at least you tried. Focus on the positive. You can do that, you can do this.* I smiled, forcing my cheek muscles to contract, trying to inject some cheeriness to the expression. My lips stretched up and away, revealing yellowing teeth in a bed of gums already withdrawing upward. I bared my chompers in a garish clown approximation of a grin, and only succeeded in scaring myself.

So. Smiling, out. I ran through simple facial exercises from my acting classes — frowning, lifting the eyebrows, flaring the nostrils, squinting the eyes, forming the mouth into a wide O, fluttering the lips (exercises once done by rote, not at all easy now) — but there was a fractional slowness to the response. The muscles and tendons were half a step behind the impulse, giving my face the sleep-stupid expression of a gasoline huffer. The effect was of a rather clever monkey trying to imitate a human. A rather clever, rather deceased monkey. I pushed at the skin with my fingers to try and massage some fluidity back into my face, but it was like shaping old clay. My fingers were also quite white, I noticed, unhealthily so. This is what happens when blood stops pumping.

Leaving the face for later, I shed my coat. My forearms were striped with red, the results of the quick skirmish with the attendant. His aim had been better than I had realized. I wet a towel in the sink and dabbed at the wounds. Scales of skin fell away to the bathmat beneath my feet. His makeshift weapon had sliced deeply, but no blood issued forth, only the grayish-red of muscle. The lacerations were tacky and clung to the towel, tearing threads of terry cloth away as I continued to wipe. I guessed whatever blood I had left in my body had clotted and was drying up in the veins. I dug through my medicine cabinet and came up with a roll of medical tape I sometimes used to support my right knee (hurt in a racquetball accident and kind of iffy since). I tore the tape with my teeth into two lengthy pieces and wrapped each arm tightly. It wasn't a great job, but a loose-fitting shirt would cover any bumps.

That done, I set to peeling the bandages away from my chest. The flesh was still partially iced to the fabric, and frozen kernels of skin shucked away as I pulled. Freed, the epidermal shutters swung open and a chuck of veiny beef popped out and plummeted into the bathroom sink, followed by a rope of sausage, the whole mess slapping the basin with the sound of raw chicken being thrown against a wall.

I had forgotten about the previous placement of my innards. Funny how you can completely ignore the little things.

Like intestinal geography.

Scooping the guts from the sink and letting them dangle to the floor, I stared at the heart, cradled in gore-spattered porcelain, forgotten, sad. The metaphysical ramifications of looking at my own heart from the outside battled with an overwhelming sense of incompleteness. Whatever else was happening to me, the fact of my heart somehow not being a necessary part of my existence anymore was obscene. This unhappy hunk of gristle and tripe was supposed to be the meat of my matter, the fundamental engine of my human machine. The mythological bassinet of my soul.

A sound caught my attention, a lapping. Looking down, I saw Sofa taking exploratory licks of my bowels. I pushed her away with my foot and shut the door.

I turned on the taps and bathed my heart until the meat was luke-warm, gently wiping off tendrils of pus with a hand towel. I stuck a finger in an aorta and slowly spun it on its axis under the running water, lettering moisture into every space, filling its ventricles. I lovingly squeezed the water out, now discolored and chunked with rubbish. I tamped the organ dry and stored it in the medicine cabinet for later.

Looking back to the mirror, I took an unobstructed look at the monstrosity I clearly was.

It was a dog's breakfast. The lungs bumped slackly against the walls of the ribs. My various organs looked to be intact, but then again, how could I tell? Was I even aware of the proper feng shui of human innards? I would have to find an anatomy textbook to make sure (I had a Grade 12 biology text in a box in the basement, I remembered), or download autopsy images online for comparison's sake. Regardless, everything save the heart and that one errant kidney appeared to be more or less where it should be. My stomach, without the cushioning of intestinal tracts, swayed at the end of my esophagus. I bounced on my toes, feeling the weight pull at the back of my throat.

My stomach let forth a gurgle. It was a tiny squeak; in other circum-stances it would never have been heard at all. But I had never heard it complain in the open air, and far preferred the muffled murmur of a bellybowl sheathed in dampening layers of muscle. It was a gruesome burble, evil, raw, festering, the digestive howls of Satan's tract.

There was a contraction and ripples of movement passed down into the upper intestines, now hanging far past my knees. Whatever I had eaten pre-death was still in there and wanted escape.

Would I shit all this out? Did I shit at all? Was that me from now on, the incredible non-excreting boy?

All at once, I was tired of the freak show. I didn't know what would happen next, but gawking was not constructive time management. I once more bundled the muck back inside me, ignoring the blan-kets of gore that abandoned their posts and took up residence with the mildew of the bathroom carpet. The most pressing issue was the hollow; I had no intention of proceeding through the rest of my life as the visible man, and I had an idea of how to fix it, if only temporarily.

I wrapped my heart in a thick hand towel, grabbed several more from the rack, and walked out to the kitchen. Rummaging through my tools drawer, I withdrew the heavy-duty stapler I used for minor household repairs. I retrieved an old wooden cutting board from my cabinet, and then moseyed downstairs to get my dad's old nail gun, the one I used when a big staple wasn't enough.

Using the detachable spout above the kitchen sink, I gave my interior a hot spraying, sponging up the water and slop with the towels. Once I had the area relatively clean and dry — you might be surprised how presentable you can gussy up your chest cavity when the blood stops pumping — I placed my heart in approximately its original place, using a decorative mirror from the hallway to help guide my hands. I had to use one hand to push my lungs apart and away. I lined up the aortic halves of the heart with the remnants that protruded from my walls. This was not strictly necessary, as I functioned perfectly fine without it — I had only an elementary school conception of the proper placement of the various tubes and pulpy conduits anyway — but I felt it might help me from a psychological perspective. Pinching the aortas and veins together with my fingers, I squirmed my stapler into place and fixed the whole mass together. The effect was Frankensteinian, but I felt better knowing it was safe and secure within me.

For an instant I considered the possibility of infection, then silently mouthed a laugh. There's absurd, and then there's *really* absurd.

Only later on did I consider that what I was in the process of doing should have really hurt. I should have been screaming to wake the dead; in the annals of pain, self-inflicted heart surgery should have been right near the top of the list, alongside labor pains and shooting Mountain Dew out the nostrils. It wasn't as if I lacked for tactile sensation, but my brain compartmentalized the torture, kept it behind a curtain. It was as if I was watching a drive-in movie from outside the fence, listening to a buzzy soundtrack on a half-assed radio while a projector lit the action onto a distant screen.

The next part was trickier. I climbed up onto my kitchen table and lay on my back, my flaps loose and open. I had likely lost some essential packaging en route, and could use a thorough stuffing before the final step. I wadded up the few clean towels I had left and crammed them into the nooks and crannies of my physique. I took care not to pack too tight, but with the loss of the ribs, the next stage was going to need a little support.

I carefully placed the cutting board atop the towels, fitting it up between the remnants of ribcage until it was good and snug. Aiming at an angle, holding the mirror in my left hand and the gun in my right, I shot a nail into the board, piercing the wood and embedding itself deep into the marrow and bone of my sheared ribs. I put two more nails in, then switched hands to repeat the process on the other side. This was not as successful, my aim too shallow; the first nail glanced off the surface of the board and shot into my bicep. Cursing (as much as a mute can curse, which is quite a bit), I adjusted the angle and set the next two nails in solid. My makeshift ribcage was not pretty, but neither was the real thing, and as I lacked any skill in sewing, carpentry was my only option. I pulled the one-inch spike from my arm and tossed it away.

I folded the doors of flesh over the board, stretching them tight to minimize gaps, and nailed my chest together. I made sure not to use too many nails, to reduce the chance of tearing. I rolled onto my side and carefully left the tabletop, acclimatizing to the new weight. The construction appeared firm. Checking out my handiwork in the mirror, I chose to ignore the haphazard pattern of the nails — my high school carpentry teacher would have freaked at the slipshod work on display — and congratulated myself on a job, well, done. The edges more or less met at the middle, and the skin appeared amenable to the metal pins perforating it. My nipples were stretched and lop-sided, but I could live with that. There were a few bubbles of air, but a quick banging with the stapler solved that problem. At least now I could wear a shirt and not have to worry about constant bandage readjustment and repair.

So, physically returned to near normality.

Next, the voice.

The role likely had a fair amount of dialogue, unless the character was a deaf-mute — how great would that be? Either way, I'd have to make at least some noise during the process, if only to meet the casting agents. I would have to learn to speak.

With the musculature so ravaged, getting any noise out at all would be a miracle. I focused inwardly on my lungs and diaphragm, picturing them working together, the bags opening and closing in a continual and unbroken rhythm. Inhale now. I forced the walls of the lungs to expand, and felt a thin stream of air pass my tongue and enter the throat. Now, exhale. I tightened the muscles, squeezing the sacs empty. Exhaling was definitely easier. I practiced this for a few minutes, just moving the air in and out, trying to make it appear natural. The breaths shuttled back and forth, up and down my throat, hissing forth into the air with a sound like a decaying pump organ — moldy, dank with disease, leprous.

Emboldened, I tried to make a sound. I didn't work on clear words, just tried to get some noise to exit my mouth.

Anything.

Any noise at all.

Just a peep.

You don't know how difficult it is to talk unless you have to retrain your vocal cords to vibrate.

Really.

Fucking.

Difficult.

I moved my mouth into different positions, forcing the air out, trying to get even a whisper of sound beyond the sickly death-rattle I was so far very, very good at. I should have been sweating under the exertion, but my skin remained smooth and clammy. Finally, my lips puckered in an imperfect oval, I was rewarded with a quiet but audible "ooh." Not willing to stop and celebrate, I kept up the rhythm of air, devoting myself to my throat, feeling the muscles and tendons re-familiarize themselves with the patterns of speech. The oohs got progressively louder, to oohs to oohs, and eventually to a full-throated *OOOO-AAAAHHH* that filled the room and warbled off the walls.

It wasn't my voice exactly; there were tonal similarities, but the sounds were barely human and growled with feral terror. I kept it up, screaming at full volume now, not willing to relinquish my triumph. It was only one vowel sound, maybe an arguable two, but ees and ays could not be far behind, and then consonants. I stood up and marched around the table, keeping the beat with my footsteps as I modulated my mouth and throat to get new sounds.

Step. *AAAAAYYYYY!*

Step. *EEEEEEEEEE!*

Step. *EYE-EYE-EYE-EYE-EYE!*

Break. I had limited time, and needed to modulate the voice to a more manageable, conversational tone. I curved my tongue against the roof of my mouth to get a hiss of air going, and contracted my lungs, forming my lips and tongue around my name:

Sssssshhhhh-eeeeelllll-eeeeee.

It was a gruesome utterance, a word of putrefaction, splatting heavily on the floor like clotted cream gone rancid.

I tried again, smiling around the word this time, picturing kittens frolicking in a meadow with baby goats, dolphins performing back flips in a tranquil bay.

Sssssshhhhh-eeeeelllll-eeeeee.

The sound of orphans being strangled in their cribs soaked into the walls. The goats head-butted the kittens into red mush, and the dolphins lined up to be mercury-laden breakfast treats for Chinese children.

One more time, quick and tight. Try to flatten it out, squeeze the horror out of it. Pop the lungs, don't drag it out.

Sheelllleee.

Shelley.

Shelley.

Sheldon.

My voice was grated, raw, shards of glass rubbing against shale and hamburger. I called to the cat a few times. "Sofa. Sofa. Sofa. Hey, Sofa. Come here." I played with the modulation, managing to turn it from a bloodless whisper into a parody of friendliness. A pederast inviting the paperboy in for a cookie. Sofa eventually returned from wherever she had hidden herself and weaved her mass through my legs. I considered this proof of success.

I looked at the clock on the wall. Seven o'clock. In another hour or so, the sun would have fully risen on my first full day as a member of the undead. I'd call Rowan at half past eight to make sure I had enough time to get past her army of underlings and toadies.

In the meantime, the voice needed major calisthenics if I were to pass muster. I passed the time by petting Sofa on my lap while practicing some vocal warm-up exercises. I'd run through some tried-and-true tongue-twisters, childhood classics to limber up my aural mechanisms. I inhaled deeply, expanding my lungs to their absolute limit, then pushed the breath out over the words "Peter Piper picked a peck of pickled peppers," my lips and tongue imperfectly meshing. It all came out *peerpiperpitapetotpittedpedders*, each syllable dripping from my lips in tones of black death.

"She sells seashells by the sea shore." *Shesellshellabaseshory*. Angels wept bloody tears as my syllabic modulation killed all in its path.

"I am the very model of a modern major general, I've information vegetable, animal, and mineral." *Iamfhjdrlibbitableinmeraralraww-wwwwrrrrraaaagh*. Sofa, before a subdued admirer of my linguistic proficiency when I practiced, bristled at that one.

Oh fuck it. Talking slow was the only option, and no matter what I did to make my utterances sound even remotely human, the sound of my voice rattled like dirt falling onto a freshly planted coffin.

"Oh . . . that this too . . . too sullied flesh would . . . melt," I said slowly, metering out the beats with my breath and forcibly enunciating every syllable. Not too bad, that time. The words of Shakespeare's Dane had never sounded so bereft of hope, but at least it suited his melancholy mood. Now, all I needed was an impresario who wanted to mount an all-singing all-dancing all-undead adaptation of *Hamlet*, and I was set.

"What the fuck?"

For an instant, I was illogically proud of the sentence. It sounded normal, human. Definitely something I would say. I glimpsed a shadow against the wall, moving quickly toward me, and realized I had not spoken. A baseball bat — a memento from childhood, I recalled, a fatherhood gift that never instilled a love of sports but kept alive a long-gone love of a parent — crashed against the wall behind me, narrowly missing my head, clipping my earlobe.

Startled, I threw Sofa at the blur.

Three minutes later, drenched in offal, I took stock.

My hunger was sated.

I was happily chewing on a forearm, said limb noticeably unattached to an owner.

My, I guess you'd call him boyfriend of three months or so, Fisher something, something Fisher, lay strewn about the table and chairs and floor and sideboard. His blood Rorschached the wallpaper.

Sofa was taking an experimental sniff of Fisher's appendix and walking about the carnage, leaving charming little red paw prints behind her.

Great. Just . . . terrific.

Fisher had been nothing serious, a playmate, someone to talk to and occasionally swap spit with. He had a sad lost-puppy look to him that I have never been able to resist. Fisher and I had hooked up every few weeks. We had nothing to connect us, but his story of parental rejection, so common among those of our tribe, made me more accepting of his faults. He was shallow and immature and flighty but then so was I for a time. I decided to let him have some fun, perhaps I could serve as a mentor, and if we got our collective rocks off once in a while, no harm. He was intimate enough that he had a key, and had slipped in during the night, maybe wanting to surprise me after my "big audition" with a celebratory/pity boink. He must have been under the covers in my parents' bedroom when I walked through the house — the bedcovers were mussed up when I bothered to take a closer look. Somehow I had overlooked him in my search for memories. Fisher had awoken during my yelling and screaming (the earplug I spat out as I sucked at his auditory canal reinforced this notion), and had taken the bat from out of the bedroom closet as a makeshift weapon. He came into the dining room — why didn't he call the police, you ask yourself, and I wish I had an answer; maybe he didn't want to explain why he was in a house he had no business being in — and seeing the drained, anemic demon sitting at the table and squawking nonsense, reacted rather appropriately under the circumstances.

His bad luck to have poor aim. His bad luck the surprise kicked in impulses I didn't know I had. My bad luck to have to clean up the mess. My *good* luck the curtains to the large picture window I stood in front of, a speck of Fisher's delicious pink arm muscle poking out from between my lips, were closed. I had torn him apart like he was made of tissue.

I checked the clock. 8:20. Pissed off, confused, irritated, but strengthened by unexpected breakfast, I went in search of trash bags and cleaning solvents.

At 8:30, I sat at the table and made a call to Rowan's office. The phone wasn't working, no dial tone buzzed in my ear. I shook the phone in annoyance, and the casing cracked slightly in my fingers as I thoughtlessly gripped the handset tighter. *Gotta watch that*, I thought, and switched the phone to my good ear. The dial tone was clear and strong.

I dialed the agency. A prim male voice answered on the first ring. "Masters Talent, how may I direct your call?"

I lifted the corners of my mouth and tried to force an airy, businesslike nonchalance into my voice. I brought air in, and pushed in out past the vocal cords. "Rowan . . . O'Shea . . . please."

Outside my house, all small mammals within earshot shriveled into fetal balls. Sofa, being a bit more in tune with the dark side (I suspect all cats are), shivered a bit at the noise but stayed put.

A long silence ensued, then: "I'm . . . I'm sorry, could you repeat that?"

Again, quieter, with less conviction. Focus on clarity and a feeling of goodwill toward all. "Rowan. O'Shea. Please."

Another pause, then a gasp. There was a sandpapery sound as the receptionist hastily covered the mouthpiece with his palm. In the background I could hear a woman's voice ("Carl? Are you okay, honey?") and what sounded like hysterical sobbing. The phone was dropped, and over the clunks I heard footsteps and a scream echoing quickly away as Carl scampered from his desk.

I hung up, thinking. I had a direct number to Rowan's personal cell phone on speed dial — "For emergencies only, and I mean that, mister, this is not a line to complain that the stage manager screwed up your latte order, you had better be on fire if you call!" — and I figured a bypass of the usual route to her ear might be in order.

She answered on the sixth ring. "Sheldon, did you just call here?" She had caller ID, an option I had always detested, preferring anonymity until I had said hello. "What did you say to Carl, he's crying in the washroom. I don't know, get on the phones!" This last she shouted at an agency sycophant, not bothering to cover the mouthpiece or move the phone slightly away from her noisehole. "You like your job, you little fuck? Get on those fucking phones now! And tell Carl he's fired! Christ, Sheldon, what'd you do? Thank god Carl's a temp."

"Rowan," I said. "You called about—"

"What the fuck?" Rowan yelled. Then, more cautiously: "Who the hell is this?"

"It's Sheldon," I groaned.

"Shel? Holy shit, hon, you sound like grim death."

"I . . . have the flu."

"Well, sort yourself out quick or you'll miss the last best hope you have of making a real honest-to-goddamned living." It figured Rowan would be immune to whatever it was my voice did to people. She had been given an empathy vaccination when she became an agent, killing the emotion-processing modules in her brain and thus making her a highly effective contract negotiator. She was a fearsome opponent who would claw, scratch, and bite anyone to death, all on your behalf. Unfortunately, this meant my failure to become anything more than a bit-part character actor in Canadian/American co-venture syndicated television series was entirely my fault.

"Take some ibuprofen and get yourself down to the Intercontinental on Front Street for two o'clock, the Wellington Room. This is your shot, and I don't mind telling you, if you blow this you are permanently doomed to a life of mediocrity and shame. I love you, boyo, but it's truth telling time: you're looking at being a mid-thirties failure, and a future career as a Wal-Mart greeter is your only viable long-term option if you don't nail this part." This was standard boilerplate, Rowan's version of a pep talk.

"What's the. Role?"

"It's a remake of *A Cry from the Basement*, an Argentinian horror thingy from the nineties. I don't know all the details, they just want an excuse to slaughter a Benetton ad's worth of nubile young co-eds for the Halloween weekend box office. Something hard PG-13ish. You're the older brother of this girl who gets killed in the first few minutes, you desire revenge, blah blah blah. You team up with a few teens who die in various creative ways, you get off a one-liner or two, maybe a pun, the least annoying most blonde bimbo fresh from the Disney pantheon of sweaty adolescent fuckables looking for 'credibility' somehow helps you shave the killer's face off with a belt sander or something, blood spurts, music swells, cue Lady Gaga theme song over the end credits, and *voilà*! Your dimly lit face on marquee posters everywhere, promising vengeance on a mass scale. Instant cash grab for the Halloween crowd, a guaranteed two sequels if it makes a profit and how the hell could it not? This is gold, Sheldon, pure Peruvian flake, two months' work with two hundred thou at the end for you minus my customary twelve percent."

Two hundred thousand dollars.

If my heart had been capable of it, it would have stopped dead.

"Shelley? Hey, you there?"

I sat there, letting the phrase *two hundred thou* mambo its sexy self through my brain. "Jesus," I finally mouthed, and then took an inhale to repeat the word aloud in a subdued croak, all thoughts about resurrection forgotten as the dollar signs shook their gold-dipped fannies at me. *Two hundred thou.*

"You're damned right, Jesus! Someone's looking out for you now, so don't fuck it up royally, get yourself tuned up and go knock them dead!"

What was I thinking? I knocked my head back and forth, fancying I could hear the brain slosh about. Maybe I *did* hear it; I was decomposing, who knew what was going to happen upstairs once my head had dried up completely and my cerebellum lay gasping on the floorboards of my skull. *I can't go on an audition*, I thought. *Not now. Not like this, certainly.* A zombie getting a job? The day just kept getting more ludicrous.

"Rowan," I began. "There's this. Thing . . ."

"Okay, I'm sensing hesitation here," she interrupted. "You're telling yourself that this is selling out, am I right?"

"Not . . . exactly, no."

"Well, you *are* selling out, but remember this, you have a mom or dad in a care home, right? Something like that? You think of them for a second, and you think about how you're going to afford to keep them alive without this job. This money could take *all* that pressure off your back. Go back to being an unemployed actor with your ethics and primitive concepts of morality afterward. Consider this an investment in your parent's life. Or whatever remains of it. If it tips the scales, I'll drop my percentage to eleven, that's how sure I am of this."

Mom. Goddamn it. Even now — medically delusional, incoherent, brimming with unfocused hatred and lashing out at every person who walked past her room — even now, Mom still managed to push a mountain range of shame in front of my path.

"I'll be. There," I managed, hanging up. Even in death I couldn't catch a break. *The zombie heads out for work*, I thought, imagining a child's picture book image of a brightly painted cartoon man in a suit, his skin gray, his hair falling out in patches, perhaps a few scabs over the face, waving goodbye to his cartoon zombie wife and cartoon zombie child as he headed out for another busy cartoon zombie day under a gaily smiling cartoon sun. I slumped down and lay my head down on my arms, noticing after a time that I was leaning in a tacky red pool of Fisher plasma. I wondered if I could weep, but decided it wouldn't be worth the effort to try.

Groaning, loudly and purposefully, I stood and tried to work out the most effective, least damaging method of bathing in my condition.

Bargaining

Infestation.

I don't believe anyone could have a real conception of horror until he has witnessed a fly hatch under his own skin and burrow itself out.

Certainly caught me off guard.

I don't know why, neither did Rhodes or the specialists, but my body has proved remarkably resistant to insect life. Small favors. Normally, after the body has ceased its normal functions, the process of decay — a process, the internet gleefully informed me, that is continually ongoing no matter how healthy you are — takes a step forward as the insect kingdom decides your festering remains would be a decent place to annex for themselves. That's in addition to the legions of microscopic organisms already making a comfortable living in your epidermis, your follicles, the folds of your scrotal sac.

It was Rhodes, dear Doc Dementia, who first called my attention to my next bodily dilemma. He had worked tirelessly at repairing the natural sloughage of my skin as the restraining cables, freed of any renewal process that tended to repairs, relaxed and gave way, pinging like a chorus of snapped guitar strings. He had made a few minor incisions under the skin of my left arm, attempting to squirt crazy glue or some such shit into the widening gaps and thereby keeping my skin actually on my body. He pulled a mirror close and let me look as he pointed at the pockmarks that lined the underside of my flesh, poking at them with the tip of his scalpel and giggling at the wholesale lunacy of his circumstances. The dots wiggled and squirmed, and as I watched, Rhodes gently pried one loose and held it close to my eyes, where the tiny maggot thrashed in protest.

The city roared by me, simultaneously the bleached white of new tank tops and the filthy grunge of second-hand wife-beaters listlessly taking up space in a Salvation Army bin. There may have been a soft covering of shimmering angel droppings blanketing the city overnight, but as people stirred in their beds and realized that there wasn't near enough of the precious white to declare a snow day, they trudged their sleep-addled selves toward their cars, cursing all the while, and angrily ground the new-fallen snow into slush and crud. Toronto had enjoyed a night of calming winter wonderment, but the city was fully awake now, cranky and out of sorts, and all the intrinsic winsomeness of nature was hastily metamorphosing into urban municipality excrement under incalculable tons of foreign-bought steel and Canadian salt rust.

I was slightly better at tempering my speech, infecting my consonants and vowels with only a smattering of the mausoleum. After finishing the cleanup of the dining room — I could save the furniture, but the wallpaper would have to be stripped and the rug was a goner — I chugged away at my voice for a few more hours, concentrating on keeping my breathing at a regular tempo yet attempting through repetition to make the operation of my bellows an unconscious rather than a noncompulsory act. I could never again achieve fully autonomous motion but if I could somehow operate the lungs, keeping them fulfilling their oxygenerational duties with only the merest hint of conscious decision-making on my part, I could then focus on content rather than audibility. If I kept the tones as low as possible but outside of whisper range my voice would possibly still cause stomach upset and nausea in the listener, but at least the sense of imminent death that ostensibly destroyed the sanity of Rowan's assistant was tamped down to a more tolerable undercurrent of nebulous foreboding.

I hoped.

I tried my newfound articulatory confidence on the operator when the bus arrived, spewing sludge over my legs as it slid to a halt twelve feet past the stop, turning a dapper pair of slate polycotton khakis into a soggy gray waste of a hundred dollars. Suppressing my natural inclination to let the driver know of my dissatisfaction with his job performance thus far — happy or not, I still needed to get to the audition, my car being trapped in the garage by a waist-high snowdrift pressing against the door, and wreaking havoc on the driver through sonic assault would not get me there any faster — I hawked up a garbled "Good morning" as I slowly walked up the stairs and paid the fare. He blanched slightly and stifled a burp, but smiled a weak grin in response.

How the audition would go, I had no idea. I'd probably have to speak up a bit.

My luck as it pertained to bus seating accessibility held fast, and I nabbed the only remaining seat near the rear exit. I mmm-hmmm'd an acknowledgment of the day's goodness to my elderly seatmate's pleasant salutation and watched as she clutched at her chest for a moment. Satisfied that this was not the big one, not today anyway, she took on the deadpan stare of the seasoned bus rider and gazed blankly out the window, the lives of others slowly scrolling by.

I prodded at my meatball surgery scars through the Gore-Tex of my coat. The cold wasn't worrisome to me, but shuffling through downtown Toronto in a thin shirt at minus twenty plus windchill might draw unwarranted attention from even the jaded populace of the Big Smoke. The construction seemed to be holding, but I'd have to avoid bending forward at the waist too quickly or the skin would tear around my ramshackle rivets and the whole of me would burst forth like a Wes Craven piñata.

The bus ground to a halt and more denizens entered, brushing snow off shoulders and stamping feet clean of muck. A few more stops and the bus was crammed full, stopping only to allow citizens outside to realize the futility of attempting to wedge themselves into a mobile sweat lodge. The stink of wet wool and steamed armpits suffused all available air, dulling the senses of the passengers and effectively disguising the scent of rotting meat I was sure emanated off me. I had finally decided a sponge bath was the most appropriate course of cleansing available to me considering the delicacy of my circumstances, but you can never get truly clean by wiping yourself down with a damp washcloth. I had applied a layer of talcum to my body after toweling off, and doused myself with brand-name odor suppressant after choosing an appropriate ensemble, but I was certain the aroma of interrupted eternal slumber radiated off me.

Bodies bumped and swayed against each other, the bus gradually making its way into the heart of the city. I allowed my mind to drift. Normally I would be preparing for the reading by running lines in my head, or working on possible character motivations and sense memories I could draw from. Blind line readings were both a blessing and a curse for actors as they allowed for a great deal of on-the-spot improvisation and immediacy but did not permit in-depth preparation. The only thing you could work with was you, and if your you wasn't up to snuff, we'll call you.

It wasn't my audition and the prospect of actual money and long-term career advancement that ate up my thoughts. Partly it was the remnants of Fisher moldering in my bathtub. A little more than partly was my absolute intention, when the day's tasks were completed, to have another nosh on fresh rump roast of paramour.

I wondered at my lackadaisical attitude toward Fisher and his demise at my hands/teeth. Was it symptomatic of the condition that I necessarily forego empathy with my food? My fondness for animals was a prime motivator for my on-again/off-again bouts of vegetarianism, but I thought that option now off the table. Or was it that, after four months, I still had no emotional connection to the dazzling young lover who occasionally shared my bed and made me passable egg-white omelets in the morning?

Was I a standard zombie, or an awful human being?

I had rarely formed meaningful attachments as a child. Eileen was a major impediment to happiness, her allegiance to all things biblical forcing me to sublimate my natural instincts to maintain a semblance of household harmony. When I left home, her claws were still embedded in my spirit, and the sense of freedom I felt at walking away from her front door was triumphed only by the sense of shame of wanting to be myself. And so the charade continued; Eileen's duty-bound son Sheldon was only another persona for the CV of a struggling actor. It was easier to find a decent agent in a city teeming with actors than it was to confront eighteen years of evangelical shame. It took me another three years to summon up the courage for a sexual encounter that would wipe clean Mom's indoctrination techniques, and her force of will has kept a constant presence within my id and ego ever since.

I tried to recall why Fisher and I had ever hooked up. For me, it was obvious: he was a fit young object of desire who approached his recent coming-out with the predictable enthusiasm of the unexpectedly paroled. Fisher was excited to be himself for the first time in who knows how long, possessed of inexhaustible ardor and a body like sculpted chocolate. We met at a production of Pirandello's *Six Characters in Search of an Author* I was performing in at the Berkeley Street Theatre. It was opening night, and my portrayal of The Father had not gone over well — the part is nothing but goddamned monologues concerning philosophical theories of identity, and I had unthinkingly repeated a few lines when I had lost my place, hearing the giggles out in the dark and flushing with ignominy. I was ergo fully in the cups when the director, Hamish, minced up to me and introduced the appetizing youthful gentleman next to him as "the luscious Fisher, my newest discovery, an actor of raw talent and limitless potential." Just "Fisher"; no indication of first or last name, no hint of a nickname, and never once had I felt compelled to dig any deeper.

I told Ham to fuck the hell off and die for once, and blurted to Fisher to run for the exit and don't look back, that unless Ham's newest discovery had ten inches or more on his person, his raw talent would be stuck doing understudy roles and chorus parts until Ham "discovered limitless potential" in someone else's boxers in the back alley. Ham huffed a pithy exit line ("Fuck you, you dried-up queenie cunt," I think, very original) and flounced away, dragging his protégé behind him. Fisher caught up with me outside as I was haggling with a cab driver over how far ten bucks would get me (tip included), and offered me a ride home on his Vespa. One lift turned into a night's worth of heavy panting, we shared a laugh over the scathing online reviews of my performance the next morning, and Ham's ward became my newest distraction from a life of immeasurable disappointment.

Fisher's attraction to me was an inexplicable happening, given my (only in comparison) advanced age and severely bitter frame of mind. He never explained it, I never pushed for more, and whatever it was quickly became a comfortable arrangement. He'd disappear for a few days at a time, but I recalled my own shame-based explorations into a newfound land of sexual liberation and never begrudged him his carnal autonomy. I was just depressed enough with my placement in the cosmos to simply be thankful for diversions.

But that was all there was to it. I rarely inquired into his personal life before the switch, as he put it, and most of his new friends were my acquaintances already, so for me life continued much as it did before, albeit with more anal. Fisher was my coital version of Sofa; sometimes there when I needed comfort, sometimes not, and always, when he was hungry or horny, I became the center of his universe for a brief period. We were not soulmates, we were hardly two ships that bumped rudders in the night, we were not star-crossed lovers, we did not each fill that emptiness in the other, we were not each other's missing piece.

We were venereal associates.

So in retrospect it was not surprising I harbored no deep yearning for Fisher beyond superficial. What was unexpected was how effortless the shift was from the sexual to the nutritional. Fisher was always an object, rarely anything more.

Before death, he was entertainment.

AD, he was brunch.

Did a lion worry about lack of remorse when felling a gazelle? Did a Great White ponder the seal pup's last desperate thoughts? Does a country singer get a lump in his throat as he unloads an M-16 into a rabbit warren? Why was I upset about Fisher in the abstract but not in the particular?

Most of my brain, however, was consumed with worry over the television news report I had watched that morning while I busied myself with removing all traces of Fisher's effluence from the house, wiping down all countertops and walls with generous spritzes of cleaning fluid. The morning anchorperson droned on in the background, his soothing baritone reporting on pods of whales that had beached themselves in Australia and some U.S. senator who was hellbent on removing all environmental restrictions and drilling for oil wherever she damned well felt like it — her words — before switching over to local matters. The anchor, tie expertly knotted, hair coifed to exacting standards, teeth whiter than the feathers of doves, wrapped up a softer-than-soft news segment with an update on a paperboy who heroically insisted on continuing his daily rounds despite having lost both his arms in an industrial accident (lawsuit still pending), before launching into his serious voice once again.

```
     In what police have labeled a "strange
     case of grave robbing,"
```

I snapped to attention, my joints arguing at the suddenness.

```
     a morgue attendant was viciously assaulted
     at Toronto General Hospital late last
```

night. Cherie Elin is live on the scene
and has this report. We'd like to warn
our more sensitive viewers beforehand,
some of the details and images may be
disturbing. Cherie, what can you tell us?

The picture switched to a two-shot, the anchor now situated on the left within the safe confines of the studio, to the right a digital box displaying a young woman standing just outside the hospital lobby. The blizzard was in its death throes, and her face was being battered by the elements. Her hair, like the anchor's, was immoveable, withstanding the punishing wind with ease.

Lorne, a hospital is usually perceived as
a place of healing. Early this morning,
that belief was shattered as the Toronto
General Hospital became an ironic scene
of gruesome violence.

The report switched to voiceover, and images of the morgue flashed onto the screen. There was a lot of red splashed about.

At approximately 1:30 a.m., Craig Neal,
an attendant at Toronto General, was
forcibly attacked by an unknown assailant
or assailants while in the course of his
duties. Neal sustained major trauma to
both arms, but it is the opinion of specialists that he will eventually make a
full recovery.

Switch to a full-body shot of Craig sitting on a cot, looking miserable and doped up, both arms swathed in full casts. The moldings jutted from his shoulders, metal rods holding them upright from a thick belt around his waist.

Even stranger than the attack itself
is Neal's repeated assertion to this
reporter that there was in fact no

outside attacker involved, and that the
wounds he has sustained are the result
of an altercation with one of the hospital's recently deceased arrivals.

Close-up on Craig speaking into a microphone held before him,
his eyes watery, words pharmaceutically slurred, his story absolute
proof of his insanity.

"Yeah, I swear, this body came in, we
were starting the autopsy, it, he, this
guy we had cut open, I took the heart
out, he, he just got right up off the
table and attacked me. He grabbed me and
broke both my arms."
    "What happened next?" the reporter's voice
asked off-camera.
    "I passed out."
    "But a body attacked you, is that what
you're saying?"
    "Yeah, a body. He got up, broke my
arms, and left. Oh, he bit me, too."

Craig wiggled the fingers of his left hand, bluish little sausages
squirming at the end of his cast.

"Kind of tingles a bit. Can't feel much,
though. These drugs are awesome."

The picture switched to generic shots of the hospital's interior
hallways.

Despite Neal's story, hospital officials have stated in a press release
that there is no truth to this account,
which they have put down to an unfortunate misinterpretation of the night's
events brought about through a combination of the trauma of the attack and the

pain medication Neal was on at the time
of our interview. They stand firm that
there was one or possibly two assailants involved, but that is the extent of
their knowledge at this time. Officials
have also refused to remark on the rumor
that a body was taken from the morgue,
but Captain Melissa Palmer confirmed the
disappearance in her statement.

The captain's face filled the frame, the bottom of the screen dotted
with handheld mikes.

"At this time, we do not have any leads
as to the reason for this attack. I can
confirm a body has gone missing from the
grounds of the hospital some time this
morning. We are working on the hypoth-
esis that the two events are connected,
and that the victim either witnessed the
theft or was ambushed beforehand. At
present, he is in no condition to provide a full account, and we hope to gain
a better picture of the incident in a few
hours. That's all for now, thank you."

Switching back to the two-shot, the anchor wore his concerned-
for-the-safety-of-the-citizenry face, the reporter just looked tired. She
consulted her notes as she completed her report, barely holding on to
the papers fluttering in her hand.

At present, Lorne, the police have not
released a name in connection with whomever's body was taken, but an anonymous source within the hospital has
stated that the body was admitted under
the alias "John Doe," which is common
code for persons of unknown identity.

> The hospital's surveillance video has
> been seized to aid the investigation,
> but police will neither confirm nor deny
> that a man was seen leaving the hospital
> and running into last night's snowstorm
> soon after the attack.

The anchor thanked her for her diligence, and assured the viewers that they would have more information on the story the moment it became available. Then, more soft news, a Pomeranian who could bark the tune of "O Canada."

I let this sink in for awhile as I fed Sofa, gave her five uninterrupted minutes of head-scratching pleasure, and went to the bedroom to decide on a suitable audition ensemble, something loose to hide my lumpy torso. The police might be able to get a picture from a video, but without a name they'd still have a difficult time tracking me down.

I looked about the bus at the riders, at the press of humanity I was suddenly no longer a member of. Was I alone in all this? It seemed ludicrous that I could be the *only* heartbeat-challenged person on the planet. But someone had to be first, right? The odds were against it being me, but there *were* odds. It stood to reason *someone* had to be a patient zero. I made a quick mental note to purchase lottery tickets on the way home.

And if this were all actually happening — if this wasn't all some bizarre last-ditch effort of my dying brain to give me one last astonishingly realistic dream before it turned out the lights and sent everyone home — what did it mean for reality outside of myself? If people could arise from the grave and walk around, take the bus, make small talk, interview for employment opportunities; if people could do this, what other mythocultural beings might be wandering about the face of the Earth? I searched the faces of my busmates, looking for anything out of the usual. There was a particularly gothy-looking emo kid near the front: was he a zombie who had found a way to live in plain sight? Were those reputed "haunted houses" that seemed to find a place in every neighborhood's folklore actually infected with the spirits of long-dead inhabitants too stupid to float into the light? Could there be honest-to-goodness vampires haunting the suburbs? Worse, would they be sparkly? Could clans of werewolves be running through the forests, feasting on Boy Scout campsites? Was a family of Sasquatch running the Mountain Equipment Co-op? A Minotaur eking out a living as a short-order cook? Were outer-space aliens to blame for every unexplained disappearance since they taught the Aztecs complex binomial theorems far beyond the comprehension of MIT graduate students?

Maybe I am death itself, I mused. The physical manifestation of the Grim Reaper, on Earth to claim souls for harvest. At this point, was that so absurd a suggestion? I *had* always liked wearing hoodies, but shouldn't one have been supplied beforehand? Did I have to purchase a scythe at Canadian Tire? Should I keep the receipt?

I needed a test. My seatmate was not wearing gloves, and had her hands lying flat on her lap. I daintily placed a fingertip atop the right hand and watched her closely, seeing if she would keel over at my touch.

She moved her hands away with a sniff. I reached over and placed my whole hand over hers. "Do you mind?" she asked. This wasn't working. I pressed down, harder; maybe it would take a moment to kick in.

"I have got mace in my purse, asswipe," she wheezed, "and I am not afraid to use it." I pulled my hand away and offered a smile of apology. She sniffed and edged away toward the window.

So. *Dead* then, but not *death.*

The old woman pulled at the signal to stop and pushed herself past me and into the aisle. As she shuffled herself around my knees, her hands, ungloved, brushed against my jacket and I got a whiff of her scent, buried underneath layers of *eau de toilette* and Gold Bond Medicated Powder. Pungent, animal. My mouth was immediately saturated with saliva, and a thin stream of drool escaped my lips and trickled down my chin. My breakfast of Fisher had kick-started my autonomic reactions concerning food, apparently. I could see the blood beneath her skin, briskly swimming corpuscles doing laps around her ancient pool. Her heartbeat throbbed arrhythmically in my good ear. The world around me blurred red, and all was blood and hunger. I leaned forward, my mouth cranked itself open, my jaw popping as it gaped past the manual's recommended limit and my teeth bared themselves and snapped at the air where the woman had been seconds before.

I forced my head back, clamping my hands over my mouth. Wiping at the spittle with the back of my hand, I became acutely aware that I was encased in a tin can and surrounded by walking sundries.

Jesus fuck, I cursed to myself. Instinctively, indifferently, I had almost turned the bus into a public transit slaughterhouse. I slid over into the empty area and put my forehead against the window, barely registering the cold against my skin. Another passenger made for the space I had vacated; a businessman in full regalia of the middle class, leading into the space with his ass. I barked an order his way: "Saved, buddy." He shot up to a standing position and clutched at the overhead rail, his eyes closed and his skin drained. He opened his eyes and looked at me: I directed my lips to curl upward at their ends and gave the gent a toothy grin of friendship. He passed out, slumping back into the seat. I left him there, unconscious, ignoring the stares of the other riders, satisfied that I had some privacy now.

I wasn't even hungry, that's what bothered me. I felt revitalized after Fisher, energetic almost, and fully satiated. I might have looked a little healthier — the mirror attested that I was as pale and saggy as before, but just maybe a bit pinker, skin tighter, hair more lush — but my thinking patterns were clear. Plainly, eating again so soon was unnecessary to my successful functioning. But the gluttonous gourmand portion of my undead brain wanted more. I'd have to watch that. The morgue doctor was bad enough, and what happened with Fisher was *really* bad, but both were containable if handled correctly.

A public feeding frenzy, however, would not be in my best interests. There'd be police, and bullets, and torches held aloft by angry villagers. If I were caught or contained, black op helicopters would fill the sky, men in hazmat suits would drop on bungee cords. The city would be sterilized. I'd be encased in a bubble, followed by a period of forced confinement and medical probing, followed by likely dissection.

No, I couldn't let that happen. Perhaps I was a menace, maybe I was the beginning of the end of life itself, but until I had figured out a course of action that didn't involve my becoming a Mary Kay makeup test bunny, I would do my damnedest to remain free. I would have to keep my feeding habits more on the downlow. Fisher would probably be enough to last me a while, if I rationed him out over a few weeks. And after I had sucked out his marrow and gnawed his bones to dust, then what? Kill again? Who? A neighbor? Who could I kill out in the suburbs that wouldn't arouse suspicion and panic? I wasn't going to move, I needed a base of operations.

No wonder there were likely so few zombies out there; it was exhausting figuring out how to cope in a world of the living while maintaining a surreptitious feeding schedule of fresh manmeat.

I closed my eyes to shut out the hunger, feeling the skin and hairs scrape across my now-dry lenses. I'd have to pick up some eye drops afterward.

TRANSCRIPT: Audition file - "Lester Ulysses"
Gary Jackson "GJ"
Director "D"
Casting Agent "CA"

D: Who's next?

CA: Um . . . Jackson, Gary Jackson.

D: Who?

CA: Exactly. Rowan recommended him, Rowan O'Shea
        from Masters? I owe her a favor. She says this
        guy is one of her best, but then, she says
        that about everyone in her stable. We could do
        worse.

D: I don't know, let me see the shots. Interesting.
        Good hair. Not exactly a looker, is he? Then
        again, I do like his eyes, they're very dark.

CA: Hooded.

D: Yeah, sunken. Gives him some menace, some char-
        acter. We could work with him. Be nice to maybe
        have someone with talent on this thing. Might
        be too old, though. Alright, let's see this
        guy.

CA: Send in Mr. Jackson, please.

D: Jesus . . . Jesus wept.

CA: Mr., um, Mr. Jackson, are you feeling all
        right?

GJ: . . . Never better.

D: Oh fuck! I mean . . . no, I mean fuck! Man, are
        you kidding me?

GJ: . . . Pardon?

CA: I think I'm . . . excuse me.

D: Fern?

CA: I'm going to be sick.

D: Wow. Gary, I mean, wow. I know you guys are
        sometimes method, but jumping fuck, man.

GJ: I haven't been—

D: Do not apologize, I totally get it. Your agent,
        she tells you, go for the second lead, but you

	know, you just know that the hero, it's boring stuff. So you get all gussied up and come to read for the bad guy. Spectacular. Hat's off to you, you know? I've seen commitment, right, I was second unit on *I Am Sam*. Penn, man. Commitment, right? That guy was focused. But you, right now, blow away anything I've seen. You hear the part is that of a batshit loony murderer, and you just go for it. Bravo, man, bravo.
GJ:	. . . Thank you.
D:	Chills! I'm gonna have fuckin' nightmares, you are brilliant! Already I have goosebumps.
GJ:	Is there. A script?
D:	Script, yes, right. Fern! Fern, get back in here!
CA:	I'm sorry, I guess I . . . caught that thing that's going around.
D:	Give the man the script, the details.
CA:	Oh. Yes, of course, Mr. Jackson, I apologize.
GJ:	. . . That's fine.
CA:	Jesu— No, I'm okay. Here's the pages.
D:	No, give him Lester's piece.
CA:	Lester? No, you mean—
D:	I mean Lester. This guy comes in here like this, the least we can do to let him read Lester.
CA:	Oh. Uh, okay. Has Rowan given you any details?
GJ:	. . . Basics.
CA:	Uh . . . oh boy here it comes again . . . no, no, I'm fine.
D:	Have some water. Here.
CA:	Thanks. The part you're reading now, Gary, is Les, Lester Ulysses. He's a, a, when he was twelve, his father was torn to pieces right in front of him by an angry mob who thought he was a rapist who had been terrorizing the neighborhood.
D:	Yeah, it turns out that the rapist was actually, get this, he was the guy leading the

mob, right? Pillar of the community, alderman, loving family man, churchgoer, and kiddie rapist. Total mindfuck on the audience, and the kid's completely traumatized as a result. Turns out that Dad was a traveling salesman, the kid tagging along, and the police can't find any other family for poor little Lester. So they ship him off to an institution. For twenty years, because they want to cover up the town's dirty little secret. The real rapist, he killed himself out of guilt, so there's no loose ends. Les's been holed up in this hospital, practically catatonic because of what he saw, but get this, the daughter of the real rapist, Alyssa, who never knew of her father's crimes, she's working at the hospital as a volunteer. She meets Lester, and gets him to come out of his shell, and they strike up a friendship. Lester even develops a bit of a crush on her. But, and this is where the movie really goes all out: Lester figures out who she is, and it brings everything back. He goes bonkers, breaks out, and starts killing the children of the people who killed dear old Dad.

GJ: Sounds . . . convoluted.

D: Believe me, it'll work. Look, I know the plot's a joke, but they all are when you think about it. What I want to do is bring the audience back from their safe little torture porns and shove the dread down their throat. It'll be old school menace, like Hitchock and Lynch, but with more gore — you gotta have at least some, am I right? It's not about plot, it's all about atmosphere, and if we can milk the tension enough people won't give a flying fuck about who's killing who for why. And it's a terrific part. I mean, the guy's a whack, no question, but there's a pathos to his rage, misdirected though it may be. This is a real Norman Bates type, but even creepier. The audience is going to go nuts for him, they'll feel bad even while they root for his death. Killer!

CA: So, in this scene, Lester, that's you, has got Alyssa tied up in her parents' basement. You've just killed her best friend, and you're busy decorating the room in her skin. Alyssa is understandably upset, and you're going to explain your rationale to her. I'll read Alyssa, and you just start on your own time.

D: Okay, Gary. Take us there.

GJ: . . . You don't understand, Alyssa . . . There's a . . . a gnawing at the . . . root of my brain . . . It's an insect . . . an army of them . . . and they . . . have been chewing . . . away . . . for two decades . . . I have to . . . stop it.

D: Jesus he's good.

CA: But why, Lester, why? Why did you have to kill Colby?

GJ: Her mother . . . took away the . . . only thing in my life . . . She murdered my . . . father, she raped . . . my childhood . . . she has to under . . . stand what that feels like.

CA: You're a monster. Colby never did anything to you, and you're using her intestines as crêpe paper.

GJ: You . . . said at the hospital, you . . . liked my art . . . It keeps me sane.

CA: You're insane, Lester. Please let me go.

GJ: Not . . . until you . . . know the truth, the truth . . . of who you . . . really are.

D: Cut!

CA: I'm sorry, I have to—

[sound of retching]

D: Fern, come on!

GJ: . . . Was that all right?

D: Alright, he asks. Fucking yes, it was all right!

Holy Buddha, you, you own the screen! The into-
nation, the weird pacing, my God, you're the
next Chris Walken!

GJ: . . . Thank you.

CA: We've got your, your number, and we'll call you
next—

D: No, fuck that, I want him.

CA: Zed, we have to talk about this.

D: What's to talk about, the guy is perfect. I
mean, look at him! Gary, my man, you are in.

CA: Zed, it's not that simple, we still haven't
heard from all interested parties.

D: Linda, who's director here? Don't answer, I
am, and this is who I want. The backers want
someone else, we'll show them this tape, they
will fucking flip for him.

CA: Zed, I'm sorry Gary, but Zed, we can't cast
him, he's . . . hideous. The producers won't
stand for it, they want Hollywood horror, not,
not horror horror. No offense, Gary.

GJ: None. Taken.

CA: Oh—

[sound of retching]

D: Man it's getting ripe in here. You just answered
yourself, Fern. This guy could be the new standard. This could be our *Saw* or *Hostel*! Gary,
you are ground zero for the next generation of
horror, man, you are *Faces of Death Thirteen*.
And if you can just dial it back by ten percent
or so, we'll have people terrified almost to
the point of vomiting, but almost, right?

GJ: I . . . appreciate . . . your support.

[sound of retching]

D: Jeez, I'm sorry, that one got even me. Holy
shit, dude, you've got the part.

GJ: Terrific . . . That's great . . . news.

D: Please stop man, you've got it, you're killing
       me here.

GJ: I'll have Rowan call . . . you.

D: Goosebumps!

   [sound of retching]

Guilt

"Who is that?"

I inhaled slowly. "It's me, Mom. Sheldon."

I sat still in the darkness, not daring to turn on the light.

I loathed this place.

Ubiquitous off-white walls that defied the laws of physics, absorbing light rather than reflecting, plunging the rooms into impenetrable gloom. Hanging sheets surrounding each bed, provided to furnish patients with the barest illusion of privacy. Twenty-year-old television down the hall, always on, always tuned to the weather channel, informing sorrowful visitors that while their personal realities were slowly cancering away from the inside out, there was a warm front preparing to hit Edmonton and Puerto Rico was absolutely lovely that time of year. Plastered sincerity of the nursing staff, repeating the same words to family members since the beginning of recorded RN time. *There is nothing we can do anymore. She's slipping. The best we can do is to keep her comfortable and safe.* You could smell the lamentations for the dead that permeated the wood and brick, no matter how many layers of fresh paint were applied, how much bleach sprayed about to combat germs that were going to kill us all anyway. The perfume of misery wafted throughout the ward, clinging to all who walked through with the tenacity of a sad-sack relative who needed money, bequeathing visitors formless nightmares when they returned to the safety of their homes. Misery and desolation, layered with a patina of forgetfulness.

Mom's breathing was harsh, ragged and moist, like an old quilt damp with mildew being slowly ripped apart. Her body, never big to begin with, looked smaller, like it had begun wasting away, melding itself with the mattress and sheets through osmosis. She rarely left the bed anymore, and the nurses had just about given up trying to convince her to walk even to the washroom. Her complexion, once her best feature, as unblemished as polished ivory, now a companion to the room, pallid and uninspired. Her dentures floated in a glass beside her bed, her toothless mouth a cavernous gouge in her face.

We looked more alike now than we ever had in life.

She stared at me from her bed, squinting. "Is that you, Sheldon?"

"Yes, Mom."

She moaned at the sound and lay back against the mattress. She placed her hands palms down on her chest, covering the tiny wooden cross that had hung from a dull silver chain about her neck since before Dad had passed.

I was visiting well outside prescribed visiting hours, as the nurse had tersely informed me when I tried to sneak in unnoticed. Not an easy accomplishment when your knees refuse to bend without cracking, and your ankles refuse your commands to walk on tiptoe. I kept a scarf wrapped around the lower half as my face as I stopped at the nurse's station, a toque pulled low over my forehead and a pair of ski goggles over my eyes. I took in a breath and emitted a full vocalization of my intentions to visit my beloved mother, and Nurse Luckless vanished into unconsciousness, panic frozen on her face.

Mom's roommate N. Nowlan (his name designation on his chart — sometimes, when you're bored enough, you'll read anything you can) would not have appreciated my efforts at silence, having been in a coma long before Mom moved in next door. The seesaw rasp of his ventilator and the intermittent submarine *pings* of whatever else was hooked up to him would cover any noise I would make. N. Nowlan had never had a visitor, not once had I seen anyone other than a bored nurse even look at him with anything other than muted disinterest.

Not for the first time I marveled that we put down animals for having broken limbs, that my mother had my dog euthanized for shedding too much in his old age, yet we keep people alive through machinery long past sensibility. What was the point of preserving loved ones as living taxidermy other than sentimentality and fear and guilt? I wasn't any different; Mom's mind had been unhurriedly deflating for years, it was only through some ill-defined sense of responsibility that I had exhausted my savings to keep her in a level of comfort she'd never recognize. And here I was, beyond death, yet still umbilicaled to this shriveled husk by a spiritual cord that nourished me with nothing save self-condemnation.

A pang of hunger nipped at my insides. I looked at the desiccated shell in the next bed longingly, a gourmand at an all-you-can-eat buffet. *Would anyone miss him? Would anyone even notice if I took just a nibble? Could this be a source of easy food, coma patients and the like?* The thought nauseated me, but not as much as it would have the week before. I was clearly going to have to continue my existence for a few more months at the bare minimum, and there would have to be a feasible menu. I tabled the notion for later review — whatever was happening, had happened, to me, it was still too early in the process to begin sketching out my meal plan.

"How are you?" she asked me.

"Fine, Mom. Relatively." This promised to be a rarity. Actual comprehension. Perhaps we could have a conversation without the need for guises. Over the past year, I had pretended to be her brother Everett, her father, her mailman, her classmate from junior high. I hadn't been myself with Mom in a very long time. Or ever, come to think of it. Even as a toddler I was guarded against her, knowing that she and I had deep character divisions, knowing that it was up to me to take on a guise and make her happy. "It's been . . . interesting of late. I've actually got some news. Good news."

"My Sheldon," she slurred. "My little Menno-knight. Always by my side."

The old pet name brought a smile to my lips. She called me that after Dad passed, spelling it out for me so I knew how special an appellation it was. A knight was a brave soldier, she said, someone who would always protect his loved ones. Later, when I was older, less tolerant of her passive-aggressive smothering, I grew to hate it. I would amend it to myself, Sheldon, the Menno-not. Now I cherished the memory, distorted though it was, and took on the role of loving son once more. "That's me."

"How have you been?"

"Oh, fine."

"Was school all right today? Did you learn anything?"

"Math was tough today," I decided. "Had a test. Aced it."

"Good boy. So smart." She stroked my cheek with the back of her hand. "So handsome."

"Aw, Mom."

"Any pretty girls you'd like to tell me about?" I squirmed in my chair. "Look at you. So shy. You'll like girls soon, you know. You don't think you will, but all that changes. Soon, you'll look at girls and can't imagine a life without them. All knights do."

"Jeez . . ."

Her eyes drifted off. "I've been lonely, waiting for you."

I braced myself, sensing a shift, the fading from one memory to another. "Sorry, I had to work."

"We all have excuses, don't we?" This was said to herself, talking to me without noticing me. "Everyone has excuses, no one ever takes the blame. That's the way it is." Her eyes focused on me briefly, flitting with contempt, before looking away, her sight already fuzzed over with memory. "I always worry about Sheldon."

"Goddammit."

"Don't blaspheme, Roland, you know how that upsets me."

I was suddenly glad I lacked the ability to inadvertently vocalize a sigh. Not that she'd remember the slight. Mom's memory had been getting steadily worse as delirium clearcut her brain, carving off large chunks of her past. She'd had good days, especially when she first arrived. She understood the nature of her surroundings, the purpose of my visits. Our conversations then were not all that different from talks we'd had over the previous thirty years. Mom was an insular creature, always focused on her own self and how the world outside continually failed to live up to her exacting expectations. Chats were drastically one-sided affairs, and I often mused that I was not at all necessary to the dialogue, as her running commentary included her perceived responses from my end.

"You know Margaret Evans, down the street. She has that house with the fence, the one that should have been painted green. Her daughter, Felicia, you went to school with her, she was a year or two behind you, you know her, hee hee, she's now a doctor, something to do with the eyes, an—" and here Mom would consult her notepad to freshen her memory "ophthalmologist, isn't that something. Well you could have never predicted that, she was always a mean child, she pushed over our fence once — I'm sure it was her — but she's rich now, so there you go."

Many times I pitied the poor people who crossed her path — librarians, cashiers, mail carriers, food court service personnel, grocers, Jehovah's Witnesses, the homeless — as she would launch into her structureless stream of consciousness without hesitation, assuming the person unlucky enough to cross in front of her eyesight was already a participant in her nomadic tête-à-têtes, knew of the people she mentioned, summarily agreed with her assertions. Her lapse into dementia was thus so subtle a process that it went nigh unnoticed by me until the day she prepared a mighty Thanksgiving feast of turkey, mashed potatoes, squash, corn, and apple pie, all for me and my decades-dead father, all on July 17th.

So at first our visits were actually comforting in their inanity, and I convinced myself that her condition, while severe enough to merit a move to a home, was as bad as it could get. She'd berate me for not visiting enough, and then switch topics to whatever she had seen that day on the news. She'd ramble on while I sat next to her, holding her hand and reading scripts, memorizing lines, or channel surfing. It was inconvenient, but tolerable. Quickly this changed, and each visit became the first in a good long while. She'd claim through angry sheets of tears that I hadn't been around enough, even though I had visited two days previous. Then she began to smile when I came around, glad to see me, how had I been, but it was a front, politely covering up the fact that she had no idea who in the world I could be. The talks at this point invariably swirled around bizarre delusions that festered beneath her surface. Fears of persecution ran rampant through her few remaining neurons. Asians were destroying the free market system. Her sister Carrie stole her favorite teacup. Her neighbor Mr. Wallis poisoned her cat, she was sure of it and she'd confront him on it the next time she saw him. Mr. Wallis was a WWII veteran who had retired and passed away long before we had ever gotten a pet, a beagle named Cooper that mom had never cared for but was the totality of my world for years after Dad's accident.

Accompanying these imagined persecutions were lengthy sermons on her concept of God as indefinable cloud of wrath, scourge of evildoers, fornicators, homosexuals, and actors. Each visit was a front row seat to the very worst in human prejudices, a ticket to a terrifying

Baptist revival, a marathon viewing of Fox News. Her diatribes were so predictable I could mouth silently along, lip-synching to the righteous arbiter of morality. Karaoke hatred.

And still, I welcomed her insanity as a long-overdue form of freedom. No longer did I have to hide my lovers under the guise of "acting partners." Mom's lunacy set me free of her chains, at least hypothetically. And very soon, the nurses told me, her memory would be sanded down to a smooth plane of nothingness, at which point we'd have "the talk" to discuss her move to the tenth floor, the floor of the walking dead, the ward of the tattered ambulatory cadaver, where residents freely roamed the halls, bare of feet, clad in old nightgowns and PJs, muttering softly to themselves about past triumphs and woes in never-known glossolalic languages until a passing Samaritan found a few precious minutes to guide them back to their rooms.

Maybe I should check myself in.

"Sorry, dear," I replied, taking on Dad's role. "It's been a long day. At the office."

"No excuse," she muttered. "What if Shelley heard that kind of language coming from his father? Can you imagine how damaging that could be?"

"I'll watch my tongue, dear."

"Such a good boy." She played with her crucifix for a few moments, intent on making it dance across her chest. "I don't think he likes girls, Roland," she said offhandedly. "Not one bit. A bit of a sissy, that one."

My mouth went drier. "What makes you say that?"

"Oh, a mother knows." She smiled to herself, suddenly a young woman. "He hides it, but I can tell. Thinks I don't notice when his *friends* come over. Oh, they're just from my class, that's what he tells me. Lying to his mother. Shameful."

"You've known? All this time?"

"I didn't want to admit it to myself. And think of the scandal! Do you think I could show my face in church again? No, better he hide it in shame, alone."

"Couldn't you have just . . ." I struggled with the words. "Couldn't you. Accept him?"

"Certainly not! We don't just pick and choose which sins we ignore. If he would just tell me the truth, we could go seek help."

Knowing it to be an impossibility, the veins in my head nonetheless began to throb. "Maybe he's just. Afraid of what you would say."

"Oh, how can you say that? I love him, Roland. I just want his soul to be safe. He could always tell me anything. I'd forgive him, I know I would. And together, we'd walk out of the darkness." Her words spiked with barbs. "It's all your fault, anyway. Don't think you've ever fooled me."

I stayed silent, uncertain how to end the topic. Not sure if I should.

"With your trips out of town. You know."

"Trips?"

"When was the last time we had sex?"

Oh, God. I leaned in. "Hon, what are you. Saying? What trips?"

"You think I didn't know? I thought you'd stop when we married. I guess I'm the fool, aren't I? A few kind words, too much wine, and there you go, forty years of denial. What a joke I am."

"Stop what? What trips? Where did I go?"

"I hired a detective to follow you!"

"What did I do?"

"Sheldon, when did you get here?"

Fuck!

"It's good to see you, dear. I've been so lonely."

I clasped my head in my hands. *So close*, I thought, but close to what I still wasn't sure. "I'm fine, Mom. Just been . . . real busy."

"No." She pulled her blankets up to her chin, her eyes shot through with fear. "It's not you."

"It's me, Mom. It's Sheldon."

"It's not you. I know who you are."

"It's Sheldon, Mom," I tried again, struggling to keep my voice down to a harsh whisper. "Your son."

"You're not Sheldon," Mom said, her eyes suddenly wide but focused on the wall behind me. I could count the veins beneath the opacity of her skin. Hell, I could hear the blood sluicing its way through her system. I clutched at the armrests and the metal dented under the pressure. "I know my Sheldon, you're not him. He's a fornicator and a homo."

"Got it in one, Mom," I mumbled.

"I speak to God about Sheldon," she continued. I shifted my lips in an effective mime show of her harangue. "I speak to Him every day and I pray every night that He might show Sheldon the error of his ways. He lives a life of sin. He doesn't know that I know. I thank the Lord his father died before he could see the abomination his son has become."

"Your husband was gay," I interrupted. "I'm pretty sure. You just said so."

"Roland was a good man. I kept him from temptation."

"Whatever you say. Mom, I've got some news. I don't have. A lot of time here."

"He was a good boy once. I don't know what happened. He strayed."

"I got a job, Mom. A good one."

"He became an actor. That's what made him queer. All those liberals. That's how they get you."

"It'll pay enough to. Help you stay here."

"I asked him to pray to God for guidance."

"Maybe I could have you moved. To a better place."

"Do you know what he said to me?"

"If I'm an actor. Then this is what God wants."

"'This is what God wants.'"

"God doesn't make no mistakes."

"'God doesn't make no mistakes.' Even then, he was lost."

"I was there, Mom. It's me."

"I love you, Sheldon. That's what I said to him."

"Now you're just. Flat-out lying. What would God think about that?"

"I love you, but God will surely punish you for your sinful ways."

"You might have. Had a point there," I admitted. I took her hand, feeling the throb of her blood push into my palm. It was like cradling an injured sparrow. "Mom, I have to go now. I don't know if you'll understand. I just wanted. I don't know what I wanted. But you'll be fine. I'm going to make sure of it."

"I love my son," she said. "I always tried to make sure he knew that. Please believe me."

I held myself still, barely able to keep from squeezing her hand harder. "I know you did. What happened to him. Was not your fault."

"Sheldon was not the easiest child to like. So many problems. So intelligent. Always asking questions."

"I'm sure he just. Couldn't help himself."

"I don't want you to take him."

"I won't," I said. "I won't take him, I promise."

We sat in conflicted silence.

"Take him where?" I asked.

Her hand tightened around mine. "Please tell me you won't take him. Take me, please." I pulled my hand away. Mom breathed out a whine and scratched ineffectually at me. "Don't take him, he's a good boy. He's just confused."

"Who do you think I am, Mom?"

Her clawing became more agitated, pulling at the sheets. She whipped her head back and forth, her sparse hairs getting caught in her mouth. "I won't let you. You can't have him. It was all my fault, I should have been stronger for him." I took her hands and held them still. She fought at the familiarity of my touch, gasping in rage, but there was no muscle behind the battle. She quickly went limp, but her eyes glared at me, seeing me, seeing something. "I hate you." There was no confusion in her eyes, no fear or pretense. For perhaps the last moment of her life, she was focused on the now.

"Where do you think. I'm going to take Sheldon?" I asked.

"To Hell."

"Mom, it's *Sheldon*," I hissed. She writhed and groaned at the sound, but I refused to let her go. "Please see me, Mom. Just this once. I'm right here."

"You're a trickster," she snapped. Her teeth were bared in her fury, she was a dancing skeleton in my arms. "You're the devil, but I won't let you take him."

"It's me, Mom. *Please*."

"I'm not afraid of you. I spit at you." A weak stream of drool slipped over her lower lip and moistened her collar. "I spit in your face for the glory of God."

"Who am I, Mom?" I yowled. Her face flattened under the force of my yell. N. Nowlan's heart rate monitor rushed faster. "Tell me! Who do you think I am?"

"You're Death," she said, and she collapsed to the bed, eyes shut.

I shook her by the shoulders, snarling. *I should eat her.* The idea ran screaming through my skull. *Eat her. Destroy the bitch. That'll show her who's death and who isn't.* I lifted her hand to my nose and took a sniff, glorying in the aroma, the meat so tender, bones so fragile. *Like chewing on salmon bones.* The thought made me grin. I placed her fingers in my mouth. They lay slack atop the points of my incisors, the skin dimpling. *It's what she deserves, after all. They all deserve . . .*

I stopped, letting go but keeping my teeth tight around the fingers so that the arm swung from my mouth. *Who deserves it? Who deserves what?* What was I contemplating here? A feeding frenzy? Indiscriminate killing? I had my mother's hand in my mouth, I had almost eaten my mother. Was I serious? For fuck's sake, something was seriously wrong with me, and I had better come to grips with its implications before I took such an enormous step. There's survival for the sake of survival, and I understood that the eating of live flesh was somehow now an essential part of my being. I wasn't yet prepared to search for an efficient means of exterminating myself, so I was going to have to find a way to manage my appetites somehow.

But eating one's own mother? Out of spite? That surely toed a line in someone's sandbox.

Lost in a moral quagmire, I ignored the scrabbling of fingers in my mouth. The fingers grabbed at my tongue, gained purchase and pulled me downward, finally getting my attention. My mother clasped my tongue in a death grip, her nails scraping at my taste buds. Her eyes blazed a dark insanity.

"I've got you now, fucker," she wheezed, showering my face in spittle and venom. "You thought you could kill me, but I'm stronger than you thought!"

"*Gluawop!*" I said, gargling around her digits. I batted weakly at her arm to loosen her grasp but she hung on, sliding off the bed as I stepped backward and pulling me to my knees to avoid losing the tongue altogether.

"I'm taking you with me, Satan!" she yelled, astoundingly powerful of voice. "Take me now, Lord, while I still have the strength!"

I screamed in panic, snapping her back into unconsciousness. I thrashed my head away, spitting out her fingers. There was a slight copper taste in my mouth, overlaying the flavor of her flesh, sparking my fear. The panic threw fuel on my hunger and I roared in confusion. N. Nowlan's body shivered once and his monitor flat-lined. I stumbled to my feet and flew toward him, throwing off his blanket and taking as enormous a bite as I could out of his upper leg, another, anything to quell the beast. I pulled him to the floor in my fluster, knocking over his IV and leaving him splayed on the cold tile. I loosed another scream, deeper, the nutrition of N.'s ligaments taking instant effect. I hefted his body in a fireman's carry and rushed out and down the hall, knocking over carts and trays, continuing my shrieking, hoping that it would keep people out of my way.

I ran freaking into the night, only composing myself when I

reached my car and had to drop N. into a snow bank and search my pockets for keys. I jammed the body into the trunk and threw myself into the driver's seat, tearing out of the lot, crumbling with shame as I savored the remnants of N. between my teeth. But overlaying that flavor, far worse, was the vinegar tang I still tasted of the one drop of my mother's blood that had seeped out of her finger.

Tasted it, and liked it.

It's the eyes.

That's what's most unsettling for people upon meeting me. And re-meeting me. What I mean to say is, they never get over it.

My eyes used to be a lovely brown, deep, hued like a mug of Sumatra. Almost black, but just so. Unsettlingly dark, but projecting the intrinsic warmth of an aged ski lodge or neighborhood pub. My best feature, often remarked upon by casting directors, boyfriends, and strangers alike.

Now, my eyes are still my most arresting feature, but for a far different reason.

You'd be surprised how easily an eye can be damaged if you never blink.

I mastered the undead art of simulating breath, but only as a means of communicating with others. Without the impediment of speech — so necessary in society — I never would have bothered to relearn the unexpectedly onerous art of lung and larynx manipulation to achieve aural interaction.

So it is with the eyes, or rather, the blinking of eyelids. An almost completely unconscious impulse that occurs upwards of twenty thousand times a day. If you don't blink, you don't provide your optic organs with a mop and sponge to clean and protect their valuable finish. And if your lachrymal glands are on the fritz and can't produce saltwater, or your eyes don't register discomfort at the myriad motes that bombard it constantly, you don't blink. A grain of sand, fine as dust yet harsh as barbed wire, can affix to the lens for days without notice.

Thus, I present my eyes. Windows to my soul. Festooned with wounds. Scratched, streaked. Scuffed, lacerated, scraped, pitted. Once-penetrating ocular marvels reduced to globes of mottled limestone with underlying streaks of brown shale, as if someone took steel wool and scrubbed my lenses to remove some particularly vexing sties.

A daily regiment of saline squirted into each eye at regular intervals helped stave off the erosion for a few months. I wore safety glasses at first when I walked outside, then a fashionable pair of ski goggles, and then tinted flight goggles I had absent-mindedly pocketed and taken home after a day's work as an obviously doomed fighter pilot on an episode of *The X-Files*. Something had eaten at the power couplings to the engine, a rust monster or something, which thereupon hurtled my character into a mountaintop at mach 5, and only Mulder and Scully could stop it. I was the wingman, not the main pilot. I had two lines: "What the—" and "Ahhh!" I gave it my all but, as Rowan related, I had the scream of a prepubescent child undergoing a tantrum. The sound effects guys foleyed in a stock scream over my agonized face as I smacked into the rocks and the jet exploded around me. I didn't feel so bad about keeping the goggles after that, even if I never had a practical use for them. Until now.

I can still see. Hazy, milkwater world it now is, but still recognizable. Clearer than you might expect, as pupil and iris are all but absent underneath the abrasions. But I would fail any driving test.

It was a repulsive carpet, fashioned with depressing swirls of orange and green. It did, however, effectively disguise the crusted beads that led out from the door of apartment 4E and down the hallway to the stairwell. You'd notice only if you were looking for them.

The door was unlocked. It moaned soulfully as I pushed it open.

Nice touch, I thought, and entered.

The smell was immediate, intense and luscious.

I entered the tiny foyer, a five-foot square space of tile that butted up against the kitchen to my left, a hallway to my right, and a living area directly in front of me. Out of habit I shuffled the snow off my feet, but there was no such need for formalities. The apartment was a tomb.

"Craig?" I whispered to the crypt. "Mr. Neal? You here?"

It had hit me that morning during shooting. I had just taken a shotgun blast to the back, and supposed hero Duane Linwood (late of the Disney Channel's *Tales of a Tenth Grade Superstud*) was triumphantly holding the gun aloft over my prone form. The evil (i.e., me) was dead, was the presumption, as few ever came back from such injuries. Ah, but good old Lester hadn't become a maniacal slayer of buxom lasses without gleaning a few offbeat survival techniques, and had fortuitously been wearing a bulletproof vest (knowledge of such to be revealed in a lengthy epilogue by a grizzled forensic examiner whose sole filmic purpose was to glimpse at my remains, mutter exposition, and then act surprised when he turned around to discover that Lester's body had mysteriously vanished. The end?). Lester would then arise, as if from the dead, and come at Duane with one of several deadly contrivances he had hidden around his cellar dwelling. Such is the life of near-indestructible killers, always one more trick up the sleeve, one more boo to the audience.

As I lurched upward, a noisy and graceless process (later edited into a resurrection of sly fluidity during post-production), I gargled out my line: "You think you've defeated me? A boy like you? I have spoken with the devil himself and come away smiling. I can never die." Deathless prose. Then, according to script, Lester was to frisbee a rotary saw blade directly at Duane's awaiting head. It would graze his temple, eliciting torrents of blood (they'd trim it back to keep us PG-13, then release the extra blood in an unrated DVD), but he'd come back unbowed with fists a'blazing. We'd trade barbs and blows, a fight to the death in dimly-lit crowded quarters, ultimately ending in Lester's throat impalement with a handy piece of rebar.

Duane waited expectantly for the rubber blade to hurtle toward him, trying not to flinch. The prop saw sat patiently in my grip, awaiting its moment to shine.

All I could think was *shit shit shit shit shit.*

Back from the dead. That was me. And in all the confusion, all the ridiculous planning of career opportunities and dietary options, I had forgotten one of the basic tenets of the zombie genre; if you're bit, you change.

Craig was bit. Craig, the morgue attendant. Craig, the guy who had removed my innards before I snapped his forearms, had gotten a heaping dose of Sheldon. And that simple fact, I had bit someone and let him live, *that* had slipped my mind.

I strode off the set over Zed's objections, muttering apologies. *Calm down*, I told myself. *You bit Mom, remember?* I had called often to check in on her condition, not daring to show my face again. The nurses reported no change, she was still delusional, still ranting. Of N.'s disappearance there was no mention, and I could not hazard asking about him. I figured they must have had some primo lawyers keeping the whole disappearance quiet, or N.'s family had simply shrugged in relief at not having to pay for a funeral.

This meant nothing, I knew. So Mom *seemed* fine. I had only pierced her finger, probably, the pinprick of my incisor; the infection could still be festering, biding its time. Craig, I had sliced open a jagged seam along his hand and drooled contagion within him.

I started scanning online news sites, searching for any mysterious deaths being reported, any recent missing persons cases left unsolved, any pets run away. In Toronto, this only gave me hundreds of possibilities, a proverbial haystack of needles. Fucking useless, is what I mean to say. No way to be sure, although I could reasonably ascertain that there were no reports of a body being found with strange cannibalistic bite marks about its exterior. Small favors.

I tracked down Craig's address, using a pay phone to dial every Craig and C. Neal in the book, asking for the gentleman who worked in the morgue, hanging up at every *huh, what,* or *who.* Only two numbers gave me possibles, both calls picked up by answering machines. One was for a fairly ritzy address in Bedford Park, the other for an apartment in Scarborough.

I went with the apartment.

Now, entering at three in the morning, I figured I had guessed correctly. It was dark inside, but from the light of the hallway behind me I could glimpse suggestions of carnage.

The bloody handprint on the wall was a dead giveaway.

"Craig?" I tried again. "Buddy?"

I closed the door behind me, locking it and fumbling for the light switch. Speckles of red spattered the carpet leading down the hall. I ignored them and walked into the den, keeping low until I reached the curtains to pull them shut. The apartment was on the fourth floor of a nine-story complex, but it was one building of many, all with open windows looking in my direction. There was no sense in leaving myself open to any possibility of detection. From this vantage point in the suite, something was clearly amiss. Standard couch, standard coffee table, standard flatscreen television atop standard pressed wood entertainment unit. All overturned or broken. Very little blood, but salt-stained boot prints were stomped into the white carpet. A lot of them. A few pictures hung askew on the walls, images of happy times. Craig and a woman on a water slide, Craig and the same woman on a beach, the duo and a newborn child posing at a hospital bed, the woman's hair bedraggled, Craig looking exhausted, both beaming.

I looked toward the hallway, toward the bedrooms.

For the first time since death, I was truly afraid.

I walked down the hall, avoiding stepping on the trail of blood that led my way. Odd I should feel squeamish.

The handprint was next to an open doorway. The tracks led inside, drops getting larger, becoming splashes, then a lengthy swatch of red that ended at a pair of legs dangling over of edge of a bed. Shapely legs, legs someone had cared about, legs now ornamented with ragged bite marks.

I turned on the light.

The woman from the picture.

I recognized her from the color of her hair. There was nothing else to go by.

The face of some loveliness was now an orifice. The skin had been ripped out from the middle and now hung in curtains on either side of the head. I could picture Craig, insatiably hungry, pushing his fingers in like an eager child opening a bag of potato chips. The skull had been forced inward until the bones had given way, its contents scooped out like a jack o' lanterns until there was nothing left. It was late winter outside, but already a few industrious flies were setting up shop within the hollow of her thoughts.

I stifled an urge to take a nibble and moved on.

I left the bedroom and went to the next door, also open. I left the lights off, but from the glow of the shuttered window I could see it was a child's bedroom. Dora the Explorer wallpaper trim, a small bed still equipped with guardrails to prevent nocturnal fall-out, a Spongebob plush on the floor. What was left of Craig's daughter was heaped in the corner, shredded beef. I closed the door before my hunger could make demands that my self-control could not withstand.

This was not the work of something that cared about being caught. This was raw appetite. If I had harbored a hope that Craig would be like me, perhaps prove a kindred spirit, someone to talk to, form a support group with, that hope was long gone. I was alone, and making a friend an impossibility. Anyone who suffered the side effects of my personal plague was doomed to a post-death existence of mindless eating.

Of Craig himself there was no sign. I checked out the rest of the apartment to be thorough, but aside from further boot prints, I found nothing.

Judging by the scent, Craig's first foray into cannibalism had been recent, not more than two days previous. Craig was out on the streets of Toronto, shambling, feral, ravenous, and clearly insensate. There should have been something in the news by now. Craig didn't seem one to lurk in the shadows; he would have locked onto the nearest source of nourishment and begun bingeing.

How did he even get out of the building? I imagined myself as Craig, lying in bed, feverish, telling the wife it was nothing, just a bug picked up somewhere from work. He'd be fine in the morning. She's too trusting, too scared to call an ambulance, doesn't want to jinx Craig's recovery. Then, for a brief instant, he leaves the world, checks out, dead. It couldn't have been too long an interval, she would have called someone. Then, the demon rises, Craig no longer, now only monstrous appetite clad in flannel pajamas. It surprises Craig's wife, crushes her skull, slurps out its contents. It hears the cry of a child in the next room and instinctively follows the noise, helpless to stop, unbound by morality, compelled to honor its bloodlust. There is no sense of satiation, no ability or desire to stop when full. Perhaps Craig was still inside somewhere, screaming, an unwilling voyeur to his body's new self. And then . . . what? Could it find its way out of the apartment? Could it master a doorknob? Did it understand the concept of "doorway"?

I looked again to the footprints on the carpet, noted how many of them there were. How fresh they seemed. The signs of struggle in the den were too clean. Only a few traces of blood. Nothing to do with Craig's family.

Someone else had been here.

There was nothing I could do. Whatever had happened, Craig would never return. I toyed with calling the police, but gave it up, too dangerous. Let someone else find this, the damage was already done. Craig's wife and child weren't getting any deader.

I left, locking the door behind me and exiting as rapidly as I could, watching out for any insomniacs who might be strolling about the halls in search of late-night conversation. I walked around the building, not sure what I was looking for, not finding anything but a nagging paranoia. I looked up at the buildings that surrounded me, suddenly feeling exposed, watched.

Other than the omnipresent hum of traffic somewhere miles away, nothing stirred.

I walked back to my car and drove home, keeping to the speed limit, thinking of legions of the dead attacking the city, thinking of Mom, thinking of my depleting stocks of food. Soon, the food was all I cared about. I scanned the sidewalks, turning onto the expressway to reach the perimeter and take a leisurely hunt for transients and runaways.

The negligible distinctions between my actions and Craig's didn't bother me one bit.

"Hey, Gary, Gary, man, I just wanted to say, sir, you were amazing today."

"Oh. Thanks."

"No, please don't brush me off, I'm not trying to make stupid small talk here. You were . . . *amazing*. You owned the set, man, and I am an admirer. I mean that."

"Well. Thank you very much . . . Duane."

"Friends call me D.J."

"Thank you. D.J."

"No, thank you. It was a master class out there with you today, could you feel it? The way we fed off each other, the energy? Man! Hey, listen, would you — oh hey, where are my manners, you wanna partake? I got plenty, the producers gets me refills whenever I want, so no worries there."

"No, thanks."

"That's cool, thought I'd ask. Um, you don't mind if I—"

"Go ahead."

"*Gracias*, amigo."

I waited patiently by my dressing room door while Duane Linwood expertly tapped out a nostril's worth of white courage from a handy silver tube he wore around his neck like an amulet and did a quick line off the back of his hand. "Eeeee-oooo! Good god but that is fine, fine shit. I don't know where you Canadians get your stuff, but this is primo. Congrats to you."

". . . Thank you?"

"So, where was I? Hey, can I have a bite of your sandwich there? Looks good, what is that, beef?"

"Uh. No, sorry. I have these made special. Dietary needs. You understand. For . . . diabetes."

"Ooh. Right right right, sorry, man, no worries. Wow. Don't know why I'm so nervous. Whoo! Nice stuff, nice. What I was saying, I know that you're a loner, lone wolf and all, right, cool, and I wouldn't want to upset that, I get it, you're a professional, need your space. Say the word, I back off, right, 'cause I respect you as an artist. Sometimes, man, I envy that, the ability to just fade out and enjoy the privacy, but my entourage, you've seen them, the douchebags in my room with the Bluetooths in their ears? They don't get that sometimes. Always wanting to be around, never giving me space. Gets to be a bit much, am I right? But see, a few of the guys and gals are going out for drinks in a bit, some dance bar downtown. Just to unwind a bit since there's little scheduled tomorrow, just some pickups. You . . . you wanna maybe come?"

"Oh. I can't. Tonight."

"Please? It'll be fun. And I really want to probe your mind, y'know, I'd love to talk about your method. That is, if you're okay with that. I just really admire what you're doing and I'd love some tips, right? One pro to another?"

"Well—"

"C'mon, please? Please please please please please?"

"Fine."

"Great. Tell you what, I'll come get you a few minutes after final wrap, give you some time to wipe the blood off your face, and the whole bunch of us will take the studio limo."

"You have. A Limo?"

"Perks, man, they are *awesome*. Anything I want, they get. Being a star, so hard sometimes, right? So, see you later, all right?"

"Right."

"*Awesome.*"

The words are there, but you're not seeing the bigger picture, the overall tableau of this conversation. You're not seeing the gleam in Duane's eyes, the wetness of his lips, the restlessness of his body, legs crossing and uncrossing and shuffling, arms unsure where to put themselves. Part of this was the cocaine; tabloids had so far not cottoned on to Duane's sizable addiction, but it couldn't be far off, the way he was snorting back a middle-class Canadian income every day. It wouldn't be much of a surprise or scandal — wow, a Disney television teeny-bopper doing drugs, what an absolute shocker of a coup — but this kid didn't have *anything* to fall back on. He certainly didn't have enough talent to make up for it; there was little to no chance of rehabilitation and public resurgence in Duane's future. If he was lucky, he'd get a few more years of partying and maybe one or two more movie roles before his winsome good looks eroded and the offers dried up. If he were smart, he'd have the sense to take his winnings and retire gracefully; if he wasn't (certainly the lottery ticket I'd play), he'd grab at any passing lifebuoy, anything to keep himself in the public eye. *Skating with the Stars*, *Celebrity Rehab*, movies on SyFy and Lifetime, anything to hold on to that one last mote of public recognition.

But even factoring in the dependency, it accounted for maybe half of Duane's excitement. You're not seeing the flash flood of red that filled his cheeks as he asked me to come out for drinks. Duane was in the closet, but he had his hand on the knob. And he had enough savvy to sense me out as a fellow member, and enough cunning to try to use that to his advantage.

You're also not seeing the startlingly realistic traces of blood on my lips and chin, remarked upon by the brilliant Duane but passed over in his trepidation. Had he been slightly more observant, he might have thought to himself that all our scenes today had been mainly dialogue and close-ups, and that the rain of gore and red-dyed corn syrup inherent in the final half of *Basement* (working title) had already been completed two weeks previous, reshoots permitting. You're certainly not seeing into the room behind my closed door, with its personal cooler filled with tidbits of the meatiest hors d'oeuvres available from the human body — a slice of upper arm, a hunk of buttock, two earlobes. You may be seeing the sandwich in my hand, wondering *how*; through trial and error, I learned I *could* ingest bread if it were sliced thin enough and if the filling was one hundred percent human. In this manner I was able to more fully interact with others, taking my lunch with them or snacking in full view. The impulse to bite every person on set was only getting stronger as the days multiplied into weeks. It was far easier to get through the day if I had a little something to nibble on between takes, either in sandwich form or, better, in the privacy of my (thanks to Rowan) personal dressing room.

My main supply was kept at home in my downstairs freezer. My stockpiles of Fisher and N. had long since been exhausted and disposed of, and I was now subsisting on Anonymous Hobo Number Four, numbers One, Two, and Three having been summarily excavated of every tiny nibble of sustenance I could suck out of them. (It's surprising how little there is left of a body, how little actually has to be lugged to the curb for morning garbage pickup when you eat practically every part. I had always been a finicky eater — I didn't enjoy chicken on the bone, I didn't like eating with my fingers, I didn't even like apple peel, something about the crunch — but my new appetites were not concerned with such niceties. I now ate everything possible in the human buffet, and gnawed incessantly on everything else until I had fully exhausted every possible nutritional soupçon from whomever was dinner that day. I had hid the final indigestible bits of Fisher in a garbage bag under old coffee grounds and eggshells, and filled the rest with food I wouldn't be needing anymore in the fridge. I instructed myself to start composting in the spring, to lessen possible discovery.)

Whoever said that only in death do you appreciate life was stirring an enormous crock of shit. I wasn't having any fun at all. Life sucked, death sucked worse.

Hobo Numero Uno was the worst. Far worse than Fisher and N., both of whom I write off as being the accidental end result of nights of confusion and/or terror. H1 was my first intentional, an authentic hunt for prey. I didn't suppose there was an actual factual Hell in which I would burn for my acts, not anymore — I was proof that, if Hell wasn't full, Cerberus was being more selective of late at the door — but that didn't alter the moral conundrum surrounding the act that was cannibalism.

It was Sofa that started it, if one can possibly use an overweight feline as a scapegoat for murder.

I had finished up with N., licked the plates clean of his flavor. Initial photography wouldn't begin for another week, and I had been working on memorizing the script and crafting a suitable background for Lester Ulysses, the confused and curiously innocent serial killer who lured millennials away from their dorm rooms and into his cellar for an evening's worth of vivisection. The pangs had been pounding away at the foundations of my resolve for a good twenty-four hours. I found myself eyeing Sofa as she toyed with the tassels on my kitchen window curtains. She batted away at the strings, purring, content to sublimate her natural aggression and killer instincts into an amusing distraction. Maybe I needed a hobby, I thought, a diversion to keep my mind occupied. The work wasn't enough; maybe stamp collecting? I scooped Sofa into my arms as I thought this over and placed my hand gently about her throat. She amped the volume of her purrs and went limp, exposing her belly for a satisfying scratch. I began to squeeze, and while I considered whether a forced interest in model trains was likely to keep my yearnings at bay, I throttled my cat. Only when her protestations reached a shrieking climax did I regain focus and realize that I had my teeth firmly around her neck, pressing through the soft fur and dimpling the hidden meat beneath. I wrenched my head back and snapped my fingers open. Sofa fell to the tile and sped from the room to the basement, hissing all the way.

If I didn't eat soon, I was going to lose control. It was a constant ache, a cloudy yearning akin to that of addicts coming down and wondering where their next fix is coming from. You don't want it, you despise it, you detest yourself for wanting it, but in the end you cave in and feel remorse for thirty seconds, then you're satisfied, and then the craving starts anew, stronger and sharper. I didn't even have the brief respite of sleep provided to the drug addict, sleep being something I hadn't done for quite some time.

I needed to feed, and quick. Morality be damned; when I was perilously close to eating my cat, the ethicality of homicide could be put aside for a time.

But where? And more crucially, who? I lived in a Toronto suburb, in a predominantly lower middle-class tax bracket. People thereabouts tend to notice when their loved ones don't come home at night. I had already experimented with animals — I had cleared the area of unlucky squirrels with some traps, I once happened across a roadkill raccoon — but while such meals eroded the pangs, they were stopgaps, like craving Black Forest cake and getting a Twinkie. And animals, unlike humans, had to be fresh; day-old animals wouldn't cut it with my gag reflex. When it came to meat, I would accept no substitutes. To satisfy my hunger, I'd have had to go through at least a full beagle every day, and I couldn't see daily trips to the SPCA as not raising suspicions.

So. Hitchhikers, then. Cheap and plentiful, if you were patient.

Like fishing.

I began taking drives out of the city at night, looking for the perfect confluence of lone hitcher and lack of witnesses. I picked up H1 about an hour outside of Toronto the first night, thumbing his way southwest from the Maritimes. He was just a kid, said his name was Jamie. His story of running away from his abusive stepfather and wanting to go live with his real father in Minneapolis read a little theatrical to me, but I wasn't in a position to judge. He needed a place to stay the night, and I offered him the guest room. He gave me a suspicious look, but I had disabled the interior light so that he couldn't get a good look at my condition, put on clean clothes and lined my garb with dryer sheets, clean scented. We drove in the dark as I contemplated the next move. Was it late enough that people wouldn't see us arrive? I had a connecting garage, but people might still glimpse Jamie in the streetlights as we drove down the street. Would the neighbors wonder why I was taking my car out at weird hours? Why hadn't I simply killed him as he first sat down in the car? How did serial killers pull this off night after night? And could I use this life experience as research for Lester?

Useless questions, I knew. I could feel the throbbing of his pulse in my bones, like the heavy thump of house music. His aroma as he sat next to me fiddling with the radio played havoc with my scent receptors, suddenly alive and jumping. If it wasn't Jamie tonight, I was going to wander next door and slay the eight-member Russo family as they slept. Or I'd cross the street and devour the nameless motorcycle enthusiast who couldn't see the value in installing a goddamned muffler on his Harley. Or I'd eat Sofa out of hunger-induced hysteria.

We pulled into the garage, and the automatic door rumbled shut behind us. I exited the car as quickly as possible while Jamie worked at getting his pack from the back seat. Walking around to the passenger side, I opened his door, pulled a startled Jamie to his feet, and sank my teeth into his jugular. I kept my teeth tightly together, jerked my head back, and mutely groaned with ecstasy as I munched on a mouthful of his tendons and gristle and muscle and trachea.

The kid fell back against the car, snatching feebly at his throat, trying to stem the gush. I opened wide and let the bloodspray hit the back of my throat, gulping greedily, a child playing barefoot in the sprinkler. He fell, and his life ebbed out onto the concrete as he stared at me. I dipped my fingers into the pooling red and took a quick suck. I'd feel bad about this later — I'd anguish and bemoan my fate and curse the heavens — but I won't deny that this was now my nature.

"I'm sorry," I told him, not bothering to soften the death in my voice. "I don't expect you to understand. This is just who I am now." This was a line from the script, a trite bit of nonsense meant to humanize Lester to the audience, but I nailed the sincerity. I felt Jamie deserved something for his troubles, even if it was only a bit of stagecraft.

"It was either you or my cat." That was an ad-lib.

Jamie's eyes went blank, and I left to fetch Dad's old ax.

The next kills were easier. I seized them as they first opened the car door and leaned in, tearing out their throats before they could let out a decent scream. In a nod to mercy, I felt that I could at least make it quick and not toy with my food. It became my signature move, a sudden lunge before they could note the plastic sheeting over the seats and floor.

Between keeping myself on a strictly regimented diet of raw earthling and having to appear in public, it was all I could do not to unleash myself on the nearest actor and feel the galvanizing zing of fresh lifeblood coursing down my gullet. The new pages of dialogue weren't helping to ease the tension, either. The dailies were proving my statements about Duane and his cadre of he- and she-pretties correct; there was barely a shred of acting talent to be found in front of the camera aside from yours truly. I've never been one to brag, but I was bringing it. The director, Zed — despite constant allusions to the work of Kurosawa, Tarantino, Hitchcock, Kubrick — was a twat, practicing utter hackery, betraying his music video beginnings by emphasizing camera angles and blue lens filters over content. You direct one Beyoncé video, get nominated for one MTV award, suddenly you're an auteur with twenty-five million dollars to fritter away. Zed was a poor leader of men, unable to corral his actors into actually trying or to encourage his cadre of set designers, lighting technicians, cameramen, and key grips into doing anything but the absolute minimum necessary to collect their pay. All told, it was a dismal set, professional journeymen biting their tongues as over-indulged starlets pretended to the glamour, preening and gossiping and demanding when they should have been, I don't know, acting.

At least Zed understood that when I was onscreen, the feeble efforts of his main cast were drowned by my sheer presence. Death had provided me an unsettling and savage charisma I had lacked in life, leastwise in the sphere of fictional cinematic serial killers. Around me, the cast seemed to step up their game; in actuality they were simply reacting to the feral dread I instilled. I had gotten so good at tonal modulation that I could bring a woman to tears with a mere whisper of her name. My voice was a doorway to terrors long thought extinct, buried deep within the subconscious over countless generations of civilization. I was a trigger that allowed primeval fears to resurface and rattle bones and hiss curses as they pranced up and down the spines of anyone in earshot.

Accordingly, the movie was now mine front and center, and only my lack of stature kept my name from being placed above the title alongside the likes of luminaries such as Duane J. Linwood and Raven Sullivan, oldest daughter on the CBS dramedy *The Diner*. Zed pushed me on the backers as being the next Robert Englund, the new Kane Hodder, hell, the next Christopher Lee or Anthony Perkins. He also demanded that my role be substantially beefed up, driving the screen-writer batty as he mangled the plotline to give me more screen time yet not push the "stars" off to the side altogether. After all, they were there to get gullible paying asses in the seats. I would keep them there.

But Duane (D.J. to his friends) was becoming a wee bit of a bother. I had thus far managed to keep myself relatively apart from the rest of the cast and crew save when we were on set. I had Rowan make it part of my contract, that there be as little contact with people outside of filming, a concession to my craft that would better allow me the time and isolation to hone my preparation and work my method upon the character. I was also to be in sole charge of my own makeup, lessening the possibility that people come into direct contact with my skin. I had insisted on this after the special effects artists had made a silicone cast of my face for some grueling damage Lester took at the hands of Raven late in the film. They coated my head in goop, wrapped the mess in plaster bandages, waited until it hardened, and then cautiously cracked it open. They were pros, they wouldn't let any normal subject come to harm, but they couldn't know I felt my skin tug loose from its moorings at the bottom of my chin and near the cheekbones. I let them finish, praying for adhesion, and instructed Rowan to demand I be allowed to do my own makeup for the duration of the shoot.

What utter bullshit, but actors are known for such idiosyncrasies. Wanting alone time, makeup demands, eccentric catering requests; these were nowhere near the weirdest contractual obligations ever made on a film set. I could have demanded that homeless children be rounded up and served to me cold and writhing on platters of stainless steel and garnished with peppermint; it would still be more reasonable than Brando's stipulations near the end.

Nevertheless, Duane was a problem in the making. He was a boy, barely old enough to grow sexy stubble-beard over his baby fat, yet a boy already used to getting everything he wanted, and double portions to boot. And what he wanted by the end of this evening, I was sure, was me. He could gussy it up, sheath it within the guise of a mentor/ student relationship, the inexperienced newcomer idolizing the wise old professional, the whole *All About Eve* or *Showgirls* thing, but Duane wasn't smooth enough yet to hide his real intentions. Duane was a young predator testing the limits of his pack leader's strength. This wasn't about sex; this was a power move. Duane was thick as beef stew, but he wasn't completely without a native cunning to better serve his own ends. He could hardly be unaware of the buzz I was getting, and it frightened him. *Basement* was his shot, his one great step away from family television movies and guest appearances on sitcoms into something approaching a serious career. He was the hero, I was the villain, and that was to be that. But when *Fangoria* came to visit, when the bloggers from Chud and Dread Central and JoBlo and Ain't It Cool found their way on set, Duane was all but ignored. The villain always gets the attention, both on and off-screen. Ergo, as the natural order of things was in danger of being rearranged to his detriment, Duane would fall back on a tried-and-true method of career salvation; he would tempt me, romance me, hold me in thrall to his sexual prowess, and then he'd whittle my role down to nothing.

What an ass. I could have told him, even Johnny Depp fell to Freddy in the end. Kevin Bacon didn't prove immune to Mama Voorhees and a spike through the neck, so what possible chance did an Efron-weight like Duane have? He'd be lucky to survive the night.

I should simply have gone home, claimed to have forgotten the invitation. Would have been the safer choice. But I was lonely. Sofa was only so good for companionship. On the set, only Zed talked to me off-camera, and he was an idiot. The crew mostly kept to themselves, and the rest of the cast was insufferably young and pretty. I was little more than a special effect to them, a lurching horror they screamed their lines at on-camera and ignored at all other opportunities. High school all over again. So Duane's sudden attention, while self-serving on his part, was a chance to have meaningful if shallow interaction.

Also, I was flattered he'd go to the trouble of seducing me.

I had to make sure that I could control myself. I ate every last morsel of roadside vagabond as I carefully applied a base to my cheeks. I never had to do much in the way of makeup for the movie, but to actually go out and walk among the normals, I'd have to give my face a bit of false vitality. The food would help keep my urges tamped down.

He knocked on my door at seven, rapping shave and a haircut with his knuckles. I slowly swung the door open and took him in. He had changed into a tight white T-shirt and jeans combo, topping it with a trucker hat emblazoned with the studio logo. The shirt clung alluringly to an absurdly prominent set of abs. His arms were overly Soloflexed, veiny, and they pushed against the confines of the cotton. It was cheesy, but I had a soft spot for the look. I could never pull it off myself. He was a finely shredded slab of ham, I had to give him that.

"You 'bout ready, dude?" His eyes were wide, fixed, and hyper-focused. He hopped from foot to foot, perhaps to make sure the sizable cocaine reserves swishing through his bloodstream weren't settling in his feet.

"Of course, Duane. I'll just. Get my coat."

"D.J., remember?"

"D.J. Yes."

"Hey, are you still in makeup?"

"No." *Damn.*

"Right."

"Shall we go?"

Duane practically pushed me into the back seat of the limo and climbed in next to me. It was an opulent affair: fully stocked bar, television, DVD player. We were, I noticed as the driver put the limo into gear and pulled away from the curb, the only people inside.

"Weren't there others. Coming along?"

"Hm?" Duane put on a dumbshow of forgetfulness. "Oh, right, the others, they, they all had to cancel. Some other thing, somewhere. Chicks, right? Always a party somewhere else."

"A shame."

"Well," Duane continued as he tapped out a healthy amount of snow on the back of his hand and did a line, "it's just you and me, then."

"No entourage?"

"Gave them the night off. Ordered them to have fun without me."

"Where are we headed?"

Duane took another snort and lay back on the chair. "Oh, I don't know, man. You know, I'm kinda played out right now. You just wanna come over to my hotel room, watch a movie or something? I've got a Wii."

Subtle. "I thought you wanted to. Talk about acting."

"Oh sure, that too."

Why not? "Why not?"

"Cool." He opened the bar and fetched himself a Bud Lite. He twisted off the top and took a tiny sip. "Mm, that is good, nothing better after a hard day." Even dead, I shuddered; Americans have no concept of good beer.

After a half-hour or so of idle talk, as Duane got more and more hyped up on his alternating drug and beer technique and I became increasingly irritated at being trapped in a leather-lined rolling coffin with a drugged-out idiot, the limo pulled into the parking garage of his hotel. It had not escaped my attention that at no time during our trip had Duane prompted the driver with a destination. What a putz. I *was* oddly warmed by his presumptuousness. I don't know that I'd even been stalked so flagrantly. It was like watching a lion cub cut his teeth by tackling his father on one of those nature channel documentaries. Adorable, but useless.

I took a seat on Duane's couch while he went to his bedroom to change. Idly, I tongued a remnant of drifter that was lodged between my molars while I took in the room. For a spontaneous evening out, the room was suspiciously guest-ready. Champagne chilled in a bucket with two long-stemmed flutes nearby, candles already lit upon our entrance. The daily rent on the place could cover an average mortgage for a few months, I was sure. But the hotel provided a fireplace, a widescreen television, a hot tub, a panoramic view of the city, a salt-water aquarium stocked with polychromatic endangered fish, and an unwritten policy of allowing celebrities *carte blanche* when it came to unruly/antisocial/borderline-criminal behavior. The kind of behavior that ruins lesser careers.

Duane bounced out of the bedroom, his outdoor ensemble swapped for white boxer shorts and a clean sleeveless tee. His biceps were festooned with ink patterns, barbed wire and Japanese calligraphy, *très* trailer trash chic. I gave him an approving smile and raised eyebrows, as I hadn't yet re-mastered the sarcastic eyeroll to the ceiling. He giggled. "So, you ready for some tennis?" He caught the confusion that crossed my face. "The Wii, buddy. Remember?" He mimed a backhand swing. "Gotta warn you, I'm pretty good."

I nodded. "I'm sure. Actually, D.J., I think I'll beg off. But you go ahead."

Duane put on a pout. "Well, that's no fun, not by myself." He sat in the recliner across from me. "So, hey, let's talk, right? I don't know anything about you."

I leaned back. "Ask away."

"So, what's with all the lumbering? I've watched you — you are always in character. I get it, the acting mystique, keeps the rest of us on our toes when you're around, right? Like Val Kilmer, the method, living your character all the time, that shit? Did you see *The Doors*? Rocked, man. That dude Morrison, he was fucked up. Don't get me wrong, fucking genius, no question. Fucked up, though. Right?"

Not sure to what question I should respond, I chose the silent nod as the best course of action.

"Cool. But," he said, getting up to grab at the champagne bottle and slouching himself nonchalantly onto the opposite end of my couch, "you're alone now, yeah? No cameras, no techies, no director. You can relax a bit." He filled the glasses to the brim and handed me one as he sipped from the other. "I won't tell, honest," he teased.

I put the glass aside. "Would that I could. It's not an act. My walk. I have early onset arthritis. See?" I flexed the fingers of my hands, hearing each knuckle crack as the movement snapped through the crusted blood in the veins. Duane shivered at the sound and took a long swallow of his drink as I continued. "I've suffered from it. For years now. It's like progeria. Advanced metabolic aging. Very rare."

"Is that why you talk like that? With all the stopping?"

"Yes. The arthritis has affected my. Lungs."

"That is harsh. I thought that was a, what's it called, an affectation."

"Afraid not."

"Wow, I'm sorry. But man, it works here. When the camera's on you, when you get that voice really going, it's like . . . you'll think this is stupid."

"I promise I won't."

Duane tucked his legs beneath him, curling himself up. "When you talk, it's like, all I can think of is when my gerbil died. I let Benny run around in my bedroom, and he ran into a heating vent. I couldn't get him out. I was too scared to tell my dad, he'd be so mad, so I, I left Benny in there. I could hear him scratching around, but he couldn't find his way out. Maybe he was stuck or something. I could hear his scratching when I went to bed. It got quieter and quieter, and then a few nights later, there was nothing. And I knew he had died." Duane wiped at his eyes. "Stupid. Stupid kid, too scared so he lets his pet die. And stupid me, still getting worked up over it."

He snorted and wiped the corner of his shirt under his nose.

"Anyway, that's what your voice reminds me of. Every time. When you talk like that, I hate you. The others too. I can't help it." He smiled weakly. "But that's acting, right? That's what you're supposed to do, picture dead relatives, get your emotions to the surface, right?"

"Duane, I . . . I had no idea." A huge lie, but what else could I say? I was suddenly aware of how much closer he was to me on the couch. His skin might as well have been cellophane; all I could see was engorged blood vessels awaiting my inspection and a healthy, veal-tender musculature. He kept talking, but all I could hear was the thick red molasses parading through his body, the *ba-bump ba-bump* of his accelerating heart rate, and the grinding of my teeth.

His eyes crinkled with worry. "Hey, I didn't upset you, did I? It's not like your voice always does that. Only when you're acting. Usually. Otherwise you're fine. I mean, not *fine*, but . . . you know.

"Wait, are you dying, Gary?" he whispered. He looked about the room, as if paparazzi were lingering on the periphery, behind the credenza or perched in the fronds of a fern. "I mean, like, it's cool if you don't want to tell me, I understand. Suffer in silence. I just thought you seemed kind of lonely on set. I can keep a secret." All I could smell was meat. "Is this why you're lonely? Afraid? I've seen you looking. You look like you want to take a bite out of me. But you're holding it in. You're afraid, and alone. I'm lonely too, right? Maybe we can be lonely together for a while. Make each other feel better."

My hands tightened into the cushions of the sofa and I willed myself to ignore the hunger screams. The drifterbaloney I had snacked on beforehand had obviously reached its expiration date, and I could feel my stomach muscles contract, physically pushing my stomach closer to Duane in preparation.

I forced myself to stand up. I'd completely misread the evening. "I think it's time I go," I said. "I need to go. I have to. Feed my cat."

"Oh, hey, I'm sorry." Duane bounded to his feet and stepped in front of me. I tensed instinctively at his nearness. "Did I come on too strong?" He looked genuinely hurt. "I do that, I'm sorry, please don't leave. I got a little excited, and fuck!" He started slapping himself across the cheeks. "Stupid, stupid. Damn, I'm so high right now I could visit the space station."

He halted his self-flagellation and placed a sweaty hand on my arm. The heat from his palm burned through my shirtsleeve and seared its imprint into my skin. My head swam with excitement and the world faded to red. My tongue took a run and shoved mightily against the back of its enamel prison, trying to pry open the teeth. It didn't matter that Duane was a high-profile celebrity whose disappearance would be definitely noticed. His vanishing would be the front item on *Entertainment Tonight* for weeks, but fuck it, I was going to binge on B-lister and screw my career, screw my mother, screw this whole goddamned excuse for an afterlife, all that mattered was giving in to the immediacy of this moment. There was no future to consider, there was only the splatter of blood between my jaws and the slowing pulse of his heart as it lay in my palms.

My stomach let loose a thunderous peal of ravenousness.

Duane's eyes swelled and he started to snicker. "Holy jeez, wow! That was vast! That's so epic!" He began to laugh as the clamor from my belly continued. "Man, when was the last time you ate? Holy shit!" I was on the verge of removing his Adam's apple as an appetizer, but his laughter cut the mist. I felt my appetite calmed by his high spirits. It was also contagious, and soon I was laughing along, albeit as silently as I could.

"I'm sorry about that," I said finally, after Duane's guffaws had subsided. "I guess I'm a little hungry."

Duane wiped at his eyes. "Look, please don't leave. I just thought . . . I was getting a vibe from you. You've got this whole mysterious older father figure thing going. I thought—"

"Don't worry about it," I said. "No harm done."

"Was I wrong? About the signals?"

"Sort of," I said. "It's not that you're. It's not that I don't. Find you attractive." But only as lunch. "It's . . . complicated."

"You're bi?"

"Christ. Not *that* complicated."

"What, you have a boyfriend? Girlfriend?"

"Yes." I grabbed at the excuse like a plane crash victim flailing for a floatation device. "He, well. We're maybe getting serious. I don't think I should betray him. It's not that I . . . ." Why was I continuing this? *Go home!* I screamed at myself. "D.J., I find you very attractive. But the timing is bad."

Duane sidled closer. "If you're worried I'll tell about your condition—"

"No, I'm sure you wouldn't." *You wouldn't survive the night.* My bowels spasmed with wrath. I imagined his tongue in my mouth, wrapping around mine before I bit down, feeling its wriggling as its severed nerve endings reacted to my saliva. "How about a raincheck? A maybe, after the shoot?"

Duane broke out the famous smile that adorned the covers of every cheap tabloid and teen magazine of note. "Raincheck, sure. Hey, tell you what, I'll lay off the snow for the evening, all right? I'll go put on some pants, we'll order some food in, calm that—" he patted my belly, and I nibbled on my lip to keep from nibbling on his "—fire in your oven there. I'll even send someone to feed your cat, okay?"

That made me smile. "No, she'll be fine. But thank you."

"So, we cool?" I nodded. Duane sighed in relief. "I'm gonna go put something on, okay? You promise not to leave?"

"I'll stay. Right here."

"Great, that's great." Duane walked out to the bedroom, chortling as my abdomen let loose another bellow of anger. I made for the door, hoping that he would forgive my silent escape, or that he'd get so high that he'd imagine he dreamed the whole conversation.

"So," he called from the bedroom. "I guess you figured out I'm gay, right?"

I stopped my exit. Son of a bitch, I didn't want to leave. "Hadn't noticed," I called back, getting a loud *Haw!* in reply. I could hear him open the doors of his closet as I quickly walked over to the aquarium, my guts chanting *food food fooood*. The tank's inhabitants darted about as I inspected them, each individual fish glowing like a heat-lamped McNugget.

"So, you like Italian?" he yelled out. "To eat?"

"Uh, I guess that'd be okay," I called back. I think one of the hitchhikers had been Italian. He tasted a little richer, anyway. I rolled up my sleeve, picked out a tantalizing medium-sized parrotfish and thrust my arm into the tank. "Or Chinese, if you prefer." Hadn't eaten an Asian yet.

"Yeah, I could go for kung pao," he said over the jangle of metal clothes hangers.

"Really, anything's fine," I yelled out as I felt slippery scales slide around and then between my grasping fingers. "Sushi would be great right now!"

"Ugh, raw fish, no thanks."

I snatched the fish from the water and crammed the whole thing into my mouth, groaning with pleasure as its life essence swam down my gullet. I reached in and snared a clownfish, sucking Nemo down with gusto, following that with a few quick snails that had been busy cleaning the glass. The urge to feed abated somewhat. I could hear the shuffle of pants being drawn up over thighs and arms needling themselves through sleeves as I went after an angelfish for a quick dessert, not even bothering to chew this time. Spasms of gratification spiraled through me as it frantically flailed its way down my throat. I walked away from the tank and pretended to admire the depressed artist artwork adorning the wall above the fireplace while I hastily rolled my sleeve back down and patted the dampness of my hand off on a nearby curtain.

"So what's her name?" Duane asked as he re-entered the room. I kept my attention on the artwork, my hand in my pocket to sponge off the last remnants of moisture. "Your cat?"

"Oh. Sofa."

"Cute."

"Yes, she is. I like this" I waved vaguely at the painting, a Thomas Kinkade ode to idyllic plains of wheat, perfect for a hotel room in its enthusiastic embrace of banality "thing," I finished.

"Oh yeah?"

"No, not really." I turned to face him. He had changed into a stylish sweater and tattered blue jeans, leaving his feet bare. "No, it's shit. Just making conversation. I'm just. Nervous, I guess."

He smiled. "Didn't have you pegged as a cat person, Gary. Got more of a reptile vibe from you. Seems more your style somehow. No offense." I shrugged a *de nada*.

We sat back down on the couch, Duane keeping a more respectful distance between us. He flipped open his cell and called down to the concierge, getting a suggestion for good Chinese takeout and leaving the entire contents of the order up to the attendant's discretion. "Just surprise me, 'kay? But make it for two, right? And I want chopsticks included, and there had better be a few fortune cookies in there."

Aside from the unremitting snarls from my stomach — occurrences I blamed on my condition — the rest of the dinner went by smoothly. While Duane remained true to his word and refrained from his nose candy, I made sure that he felt free to have beer, ensuring he was just buzzed enough not to notice that he was doing all the eating on his own. I snacked on fresh fish during his occasional trips to the bathroom, and by the end of the evening the tank was a far more sparsely attended affair.

As the evening wore on, I let myself relax. I hadn't realized how starved I was for emotional contact with someone, anyone. Sofa could only do so much for my self-esteem. After Dad left the two of us with a small insurance policy to fill the large hole now in our relationship, Mom's demands on my time pretty much ate up any chances I had at a high school romance. Because of my fear I had never formed any lasting friendships as a teen, my sexual desires stowed away in a footlocker beneath my bed, and a calendar of constant auditions and temporary employments furnished me with a social life made up exclusively of professional acquaintances and, if not exactly random, a less-than-predictable sexual schedule. It was easier, I told myself, to function as an actor if I had the freedom to up and leave on a moment's notice, using Mom's slide into incoherence as a crutch to justify my lack of stardom. I kept people at arm's length, even the occasional delectation such as Fisher. As with Mom's constant nattering on how disappointing I had turned out to be, I had acclimatized myself to a life of loneliness without realizing it.

Maybe that's what made me a good candidate for zombiehood — far easier to see humanity as a selection of edible foodstuffs when you lack any emotional attachment to what's on your dinner plate. I wonder how farmers do it. Can you truly enjoy a steak when you've first been its nursemaid and protector? Does the milk taste foul on the tongue?

Were all farmers psychotic? Was I?

As Duane and I talked and laughed — Duane actually had a nicely twisted sense of humor, at odds with his Ashton Kutcher–lite persona; he acted out a few *Goon Show* sketches, and I could not help but admit my admiration for his knowledge of British comedy — I moved past my preconceived notions of his intentions and began to see him as he really was: a handsome, endearing, slightly goofy boy, unseasoned, easily manipulated through flattery, still feeling his way through himself. He was leaning toward self-destructiveness, egged on by a modicum of success and a delegation of flunkies all too willing to leech off him until his money was spent and his prospects dried up. He probably had father issues, which went some way to explaining his desire to hang out with me. But there was a spark in him, an animation that could survive if he somehow withstood the perils of extravagant affluence.

"This was fun," said Duane at the door. I had begged off his offer for a late movie; there weren't enough fish left to keep Duane safe, so I made an excuse — *it's late, my condition, I need my sleep.*

"Do you think we could do this again?" he asked. He nudged me with his shoulder while he looked at the floor. "I could stay in town for a little while longer after the shoot's over. We could maybe hang out? If you want?"

"That'd be nice, Duane."

"Call me D.J."

"I prefer Duane. I had fun tonight. The first time in ages. Thank you."

"I'll call down to the limo. You just tell the driver where you want to go, he'll take you."

"Thanks."

"You'll call me?"

"I'll call."

Without warning, he raised his arms and hugged me to him. I gritted my teeth and sealed my lips. Duane squeezed me between his biceps, tightly, humming pleasure. Saliva filled my mouth; the warmth of his circulatory system, so near, so easy. I held him close, my sandwich board of a ribcage pressing in. My mouth opened a crack and my teeth brushed against his neck. I let the tiniest hint of air escape my lungs and play with the hairs on his nape. He shivered, and my jaw cracked open.

"You kind of smell, you know," he said and giggled. "You smell old. I hope it's okay I said that."

I thought a curse, and let my maw swing open.

"I'm glad I met you," he said.

I closed my teeth and curled my lips down over them. My grip relaxed at my orders. We loosened ourselves and regarded each other.

"See you tomorrow," I said. I opened the door and stepped into the hallway. There was a pressure in my heart, odd not least because of its being on the fritz. I turned back; Duane still stood in the doorway. "And thank you for this," I said. "It. It has been a while for me. To talk to someone."

He gave me a puzzled smile. I waved a hand goodbye, and walked away to the elevators.

The limousine driver was as good as Duane's word, hopping to attention as I approached and holding the door open for me, asking me my destination. I gave him the address and lay down on the stretch seat. I had some new lines to go over before shooting started the next day, but since I no longer slept, I had plenty of time for memorization later. I just wanted to luxuriate in the immensely rare experience of being . . . content. We drove through the city at a leisurely pace. I had the driver switch off the interior light, and the beams of streetlights and passing cars cavorted around the walls and ceiling. I let myself enjoy their dance as we crossed the boundaries that separated the downtown from middle-class neighborhoods and made our way toward home.

"Hey, sir," the driver said as we turned into my street. The frolicking lights on the ceiling had new shadings to their personalities, adding reds and blues to their manic tango. "Looks like something's up on your street."

I sat up. At the end of the block, surrounding my house, a blazing array of lights lit up the neighborhood. Shadows flitted back and forth between them, beings with serious intentions.

"Drive past," I ordered. "Just keep going. Don't speed."

The four cars in front of my house had all their emergency lights on. As we idled by, a policeman marking the area with yellow tape gave us the once-over, then resumed his work. I could see heads bobbing in the windows as people made their way through my kitchen and dining room. I looked through the back window as the house drifted away, and saw a cop emerge from the front door with what looked like my old cat carrier in his hand.

Oh, you fuckers, I thought. *Goddamn. Sofa.*

"Trouble, sir?" the driver asked.

It's been a while, hasn't it? my appetite warned me. *You're going to have to kill him now, to keep this quiet. Might as well do it, the jig is obviously well and truly up.*

"Shut up," I told myself.

"Fair enough, sir," the driver said, unperturbed, a pro.

"Take me back downtown."

"Any particular address?"

"Just drive."

Back to Duane? Useless, a short-term solution. The game had changed. I needed new contestants if I wanted to keep playing.

I thought out the field, looking for options. There was only one path open.

Fuck.

I gave the driver an address, telling him to first head for the perimeter and drive around for a few hours, take the scenic route. And leave the divider down; I wanted to make sure he didn't make any calls in to his dispatcher. He was an old hand at this and nodded agreement, putting on a jazz station at my request and keeping silent the rest of the night. We drove the perimeter five times before daylight hit the streets and we re-entered the city.

Let's not put too fine a point on the question and just confront it head on: do zombies shit?

Short answer: yup.

Long answer: not pleasant.

As near as I've been able to determine, most of my autonomous functions have shut themselves down and now only operate voluntarily. I can manipulate the lungs to achieve a semblance of sound, I can blink, but these actions may only be achieved through conscious decision. I can propel my muscles to achieve movement, but they respond sluggishly, as if they have been kept in cold storage and have not thawed completely. My tongue, that most powerful rope of fibrous tissue, must be exercised regularly to remind itself of the positions and routines necessary for verbal communication lest the words become mushy and unintelligible, a dancer who has forgot his steps, a singer who's forgotten the tune. I cannot exert any influence over my liver to secrete amino acids or filter out impurities in my food. Were it still attached, I would be unable to regulate my heartbeat. I have no control over blood flow, or rather, the embalming fluid Rhodes replaced it with. My hair is static, which saves on hairdressing fees, but I must be careful when I brush, as I only have so many follicles left at my disposal, and the loss of each individual strand is another blow to my vanity.

Yet my brain keeps on truckin'. Better than before, as now, without having the impediment of being in charge of so many now-useless operations — without having to act as traffic cop to the highway that is my body, keeping the lanes clear, calling in reinforcements in case of accidents — my brain is free to better supervise those few still-active bodily activities. The electrical impulses that keep my muscles active are still operational, although the muscles must work harder to compensate for the lack of natural lubricant, resulting in a jerking motion as they grate against themselves. The point is, they still work, rusty but serviceable, despite all scientific evidence that suggests they should have atrophied long ago.

But it is my digestive system that concerns us now, and thanks to the process of interrupted eternal slumber it is now a supercharged dynamo of evolutionary perfection. My stomach is a roiling sulfuric acid bath, efficiently melting adipose tissue and vagabond sweetmeats into pulp and shoving the whole mess into the waiting tunnel of the intestines where it luges downward, various proteins and foodstuffs absorbing through the walls, until the final slurry reaches the anus and hammers at the gates until I trigger the release mechanism and plaster the sides of the porcelain bowl with waste. The first time it happened, an hour or so after Fisher, I barely made the toilet; thankfully, the clench/unclench apparatus of the sphincter is still under my control, and I have made it a habit to modulate my intake to synchronize my movements with natural breaks during the day, and to memorize the locations of all available toilets when I enter new surroundings.

I don't actually need to eat as much as I do. If the size of my deposits is an indication, my digestive tract removes very little from my food in the way of nutrition. But my brain demands food nevertheless, and all the rationalization about dietary necessities is an unproductive exercise when put up against the monstrous mass of my appetite. Rhodes, having looked at magnetic scans of my cerebrum, claims that while much of my brain works at peak efficiency, my hypothalamus is swollen, malfunctioning, likely resulting in a condition classified as hyperphagia, the incessant desire to eat without any feeling of satiation.

Who knew death could lead to an eating disorder?

The less said about pissing, the better.

When in trouble, when in doubt, don't just simply scream and shout.

Call your agent.

A piece of advice I had always followed, and saw no reason to ignore now.

The monstrous regiment of personal assistants proved no problem. Ordinarily Rowan would never see a client without an appointment that had been delayed until a later date at least twice, then canceled altogether in favor of a quick text. An unpredicted barge-in by a raging thespian was an event rarely heard of. Trained in the deadly art of client obfuscation, most assistants at Masters Talent were expert in diverting perturbed and aggressive clients from their appointed tasks, i.e., taking up Rowan's precious time with niggling whines on the state of dressing rooms, the unfairness of contracts, the brutality of directors, the ineffectualness of Rowan, and any other number of complaints that an agent was logically expected to attend to with all due haste but in actuality were simply placed on a TBR pile and ignored as the blatherings of a put-upon *auteur*. The agent's minions — if the agent had minions, of course; if the agent worked alone, she was likely a worthless ten-percenter, the poorly carved weasel at the top of an otherwise nicely crafted totem pole — the auxiliaries and subordinates formed a mythical labyrinth of brutally efficient impediments, thick walls constructed of *she's busy* and *she could pencil you in for sometime next month* and *oh what a shame you just missed her*. And actors were a notoriously flighty species; a few well-placed promises that Rowan would personally see to all these horrible problems was usually enough to placate even the most ill-tempered diva.

This was not the usual complaint.

Ordinarily, I would have been utterly lost in the maze of lickspittles and would eventually turn tail and flee to the nearest bar rather than hear another meaningless guarantee of Rowan's personal commitment to each and every one of my very very very important concerns. But I was in no mood for appeasement and flattery.

The first obstacle, a lowly subordinate stationed in the main lobby of the Masters building, posted behind an enormous half-circle of mahogany that sat between two banks of elevators. A charmingly demeaning Hɪ Mʏ Nᴀᴍᴇ ɪs Tᴇᴅ Mᴀʏ I Hᴇʟᴘ Yᴏᴜ? name tag was affixed to the chest pocket of his short-sleeve dress-casual. Tᴇᴅ was by default the first line of defense between the outside world and the entirety of the building's one paying inhabitant, the multinational conglomerate L.D. Inc., Masters Talent being only one of its hundreds of subsidiaries. Tᴇᴅ, after determining that it was Rowan O'Shea of Masters Talent I was seeking and not Rowan O'Leary of Masters Tax Consultants, tried his best to reroute me with assurances as to Rowan's astonishingly busy schedule and it being a nigh impossibility that she could ever see me without a pre-approved meeting time. He blinded me with a grin of practiced insincerity that glinted off my ocular blemishes. Being in no mood to have my panic attack hijacked by a pretty-boy auxiliary with delusions of competence, I laid him low with a baring of my teeth and a guttural snarl straight from the breadbasket of Shiva, destroyer of worlds. He immediately rethought his vocational choice and allowed me passage to the elevators, where a wet cough of fury cleared the compartment of persons and permitted me to ascend to Rowan's fourteenth floor offices in solitary bliss.

Some last vestiges of commitment to the job must have remained in the far dark corners of Tᴇᴅ's terrified wits; he had called ahead to have the second layer of Rowan's army of gofers meet me as the elevator doors slid open. This second test was a dark-eyed trio of albino short-maned harpies in steel blue business suits, their hair dyed black, lips shellacked with crimson, all sharp angles and vibrating ᴘᴅᴀs.

"Can we help you, Mr. Funk?" number ɪ asked me as the doors unsealed and the pressurized air guided me out.

"I need to see Rowan," I said, my voice mild as Indian summer.

"Ooh, Ms. O'Shea is *very* busy today," number 2 admonished.

"I appreciate that. But this is an emergency."

"If you'll just step this way," number 3 purred, gently tugging at my sleeve and motioning down the hallway to the opposite side of the building, "we can take down your information."

"Maybe we can help in her stead," suggested ɪ as she walked ahead, as if this thought just occurred to her.

"She has been mentoring us intimately," said 2, following behind.

"Think of us as her eyes and ears," recommended 3. "Whatever it is you believe she can do for you, we can do for you."

"And vice versa," ɪ chimed in.

"You *really* should have called," 2 clucked.

"You can't expect Ms. O'Shea to drop everything for you, now can you, Mr. Funk?" 3 asked as we reached the far doorway, unremarkable except for its unremarkableness. Not even a number graced its plain chalky laminate.

"But she's hearing good things about you from the set." A key popped out of hiding.

"She likes what she's hearing, your ratings in the office have shot right up." It entered the lock.

"She's lining up a lot of work for you." A muffled clunk of tumblers falling into grooves.

"Whatever your concerns . . ." The lock turned over.

". . . we're sure we can work them out . . ." The knob is grasped and rotated.

". . . together." The anonymous door swung wide, and an anonymous white room decorated with an anonymous white metal desk and four anonymous white folding metal chairs greeted us.

I turned. The triad faced me, blocking access to the hall, shoulders lined up, a bulkhead of pressed virgin wool and fearsomely plucked eyebrows.

"I am afraid that I can. Only speak to Rowan," I said, panic threatening to overtake my standard submissiveness. "If you could all just. Step aside."

No one moved.

"Please?" My last concession to polite formality. I let the deferential adverb hang for a few moments while I fancied I heard the stormtrooper stomp of SWAT teams pounding up the stairwell to arrest me. The threesome stared, unmoved by my insistence. My intestines roiled, and I reflexively took a gourmand's gaze over the stock, at the particularly juicy indentation at the base of the neck of number 2 as well as 3's well-toned leg meat and 1's zesty-looking earlobes.

I closed my eyes against the hunger and bellowed a quick explanation as to just how vitally important it was that I see Rowan right this instant.

I opened my eyes a crack. 3 had passed dead away. 2 was slumped against the wall, eyes blinking in tandem with her pulse, her hair bleached bone-white. 1 stood her ground, but this may have had more to do with her wearing flats where her mates wore heels. Her eyes had rolled back in her head, giving me a tasty glimpse of the bloody veinage that squirmed across the field of optic snow, and a fine strand of saliva wormed out her mouth and onto her front, darkening the blue of her blazer.

Victorious, I hurried back the way we came, toward the door made of clouded blocks of glass, labeled in unpretentious (yet simultaneously incredibly pretentious) simple black lettering:

Masters Talent

I had only stepped through the portal twice before: once in my initial meeting with Rowan when I was still considered an up-and-comer with loads of pizzazz and gobs of chutzpah, and the second time at a holiday party for clients a few years back when I found myself in town, out of work, and just desperate enough to attempt to schmooze my way into a new job. It had worked, actually, as I had finagled my way into three months' work as Spartan Soldier #17 on *300*. For ninety days I wore body paint and sandals and screamed myself hoarse behind Gerard Butler, that most Scottish of Greek leaders. It was a production far more devoted to CGI than acting, and while the paycheck was fine, dandy even, I wasn't too upset that all the blurring action choreography and red-tint filters rendered me unrecognizable in the final print. Although you can make out my arm getting sliced clean off in the battle against the Immortals. Again, the sound effects technicians dubbed my scream, which hurt; I thought I had put forward quite an anguished roar that time.

I pushed against the glass and strode as erect as I could into the foyer and up to the crisply attired young woman set behind an intimidating oak desk. She spoke rapidly into her headset as I approached. Rowan was one of seven major agents at the firm (ancillary agents abounded in concentric circles of Hell outside the building); their individual doors were unlabeled, their hallways unmarked, and my memory as to which avenue she lurked down hazy. I reached forward and ripped the headset off the woman's skull, pulled her close before she had a chance to react, and whispered for her to point me to Rowan's door. She extended one trembling finger toward the third passageway behind her. I left her convulsing in her chair.

Were I in normal circumstances, I would have swallowed nervously, smoothed my hair, thrown back my shoulders, and feigned confidence through a brisk knocking of knuckles against the door. Being in an extremity of agitation, I bulldozed my way in, wrenching the doorknob loose.

"Sheldon," Rowan said, rising from behind her desk. "Please come in, have a seat. It's been far too long."

Give it to Rowan, the woman was unflappable.

I tossed the doorknob to the ground. "Sorry about that."

She shrugged, as if such destruction was a daily occurrence. Maybe it was; actors get pretty emotional at times.

Rowan walked around her desk and leaned against its front, crossing her legs at the ankles. She was only a touch over five feet tall, I loomed over her, but the immensity of her ego always made her clients feel like they were three-foot first graders being lectured to by a stern parent. The severity of her hairstyle helped, her locks pulled back in a tight ponytail, stretching her facial skin to deny her age. Her tales of negotiation theatrics with Jack Nicholson and Meryl Streep put her at possibly in her mid-fifties, but her translucent skin was so expertly textured by loving complexion professionals she could pass for a harsh thirtyish. Her scent, however, put her at fifty minimum; I could smell the doses of mild botulism that filled the aged trenches in her forehead.

She motioned to the swivel-back, and I took a seat. The leather was as soft as butterscotch pudding, and I fought the urge to sink back into luxuriousness and let dried hide of cow erase my worries. I forced myself to sit erect — not easy as the leather pulled at my lower half like a desperate lover.

"Well, you've made it past the armaments and invaded my castle, Sheldon, kudos all around." She flicked a stainless steel cigarette case opened and offered me a coffin nail. I waved them away, and she shrugged and lit one for herself. Smoking was another power play in her arsenal, a subtle nod to her ability to control fire itself. She inhaled a cloud, blew it out contemplatively. "Not many have had the balls to deal with so many impediments, Shel. I should fire the lot of them—"

"I wouldn't be too hard on them," I said over her speech. Now that I was in the inner sanctum, I felt absurdly guilty for the way I dispatched them. "They were . . . slightly unprepared. For the nature of my problem."

"—but first let's get to why you're here. Shouldn't you be, I don't know, at work or something? Isn't there a film set I busted my ass to get you an audition for expecting you? I assume that whatever is in danger of sabotaging your career is frightfully important, it *always* is, but rarely" she pointed at the knob, lying against the deep burgundy of the carpet and staining it with oil "do my clients take it out not only on my staff but on my furniture. I'll bill you for that of course — you're hardly Russell Crowe." She crossed her arms and stared at me. "So, what is so important that it couldn't wait to even take off your makeup? And good job on that, bee tee double-you, real horrorshow. I must remember to send the makeup artists a congratulatory muffin basket."

"Well—"

"Is it that ass of a director?" Rowan lapsed into her usual patter pattern, a flood of information targeted to overwhelm neural pathways and render listeners confused yet hopeful about their employment future. "I do realize that he is a complete and utter buttfuck, but you, I have on good authority, are doing marvelous work. Much better than I ever gave you credit for, frankly."

"No, it's not that—"

"Good, because I'll tell you something, and I was planning to surprise you with this, but your dailies have been making the rounds (thanks in no small part to yours truly) and there is some real serious interest brewing around you."

"That's great, but—"

"Heavy, heavy hitters, Sheldon. We're talking upper tier stratosphere here."

"Rowan, I—"

"Ask me who."

"I don't have time for—"

"Rhymes with Beter Backson."

That stopped me. "Peter Jackson?" Rowan nodded, a smile barely creasing the limits of her Botox. "Peter Jackson wants me?"

"Well, no, not *exactly*, but he is producing a little sci-fi piece out of New Zealand, and the director has put out feelers for someone just your type to play the leader of the Martian resistance. It's a nine-eleven allegory, something bullshitty like that, but it's a part that'll get you really noticed. He likes your lurching gait, as he puts it."

I shook my head, my neck bones grinding in protest. "That . . . that sounds really great, but I have. A bigger problem here."

"Good actors, too. The script's drawing real attention, we're talking A-plus talent."

"I am in—"

"Willem Dafoe's handlers have leaked his interest in the main human lead, but hey, he's Dafoe, so—"

"*I am in trouble here!*" Rowan bent further back against the desk as I yelled, holding on to the edges to remain standing. How she didn't die from fright spoke to some deep sociopathic stain on her character.

She straightened back up and blinked a few times. "Sheldon," she said evenly. "There is no cause for shouting here." I reflexively muttered a bashful apology. "I have always looked out for your best interests, Sheldon, even when others suggested I toss you under the bus. And proving my instincts correct yet again, you have finally become a moderately profitable investment of my time. But if you persist in this behavior, I will have you removed from this—"

And she stopped as I struggled to my feet.

And she stared as I opened my shirt.

And she gasped as she took in the misshapen torso, the sagging gray that threatened to slough off the bones if shaken too hard, the staples that held the overlapping elephant ears in place.

And she walked forward and felt at the meat, wondering out loud at the fantastic job those makeup boys could do nowadays, but how did this fit into the plot of the movie?

And her cigarette loosed itself from her gaping lips and fell to the carpet, smoldering as I reached up and fingered my digits in between the staples and pulled outward, the skin ripping open, a lone staple *poinging* its way free and rocketing past Rowan's head.

And she placed a hand over her mouth as organs and fetid towels slipped wetly forward and out, dangling like decayed deli meat, dribbling muck.

And she closed her eyes as I wrenched off my makeshift ribcage, slid my hand inside, and yanked free my heart, holding it out to her as an offering of supplication.

And she whimpered, once, a sound of the actuality of her existence flexed to the point of snapping, as I took her hand and drew it into me, pushing her fingertips through the gap between my lungs and against the inner wall of my back.

And her reality fractured with an audible *crack!* as she kept pressing and leaned past my shoulder to look behind me at the imprint of her fingers elongating my skin outwards.

"Jesus," she breathed. "Oh Jesus God fuck." She flailed back away from me, grabbing at anything to hold, finding her chair and flopping down as her knees went numb. "Fuck." She took another look at me, my chest gaping, too real to be an effect, too sloppy and loathsome, too unprofessional-looking to be anything other than an authentic carcass standing before her, and put her head between her knees. She panted, whispering obscenities.

"I am," I rasped, "in real trouble here."

And I laid it all out bare for her as she wavered and teetered in her seat, clutching at her desk for support, keeping her head down and staring at the floor. The bus. The attendant. My mother. The vagrants. D.J. I carefully relocated my innards back into place while I unspooled the tale, using a few roles of packing tape from Rowan's closet to keep the casserole in its dish.

"And that," I said, handing her the last roll to hold as I stuck the tape to my stomach and spun myself slowly in place, arms lifted, swathing my torso in thick layers of sticky cellophane — her hands didn't even shake at this point, I noted — "is that." The tape ran out, and I lowered my arms and put my shirt back on. Rowan still held out the empty roll for me, her eyes wide, lips pursed, and eyebrows raised.

I placed a hand upon hers and pushed her arm down. The roll slipped from her fingers and joined the doorknob on the carpet. "Are you okay?" I asked, knowing the stupidity inherent in the question but unable to come up with anything else to say.

"Um." Rowan blinked, once, twice, three times. And then again, three times. "Um. Um." She turned to her desk, turning her back to me, then fearfully looked over her shoulder. Her hands blindly fumbled over the surface, knocking over penholders and paperclip dispensers until it found the intercom. She settled herself down, making sure I had not moved closer, and pressed the button.

"Ms. O'Shea?" a voice crackled.

"Who am I speaking to?" Rowan snapped.

"This is Taylor, ma'am," the voice informed us.

"I don't know you, Taylor, where's Marianne?"

"I'm Mr. Barton's assistant, ma'am, he sent me out to see what was going on. It's kind of crazy out here. Security is here, they're asking for you. Should I send them in?"

"Where's Marianne?"

"They're very insistent, ma'am."

"I want Marianne, Taylor, put her on."

"Uh . . ." There was a rustling noise as Taylor cupped his hand over the receiver. Through the door, we heard Taylor yell for an update on Marianne's condition. A few muffled shouts were returned. "Ma'am," he said, "Marianne, uh, she's, she's . . . she can't come to the phone right now."

"What's her problem?"

"I think the security guards could—"

"What is her problem, Taylor?" Rowan snapped.

"Yes, ma'am, she is . . . she is unconscious, I guess you could call it, one of the guards is looking after her—" From outside, a yell, something like *she's freaking out.* "Ma'am, she's convulsing, and her hair is all white. There's a, ewww, there's a lot of vomit. The security guards really would like to see you, they're very—"

"No," Rowan shouted. She closed her eyes and breathed in through her nose and out her mouth for a count of ten. "Under no circumstances," she continued, "is anyone to come into this room, do you hear me, Taylor? Repeat that back."

"No one is to come in, yes ma'am."

"Anyone comes in before I call, you're fired, *comprende?*"

"Yes'm."

"Now, call an ambulance for Marianne and keep the guards out there on standby until my say-so."

"Should I get another ambulance for Carrie and Lily?"

Rowan shot barbs at me. "What the hell did you do out there?" she hissed. I shrugged. "Yes, call an ambulance for whoever needs one, do what needs to be done. Just keep people away from this office until I call." She released the intercom button, switching off Taylor's acknowledgment in mid-grovel. Outside, voices sang out in anger. The guards really did want to storm the room. Rowan looked at me, considered something, then pressed the button again. "And call Ed Judger, get him on the line for me, tell him it's urgent." Already I could hear Rowan switching gears, moving boxes to make room for new information.

"Who's Ed Judger?" I asked.

Rowan stood up and walked to the other side of the desk, sitting back down in her seat of power. She closed her eyes again, appeared to offer up a silent prayer, and opened them again in full agent mode. She looked at me, taking me in fully and appraising me as her client and product. "What do you want, Sheldon?" Rowan asked, ignoring my question. "From me. What do you want? Where do I fit into this? Forgive me, won't you, for worrying about my own needs before those of the walking dead."

I mimed a sigh. "You're the only person. I could turn to. You could protect me, maybe. If this gets out. I'm dead."

"Figuratively, I take it." Her sardonic nature was re-emerging. I took this as promising.

"I'm not saying I shouldn't be. Held responsible. I've done horrible things. I'm Dahmer bad. I reacted poorly to my situation. I should have thrown myself in a fire. Or shot myself. Something. But if they get a hold of me, it's not. Going to be the same. There won't be a trial. Look at me. I'm a walking science experiment. I'll disappear. They'll torture me, dissect me. Until there's nothing left. I'll be a brain in a jar. I'll be *aware* of this. The rest of my life. My existence. Will be an eternity of probing. Literally. An eternity. This can't get out."

Rowan crossed her arms while she considered this. "I take it that destroying your body now somehow is not an option? That would make my job easier. I've already made a good chunk for your work, and your disappearance could elevate your profile, bringing in more dollars for the movie. We could get you to one of those car crushers junkyards have, garlic press you out of my misery."

I shook my head. "My mother would be left alone to die. Even she doesn't deserve that. And my cat. All alone." I had a fleeting image of Sofa in police custody, yowling from a cage, waiting for the injection. "And you'll probably disappear too," I added, in case she'd decide to exterminate me behind my back. "This is probably a matter. For Homeland Security here. Whatever it is that has happened. They couldn't take a chance on anyone else. Knowing. Sorry."

"Well, this *will* get out," Rowan said. "That's a guaranteed fact at this point. They're already searching your house, something led the police to you, and I'll assume that they'll find something. They may not find the remains of everyone you've," and here she allowed a brief instance of human emotion to crack her armor in an abrupt but noticeable full-body quiver "*eaten*, but they will find something. All we can do now is damage control. Honestly, you should have come to me with this weeks ago, months, we could have been fully in front of the situation."

"You're taking all this very calmly," I said. "I thought you'd need some. Time to process."

"I think I've got the gist, assuming I'm not hallucinating all this.

Maybe I've completely lost it, don't think it hasn't crossed my mind, but I think that people who've gone gaga aren't usually aware of it as such, so I'm in a quandary. In any case, the way it is is the way it is, and I will deal with it." She withdrew a calfskin journal from a drawer. She began jotting down notes as she talked. "You're my client, you have come down with a, a rare illness, something incredibly rare, something foreign, from Africa say, you got bit by a tsetse fly, that's believable, and in the feverish delirium brought about by your condition you committed a few unfortunate, random — but perfectly understandable given your impaired mental state — acts of homicide. That's how we'll play this, I think. We'll need a doctor, no, two, three, that should be enough to start."

"Illness?" I interrupted.

Rowan sighed, a sound I was very familiar with, the exhalation of barely restrained impatience with a dull-witted client, and looked up from her writing. "Sheldon," she said, putting me in my place with one simple inflection of my name that equated me with an implied subclass of short-bussers, "you can't expect people to simply accept your state as a zombie without building up to it first. People will need time to adjust, not everyone is as flexible in their perceptions of reality as I am. Of course, again, this could all be one big delusion and I'm actually in a rubber room somewhere painting landscapes with my feces, but that's for future therapy to work out. So, how many?"

"Many?"

"How many people have you killed? I'll need a number to gauge what kind of trouble we're in. The real problem is that you're not famous yet — that would have really helped a lot with the press."

I shook my head in wonderment at Rowan's thought processes. She started slightly at the noise of my vertebrae eroding against each other and made another note in her book, circling it twice. I heard the word *plastic* escape her lips. "Eight," I said. "No, maybe seven, it depends, my mother, I . . ." I shuddered, unable to complete the thought. I wondered that no one at the ward had called to inform me that my mother had gone a wee bit bitey as of late. "Judger?"

"Ed Judger," Rowan said, a touch impatiently, "is one of my counterparts in L.A., a very, very influential gentleman, particularly when it comes to putting the best spin on things. We're going to need help from the higher-ups, and he is a man who makes things happen. I'll set up a meet for you."

"Spin?" I repeated. "Rowan, we're not talking about a. Drunk driving charge, or a drug bust. This is pretty much. Pre-meditated murder—"

"—that you were unable to control because of the organic nature of your affliction," she finished. "Believe me, this can be spun. People are going to see you as an object of pity and pathos when Ed gets through with you."

"But I'm a zombie!"

"And last year's Best Actress winner collects Nazi paraphernalia, but you haven't heard any of that thanks to Ed, and you did *not* hear it from me. And you are *not* a zombie; let's get that straight right now. No, what you are is . . ." Rowan leaned back and rotated her hands, searching for terminology ". . . living impaired? A natural evolution? A miracle?" She looked me over. "No, not a miracle, people like their supernatural marvels to look a little less off-putting. I'll put someone on this, we'll think of something more user-friendly."

"I'm a freak."

"Save the self-pity for your autobiography. Which you *will* be writing, come to think, so you might want to start making notes for the ghostwriter. It's never too early to start thinking about merchandising rights. How do you feel about T-shirts?"

"Whoa." I held up my hands, the motion pulling the tape tighter, tearing it in several places. I pressed the adhesive tighter to the skin. "Dammit. This isn't, I can't, no. I need help. That's why I came to you."

"Sheldon, I am your agent," Rowan said, smartly crisp and professional, still making notes and not looking at me. "I am not your friend. You cannot crash at my place until this blows over. I cannot help you in any capacity as anything but an agent, and what agents do is fight fire with fire. We need to be in control of this, and the only way I can see to protect you as a client is to launch an all-out media assault. I'm talking interviews, television specials—"

"What?"

"Ed knows people who know people. I'll float the idea by him, but I'm sure he'll come up with the idea himself in any case. This is going to take some time, we'll have to get you set up somewhere. Your house is not an option, obviously. We have a few bungalows in town we keep for guests, I'll set you up in one. The question is how, how, how?" She accentuated each *how* with a sharp jot of her pen on the paper. "How to keep the police off you until we're ready to go. Any ideas?"

"None spring to mind."

"Right, let's talk this out. They are looking for Sheldon Funk, right?" I nodded. "Would the police have anything connecting that name with Gary Jackson?" I thought, then shook my head no. I didn't have any ID under Gary's name, and I'd left all my resumés with the casting director in New York. All my Gary persona was digitized on my laptop, currently sitting unnoticed in my dressing room. I told this to Rowan. "I think we're clear then, at least for a little while. We'll keep you under wraps while the movie's being edited. Maybe we can time this to boost interest when it gets released. They want to get an early release out for Halloween, so we'll need to keep you down low for three months or so." She tapped her head with her pen. "Anything else? What are we missing?"

"My mother—"

"We'll move her somewhere, we've got a few places where celebrities go to dry out."

"She," I started. "She. She may be. I don't know what happens for sure. If I bite someone."

"You bit her?"

"It was an accident."

"Any chance she's like . . ." She pointed at me. I shrugged. Rowan pursed her lips and hummed. "Okay, I've got a doctor, well, surgeon — I want him to take a look at you, he may have some ideas on where to put her. We'll get her out of there before the police track her down, then see what's what. No promises, Sheldon — we may have to put her down in order to keep this thing contained. You need to know this."

I chewed on my lip while I thought this over, then stopped, aware that the flesh was no longer self-renewable. I nodded. Rowan clicked on the intercom and ordered the guards to leave, then called for a car service to come pick me up. "We'll put you up in a hotel right now, and I'll get the doc to take a look at you himself, that's the only way he'll believe this, anyway. Can I trust you not to go all zombie on him? Are we on the same page?"

I nodded. "Just two more things?" I asked. Rowan sighed, raised an eyebrow in question. "I need to eat someone. And soon."

Rowan leaned back and pressed her palms over her eyes. "You're killing me here."

"Believe me. I'm not happy about this."

She threw up her hands. "Well why would you be? I've done a lot of things as an agent, a lot of underhanded things, but I've never procured dead bodies before. Alcohol, drugs, prostitutes, but no dead bodies."

"Live would be better. But I can make do with a dog."

"Make do with a dog?"

"For now. A live one. Medium size should do."

"Right." She wrote as she spoke. "One. English. Bulldog." She dotted the final period with a flourish, pushing her pen deep into the pad. "And the second thing, dare I ask?"

"I want my cat back."

Why always the biting?

Despite my best efforts to change it up and maybe have a salad now and then, my body does not react well to vegetable matter; it expels all foodstuffs of a non-beastie variety. I have been able to deceive my digestive system somewhat, mixing breads and the like with my daily intake, finally getting some control over my gag reflex, but my colon can't be duped, and any substance not immediately animalistic in nature is flushed through the system whole — soggy, chewed, undigested. I have few bodily fluids left, but digestive juices have stuck around.

Additionally, I can imbibe in all animals of a non-human genus, but they must be fresh — wriggling on the hook fresh. But it's not the same, and not enough. Cold processed meat does nothing for me. I cannot subsist on raw hamburger.

No, to satisfy the hankerings, it must be homo sapiens, plain, no side fries or baked potato. Not necessarily fresh, but as with all groceries, fresher is better. Rhodes is at a loss to explain this, as it makes no logical sense, but then, what does? He's prodded and inserted and removed and examined and prodded again but there is no question that I am a medical impossibility that follows none of the usual laws of nature. We have sought out answers in biology, in virology, in radiology, theology, astrology, parasitology, every -ology there is, but the fact remains, I am verifiably deceased.

And terribly famished all the time.

I think it may be psychological in origin, the hunger for human. According to voodoo folklore, zombies have historically been "raised" from the dead to serve at the pleasure of their necromancer, but based on the lack of any physiological evidence, such "zombies" are assumed to be confused individuals who have been hoodwinked by their own ideology into believing that they have joined the ranks of the undead. They are told that they have been cursed to roam the earth and serve their master and, as that is what they've always believed to be possible, they fool themselves into the role. Say someone with this belief catches a bad case of the sniffles and falls into a coma for a few days; when they awake, they may feel otherwise fine, but if told by someone that they actually died on the operating table, their psychological makeup impels them to then act the part and shamble about the countryside, moaning, scaring the bejeezus out of children and tourists, and generally making it difficult for genuine zombies to be taken seriously.

Perhaps it's the same with me. Raised from an early age on a steady pop culture diet of late-night B-movies on cable television, I have always believed the classic zombie to be obsessed with the cannibalistic consumption of human flesh. So following the path of logic, I eat people because, subconsciously, I believe I am *supposed* to.

Of course, even if true, does it help explain the appetites of the others? Aren't there good odds that at least one of my disciples should have grown up in a pop-cultureless household? Shouldn't one of them, a person who never believed or even knew of all the nonsense, be able to subsist solely on a diet of cauliflower?

Anger

There was something in my eye.

Fuck. Worst possible time for this.

I thought it was a flake of skin, another toboggan of cells making a luge run for freedom down my once-proud tanned and tightened countenance. Despite Doc Rhodes' best efforts, my disintegration had slowed but not halted; I had to be careful I didn't move too quickly, no sudden movements, or his work might be revealed as the excellent-under-the-circumstances-but-for-all-intents-and-purposes-patchwork job it really was.

The fragment of dermis, discomfortingly bulky, clung to my left lens, direct center. I cautiously closed and opened my eyes a few times to dislodge it.

Not skin. Worse, under the circumstances.

Pancake. A splinter of slightly hardened pancake makeup, scraping up against my lens. The protective blinking acted with much the same effect as a window wiper does to a dead locust pulverized into mush against a windshield. The motion smeared the grit across my vision, my lack of tears allowing the bugbear to get its hooks in and coat every scratch with powdery Caucasian flesh-tone. I had worried about just this sort of thing happening, but the producers insisted that I not wear my goggles, "because of the glare, you understand." Rowan had a different take on the matter, fearing that the dark protruding eyeshields would only serve to make me seem even more alien to the audience. So, no goggles, not in prime time.

This was to be a different demographic; up until that point my public persona had been primarily confined to select print media. My lovely face graced the smarty-pants pages of *Scientific American*; *Time* and *Newsweek* interviews were set for the following week. But now a far different segment of the population would be studying me, one that demanded that anything odd or unusual must be packaged in as pleasing a wrapping as possible to avoid upset. A more ideologically conservative audience. The genus of gawkers that feared the unknown and demonized anything that could shatter their own personal mythos of how the universe operated.

At least they allowed me a pair of tinted aviator glasses heisted off a nearby teamster to lessen the impact of my whitening orbs to the viewing audience. Without the darkened lenses (probably not UV safe, not an area of concern anymore), the glare of the floodlights twinkled happily off my many corneal abrasions and left me snow-blind. Sunglasses on, everyone was hazy but recognizable, washed in friendly yellow. The glasses also furnished me the look of a particularly haggard Robert Evans after one hell of a bender — not an effect I was going for. The layers of pancake caulked into my wrinkles didn't help. The studio makeup artist was unprepared for the challenges a skull of dead skin offered — Rhodes had done what he could, even going so far as to once pierce the skin with needles and squirt food coloring into the subcutaneous layers of my cheeks and forehead, trying to tone down the gray and achieve a more lifelike skin tone, the result being a physiognomy of ashen pallor with unsettling deposits of scarlet located haphazardly about the terrain, a corpse with measles — and chose to shelter the whole magilla with as much base and rouge as she could get her hands on. It may not have been entirely her fault; her hands trembled noticeably as she hastily troweled the goop over me. She had the fear-shakes. When I finally looked at myself in the mirror, expecting my old complexion and instead finding a waaaay-past-his-prime man-whore, I let my guard down and loosed a dark, blood-dried chuckle from deep within my gullet that sent the woman fleeing out of the building and into the safety of the New York night. The intent was to make me look lifelike; I looked like an undertaker's practice dummy, a cautionary example funeral directors could use to frighten their apprentices. *This is how bad they could look if you don't concentrate on your job!*

The face paint now fully coated my left eye, reducing my field of vision down even further from its usual cataracted view. Dimly, I could hear the director laying down final instructions for the night through the cameraman's headphones. I reached up to rub my eye, but remembered that I shouldn't touch my face. The artist, Jimmy she was called, Jimmy had warned me not to touch my face until the show was over. *Hell,* I thought, *I couldn't look worse anyway,* and poked a finger underneath the glasses and directly against my cornea, dabbing, trying to wipe away the mote. This only smeared it further; the world was now bathed in pink. I took a bottle of eye drops out of my pocket and leaned my head back to plop a few synthetic tears in, moistening the desert plains. I blinked, and the liquid bonded with the cosmetic and transformed the dust into sticky oatmeal, glazing my lens with sickly coral.

"Motherfuck."

"Is there a problem, sir?" The voice crackled in my ear. Rowan gave me a glance, but she was busy texting and couldn't be bothered to see what was up. Franklin gave no indication he had heard me, but even if his earpiece was malfunctioning, his seating arrangement three feet to my right put him in prime hearing range. Rhodes definitely overheard the remark, and didn't bother to stifle his snicker.

"Sorry, I forgot there's. Someone listening," I said, fumbling at the portable microphone attached to my shirt collar. The amplified *thumpity-thump-thump* of my fingers against the mic filled my ear. Rowan, Franklin, and Rhodes all winced and shot dirty looks my way, and a few curses loudly emanated from the sound booth.

"That's quite all right, sir. Can we help you? We've got two minutes."

Rowan leaned in close. "Could you stop fidgeting? What's the problem, nerves?"

"There's a. There's makeup in my eye. Sorry."

"Oh, for fuck's sake," Rowan said. She pulled her collar close to her mouth and spoke into her mic. "Could we get a little help for Mr. Funk, he's got makeup in his eye, please."

"We'll send someone out right away," the director intoned.

A young woman, not the traumatized Jimmy, rushed over excitedly with a makeup kit. She lifted my glasses and peered in. "Can I wipe, I mean, can I actually touch your eye?" she asked. There was a gleam in her eyes, an edge to her smile that I was becoming more and more familiar with.

"Feel free," I said, steeling my appetite for the brush of her fingertips against my skin.

Expertly, she draped a tissue over her right index finger and, propping my eyelid open with her fingers, gracefully polished the exterior of my cornea, returning the world to its customary dull white murkiness.

"Much obliged," I said, keeping my voice low and modulated.

"No problem, sir," she said, and then leaned in quickly, past the mic, putting her lips directly in my ear. "I'm a big fan," she whispered, and nimbly dropped a card into my front pocket. "Call me, 'kay? If you want." She threw me an alluring wink and scurried away.

I smiled out of politeness, wishing I could heave a great sigh of annoyance. Corpsers. I had already garnered more than a few websites devoted to how hot I looked for an undead dude. A loose movement was quickly spreading over the grid, people calling themselves, among other labels, "corpsers," "undeadites," "necrofanatics," and most disturbingly, "Twihards," unhinged *Twilight* fans looking for another dreamy dead dude to tempt out their nascent necrophilia. I dug the card out and handed it to Rowan. "Another for. The pile, I guess." Rowan slipped it into her pocket.

"Okay, people, we are good to go," the director announced. "Camera one on Franklin, two and three on guests, let's do this, we are live in five, four, three." Two fingers were held up, then one, and then a point to the host, go.

I watched the monitor from the corner of my eye, trying not to look like I was actually watching myself but helpless to stop. The curse of the actor, always trying to ensure the camera caught his best side. Luckily the glasses disguised the direction of my eyes, although my optic spheres were by then so whitened with nicks that the pupil was only faintly visible. The camera was pulled out into a wide sweep of the set, capturing the desk, the logo, the green screen behind the host, and the four participants in the night's program: Doctor Igör Rhodes, plastic surgeon to the stars and my agency-appointed physician; me, representing myself, spokesperson for the rights of the undead, I supposed; Rowan, representing Masters Talent; and past her, Franklin Pilato, respected newsman, Pulitzer Prize–winning journalist, and Emmy-nominated host of *Speaking Frankly*, television's third-highest-rated news-related talk show, just behind O'Reilly and Maddow.

I had tried to speak to Franklin before airtime; the man was an institution, after all. I received in return a shoulder so cold I could see ice crystals coating his walrus moustache.

As the show logo faded, a movement to my right, past Franklin's opposite shoulder. A familiar-looking woman clad in a fashionable pinstriped suit hurried in and sat down, fidgeting with an earpiece. Her eyes were disturbingly bright; I put this to her improbably tiny corneas, discs of pale azure floating in a vast white sea. She was also cosmeticized to a degree that made me feel far less conspicuous. The woman inserted the earpiece and smoothed her hair over it, gifting Franklin with a brief smile of acknowledgment before turning her glacial gaze to me and fixing me with a scowl of fabulous loathing.

I glanced at Rowan, shrugging. Rowan had straightened in her seat as the woman had entered, and her lips were now pursed together, her fists clenched, knuckles white with tension.

The five of us filled the screen under the logo. Four warm-blooded people and a corpse with aspirations of humanity. Guess which one stood out. My being unaware that my mouth was dangling loosely open was a dead giveaway. I slowly swung it shut, my joints grinding together.

The camera pushed in tighter, sliding the guests off and filling the screen with Franklin's confidence. He kept his eyes on his papers until the move was completed, and then looked up into the teleprompter.

"Death. Until very recently, it was the ultimate finality of life, an experience shared by every species of animal on this planet. Since man's forebears first grasped the concept of mortality, humankind has attempted to contextualize death in myriad forms. As a definite end. As the final extinguishment of a spark. As a stepping stone to another dimension of being. As a necessary stage in the ascendance of the soul immaterial to realms either heavenly or chaotic. But aside from those few persons who argue that they have had 'life after death' experiences, a highly debatable notion to both scientists and theologians alike, there has been no way to effectively quantify what, if anything, happens to what we will refer to here for the sake of brevity as the 'soul' once our fragile bodies have ceased to function."

I covered my mic with my hand and leaned in to Rowan. "Laying it on a. Little thick, you think?" I said, struggling to clearly form the words in a whisper. It was a skill I had not yet mastered, my words clearly picked up by her microphone and broadcast to millions of viewers. Rowan stiffened and shushed me with a look.

Franklin paused at the interruption, cleared his throat, and continued.

"But now, humanity may be closer to an answer than ever before. Before very recent events, my guest's most prominent public appearance was still to come: a lead role in the upcoming horror movie *Basement*, under the acting alias of Gary Jackson. Since then, astonishing evidence has arisen that Mr. Jackson is, in fact, Sheldon Funk, a Canadian actor who disappeared from public view late last year. But the real story, far more fantastical than anything Hollywood could ever devise, was yet to come. Mr. Funk was actually discovered dead on a bus en route from New York to Toronto, and was admitted to the morgue as a John Doe. There, video evidence verifies that during his autopsy, during which his chest was opened and his heart physically removed, Mr. Funk rose from his examination table, attacked an attendant and then fled the hospital, disappearing for months until finally contacting medical authorities and revealing his condition to the public. Mr. Funk has been exhaustively examined by medical experts, including an independent panel of doctors hired by this network, and all have verified that he is, by all standard presumptions of the word, dead. And yet, he sits with us here tonight. The workings of the world as we understand them have been twisted out of shape since Mr. Funk's first appearance on newsstands a month ago. Many are calling this an elaborate hoax. Some have labeled Mr. Funk a medical marvel, or the next pure step in human evolution. Some call him a religious miracle, a claim he himself strenuously denies. One thing is certain; he has captured the attention of the world. Is he a man? Does he still retain the rights and freedoms we in our innocence often take for granted? Or is he, as one of our guests contends, a fraud, or worse, a blasphemy? Our Speaking Frankly religion correspondent Julianne Staenky has prepared this report.

"Death," a female voice intoned in my earpiece as the live feed switched to tape. "It comes in many disguises, but until now, the end result was always the same . . ."

"And we're clear," the director announced. "Four minutes until live." Franklin stood up and hurriedly walked off-stage, an assistant following him with a pack of cigarettes. The woman began texting something on her phone.

"Those sons of bitches," Rowan cursed in a whisper, covering her mic with her hand. "We've been played, Shel." She shook her head; there was a healthy undercurrent of admiration in her tone.

"What the fuck. Is this all about?" I asked her, not bothering to cover my own microphone. "I wanted to protect myself, not. Have a debate on the moral issues. Of my existence. And who is that woman?"

"This is how you play the game, love," Rowan said, placing a warm hand over mine on the desktop. "You have to trust me. This was inevitably going to happen, so better now than later, when people have had a chance to form their own opinions. We can't have that. This is a setback, but if we keep our heads about us, we will prevail. They have rattled our cage to see if we'd bite, but that's it." She motioned at the woman. "That bitch over there" Rowan uncovered her microphone for the phrase, then covered it back up; the woman looked up, face puckered in a grimace, clearly catching the insult "is Pauline Kud. *Senator* Kud from Montana. She's a tight-assed republican mouthpiece who has had you in her sights for weeks."

"Why is this. The first I've heard?"

"I've tried to keep it from you. Her people have been calling our offices ever since your death mitzvah."

"So what's the problem?"

"Senator Kud represents a sizable contingent of people who object, on religious grounds, to your presence. This whole show is no longer a coming-out, it is going to be a test of your moral right to exist. Fuck. Oh, and Igör?" She leaned past me to Rhodes, who had been patiently listening to our chatter. "You don't breathe a word until spoken to, all right? No off-the-cuff remarks, no humor. Keep to the point or you'll be lucky to get a job bleaching anuses." Rhodes nodded understanding.

I leaned back in my chair while Rowan checked her cell for messages and Rhodes looked over his personal notes of the procedures he had practiced on me. Compared to this, the weeks of prodding I had recently completed had been a breeze. After Rowan had finessed me out of the remaining shoot for *Basement* — amazing how the word "cancer" can get you out of almost everything — she had called on the talents of Dr. Igör Rhodes, cosmetic quack to celebrities and dictators. Rhodes, after the customary bout of disbelief/vomiting, took to my case with the unforced glee of a child discovering his first dead animal. His first steps were mostly cosmetic — trowel and concrete jobs to support a sagging infrastructure — but then he began to undertake a serious examination of my new makeup. It was thanks to Rhodes that I had a slightly decreased appetite, far more manageable. In a frenzy of *let's try this*, he drilled a small hole through my skull and poked around my hypothalamus area with sparking electrodes until my appetite began to wane. I preferred to not think about how damaged my poor brain now was, but given that it should have rotted into jelly months ago, there was no point in worrying. The hunger was still there, but muted, more of a mild craving for a tender forearm than a raging appetite for human brains. He also came up with a substitute foodstuff, experimental human muscle grown in petri dishes and incubators. It was like getting ice milk instead of cream, but it fooled my new self into accepting it as fresh kill, at least for a while. Why I could live only on fresh flesh, we still had not a clue.

Once the preliminaries with Rhodes had been completed, a murder of lawyers at Masters Talent's beck and call had crafted a personal letter to several leading minds in the scientific community, asking them to a special meeting of utmost importance to their understanding of the universe. I had then become the personal plaything of every yahoo with the letters P, h, and D behind his name. I was offered up to the highest-profile medical journals in the world, and allowed everyone who asked to poke, jab, swab, spray, probe, swathe, inject, fondle, and season me unmercifully, all in the name of knowledge. Only the lawyers and a niggling sense of morality kept them from dismembering the cognizant corpse altogether. After they had had their fun, findings were rushed together, papers prepared, and articles released to the general public.

The furor was immediate. I was a fraud. I was the liberal media's middle finger to an increasingly gullible middle-America audience craving the next fleeting distraction from a withering recession. Where was the proof? Where was the death certificate? In a world dependent upon sound bites and ambush journalism to make any sort of impact on citizenry, a series of papers and photographs would no longer cut it, not for something of this magnitude. Not nearly sexy enough. Pundits claimed the whole thing reeked of alien autopsy specials, seizing upon every aspect of the event and gleefully covering it with ridicule.

Conversely, there was the already-sizable contingent of theological devotees convinced that I was God's emissary, or God himself, or some type of deity. Religious shut-ins clamored for articles of my clothing. Goths claimed I was evidence that Hell was closed for business and its patrons primed to dig their way back up. I was hope for salvation and/or the beginning of the end.

Both sides were rabid, coating the other with frothy hatred.

Through it all, Rowan and Masters Talent kept me hidden from public view, moving from place to place, lawyers primed and ready to deny any and all demands for access to the freak through a stockade of bewildering legalese. It must have been costing them a fortune, but I was an investment they believed would pay off dividends. My future earning potential was enormous; I could feed a small nation on my speaking fees alone. I was the cornerstone of a burgeoning empire, employing people in different facets of the entertainment, scientific, and telecommunications industries. People now depended on me for their livelihoods, Rowan carped, so I had better not take the coward's way out and off myself in a crematorium or something.

Police interest in my case had not been difficult for the cadre of lawyers to dissolve. They had finally figured out my identity; the thoughtless teen who had taken up two seats to himself on the bus that long-ago night had ended up absconding with my identification and carry-on. He had tried to use the restroom after I had passed on and, after forcing the door open and discovering my body, searched my pockets for my wallet and then removed all my belongings from my seat. He had been smart enough to keep everything hidden for a time, throwing away most of the papers and resumes, but the boy had finally succumbed to temptation and used my driver's license as a fake ID to gain access to a Yonge Street titty bar. One phone call later from a fearsome bouncer to the lad's parents had been enough to unstopper the boy's tongue and bring the whole story pouring forth. Police had been contacted, two and two were finally added together, and they sped to my house to try to divine what had happened to that pesky walking stiff they had misplaced so many weeks previous.

After the agency's lawyers ascertained that the police sought my body in relation to the ongoing investigation and not in relation to any other disappearances in the city — Rowan kept her instructions to the lawyers vague on this point, and they were just professional enough not to press the issue — they had taken a mighty legal jackhammer to the whole construction. Starting with the police chief and working both up and down the hierarchy, the case of the missing mummy was summarily pushed to the back of the cold case file for lack of evidence, as well as being a drain on taxpayer resources. All involved agreed it was best left forgotten, one of those strange cases cops talked about in the wee hours of the drunken morn. Cops were paid, non-disclosure contracts were signed, and the incident was forgotten until I appeared on the front page of the *New York Times*, when it was too late to do anything about it.

Mom had been gathered up and moved to a remote facility for aged and infirm relatives of the rich and powerful in southern Florida, under the direct supervision and care of Rhodes himself. He and he alone could explain to the workers why she was a special case, why she had to be kept separate from other residents in a special wing, why her room was to be kept locked at all times, why her dentures had to be removed, why she had so subtle a heartbeat as to be all but undetectable.

Mom was indeed dead, with delusions of animation; it was not a miracle that she had not bitten anyone, for she had, several times. However, lacking dentures, her constant soft gumming of her attendants' limbs was a cause for irritation, not worry. Rhodes walked me through what he believed to be the chain of events. The virus, if that's indeed what it is, had entered her bloodstream through the tiny nick my teeth made in her hand when she had grabbed at me. It took its sweet time having any impact; maybe it was her age, or perhaps the myriad medications she was on acted as a firewall. The eventual substitution from infirm, incoherent, doddering woman to shuffling death instrument was so gradual that no one had noticed, and her lapse into biting at everything that moved was written down on her chart as yet another step down the dementia ladder. She was kept in restraints, pinned down with leather straps, pointless nutrients forced intravenously through a needle in her arm. Rhodes told me he had gotten to her just in time; her arm was swollen to burst from all the liquid they had thoughtlessly pushed into her. Rhodes made a quick incision in the forearm and squeezed the liquid out into a nearby slop bucket while his assistant held Mom down. She was so weak from hunger at that point, it was all she could do to silently gnaw at the air in Rhodes' general direction. It was testament to how poor a nursing home I had put my mother up in that, while the attendants and nurses had indeed noted the mysterious absence of N. Nowlan one winter's eve, they did absolutely nothing about it. Dead, for them, was dead, gone was gone, and mysteries were for the "living"; presumably, the "living" kept in better care facilities than Mom's.

Should we kill her? Many times I had wished I had the strength of will to euthanize her, rationalizing it as performing an act of mercy, plunging an air bubble into her bloodstream and ending her/my torment. These were idle thoughts, envisioned over interminable evenings as Mom warbled her merry way through her personal haze of theocratic conspiracies and prevailing discombobulation. She had no quality of life, I told myself. Better a painless slip through the veil of the sheltering sky than this unending descent into incoherence.

Even as I thought this, I knew I could never follow through. Fear stopped me. Fear of being caught. Fear of being wrong. Fear of destroying a perfectly rational being hiding behind the eyes of a madwoman. How could I ever be sure?

But that's what I ended up doing. Wasn't it the same now? By Rhodes' account, Mom was now a growling, feral beast. She paced back and forth in the corners, silent, her eyes roaming the room as she traveled the same path again and again, a tiger gone heat-stupid in captivity. Was there anything human in there? Why was I rational yet my mother/progeny a slavering chowderhead? In the images Rhodes played for me I saw nothing in the husk that haunted that room, nothing human, nothing sane, nothing beyond an animal instinct for raw flesh that we could not explain.

"Mr. Funk," Franklin said, his voice greased over with faux politeness. "Good evening to you, sir."

I jerked involuntarily, startled out of my thoughts. The report had ended and Franklin was live on-air, waiting patiently for a response. I took in a breath to speak, too loud, suddenly nervous. The breath was uneven, the dry processed ether of the air conditioning scraping against the ragged lining of my throat as it made its way down into my lungs, the process obscenely amplified by my microphone.

"Thank you, Franklin. A pleasure to be here."

"Next to Sheldon, we have Ms. Rowan O'Shea, personal representative for Mr. Funk."

"Good evening," Rowan replied with a gracious, natural smile. She could have been an actress herself.

"As well, joining us for a discussion on Mr. Funk's medical condition is his personal physician, Dr. Igör Rhodes. Good evening, sir."

"Jah, gut to be here, zank you, jah."

From the moment he'd walked into his examination room and I'd heard him pronounce *Now, vat zort of boo-boo haff ve here, hmm?* I knew his accent would haunt us all. It was difficult enough portraying me as a sympathetic monstrosity who meant you no harm, but having Dr. Strangelove as scientific backup was, in retrospect, not the best choice we could have made. It mattered not that he was, in fact, of Czechoslovakian origin, a man with an easy grin and boisterous laugh — the mangled Ws and Vs, replacing *s* with *z*, the thin black moustache; they layered our presentation with the scent of extermination camps.

"And finally, we have with us a familiar guest to the show, Senator Pauline Kud, three-term House Representative from Montana and founding member of the lobby group Priority Action Family First U.S.A.O.K."

"A pleasure as always, Franklin." Her eyes glistened in the glare, wide and unfocused, their color the pale blue of dementia.

"Mr. Funk, as both guest and topic, I'd like to begin with you. I am looking at you now from across this desk, and I am having, shall we say, a difficult time reconciling the reports I have read with the person who sits before me. You understand that what you claim, even with the backing of medical proof, can only be met with skepticism by any rational-thinking adult?"

"I understand completely. I don't believe it myself. Half the time."

I forced a winning smile to my lips to try to acknowledge the unusual humor in the situation. Franklin blanched as I bared my teeth, and I let the smile fall away. Rowan *had* warned me against smiling; Rhodes' tooth bleaching efforts had only succeeded in making my grins look all the more ghastly.

"Um. We will, we will [cough] we will get into the merits of what these reports claim momentarily, but taking your condition as fact, for the moment, I'd like to begin by asking the question that I'm sure is on everyone's mind watching tonight; what, exactly, is the process of death like?"

"Unpleasant."

"Could you elaborate?"

"Very. Unpleasant."

"If I may, Franklin?" Rowan interjected.

"Please."

"Sheldon has undergone something unprecedented in the annals of history—"

The senator nearly snapped her neck bouncing forward to interrupt. "I'd like to argue that point. The Bible clearly states that, aside from Lazarus, Jes—"

"—arguably unprecedented, then, if it moves this along," Rowan growled back. "But undeniably traumatic. What happens after death is simply outside human understanding, and Sheldon's reaction is a natural response to an event beyond our limited comprehension. How do you describe a sunset to a blind person? How do you explain music to the deaf?"

"Sheldon," Franklin looked at me, "would you say that is an accurate analogy?"

"Sure?"

He turned his sights on Kud, frosty demeanor noticeably softening. "Now, Senator . . ."

I had never noticed before through the television screen, but Franklin's skin was quite thin, like tissue paper. I watched capillaries expand and contract as blood strode its way through his system. My teeth began to ache, and I furtively reached into my pocket for a nugget of Dr. Rhodes' patent-pending shamburger and popped it into my mouth as the camera focus switched to the senator. The craving subsided as my tongue felt its way around the contours of the gobbet and, finding it satisfactory if oddly tasteless — like chewing a wad of old gum, flavor long sucked out — flung it back into the cavern of my throat and swallowed it down.

". . . if we may take it as fact, something that you've gone on the record as claiming to be a fraud 'perpetrated on the American public to achieve monetary gain,' your words on yesterday's 700 Club; if we can presume for the moment that Sheldon's affliction is genuine, how do you believe this bodes for humanity's future?"

The senator prepared to unleash her fury. "Well, we can't believe this, it is absurd on the face of it, and I won't dignify such a blatantly ridiculous question with a response. What these people are doing is nothing less than one of the most distasteful examples of public deception in American history. They make these harebrained assertions, backed up with highly questionable quote unquote scientific proof, and shove them through their well-worn channels in the liberal media to try to extort money from the gullible. It is a disgusting charade."

Rowan rolled her eyes. "Then how do you account for this show's own medical experts—"

"I mean, look at the path they've taken, Franklin, really. Is this man really dead? What would any sane person do if confronted with such a creature as Mr. Funk claims to be? Did they take Mr. Funk directly to the CDC for examination? Did they report his condition to Homeland Security? Did they even call the police? No no, they bypassed logic and went straight to the media, Franklin. That right there should ring warning sirens in the minds of all right-thinking Americans—"

"May I interrupt here?" Rowan asked.

"Yes, Ms. O'Shea, you are Sheldon's representative, and I forward the senator's question to you. What do you say to these charges?"

"Franklin, what Sheldon is, is something unique. He is an absolute one-of-a-kind exclusive individual, and as both his agent and lifelong friend, I have an obligation to both represent his best interests and protect our investment. Clearly it is not in Sheldon's best interests to be poked and prodded and locked away for study. Whatever else he is, Sheldon is still a person, not a science experiment. What has happened here is remarkable, and the entire world deserves to know the truth, that the world they think they understand is still capable of surprising them. As such, we felt, along with Sheldon, that the best way to protect his interests was to take his case directly to the public, before government and corporate entities had an opportunity to get their claws in him and use him for their own selfish interests and subsequently deny him his God-given right to life, liberty, and the pursuit of happiness. That is why we chose to reveal his existence to the world in this manner, to reach the largest audience possible, to ensure media attention so that he could continue his life free and unfettered by governmental intrusion — a platform, I'd like to add, that the senator herself has campaigned on many times in the past. Were those just words, Senator?"

Rowan's last barb sank deep into the senator's armor, and Kud's eyes bulged as her blood pressure rose in protest. My mouth watered as I watched her skin tighten, and I quieted them with another hunk of depressing fake meat, trying to relish the taste as much as I was enjoying the dialogue, but it was a poor substitute, a vegan hotdog. Tofuman. Far tastier was the senator's flailing. She had looked commanding and forceful going in, but she was already beginning to crack under the absolute insanity of her own arguments. Keeping up a wall of ideological blindness and arguing against well-nigh undisputed scientific acceptance on climate change was one thing, but it must have been exhausting to keep up the pretense when the proof was sitting eight feet away and conversing with you. I would have pitied her had I not a vested concern in my own well-being.

Franklin swung back to Kud. "Response, Senator? If all this is true, as the medical facts state that it is, shouldn't Mr. Funk still have the same rights and freedoms as anyone else?"

"Fine, Franklin, I will play along with Ms. O'Shea's little game. If we accept his condition as fact — and I do not, I want to be clear and on the record about this: he is not dead — the fact is, under our constitution, under any country's charter, living people have rights. The dead do not. The dead cannot vote. The dead cannot own property. The dead are to be properly disposed of, for religious and health reasons. Mr. Funk, should he really be dead, has given up any rights he may have ever had to life and liberty. If dead, he is not by definition a person any longer. He is a thing to be studied and then discarded."

I'd had enough. "If I may. Butt in?"

"Please," Franklin said, waving a hand in my direction.

"Franklin, Senator, the. Fact that a dead person has. Never owned property before. Is not a feasible argument. I do own property. I may vote if I choose. There is no law that explicitly. Addresses my circumstances. Until I am specifically legislated against. As a deceased individual, I will continue. To assert the rights and freedoms any. And all intelligent beings on this planet are owners of."

Rowan continued, putting her hand on my arm, comforting the misunderstood fiend for the cameras. "And we will be arguing voraciously for his rights under any and all existing laws until we have exhausted every possible avenue. Sheldon poses no threat to anyone. We have been aware of his condition since it first occurred, and have been cooperating with authorities regarding any possible contagion. He is kept under scrutiny at all times. He has some unique dietary requirements that we have had to tackle, yes, but no different from if he was diabetic or suffered from a peanut allergy. Sheldon is a victim, the target of some sort of unknown virus, and we have made him fully available to any and all medical tests deemed necessary, but we will not abdicate his right to a private existence free of intrusion from the state, a right, again, that Senator Kud has repeatedly argued is a

God-given right. With proper care, Sheldon can continue to lead a full and normal existence."

Kud's face was turning red. "But—"

"We will return to our debate right after these words."

"Clear," the director said. "Two minutes."

"You bastards!" Waves of heat floated above the senator's head. "You damned liberal cocksuckers—"

"If you can't stand the fucking heat, honey," Rowan snapped back, whipping a pen from her front jacket pocket and slinging it at Kud. It whisked through the air and hit the senator in the dead center of her forehead, a blue dot proof of accuracy.

"Makeup!" the director yelled over Kud's cry of pain.

"Ladies, please," said Franklin as the makeup girl rushed to the senator's aid and dabbed at the spot with a sponge, looking at me and giggling, mouthing *call me.* "Save it for the cameras."

"And you'll be hearing from our lawyers, Pilato," Rowan said. "This is cheap gotcha journalism. Good luck getting us back on this network — you people are cut off. No more access to the greatest story in a lifetime."

"I sincerely doubt that, my dear," he said, his rolling baritone dripping grease. "I've been doing this a lot longer than you. You'll get tremendous exposure from this. Besides, the senator has the right to examine your freak. We all do."

"I'm right here," I butted in. "You can talk to me."

"I don't talk to freaks. Miss O'Shea, if you want to at all survive this interview, you'll keep your monkey on a leash."

"In five, everyone! Four three two."

"Welcome back. If you're just joining us, we are discussing the ongoing case of Sheldon Funk, the quote unquote zombie that has—"

"Franklin, I'd like to say something, if I may."

"Mr. Funk, please, you've had your turn."

"I don't think I have."

"We will get back to you. I'd like to go to the senator first. Senator, as a representative of the American people, what do—"

"*I'D LIKE TO SAY SOMETHING!*"

"Dear GOD!"

Franklin's head flung back as the sense of his own mortality hit his eardrums, and a small flap of false hair dislodged from its lacquered spot. He gasped and patted at his heart as the loose hairpiece flopped back and forth. Senator Kud choked back a chunk of vomit, and Rhodes attended to his spontaneous nosebleed. Cameramen had abandoned their posts to deal with the sudden onset of deep intestinal cramping, and the screens now displayed lopsided shots of concrete flooring. The studio had gone quiet save for the noise of gelatinous splattery vomit from all corners.

Rowan stared at me, livid. Behind the camera lenses, through the cables and out the station into the airwaves of the countryside, the entire viewing audience of North America had likely just come down with a stomach virus.

Over our earpieces, the director wailed commands to his queasy cameramen. I waited until one of the cameras had been righted and focused on me.

"I would like to apologize for. Losing my temper just now. This is a very stressful time for me. And to be accused of fabricating my. Condition without the opportunity to. Address the claim is aggravating. I think that, before we can really. Have a substantial discussion tonight on my condition. We need to all be in agreement. As to what that condition is."

Franklin struggled to compose himself. "Well, um, what would you suggest, sir?"

"The senator here. Has called me a fraud. She asks for proof. As you said at the break, she. Has the right to examine the freak. I would like to indulge her."

Dr. Rhodes looked nervous. "I don't zink zat's—"

"It's all right, Doctor. We had planned to show. This later on. But I want this done, now. I would simply like the senator. To be more involved. She needs to see."

I stood up and removed my jacket, slowly unbuttoning my shirt and letting it fall to the floor. Rhodes helped me slide my undershirt up over my head. My upper body was now completely revealed to the cameras and Dr. Rhodes' lifetime of expertise was on full display, live and in color. Where once had been a misshapen mess of skin and nails with wood underpinnings there was now an exquisitely grotesque amalgamation of flesh, stitching, plant-based adhesives, and tracks of interlocking metal teeth. Rhodes had used steel pins and leftover rib fragments from medical student autopsies to repair my ribcage, and at my request had repositioned my heart to its customary nesting place after first having it plasticized to prevent further decay.

He had filled any excess spaces from deflated or missing organs with healthy squirts of foam insulation. Citing issues of access, Rhodes had then affixed industrial stainless steel zippers to my flaps of skin so that he could reopen and reclose me on a moment's notice. He also sliced new fissures into key areas along the front, back, and spine, again claiming such entranceways vital to his effectiveness.

I think Rhodes was just drunk on the idea of seeing what he could get away with. After decades of patching together aging Hollywood stars, Rhodes was a master of defying age and common sense. When it came to what could possibly be done with the human body, Rhodes was a genuine artist, and had finally received a canvas truly worthy of his talents.

I walked up behind Franklin and bared myself to the senator, nonchalantly holding my arms wide.

"Senator Kud, if you would be so kind?"

"This is ridiculous, I refuse to be a part of this . . . this travesty."

"It's all right, Senator. I know what it is. To be scared."

Kud looked to the anchor, getting the merest shrug in return. The senator was holding herself together as well as could be expected, but Franklin was decidedly freaked. She was alone in this.

"Fine. If it will end this fraud." Kud arose and began examining the tabs, flicking them with her fingers and making comments on the poor quality of the effect, bolstering herself with false bravado. This was her moment, she knew, the proof of her unwavering character. Her triumph over this hoax, her unmasking of a trickster with nebulous motives, would be a cornerstone of any re-election campaign. She played her swaggering to the cameras with the required ease of a professional politician.

Even then, her voice was slightly cracked at its core. I could see the blanket of denial she had wrapped her mind in begin to fray at the edges as she went on, tugging slightly at the zippers, making lame jokes about shoddy tailoring while the seconds ticked by. Finally, she could postpone the moment no longer, and quickly pulled open one of the fastenings on my front, a fifteen-inch zipper that bisected my belly.

She stepped away. She uttered the mother of all blasphemies, bleeped for the broadcast.

The bulging mass of my entrails pulsed out slightly, held in place through tight packaging and Rhodes' attempts at adhesion. There were a few lengths of twine helping to hold it all in, woven into the casings and anchored around the spine, but this could not be seen from the front.

The senator took a pen and poked at the bundle. My stomach groaned a little, not as a result but with hunger, and the noise scared a scream out of her. I smiled a little at this, and Rowan and Rhodes loudly giggled. This emboldened Kud, and the sense that she was being made a fool of made a sudden resurgence. She prodded harder now, jabbing, until the tip broke through the skin and a dribble of my lunch squirted out over her hand.

"Please be careful, Senator. These are the only intestines. I have."

"Oh my, my, my . . . my God."

She kept thrusting, harder and harder, frantically digging her hand into my innards.

"Oh, oh, oh oh oh oh oh—"

Kud's eyes rolled back to take a good long look at the interior lining of her skull, and she crumpled to the floor. The director shrieked for commercial, and the scene cut away to an animation of a baby bear tormented by three-ply tissue cling-ons over its ass.

Rhodes rushed to Kud's side and began checking her pulse. "She is fine, I zink," he diagnosed, "but the shock, it vaz too much for her. Ve should get her to lie down."

"Drop her in the green room," the director said over the loud-speaker. Two interns ran up, giving me a wide berth as they tried to hoist Kud up between them. "Makeup, check Franklin, he's got some puke in his 'stache. Let's hurry, people, we still have a show to finish."

"Think you've got your ratings yet?" Rowan asked Franklin as the senator was wheeled away — the interns had given up trying to lift her and had decided on pushing her out of the studio in her chair. Franklin glowered, but there was a spark of journalistic interest left in him. He picked up Kud's pen off the floor and tentatively poked at my colon, waving away the makeup artist. A wide, creepily joyous smile lit up his face.

"Fuck the ratings," he whispered. "We're talking Emmys here. A Peabody, even."

"A Pulitzer?" I suggested.

He took one last nudge at my guts, and then reached out and heroically zipped my skin-pocket shut. "Why not?" He signaled the makeup artist, who dashed forward and gave his moustache a vigorous combing. "Sure, another Pulitzer. I deserve it, I think. Fuck Cronkite, fuck the goddamned moon landing. Fuck the Berlin Wall. Fuck the Challenger. Fuck Hiroshima."

"This tops them all?" I asked.

"This blows them away."

The rest of the evening went much more smoothly. Rhodes assuaged my fears and was a heavily accented delight as he described to the tiniest detail how he had gone about surveying my reconstruction, zipping and unzipping me to demonstrate his techniques. Franklin was far more gracious a host; he had tossed aside any notions of exposing a fraud and was starting from scratch, playing the dual role of impartial interviewer and astonished audience-member, asking serious questions while exhibiting a childlike delight at the medical marvel parading like a trained monkey before him.

By the end of the hour, my future was all but assured. I was the next big thing, a new star in the firmament. Untouchable.

A gibbous moon hung over the mesa and stared down at us. Judging me, I thought, taking into account my wholesale value with its low-wattage beam. Exposing the gruesome fathoms of my soul to the desert winds, the low shrubs, the nocturnal animals hunting the terrain for early breakfast.

Easy for a hunk of lifeless rock ensnared in Earth's gravitational tyranny to judge. I'm pretty sure it never had to go through something like this.

Well, at least someone *is judging me*, I thought; the reams of fabricated sympathy I was otherwise receiving were eating away at my collapsing psyche.

The Menard Institute for Mindfulness and Mental Repose squatted in an ersatz Arizona oasis maintained through a mighty combination of humanity's cancerous desire to alter terrain to suit a nebulous vision of happiness and the economic influx of gobs of celebrity money. A thicket of transplanted palm trees bristled in the parched breeze as we walked by, and the censorious gleam of moonlight bounced off the water of a manufactured spring. Other than the smattering of adobe structures and the geographically impossible deposits of flora, there was nothing within eyesight but sand, rocks, and the occasional Ansel Adams–esque plateau of even more rocks and sand. There was no earthly reason to locate anything of value there except privacy, which is what its residents craved. And paid for in trash bags full of cash.

We were fifty-some miles west of Phoenix, just at the end of an unassuming dirt road that seemingly led to nowhere. It branched off the main highway and extended southward into backcountry, faded tire tracks the only proof of its existence and quickly blurring into an endless expanse of beige topography, no signage to indicate what could possibly lie at the finale of its unpromising route.

After an hour of bone-rattling travel, our Humvee having driven up and over the horizon several times, the unassuming premises of the Menard Institute emerged into view. Here, anonymous VIPs checked themselves in to purge their bodies of whatever they felt ailed them: alcohol, heroin, cancer, male pattern baldness, depression, steroids, halitosis, ego, syphilis — whatever might affect their life in any conceivably negative manner. Rumor had it, so Rowan whispered as we trekked across an unnecessary bridge over a dried canal, that this year's winner of *The Biggest Loser* was currently holed up in one of the buildings, having her body professionally excavated to remove all traces of gluten. Dr. Rhodes murmured agreement, adding that he personally had attended to the de-STDing of almost every famous musician at one time or another, and began rattling off a list. I waved him quiet between rock bands, suddenly not keen on the odds that the good doctor would keep my next actions forever unknown under the silent umbrella of patient/doctor confidentiality.

Rhodes fumbled with his keychain as we approached journey's end, the entranceway to the Marilyn Monroe Memorial Annex. No lights were visible in the building; Rhodes had given his staff the day off, and the attendants were only too happy to oblige his orders and leave their charge alone in her room.

. . . so hungry . . .

"Quiet!" I said.

We halted our walk, and I listened to the wind rattle through the brush. Rhodes and Rowan looked at me expectantly.

"Nothing," I said, unsatisfied. "For a moment there. I thought I heard . . ." I shrugged.

The keys jingled merrily in Rhodes' fingers, playing eerie music over the wilderness. Rowan retrieved a pocket flashlight from her purse, and Rhodes finally located the correct key and slid it into the lock. The door swung open to darkness. On unspoken agreement we bypassed the light switches, letting the pencil beam of Rowan's light lead us through the reception area and into the halls beyond. There, the illuminated EXIT signs bathed our faces in a dim scarlet shine, lending the passageway the look of a tastefully appointed submarine on red alert. Twelve identical doorways stretched out before us down the corridor. Small wooden half-tables leaned against the walls at various spots, normally adorned with magazines and vases of fresh flowers, now bereft of toppings.

. . . eat . . .

"Did you hear that?" I asked Rowan. She listened, then shook her head.

The room we sought lay at the far end of the passage, the furthermost point of the entire center; even in a structure devoid of any other patients, the room's sole resident was kept as far away from patients in other buildings as possible. We stopped at the door, and Rhodes pressed his ear up against the metal. From the other side we could hear a feeble scuffling, a muted chime of steel links being dragged listlessly across a tile floor.

"I zink it is fine," Rhodes concluded, and grabbed the doorknob. I stopped him and placed my hand on the wood. I couldn't hear the voice behind the door, but a word echoed in my mind.

. . . hurts . . .

Rowan laid a pitying hand on my arm. I shook it off and grabbed her handbag, growling, confused, digging out what I needed and tossing the emptied purse back into her arms, hitting her in the bosom.

Rowan backed away, counterfeit compassion erased as she groped for the bag in the dim. "Just get this done already," she said, miffed. She turned and walked back down the hall, the spotlight dancing in front of her. "I'll be outside. Mr. Zombie *obviously* doesn't need my help."

"Leave the light," I said. She looked at the small bar in her hand and then flung it at me. It bounced off my goggles and clattered to the floor, the clamor obscene in the gloom. She stalked away as Rhodes picked the flashlight up and handed it to me.

"Are you sure you do not vant me to do it?" he asked. "I do not zink anyone vould blame you." I shook my head. This was my fault, I'd deal with it alone.

I pulled the door open a crack, and three wasps flew out and buzzed lazily down the hall. I slowly opened the door and stepped through, tracking the beam across the room and its contents.

It was a spartan affair, the room's inhabitant clearly not one for finer things. There was no calming patterned wallpaper. There was no desk, no chairs to sit in. The one window had been bricked shut, no attempt made to blend the hasty masonry into the décor.

There was no bed, only a single mattress, its fabric befouled. Its user stood next to it, facing the wall and unhurriedly thumping her head against it. I played the spotlight around her head. Distracted from her task, she followed the beam as I moved it about, getting her to turn around and face me.

Mom had looked better.

After the interviews and public appearances, there was no doubt that Mom's existence had to be dealt with. Even this secretive jaunt in the dead of night was risky; the established safety zone of floor fourteen of Fulci Towers in midtown Manhattan was several states away. Taking an unscheduled break from the webcams and various devices that recorded my every move and broadcast my day-to-day activities live on the internet to whomever cared to watch — my numbers were in the millions — left me open and exposed. The trust that those around me would not leak my whereabouts to whomever would pay the most was the only thing lying between me and a date with an extra-large petri dish.

My freedom hinged on my ability to control my ravenousness; at any moment officials from the Center of Disease Control could come to their senses and have me removed from the view of society. I'd be sealed in a sterile, airtight cube of Lucite and tucked away in a laboratory corner somewhere while Nobel laureates lined up to anally probe me.

But this had to be dealt with. Rhodes had made many assurances as to his ability to keep things secret, laying out a plan to move Mom by armored van to a remote mountain spot he knew of in the Ozarks where she could be tethered within an abandoned copper mine, one mile deep. There would be no need to end things with her, he pleaded.

There were just too many ways for this to go wrong. The lawyers were artisans, but something like this could only be kept secret for so long. With Kud's political connections battling our lawyers for legal ownership of my being, we had to remove all possible ammunition that could be used against me. Mom could escape, or someone along the line could decide that the authorities might want to know about Rhodes' strange elderly patient in the middle of the Arizona desert, Eileen Funk, the quiet one, the one that never ate, the one with the skin condition, the woman no one was allowed to so much as look at. And Rhodes' determination to keep her, frankly, was too creepy even under the circumstances.

Rowan agreed with my concerns but refused to let me see to it personally until I relented and agreed to ABC's offer to hoof it on that season's upcoming celebrity dance debacle. Placated, she facilitated our sudden departure from the city, covering our actions with an emergency website shutdown. Anyone logging onto the site looking to watch me catch up on my reading or do my taxes (yes, I was still doing my taxes; for me, there was only one sure thing in life anymore) would find only a flash animation of a cartoon zombie coughing until his brain fell out of his mouth. CLOSED FOR REPAIRS would then scroll across the screen as the zombie grabbed a broom and swept the brains off to the side.

We left the tower through a freight elevator to the parking garage, where we entered a waiting nondescript sedan and drove out into the city via an exit that emerged from underneath the neighboring building. We drove to a private airfield in New Jersey where a small jet was fueling up, and then flew to another airstrip outside Phoenix.

Her face was slack, dumb with incomprehension. The folds of her skin drooped loosely as only the most tenuous strands of connective tissue kept her entire countenance in place. Her temple was an open wound from her poundings, the wall behind her spackled with bits of pink and gray. The once-mighty sweep of auburn hair was gone, and patches of her skin had detached and slithered off, revealing a skull stained pink with fluid. Her eyes were faded, laced with scars, the emerald pupils wholly masked with milky white games of tic-tac-toe. Two uneven cavities encrusted with what looked like tobacco spit took the place of her ears, gone AWOL long before. As I watched, a wasp grown fat on organic slime crawled from her ear canal and took flight. I snatched it as it leisurely bumbled past and crushed it between my fingers.

Her nightgown stuck to her body where portions of her flesh had sloughed away, bonding to her as her liquids dried and became tacky, becoming a part of her, a second cottony skin. Mom's legs were bare, and the cuff of the chain fixing her to a six-foot circle had ground its way through the meat of her ankle as she shambled around, and was gouging a trench into the bone.

She mutely opened and closed her mouth as the beam flitted across her face. In my mind I heard her groans of hunger. She was begging for meat.

They hadn't once fed her, Rhodes confessed as we made our way across the desert. Bereft of teeth (her dentures had fallen out, no one keen enough to try and stick them back in), Mom was unable to chew. She wouldn't take any of his synthetic meatshakes and had pointedly ignored the ground cadaver flesh Rhodes had smuggled from hospital morgues and medical schools. For Mom, it was fresh or nothing.

And so she stood, rotting away, mindless, empty save for appetite. Every day an aide would check in on her, make sure she was still in irons, and would then call the doctor to report: no change in condition, sir. The aide would then go home, check his online bank account for that week's absurdly hefty paycheck and leave any concerns he had about legal and moral ramifications of his actions at the bottom of a bottle of rye.

If I left her here, locked the front door and encased the entire building in concrete, would she stand in this spot forever, waiting patiently for a meal to come within arm's reach? Would she stand while her skin composted into mush? Would she stand while her organs spilled out, and collapse when her ligaments decayed to nothing? Would the brain still labor away, fresh and vital, lying in an empty skull on the ground, neural impulses firing off in the dark, no muscles to move, no eyes to see, no teeth to chew, no stomach to feed?

I removed my goggles and aimed the light at my face, seeing if there was any hope of recognition. She watched me for a moment, head tilting as if in thought. Her mouth opened, forming words only she could decipher. All I could discern of her intelligence was a mad screaming that rang in the spaces of my cerebrum. I had no response to give. I was nothing to her anymore. I wasn't even food.

My mother stood in place, swaying, expecting me to save her.

"You zee how it iz," Rhodes said from behind me, giving me a start. "Zee differences between you and it, jah?" Mom swiveled her head around at the break in the quiet, so sudden a movement I could hear the ligaments swear and curse in her neck. A blazing hunger filled her milky eyes and she stumbled toward us before falling forward, the chain around her ankle refusing to give. Her arms clawed at the floor, and I made out a larger, thinner circle surrounding her, fingernail scratches embedded in the tile. Her mouth gaped, indecently wide. From the pits of her lungs came a thin whistle of appetite, forced out as she banged her chest and stomach against the floor in her writhings.

"Unlike you," Rhodes continued, unfazed by the slavering hellbeast of motherdom, "it haz nuzzink in zee vay of intelligenze." He took on a tone of a lecturer, guiding a student through the day's lessons. "I zink you are like, who iz it, Typhoid Mary? Do I haff zat right? You are a carrier, jah, but you do not zuffer zee full effects of zee infection. Vare you still haff almozt all your faculteez, it iz completely a creature of inztinct. You haff zee ability to control your hunger, jah? Up to a point, like haffing a bowel movement. All it vantz to do iz eat. Like you, it haz decreazed motor control, but to a far larger egztent.

It haz very little balance, unt itz muzcular coordination is zeverely limited. I zink it may haff a damaged, um, amygdala, jah? Ziz iz why it iz zo aggreziff. And itz hypothalamuz is completely inert, vich is vy it iz zo hungry all zee time. Yourz iz broken, too, but I fix good, jah? But ziz here, ach, I cannot fix. I zink. Vizout an autopzy, I cannot be sure, I am only guezzing.

"Zee rate of decay iz again differing from yourz. You decay zlower than egzpected, but it iz far more like a regular corpze. If not for me, I zink it vould haff fallen apart long ago. Are you sure I cannot keep it longer? Zare are some more egzperimentz I vant to try. You zee the zkin? Zee body iz almozt completely egzanguinated, zere is very little fluid left in it, it haz no blood left, but, like you, zee eyeballz are still full. Zey should haff dried out monz ago. I cannot yet egzplain zis. And zee brain? Still moizt, you can zee zat zare." He pointed at the crown of Mom's head. The skin was peeled away, and the skull had completely cracked open. Cloudy pus seeped through the fracture. "I can keep it a little longer, jah? Juzt a few veekz, maybe? I promize, I vill kill it ven I am done."

I grabbed Rhodes by the shoulders and threw him against the wall, pinning him with one hand on his throat. His legs kicked at my knees. "You call my mother 'it' one. More time," I said, giving him a half-volume roar directly in his face, "you'll get first-hand. Knowledge of her condition. Doctor." I dropped him to the ground and turned to my mother, still scrabbling at the end of her tether. I let Rhodes stumble out of the room to tend to the cantaloupe-sized boulder of spewage stuck in his throat.

We had discussed the best way to do this, and Rhodes assured me that, as movies and comic books suggested, destroying the brain was the only sure way to achieve certain second death. Rowan had brought a revolver armed with dum-dum bullets that would expand their mass on impact and blow the contents of whatever they struck forcibly out a new exit.

Mom had halted her struggling once Rhodes had left, and now lay motionless, face down, repeatedly lifting her head and banging her face into the floor.

I brought the revolver up and cocked it, aiming at the back of her skull. Right now, I knew Rowan and the doctor were waiting for the gunshot. They would then grind their cigarettes out on the ground with the toes of their shoes and walk back in to help clean up.

The blast of the gun would be explained away as a generator going kaput in the night. There would be no questions; people at the center, understanding the importance of secrecy, knew better than to pry.

I knelt down and placed the muzzle at the base of her skull. I wanted to cry, or say something, but there were no tears, no words forthcoming, no eulogies. Mom continued to bang away, pressing up against the barrel every few seconds. The skin remained dimpled where the muzzle pushed in, forming a circular nook.

Is there nothing left? I thought. I hadn't expected anything in the way of Oedipal anguish, but couldn't I feel *something*? I had lived in this woman's house for twenty-two years. She had fed and clothed me on her own, working a low-paying part-time job as a church secretary and combining her wages with Dad's pension and life insurance to keep me safe. All this, even as she berated me over my progressively pronounced disinterest in — later explicit loathing of — all things she thought sacred: her church, her friends, her perfume, her smothering, her assurances that I was just going through a phase that the right girl would snap me out of, just you wait and see. And what a manly woman she would have been.

I placed my hand on Mom's shoulder and slowly turned her over. She stared up at me patiently, her jaw cracking as it rhythmically opened and shut; I had no pulse, no oxygenated blood to offer, and so I was of no interest to her, just another tedious rambling corpse lurking behind the diaphanous scratches on her corneas. I put my palm against her cheek, willing her to respond, to give me something beyond hunger, show consciousness underneath the appetite. Her skin was cold, unfeeling; I might as well have tried to form emotional bonds with a slab of steak. Yet there was *something* at play; she rested her head in my palm, and for an instant the mind-shrieking diminished.

. . . food . . .

I played my life over in my head, pulling out the few actually happy memories I had of this woman. Her and Dad buying me an ice cream at Canada's Wonderland, and my throwing up all over Dad's lap as we rode the Octopus. Mom laughed at that as we whipped about in our seats, my upchuck flying, spattering Dad as we spun about in the centrifuge, Mom's horrified chortles pealing over the noise of the grinding gears and the tinny pre-recorded music of the calliope. A summer trip to Prince Edward Island, spending two weeks in a cabin owned by an old schoolmate of Dad's, just the three of us, every day nothing but swimming in the ocean, Mom teaching me the backstroke while Dad played a few rounds of golf, then all of us meeting up for lunch, shopping, and whatever else we wanted to do. The first Christmas morning after Dad's death, Mom hugging me tight after I unwrapped a ColecoVision video game system, playing *Donkey Kong* for hours as Mom made waffle after waffle after waffle, singing carols all the while.

All those moments. Dust. This thing did not care it had once set me up on a blind date with a good friend's daughter, and I had agreed to go, the two of us both realizing that this was a charade that could sustain our relationship a brief time. Her mind was gone, her personality evaporated, leaving a gore-hungry It in her place. I was the only proof my mother had ever existed, I was the sole repository of her memories, and . . .

Fuck this, I thought. I couldn't do much more than I had done; I had suffered my mother in life, but it wasn't worth this, these post-death tribulations. I owed her *something*, I knew, even if this walking sack of meat was only animated tissue, its movements the only thing separating it from being fodder for worms. Even in death, a modicum of reverence went a long way. I had hated Mom for most of my adult life, I had put her in a home when she became inconvenient, I had caused her death and rebirth in my ignorance, I had locked her up to protect myself — but fuck me if I would have her last sight be the bloody remains of her own brow against a concrete floor.

I lowered the gun and blasted her shackles loose from its moorings. The discharge rang though the room and echoed down the hall. Gathering up the chain to use as a leash, I pulled my dead mother to her feet and limped her down the hall, yelling to all persons outside to back away as far as possible. I brought Mom out to the open air; she stood beside me on the stoop for a moment, sniffing at the air. Was she enjoying this sensation, freedom, however misguided?

In the moonlight I spotted the silhouettes of Rowan and Rhodes hiding behind a palm tree. The embers of Rowan's cigarette glowed feebly in the shadows as she nervously puffed away, impatient for resolution. I was certain they were out of Mom's sight, but she sensed their heat. She lurched forward, pulling at the chain, clawing at the air, gnashing her teeth in the dark. I pulled at the leash and the metal manacles clacked against open bone. She tugged harder, straining for release, the cuff cutting into the leftover skin of her foot. Slowly, as she jerked, the flesh began to slide off, the manacle peeling off her skin as if removing a stocking. Still she hauled against her tether, scarily silent, snapping at the air, her loose gums pounding together with a moist clapping sound.

I grabbed Mom at the waist and flung her over my shoulder, fireman-style. She weighed next to nothing, but her struggles to get at the walking dinners cowering behind the foliage belied her mass. It was like holding a bag of badgers. As quickly as I could I walked around the building and into the desert beyond. Soon her floundering quieted, Rowan and Rhodes outside the realm of her senses. I put her down and led her away, docile as a cow.

We walked ten minutes, until the institute was only a few spots of light on a dark horizon.

I said nothing.

I thought nothing.

Not true.

I thought of my father. Lying in his coffin, his eyes closed, his skin unblemished, white, whiter than it had ever been in life. His hair, moussed, neatly parted, but on the left side, the wrong side; Dad had always parted his hair on the right, fighting the natural fall of his hairline, giving his head a lopsided, messy look as the follicles struggled to realign themselves. My twelve-year-old self looked down at him, dressed in his Sunday best, enveloped in silk and oak, my hands itching to poke his cheek and wake him up. That's all it would take, I was sure, just one touch and the joke would be over. I thought then as I thought now,

Is this it?

What a fucking joke. This is all there is to it?

I brought Mom to a halt, and took one last look into her eyes.

"Eileen?"

Nothing.

The monster gawked at me. Its bowels screamed their emptiness into the blackness.

I rested the barrel of the gun on the bridge of its nose.

"Mom?"

. . . shelley . . .

I pulled the trigger. I emptied the other four rounds into what was left scattered in the dirt.

I yelled then. I bawled nonsense vowels into the night, the metal of the hammer snapping as I put the gun to my head and pulled the trigger over and over. The sand rippled in sympathy. The moon hid behind a wayward cloud to avoid my gaze.

I left the flashlight as a marker and walked back. My handlers stood by mutely as I dug a can of gasoline out of the Humvee. Rowan tossed me her lighter as I walked back past.

I doused the remains with the fuel, soaking the sand underneath. The heap flared into life and I watched as the zombie charred into dust, trying not to hear the pop of leftover liquids boiling and bursting through its skin. When the flames began to die down, I fed them with nearby shrubbery.

I waited until the last ember turned dark, and then shoveled dirt over what was left with my hands.

"So."

As good a start to a conversation as any. So. My favorite adverb. Full of promise. Foreboding.

I nodded, patting my hands on the sides of my thighs as I sat there, forcing nonchalance into my posture.

"So," I echoed.

"So. Zombie, huh?"

"Yeah."

"One of the 'undead.'"

"The size of it."

"Huh. That's . . . that's really weird."

"Yeah."

"You're looking good. I mean, you know. Considering."

"Thanks."

"Is that okay? Calling you a zombie? Do you have, is there a different—"

"No, zombie's fine. That, or Sheldon."

"Sheldon, right. Not Gary anymore. Takes some getting use to."

"Or Shel. You can call me Shel."

"Shel."

For connoisseurs of awkward pauses, this must have been a buffet of delights.

"I hope," I started again. "I hope you don't think I was. Avoiding you."

"No, no."

"Because I wasn't."

"No. I mean, it crossed my mind, at first. I know you acted weird and all, but I thought . . . I thought you didn't like—"

"No, no. It wasn't you. I had a great time that night. In other circumstances . . . it just wasn't safe. For either of us. It's . . . it's me, really."

"Ha. No shit."

"Sorry."

". . . Not your fault, I guess."

"Thanks."

"You mind my standing way over here?"

"No, I get that a lot."

Duane hadn't moved closer than a dozen feet since he entered the room. He orbited the area by the door of my office, wandering from the wall to the closet, fingering the coat rack, toying with the sleeves of his leather jacket, eyeing me. Just behind the door in the hallway, I knew, lurked the fearsome Iris Sleiger, my bodyguard/keeper, hand curled tightly around the knob, listening attentively for unusual noises.

Rowan insisted on a bodyguard, doubly so since Senator Kud's unambiguous promise of holy retribution for her highly public shaming. Iris had worked as a personal guard in the entertainment industry for years and came highly recommended. There were rumors she was part of the Seal team that had stormed Abbottabad and executed bin Laden, but I never confirmed this. She sold me on her qualities when her shoulders entered the room seconds before the rest of her. Her training impelled her to follow instructions, and she left wordlessly when I asked to be left alone with Duane. However, the mercenary in Iris kept her alert and suspicious, and she patted the bulge at her waist as she left. Her weaponry, always at the ready — not for Duane, but for me.

The taser couldn't possibly hurt me, but sustained electrical charges wreaked mayhem with my nervous system for a few moments, more than enough time for Iris to cattle-rope my limbs together and clamp a ball gag on me. Unlike the taser, the gun was never to be used on me, instead serving two other purposes — protection and extermination. It was large enough to dissuade on sight all but the most fervent of lunatics. And should Iris be slow on the draw and I manage to bite someone, the gun would remove any threat of contagion transmission by efficiently eliminating the infected. Iris was unnervingly at peace with the possibility of killing otherwise innocent people whose only crime was getting in the way of my appetite, which made her an ideal candidate for the job.

I sat behind my desk and made no move to stand.

Duane had called to see if he could get in to visit me. Rowan immediately vetoed the idea — not a good plan, too dangerous, too soon, Duane who, hardly an A-lister — but she relented after I promised to do the town with a Grammy winner of her choosing and full paparazzi accompaniment. I'd be whomever's evening companion for the catwalk unveiling of some fashionista's latest display of contempt for the female form, plus drinks and dancing afterward. This would be a perfect opportunity, Rowan said, to relocate myself out of the headlines and into the public sphere, to start blurring the lines between media sensation and misunderstood, sympathetic being with a right to a private life. After all, Rowan reminded me, I couldn't expect to attend the Oscars, hobnob with the Nicholsons and Bridges and Paltrows, if I didn't start living the life of a celebrity. She never fully confirmed that plan, but the message was clear; get out and shake your moneymaker. I had already turned down further daytime talk show appearances, and if I wasn't careful the public's attention might turn to more recent sensations.

Strange that the unprecedented supernatural phenomenon of a reanimated, talking corpse could only be expected, by itself, to hold someone's attention for a few weeks. A viral video of a squirrel trapped in a submarine was already the next big thing, with a movie adaptation in the works.

I had been on the cover of *People* and *Us* for three weeks running, never mind the more upscale features in *Time* and *Newsweek*. I had even done a special interview with Oprah, a gratifyingly less-strenuous experience than *Speaking Frankly*. Far more tears, way more hugging. She had done the show unwillingly as a favor (under duress) to several entertainment interests. But the show had been a smash, a coming-out party for the ages, measurably improving her network's shaky ratings. Clips of her examining my gizzards on an operating table had been a staple of news programs ever since. When she had declared that I had clawed my way out of the grave and straight into her heart, I let myself hope that it could all be as simple as she made it out to be.

That hope did not last more than five minutes. When the show ended its taping, Oprah promptly vomited over her dress. That didn't make the news. But as omens went, a solid B-plus. She apologized immediately afterward, which I thought sporting.

Ever since, the offers had been surging in: speaking engagements, awards ceremonies, magazine covers, recording and/or modeling contracts, sitcom cameos, my own line of action figures, a proposal by the WWE to fight any horror movie icon I might consider in a mid-budget movie (*Sheldon vs. Dracula!*) — and those were only the reputable propositions from entertainment industry professionals. Lower down the entertainment hierarchy were mall openings, a suggestion to host my own graveyard-themed Las Vegas variety show, an offer to battle Chuck Norris in a pay-per-view Ultimate Fighting event (in the *octagon!*), and a full script for the first in a series of "high-quality pornographic horror movies" (*Night of the Living Whores? Schlong of the Dead?*). There were also myriad proposals along a more scientific bent — offers to dissect discrete portions of my anatomy, pleas for access and samples, one suggestion to spin me in a high-grade centrifuge (at no financial cost to me) to fully separate and scrutinize all elements of my substance.

This is to say nothing of overtures of a less stable-minded bent, by far the largest of the piles and another reason for Iris' presence — offers of marriage; appeals for my insights into the geography of Hell; scads of non-sequential bills tidily laundered and bundled to persuade me to kill certain individuals, no questions asked because why would I care anyway, what with my lacking a soul and all. A Saudi oil prince put in an offer of five million to acquire my personage for his personal zoo of endangered animals, claiming I was the one purchase that could make his menagerie complete, then upped the sum to ten, then twenty. There were more than a few sexual invitations from corpsers, those lonely individuals seeking a romantic night of consensual grave robbing; my official legal status was still up in the air, and until a new definition of "person" could be agreed upon, there was every possibility that I would still be technically dead in the eyes of the law, adding a distinct scent of the boneyard to the process of lovemaking that some found intoxicating. A few missing person reports arrived in the mail (thankfully none concerning my actual victims), packaged with heartfelt accusations of my obvious involvement in their deaths and appeals to turn myself in and offer the poor families some closure.

And (with no irony detected) death threats galore.

I was an abomination.

I was obscene.

Evil.

The death of good.

The antichrist.

That sort of thing.

And so it goes. Hi ho.

"Hey, is that Sofa?" Duane asked. He pointed at the prodigious ball of auburn-striped lethargy making itself comfortable on the cat-tree in the corner.

I shambled to my feet and picked the cat up off her perch, getting an annoyed protest from her as she awoke, feeling her vibrate lazily in my arms as she quickly acquiesced to the interruption of her seventeenth nap of the day. "You remember her name?" I asked. Duane shrugged, smiling. "Would you like to hold her?"

I took a quick few steps toward him, not thinking, holding Sofa up for a cuddle. Duane staggered back in fright, knocking the coat rack over with a loud clatter of wood and metal.

The door exploded inward and Iris hero-rolled into the room, knocking Duane off his feet, her taser withdrawn and aimed at my torso. I started to shout a *Don't!* but was cut off when silver electrodes penetrated my shirt and jolted me with fifty thousand volts, milliseconds after I had released my grip on Sofa to let her fall. I stiffened in my tracks as the current flowed through me and into the floor, filling the room with the stench of burnt carpet. Sofa leapt away to her tree, hissing as she flew to the safety of its highest perch.

I held my pose for a few seconds as Iris assessed the situation, and then brushed the electrodes from my chest as she straightened up and retracted the taser's wires. We both watched Duane stumble back to his feet. "That wasn't necessary, Iris," I said.

She grumbled an answer, something about not being paid enough for such bullshit, and left the room, giving me the evil eye and leaving the door wide open. Down the hall, I could hear Rowan's shrill voice demanding details on the commotion. Iris told her to shut the fuck up and to let her do her job, everything was fine.

Duane and I stood there, both of us embarrassed as the women argued in the corridor. Shouts of anger filled the emptiness between us.

Duane made the first move, stooping to pick up the rack, keeping me in his periphery as he tidied up. I gave Sofa a conciliatory back scratch and carefully walked back behind the desk.

"I'm sorry," Duane said after I had sat back down. His skin was ruddy with discomfort, and perspiration burst through the skin of his forehead. "That wasn't, I shouldn't have—"

"Happens all the time," I assured him. I slid open a drawer and fingered out a quick niblet of meat to quench the sudden compulsion to launch myself over the desk and take a closer look at Duane's inner workings. They were another Rhodes innovation, hardened chunks of synthomeat with an edible resin made primarily of bone marrow and wrapped in cellophane, lending them the appearance of cough drops. It was far less off-putting for the public to see me suck on a hard bonbon than eating a synthetic flesh pulled-pork sandwich.

I said, "An aide of Pat Robertson's—"

"Who?"

"Big religious mucky-muck," I said as I unwrapped the brown spheroid and popped it into my mouth. The resin softened immediately and juices flowed down my gullet. "An aide of his came by last week. See if I'd debate him on. Teevee over the" I air-quoted "'ecclesiastical consequences of my existence.' There was a fly in the room. Landed on the desk there. Dimwit was so scared of me. He fainted when I swatted at it. Iris broke the door off its hinges at the noise."

Duane chuckled at that. He looked at me and took a breath, steeling himself. His bare arms rippled with gooseflesh. "May I try again?" he asked, motioning toward Sofa.

"Only if you're sure."

He walked with measured steps to the structure and cautiously scooped the cat up in his arms. She flexed her paws, gave his arm a quick squeeze with her claws to make sure Duane knew his place in the arrangement, and then let herself be seduced.

"I think she likes me." Duane scratched her below her chin and got an enormous purr of contentment from the walking throw cushion.

"She abides you," I corrected. "I don't think cats like anyone. They're only biding time until they evolve thumbs. Then we're probably doomed. I've been watching her lately. Trying to take life lessons from her. Just go with the flow. Take what comes. Evolve and adapt to circumstances. A very zen state of mind." Duane frowned at that. "Very calming," I explained.

He let Sofa slinky out of his arms and to the desktop, where she busied herself with rearranging pens. "So, uh." He sniffed a laugh. "How've you been?"

"Good. Surprisingly good. Considering all . . ." I pointed at myself, traveling the length of my body with my fingers ". . . all this. Not bad. Better than most, in my position."

"I've seen you on television. You look good. Very professional." I thanked him. "So, what are your plans?"

"My schedule is free tonight," I said quickly, too quickly. *Dammit.* "I mean, if you want. Dinner or something, I could. Find the time."

"Oh." He blushed, and I quickly unwrapped another meat treat.

"You weren't going. To ask that, were you?"

"No. I meant, what're your plans, *overall*. Where are you heading with this? I mean, yeah, dinner, that would be . . . dinner . . . maybe . . . you . . . me . . ." The silent interludes between Duane's words stretched longer and longer with each successive syllable. His mouth opened and closed impotently around theories of sentences he could not verbalize. Since coming out, I have learned that a common side effect of my condition is inadvertent tongue-twistedness in others.

Duane suddenly took his bomber jacket off the rack and began putting it on. "You know, maybe this was a bad idea. I don't know why I came here. I thought—"

"Duane, please," I said, rising. I walked around the desk and stood before him. He admirably controlled his instinct to bolt. "Duane, I don't blame you for being scared."

"Scared? Gary, I'm—"

"Please call me Sheldon."

". . . Sheldon, I'm not scared, I'm mad. Well, I am scared, but still. You took off, and I never heard from you again. You abandoned the movie, you left us all hanging, then the director tells us you've come down with cancer or something and can't work anymore, we'll just shoot the rest without you. I try to call, no one knows where you are. Then, you're everywhere. Sure, you have excuses. I think, okay, he's going through some pretty heavy shit lately, can't blame him for flaking out a bit. But not one call? No email, nothing? It's been four months. And look." He held out his hand, palm down, steady in the space between us. "No shit, I have not had one snort since you left. I'm clean, drug-wise. Put myself up in rehab and everything. Your whole 'disease' thing, your breathing, the cancer, all the lies, put stuff in perspective for me, I thought. I cleaned up for you. I thought if you would call, I could come and help. I thought we, I don't know, connected or something. But nothing?"

I stood there, abashed and somewhat peckish. "I had no idea," I managed to say. It took two times; I forgot to breathe the first time. "Duane, I'm. I'm sorry."

Duane sniffed, shrugged, faux tough-guy cool. He seemed to shrink, becoming ensconced in the folds of his jacket, an innocent child clad in big boy clothes. It was adorable. "No biggie. Like I said, I get it, you had other things on your mind."

"Still. I should have called. Honestly, it never. Occurred to me."

"I was just worried, dude."

We looked at each other, Duane's eyes abruptly waterlogged with tears. He took a step closer, shivering, and placed his hands on my shoulders. He pulled me into an embrace. He buried his face in my chest and let out a squawk of a sob as I warily put my hands on his back. My palms singed from the heat of him, bursting through the pores of the leather. I hugged him closer to me, smelling his bouquet, feeling the heat of his melancholy through my shirt. After a silent count of fifteen I gently pushed away, separating our bodies as my appetite commanded me to shove a letter opener into the dimple beneath his Adam's apple and siphon out the sap.

Duane's face was a mess of liquids. I grabbed a tissue from the desk and waited while he wiped himself off. "Sorry," he murmured, taking another tissue and blowing the wetness from his nose. "Didn't plan that. Kind of got away from me."

"No apology necessary."

"By the way," his nose crinkled, "you really smell."

"I get that a lot." We shared a smile. "Duane, can we start again?" In our brief clutch, beneath the hunger, I recollected the intimacy of friendship, the easy unity of companions. It had been a long time since I had felt that human. "I would . . . things are difficult now but. I would like us to be friends. I can't offer you more than that. But I think I need a friend."

He smiled, still sniffling. "That'd be cool."

"We wouldn't be dating, though." I smiled, lips shut so as to not spoil the moment with an odious grin.

"That's fine."

"Not in the traditional sense."

"It's cool."

"I . . ." How to phrase this? "I can't do anything. Sexual. There's nothing working down there anymore. And I can't do anything with you. Too risky."

"Okay."

"You should feel free to date other people."

"Oh. Okay, if that's what you want."

"It doesn't matter what I want. I don't want you to feel like. This is a commitment."

"Uh-huh."

"We can only be friends. When you think about it. We aren't even the same species anymore."

"So, this would be . . . interracial?"

"No, intergenus. Not necrophilia, not exactly, but close."

Duane thought it over. "I'm fine with that," he said. He straightened his shoulders with resolve.

"You should think that over. You haven't even come out yet."

"But I want to. I am planning to. I will."

"But this is more dangerous, and not. Just for your career. I like you, a lot, but . . . when I look at you. All I see is lunch. I shouldn't even be alone with you now."

"But you are," he said. "And I'm not afraid." He pulled me into another hug. "See? Nothing happening."

"Trust me," I said as I gently pushed him away. "Something is happening." My stomach wailed for another lunch.

"You know," he said, as if it had just occurred to him, "*Basement* has its premiere in a few weeks. Two Fridays from now."

"I heard." Once I'd made international headlines, Zed had rushed the film into post-production to capitalize on my notoriety. The buzz was not good; his limitations as a director were evident in every overly stylized frame. Consequently, people would come out not to see my work, but to see me. Predictions for opening weekend were over forty million (triple the budget), based entirely on my current prominence as suspected cannibal and grudging spokesman for the dearly departed.

My first taste of real honest-to-goodness celebrity, using my personal infamy to market an inferior product to the lowest common denominator of consumers.

I felt like Charlie Sheen.

Zed's people had been pestering Rowan for weeks to get me out on the carpet and do some publicity. I imagined the rows of photographers come to get a picture of the monster, hoping for a King Kong rampage because of the bright noises and flash bulbs. Maybe I'd snap and kill someone in camera view; that would sell a few million copies. "I was going to skip it. I don't think I'm up for the scrutiny yet."

"Well, would you . . . want to go with me? If I asked?"

"What, as a couple?"

"Whatever makes you comfortable."

I began to shake my head, then thought about Rowan's plans to make a spectacle out of me for her own amusement. At least with Duane I'd have someone in my corner. He cared about his celebrity, but his guilelessness ensured that he cared far more about me than he did his own image.

"All right," I said finally. "We'll go. But don't tell Zed, we'll handle that."

"Awesome." Duane looked fit to jump out of his own skin with joy. "You won't regret this. It'll be terrific. Thanks, Sheldon."

"Call me Shel." He grinned and then ran out the door.

I ran a hand through my hair, stopping when I felt a few strands spring away. It wouldn't do to go on a date without a full head of hair, not if I could help it, anyway.

I called Iris into the room. "Do you have a suit?" I asked her. "Something dressy? Maybe a tuxedo?"

"I've worked with celebrities for two years," she said, deadpan. "I have three tuxes."

"Well, get it pressed and ready. In two weeks, we're doing the town."

"You're the boss."

"I am, aren't I?" Rubbing my hands together in excitement, I called for Rowan. And then for Rhodes, as the rubbing had loosened a fair amount of skin from my palms.

"We rolling? Good. So, what are you doing?"

"Just . . . making a sandwich here."

"Sounds tasty."

". . . I guess."

"What's the meat there?"

"This? Um . . ." Sofa hopped up to the countertop and sniffed at the spread of foodstuffs I had laid out before me. She snuffled around the plate of meat, her tongue darting in and out. I shoved her away, rudely, but better a lack of courtesy than let the cat nibble on Rhodes' zombiedibles. She sniffed in annoyance and curled up at the edge of the counter, watching us with derision. "You know what it is," I said, looking past the camera.

"What?"

"It's. It's just meat. That's all it is."

"I'm going to need you to elaborate a bit here, chum."

"It's, it is a synthetic meat substitute."

"I thought you couldn't eat regular food."

"No, but this is. This is different."

"So, it's human meat, is that what you're saying?"

"No, um. It is manufactured in a petri dish and. Grown larger in. An incubator."

"Is there anything to the bread?"

"What do you mean?"

"Is it, I don't know, meat bread of some kind?"

"Meat bread? No, it's just plain Wonder Bread. No real nutritional value. It's basically paper. That might be how I can stand it."

"And what's that you're putting on it?"

"Just. Um. Sauce."

"Looks like ketchup?"

"Huh. Let's go with that. Sure."

"Sheldon, I'm dying here, give me something."

"I'm sorry, Clive, I'm just not. Comfortable with all this. We've been filming all day. Couldn't I just eat my supper alone?"

"Okay, fuck this. Cut! Rowan, I cannot work with this." The camera spotlight blinked out of existence. I cautiously removed my goggles and moistened the dry orbs beneath with red-eye reduction agent as Rowan calmed Clive down with a few choice expletives. He stormed out of the house as technicians busied themselves with cables and duct tape, each of them keeping one wary eye on my movements. It had been like this all morning, a director masking his fear with utter umbrage at my every suggestion, and techies who didn't bother to disguise their dread at all. One grip wandered too close as he checked messages on his cell phone; as I was rather cantankerous as well (Rhode's meat substitute was nourishing but hardly the same thing as fresh kill), I threw my arms up and shambled toward him, screaming *Braaaiiinnnsss!* as blood-curdlingly as I could. He urinated on himself, soaking his Levi's, screaming bloody filth while he tripped over his legs and fell, taking a light tower down with him. All my submissive apologies to him and his union representative couldn't convince him to stay on set one minute longer.

I spotted the cameraman behind a couch, filming the whole event while keeping a respectful distance from my zone of terror. *Well, fuckadeedoo*, I thought.

Rowan stood beside me and together we watched the grip flee the house, making the sign of the cross over and over again: spectacles, testicles, wallet, watch. "Well, that was just great, Shel. Anyone else here you'd like to scare the shit out of?" Not waiting for an answer, she struck me across the face with the back of her hand. If it hurt her, she didn't show it, but my head hadn't snapped back under the blow. It hadn't even budged; she might as well have been bitch-slapping a fencepost. Dr. Rhodes popped into existence from wherever he had been observing and attended to my face. After some light probing of my cheek with his fingers, he pronounced my face undamaged.

"Rowan, I am. Sorry." I pushed every word out heavily, trying to affix an indication of yawning regret to my voice. It just came out breathy and guttural, and I gave up the attempt. "This is a bad idea anyway."

Rowan blew an errant hair from her face. "Clive, we're going to need a minute here. You stay, others, out." The director called for coffee and smokes break and the techies ambled out, already convincing themselves that they were congenitally more courageous than their vamoosed workmate. I considered going after them, baring my teeth as I imagined their cries, and a spurt of saliva ejected out my mouth and onto the hardwood flooring. Rowan snapped her fingers under my nose, and I clamped my lips shut and took a seat at the kitchen table, the penitent soulless corpse.

Clive and Rowan observed me for a moment. "Shelley, I'm going to be perfectly candid with you," the director began. He bent forward and placed his hands on his thighs, taking the position of the exhausted father. "You are by far the worst actor I have ever had to work with." Rowan nodded. "Now, I am used to working with amateurs on reality television. I am, in point of fact, one of the best there is, not something I like to boast about, but precisely why I find myself today in this unenviable position. And I get it, this isn't reality television, this is a documentary. A documentary for A&E, but still, yeah, a documentary.

"But you . . . you're a nice guy." Never had I heard the word *nice* sound so distasteful. "People want nice guys for friends. They do not want nice guys for appointment television viewing. *Nice* gets you the old crony demographic. *Nice* gets you CBS. You want CBS, Matlock?"

"I think," Rowan said, "what Clive means is that you are forgetting the basic tenet of North American television, which is that life is nothing but a freak show. And you, my darling little ATM, are the biggest freak out there."

"Huge," Clive agreed. "An enormous freak on a landscape of wannabes. A medical oddity with realms of untapped potential."

"We're talking T-shirts, Shel."

"Action figures."

"Recording contracts."

"Clothing lines."

"Celebrity feuds."

"What's her name, that senator?"

"Kud."

"Right, the cow, she says you are an aberration who crawled out of the bowels of Hell to infect us all. She wants you put down like a rabid dog; are you just going to take that?"

"Are you going to man up?"

"No, zombie up."

"Better."

"Your picture on lunchboxes, for the ironic hipster."

"Attendance at awards ceremonies."

"A line of frozen foods."

"But you need to let us in." Rowan pointed at the camera, alone on its tripod, its lens an open wound. "Let *them* in. Let them see the real you. The man inside the zombie, taking his new life day by day, struggling with his desire to consume human flesh."

"The stuff of great drama," Clive added. "Shakespearean in its scope, a regular Falstaff of the undead."

"You want the world to sympathize," Rowan said, her voice purring with sincerity, "fine and dandy—"

"—lemon candy—"

"—you've got their attention, but if you want to keep it, and we do, my darling monster, we have to make you an honored guest in their homes. We must throw you in their faces and demand their love."

"No one liked King Kong at first."

"That's right. People hated Godzilla, too."

"Dracula had them screaming in their panties."

"Freddy gave them nightmares."

"Jason terrorized their fucking wits."

"And now, Sheldon my dear, my fabulous monster, people adore them. These are books and websites and conventions dedicated to how much people love them. People need to work past the fright to get to the admiration, but they need the fright *first* to lube up their senses."

"Now, I am going to call everyone back in," Clive instructed, "before we start having to pay the unionized fuckers double-time-and-a-half, and you are going to answer my questions, and you are going to be charming, and gruesome, and gross, and misunderstood, and you are going to do this now."

"Or," Rowan said, lighting a cigarette for emphasis, "I will make one phone call to the CDC and this all ends with you in pieces, your brain in a jar and the rest of you in a series of test tubes and beakers, segmented and sent to laboratories around the world. They are just praying you'll fuck this up so that they can dip their filthy little grant-grubbing science fingers into your guts and pull at whatever they find. So do us all a favor: give the people what they want and monster the fuck up."

I thought about this. I told Clive to turn the camera on, and took the cigarette from Rowan's fingers.

"You rolling?" I asked. The blinking red light above the lens answered me. "Monster up," I muttered, half-ashamed at myself, half-hoping Rowan would defecate in her delicates at the upcoming show. I stuck the cigarette between my lips and took a drag, deep, deeper than humanly possible, and kept going. I thought about what Rowan said while the smoke coiled itself over and through the moldering remnants of my lungs, so recently reinforced with experimental latex glue. I switched my stare between the two of them as the camera rolled, going from Rowan to Clive and back again until he was sweating with fear. I gave him a slight nod to make sure he was watching and lifted my shirt off over my head, giving the camera a full view of Rhode's complex network of zippers crisscrossing my torso. Selecting a tab near my left nipple, I pulled down and across, careful not to get the teeth snagged, letting the skin fall away against the countertop with a lovely squelching sound until my restored ribcage was fully open to the air. Beneath them, my lungs pressed up against the bone and formed resin, swollen with the force of my inhalation.

"Ready?" I was careful to not let any exhaust leak back up through my teeth. Clive choked out a reply, muffled by his rising gorge.

Smiling at Rowan, I took one further breath inward to stoke the embers on the smoke, the lungflesh beginning to protrude out through the gaps between the ribs like a water balloon heedlessly squeezed to bursting between the fingers of an excited child. I took the cigarette from my lips and, watching Clive focus on its movement, slowly prodded the glowing end through the ribs and against the membrane of my breath sacs, listening to the sizzle of the meat, a hot grill frying up fresh liver and onions for hungry customers. Fumes rose from the branding until finally the tissue gave way and the cigarette broke through. The smoke I had been holding back for fully five minutes flowed forth, filling the air around my head. I flicked the cigarette away and zipped open another slit, just beneath my navel. I reached inside and took a hold of my lungs from the bottom, squeezing out every last vapor, the force generating a steam-kettle whistling as the smoke rushed out.

"Is that what you want?" I asked. "Does this satisfy you?" I looked at Rowan and snarled. She lit another cigarette and blew smoke in my face.

"Get going," she said to Clive. "You're not paid by the hour, so move."

Clive stuck his head out the door and yelled an end to smoke break. As the techies drifted back in, the cameraman hoisted his rig onto his shoulder and aimed the lens at me.

"Now," Clive hissed. "Just zip up, and we'll begin again."

I shook my head, and pulled open two more zippers, watching several technicians blanch. "I'm going *au natural*. Deal with it."

Clive looked to Rowan, who shrugged, *what the hell, he's the talent.* "All right, from the top. What are you eating?"

I heaved a theatrical sigh and looked into the camera's eye. "This?" I asked as I prepared my sandwich again. I spread my lips wide, the grin severing my face. "Well, I have what you could call a. Strange diet. My body wants live flesh, but. We've managed to fool it with. A synthetic meat grown from human stem cells."

"Like, from embryos?"

I twisted the grin into a malicious leer. "Oh, could be, yes. I didn't ask. Could be. Something to think about, isn't it? All those embryos. Yummy. But for all intents and purposes, this is. Human meat, grown in an incubator. And delivered fresh to my plate. I'm seasoning it with a plasma substitute commonly. Used in emergency surgeries." I held the completed sandwich up for inspection; a thick liquid red oozed out the sides as I compressed the layers together with my fingers. "You know," I said as if the thought had just occurred to me, "I hear they're doing this with pork and chicken, too. Synthesizing the meat in test tubes. Soon, we might all be eating like this." I cracked my jaw wide and took a bite, taking over half the sandwich in my mouth at once. I groaned with exaggerated pleasure. "Boy, that is finger lickin' good," I said, winking at the cameraman. Behind him, Clive called a cut as a key grip vomited until he cried.

Announcer:

>Here to present the award for Best Makeup in a
>Motion Picture, the Oscar-winning star of *Mamma
>Mia!* and *Sophie's Choice*, Meryl Streep! And the
>breakout star of *Basement*, Sheldon Funk!

Meryl:

>Sometimes, no matter how talented the actor or
>actress, the demands of a role requires that
>extra steps be taken.

Sheldon:

>Sometimes, even the best of us need a little
>extra oomph.

Meryl:

>Huh.

Sheldon:

>Excuse me?

Meryl:

>No, nothing.

Sheldon:

>No, you obviously have something. On your mind.

Meryl:

>Well, this is the award for makeup. But I've
>always felt that any talented actor never needs
>makeup.

Sheldon:

>So, you never wear makeup in your films?

Meryl:

>Nope. Not one bit.

Sheldon:

>*Sophie's Choice?*

Meryl:

>I just stayed out of the sun for a few months.

Sheldon:

>Wait, in *Death Becomes Her*, you transformed.
>From old to young in one shot.

Meryl:

Body control.

Sheldon:

Really?

Meryl:

All Stanislavsky Method.

Sheldon:

Wow.

Meryl:

You bet, wow.

Sheldon:

Well, with a few obvious exceptions. Most actors need a little help. From time to time. And that's where the makeup. Department comes in.

Meryl:

Under the expert care of these master cosmeticians, entire alien races can be created through liberal applications of latex and body paint. These wizards can make the young look old, the old young, the plain beautiful, and the beautiful grotesque.

Sheldon:

You know, Meryl, like you. I've never had that problem.

Meryl:

You're *that* talented?

Sheldon:

No, I'm *that* ugly.

Meryl:

Now, don't put yourself down. You have a real manly quality. I find you very attractive, Sheldon.

Sheldon:

Really? You really think I'm attractive?

Meryl:

No, dear. Again, I'm *that* talented.

Sheldon:

These are this year's nominees for. Best Makeup

in a Motion Picture: Tom Savini, for *Dead City.* Gary Tunnicliffe, for . . .

Doctor Thompson stared at my daughter and I from across the parlor. "I feel that someone in this village is practicing witchcraft, squire. I fear that corpse wandering on the moors is an undead, a zombie."

"A zombie?" I sputtered, partially in character and partially over the Welsh accent I had been struggling with. "Here in Cornwall? Preposterous! I think you'll find that kind of talk. Won't endear you to the locals. I don't know what they teach in your fancy. Schools in London, but in these parts, Doctor. We do not harbor these deep superstitions you seem to suffer. To leap to such illogical conclusions. Based on the flimsiest of pretexts speaks. Volumes to your character, sir. I advise you to keep such ridiculous notions to yourself."

"Father, please!" Sylvia protested. "Hear Peter out. He is not—"

"Peter, is it now?" I thundered at him. "Have you been friendly to my daughter? Oh, I now see how it is, sir. The gallant young doctor from the great city. Aims to sweep my daughter away from the perils of village life."

"But Father, I—"

"I will have none of this in my house!" I aimed a finger at the doctor. "You are no longer welcome in this house, sir. Nor in this parish! I shall be speaking with the town fathers immediately. To ensure that you do not darken the doorsteps. Of the citizenry a moment longer!"

"Cut!" The lights in the parlor dimmed, and Johnny and Samantha slouched in relief. A dress mistress ran in and loosened Samantha's corset, eliciting a groan of intense pleasure at her liberation from the torturous confines of nineteenth-century women's fashions. Johnny mouthed *good job* to me, and I nodded a thank you as I dug my goggles out of my pocket and placed them over my eyes, sighing mutely as they immediately spurted saline over my wretched corneas. A new invention of Rhodes'.

"How was that, you think?" Tim asked by the bank of camera equipment.

"Everything looked five by five here, I think we got it," said the DP. "I'll know better when we see the dailies, but that was solid."

"Good, good." Tim hopped up out of his chair and trotted across the set, gathering the three of us in a loose circle. Iris hung back, always wary. "All right, notes. Samantha, brilliant work today, no notes for you. Go get out of those things and relax, we'll call you later for scene, uh" he checked over his clipboard "twenty-seven. No lines for you, so rest up your voice for the pyre scene tomorrow, you'll need it for screaming."

"Thanks, Tim." Samantha slipped out of her period heels and grimaced as her feet resumed their natural shape. "Christ, these things are tight. Any chance of a larger size?"

"Talk to wardrobe, tell them I demand comfort for all my actors." Tim shouted over his shoulder to the DA, "Sara, bigger shoes for Sam, right? And give the call." Thanking him, Samantha stumbled off, seizing a nearby grip and using him as a crutch as she headed for her trailer, apologizing all the way. The DA shouted into her megaphone, "Lunch, everyone. Be on the Cornwall exteriors set in one hour, we'll have set up for scene twenty-seven."

"Good work, both of you," Tim continued. "Johnny, I think you've got a handle on where Peter comes from, but I don't want too much naivety sneaking into the character, right? He's new to the job, but he's not a newborn. Tone down the wide-eyed doe bit a little."

Johnny rolled his eyes skyward. "Give me a break, Timmy. I'm forty-eight playing twenty-five, I want to make sure the innocence of Peter's youth comes out. You think re-shoots?"

"I'll know better after dailies, but I figure no. Sheldon, almost the opposite for you. We all know you're the bad guy here, but let's fight the tendency to play that up from the get-go. Work with the ambiguity of the character, don't come across as too menacing right off the bat. Think charming like Peter Cushing, keep the audience on its toes."

"Right," I said. "Charming. More Cushing, less Price."

"Exactly. Bring the Price out later, save it for the blood offering scene. And I know this is difficult for you with your, your breathing, but less pauses if possible, we want to keep the movie under two hours. Now, off with both of you, get a quick lunch and change clothes for scene twenty-seven."

"Which is that again?" Johnny asked.

Tim scanned his board. "Scene twenty-seven, Peter and Clive see each other for the first time. You're on the carriage coming into town, you see Sheldon here speaking to the townsfolk, you make eye contact. Wide shots at first, we'll shoot close-ups later if we've still got the light. Mainly second unit stuff, but I'll be there today, I want to make sure we get a grand sweep of the whole town square. Sheldon, we'll probably dub in your dialogue later, but this is not a dumbshow, I want you in full character. Do that" he motioned to his throat "voicey thing you do, I want the extras to look absolutely terrified." Clapping us both on the shoulders, he walked back to the DA, shouting instructions.

"Does he ever take. A break?" I asked.

"When he's dead, he'll take a break," Johnny said. "C'mon, you want lunch in my trailer? I'd like to go over some background beforehand."

"Sorry, I never eat. In front of people."

"Hey, no problem. Stop by when you're done, all right?"

I nodded and walked off set toward the exit, toward my trailer, toward food and sanctuary. Rowan and Dr. Rhodes popped out from wherever they had been hiding themselves and hurried along after me, Iris shadowing my every move from twenty feet away as I crossed the warehouse floor and out to the open air. Was I feeling okay? Did I need anything? Was anyone getting too touchy, should they warn Tim not to make direct contact as he did? I decided to take full advantage of my prima donna stature, barked out a command to cease and desist while I climbed the steps to my door, and slammed it.

"Tough day at the office?" a voice called out from the kitchen area, nicely curtained off from the (I suppose you'd call it) den of the trailer. Surprisingly roomy, but a trailer is a trailer is a trailer.

"You have no idea."

"I could see them flapping around behind you out there. Well, you just have a seat and relax, I've got just the thing for you."

"A gin and tonic?" I shucked off my authentic nineteenth-century overcoat and gingerly lowered myself onto the settee, nudging Sofa to the side and gracing her with a quick bout of belly scratching. My intermediate and proximal phalanges argued against each other as I toyed with her, grinding like rocks in a cement mixer. "A dirty martini?"

"Much better." Duane walked out from behind the curtain, a plate of what looked like cold cuts in one hand, a tall frosted glass of red in the other. He handed me the glass, a bendy straw thoughtfully prepared and waiting, and put the plate on an end table.

"O positive?" I asked.

"AB negative. Rhodes tells me it's the rarest."

"You spoil me." I took a sip through the straw and almost cried as the blood, pure manna, blessed my soul with energy. I gave in to temptation and gulped the sixteen ounces down in a few seconds of unending bliss. My toes spasmed with glee.

Duane took a seat beside me while I impatiently sucked the last few drops out of the bottom. "You look tired, Shel."

"I don't feel tired. I never feel tired anymore." But I knew what he meant. I pulled at my wig, testing the adhesive. "I think I'm drying out again. I can feel my limbs hardening up."

"Time for a checkup, I guess."

"Christ. I don't look forward to it." Lately Rhodes had gotten even more maniacal in his quest to keep me fresh. I think a God complex might have taken hold of him. I slipped the goggles off and popped out the colored contact lenses the doc had made to make my eyes look almost human. They had the added benefit of being made of polarized glass, cutting down the glare considerably and improving my eyesight tenfold, although anyone with normal eyes would have torn their eyeballs out from the considerable pain. Duane quickly squirreled them away into their saline container.

"So, rough day?"

I winced. "Tim touched me. Just now, accidentally. He touched my shoulder. His hand slid across the skin of my neck. Just what I need now. To eat Tim Burton. There's a career killer."

"But you held it in check."

"I held it in check. It's my fault for not having. Iris bring a lunch kit along to the set. But it's getting harder lately to control. I know exactly how he would taste. From his scent. Like pork marinated in alfredo sauce." I had begun classifying people in this way, unconsciously at first, then as a test to keep my mind occupied. Somehow, thinking about how a person would taste actually distracted me from my appetite. Duane would taste of chicken, sautéed in butter. Rowan's aroma reminded me of beef sautéed in onions. I lifted a slice of meat off the plate and sucked it down, barely chewing. "I don't know how you. Can stand to watch this," I said around a second piece, this time taking a moment to give my teeth some exercise.

Duane shrugged. "I watched a lot of nature shows when I was a kid. Lions taking down a zebra, that kind of thing. How is this any different?"

I looked at him; Duane's capacity to forgive my many faults was truly astonishing.

Duane had gone from co-star to friend to live-in roommate in rapid order. After *Basement* had premiered, Duane had come out, doing the usual rounds that go with revealing to the public something that wasn't any of their business to begin with. Admittedly, the hype was higher than usual due to his constantly being seen in the company of yours truly. I thought it was bad for me, but it turns out that for many people the only thing conceivably worse than being the living dead was to be a companion to the living dead. I can't even begin to describe the hate mail.

Or the online slash fiction about our "torrid affair." Suffice to say, some corpsers had incredibly vivid imaginations when it came to what you could do with the sexual couplings of a healthy young man and a decomposing carcass.

Duane took it all in stride. His lack of guile was astonishing, as was his inability to see just how harmful our relationship could be to him, professionally. I couldn't stand by and watch as he sacrificed his career over me, so I decided to become his protector. I arranged for him to get a producer credit on the documentary, and then finagled that into a role as executive producer for this venture, along with a supporting onscreen role as Samantha's popinjay brother, Neville. If he wasn't going to look out for himself, I'd do it for him.

"What's with the getup?" I asked. He looked the proper English fop, clad in ridiculous finery and linens.

"This old thing?" He delicately fingered the lacework draped about his neck. "I've got that scene with Sam this afternoon. Hey, check this out, I've been practicing." He stood up and cleared his throat, shifting his weight onto his back foot and thrusting his chest out slightly. "'Dear sister, you must be truly mad to go off with that cretin of a doctor. He'll do you no end of trouble, just you see.' How was that?"

I applauded. "You are indeed. A proper dandy, good sir." He had been working with a dialogue coach on his accent and was unpredictably good at it. His dialogue rolled off his tongue in plummy British tones only spoken by those with vast stores of unearned wealth. It wasn't perfect, neither was Johnny's, but both were good enough for an American remake of an unremarkable British horror film filmed in Canada. "But you'd better check with the DA. This afternoon is the crowd scene. Might be the wrong clothes."

"Ah, dammit." Duane minced about in his costume. The mincing wasn't his fault; you couldn't do anything in leggings and lace without it seeming thus. "It took me literally an hour to get all this shit on. These things really bind at the crotch." He stormed out of the trailer, yelling for Sara, leaving the door open for Rowan and Rhodes to scramble inside and ruin my meal.

Since *Basement* had been released to the public — fifty-seven million dollar North American opening weekend, only twenty percent drop-off the following weekend, a definite moneymaker for all concerned, and video sales were expected to double the international gross — I had mused over several scripts, most of which, hell, all of which played on my notoriety as founder and sole member of Club Dead. I automatically turned down anything that reeked of direct-to-DVD: *Zombie Honeymoon*; *Lunch Period of the Dead*; *House of the Dead III*; *Pontypool Changes Everything Again*. Outside of those, there were more high-profile roles, but I was still being typecast. The roles were big, the budgets substantial, and the talents involved enviable, but my roles inevitably were those of dead people wandering around among the living for a variety of reasons. I looked in vain for a more meaty character role, but quickly learned that people were not only wanting me to play zombie but unable to fathom my playing *anything* else. I once read for a low-rent romantic comedy, did pretty well, got to the final stage of auditions for the lead role alongside a few fading celebs who would take anything to remain in the public eye. Unhappily, the director became aware through channels that I was gay, and the role was denied me. This is not conjecture; rather, it was boldly stated to my face, "Gay can't play straight, no one buys it."

Finally, I narrowed it down to two remakes of Hammer horror films, *The Plague of the Zombies* and *The Abominable Dr. Phibes*. David Fincher was doing *Phibes*. It was a full lead role, the protagonist not dead but merely horrifically disfigured, but the script wasn't yet complete, stuck in rewrite hell, and shooting wouldn't begin for six months minimum. I went with *Plague*, rationalizing that my character was at least *presumed* to be alive until the third act reveal — Squire Clive Hamilton, keeping his village safe from the intrusions of modern society and scientific rationales, all the time performing black magic incantations to raise his own army of the undead. However, the role wasn't nearly as interesting as the company I'd be keeping. The movie had been a pet project of Tim Burton for years, and where

Burton would go, Johnny Depp would almost inevitably follow. Throw in Samantha Morton as Depp's love interest and my daughter, Helena Bonham Carter as my wife, and you've got a fascinating mélange of over-the-top gothic horror, star appeal, freak show, and critical cachet. All I had to do was make sure I didn't eat anyone, and work on my English accent. The whole gaggle of us then were herded off to Montreal for filming, where the metropolis, amply laden with suitably period-looking architecture, would for three months act as a representation of a mid-nineteenth-century English hamlet.

"He touched you, didn't he?" Rowan demanded, answering herself before I could get a word around a mouthful of petri meat. "That son of a bitch, he knows better than that! We could lose all funding, you know. One slip-up, one scratch, and that's it, 150-million-dollar production, guaranteed return in DVD sales, all shot to shit. Like it wasn't hard enough getting insurance for this thing. You know how much you cost us, just to be allowed to have you on set? God, why couldn't you just have a drug problem, or AIDS? *Those* are insurable, but you, the great uninsurable one, you have to be an unclassifiable. You are one step away from an act of God, that's how difficult it was to insure you."

I let her rant on while I sucked down the last of the phony baloney. She had a point: I was at all times only one good sniff of fresh human blood away from rampage, but I always went on set fully gorged, my appetite dampened to a manageable pang for anyone within my zone of reach. Besides, Rhodes had made remarkable strides in improved flavor and consistency of his laboratory loin. The blood was real, but I didn't feel too bad about that: he told me they got a discount on some Canadian bulk blood from the Red Cross, all tainted with a variety of pathogens that would definitely kill lesser, more life-enabled sorts. Recycling, really.

Duane came back in near the end of Rowan's spiel, dressed in new leggings and frilly shirt, frowning in confusion as she promised to personally gut the producers of *Plague* should anyone so much as think of touching me without following proper procedures. The actors were far braver than most, but there was never any actual contact; Johnny was instructed to wear gloves when our characters shook hands, to minimize risk, and during larger, more crowd-laden scenes, a sheet of Plexiglas was installed between the extras and myself. This was necessary not only for their protection but for mine as well: already, two extras had rushed the wall, trying to breach it to get within touching distance. One wanted my autograph — should have waited, I made it a point of habit to sign all proffered papers at the end of each and every shooting day; I got more requests than all my co-stars combined — and the other was out for blood. Not figuratively, not in a murderous rage, but rather literally wanted a vial of my DNA as a keepsake. Not that I had any blood left; Rhodes had replaced most of the fluids in my veins with an organic formaldehyde that kept me limber. The extra couldn't have known that, charging up to me with an extended syringe in his hand, only stopping when his forehead hit first the transparency and second the floor, where he was repeatedly hammered by Iris about the face and shoulders with a blackjack.

" . . . and that's what we'll do." Rowan leaned against the wall and lit a cigarette, her anger spent for the moment. She'd been getting touchier of late, prone to profane outbursts that, even for her, were startling in their length, breadth, and overall cruelty. Her façade of coolness was crumbling, her hair often untended and loose, her age wrinkles more prominent. I recalibrated my estimation of her age; she was a young fifty, possibly young sixty if she had availed herself of Rhodes' services. "So that's what we'll do," she repeated to herself.

"Good," I said, throwing a wink to Duane. "Then that's that."

"That's what, exactly?" Rowan asked, annoyed, puffing out a cloud of smoke.

"Whatever that was." I waggled a finger at her nonchalantly. "That, what you spoke of. It is that." Rowan scowled. "No, I wasn't listening. You've been on one speed lately. I can't be expected to keep up. With your rants." Fame *had* gone to my head a bit, but as Rowan had treated me (and others of my character-actor-at-best ilk) like an inconvenience for years, a poorly traded stock option she couldn't be bothered to sell, I figured a little payback through actorly bitchiness was only fair.

"I'm looking out for your best interests here. For everyone's interests. Yours, mine, Duane's."

"You look out for me? Get me a refill." I waggled my empty glass at her.

"You think this is easy, you undead bitch?" she shot back. "You think I'm not constantly fending off not only paparazzi, not only goth fans, not only freaking corpsers, but the fucking government as well, the CIA, the CDC, the ACLU? You've got nerve, Shel, treating me like a flunky."

"Hey, who works for who here?" Duane spoke up. "I don't see you complaining about the money he's making you. Talk shows, articles, toys—"

"Unt dat video game?" Dr. Rhodes threw in. "Iz zat ztill on zee table?"

"The video game appearances in *Dead Island 3* and *Mortal Combat*, thank you, the fashion shows, the swag. He's making you a mint in publicity, he's a walking fame magnet." Duane crossed his arms.

"You nearing a point?" Rowan spat.

"You work for me," I said. "That's the point. I appreciate all you've done for me. But you want to go? You're not happy? Say the word. I make one call to Masters. I get a new agent."

Rowan's veneer cracked open, minutely, and I could just glimpse the person underneath the persona. She was tired. She was angry. And scared for some reason. She opened her mouth to retort. Her cell phone jingled in her pocket, cutting off her answer. She answered, her eyes darting about as she listened to the speaker on the other end, and left the trailer to talk outside.

"Thanks, Duane."

Duane shrugged and took the glass from my hand. "She doesn't deserve you, that's all. You're the one suffering here. I just hate to see her making a mint off you and then complaining about it."

"Iz a clazzic victim zyndrome," Rhodes said, taking a seat next to me and putting on his glasses and latex gloves to begin our daily physical examination. "Narzizzizzm. She haz to make everyzing about her, jah? She iz zee zenter of zee world, to her. She cannot zee you az a perzon, only az an accezzory to her life. My professional opinion, anyvay. But I'm not a head doctor." He chuckled. "Not in zat vay, anyvay."

"It's not that I don't appreciate her," I said as Rhodes removed my goggles and shone a small flashlight in each eye. "I'm just tired of the constant harping. It's getting worse and worse lately."

"Vell, giff her zee zpaze, jah?" He rapped underneath my knee with a hammer. No response. He jotted this down on a notepad, humming to himself. "She cannot help herzelf." He prodded the muscles of my arms, watched the indents refuse to pop back out. Frown lines formed on his forehead. He pursed his lips and began to pull at the skin on my left arm, forming fleshy peaks that stayed put. "I vaz afraid of ziz. I thought ve had more time, but . . ." He let his sentence trail off.

"What's the diagnosis, Doc?" I asked.

He ran his fingers through his hair and puffed out air. "Vell. I zink I haff zome bad newz." He stared into my eyes. "I am afraid you are dead."

"That was only funny the first seventy times."

"Jah, but zere iz an ackzeleration of zee decompozition now. You and I, ve haff done zome remarkable vork here. Ve kept you together with metal unt rubber. I filled your veinz vit fluid unt kept you limber. I even made you zmell better."

"And thank you for that," I said, meaning it. Before shooting began, Rhodes had prepared and implanted subcutaneous pockets of potpourri that filtered through the slightly perforated skin and effectively masked my standard aroma of an untended monkey enclosure. He then moved on to other variations; Duane's favorite was cinnamon, I was partial to rosemary. As a result people tended to get hungry when I was around, rather than lose their appetites.

"But now, I zink zat, vizout zome major modificationz to your zkeleton and muzculature, you might not lazt zee year." Behind him, a small gasp escaped Duane's lips.

I smirked. "Being dead for eight months is. Bad for your health. Who knew?"

"You can fix him, though, right?" Duane asked. "I mean, he's already dead. You've kept him together this long. Can't you, I don't know, give him a skin transplant or something?"

"I do not make ziz ztatement lightly. Your body, Sheldon, it cannot take much more than I haff already done. Zere are limitz to vat zee body can take, even in your caze. I can keep you here, like ziz, to complete the film, jah? But after zat?" Rhodes clapped imaginary dust from his palms. "Over."

"So, what, you're going to let him fall apart?" Duane pulled at his hair. "What kind of a doctor are you, didn't you take an oath?"

"Jah, for zee living, Duane. Zee *living.* Ziz? Zere iz no oaz for ziz."

"Duane, please, don't panic." *Maybe this is for the best,* I thought. I had already lasted the better part of a year after death, and only killed ten or so people, I thought. Quite a record. I'd leave everything to Duane, I decided then. He deserved it. *I should make out a will. Can I make out a will? Is that legal now? I'd better start transferring funds while I still can.* Sofa coiled herself around my ankles. I bent down and rewarded her with an ear rubbing. "We knew this was coming. I think we should just accept this."

"No, c'mon, Shel." Duane's eyes began to swim. "You can't just give up like that. The doc here is a genius, he can do *something*, can't you?"

"Duane, no tears, okay? No one should cry for a zombie."

"You know," Rhodes said, "I *haff* been zinking about juzt ziz zort of zing. I didn't vant to tell you ziz zo zoon, but now ve haff little time." He pulled a folded piece of paper from his bag and flattened it over the endtable. It was a sketch of a skeleton, drastically altered, a scenario from the mind of a DC Comics artist. "If ve can keep your brain and zpinal column intact, vich I beleef ve can, I zink ve can replaze your entire zkeleton. Zare really iz no need for it, and zinz you feel little pain, over time ve could zvitch every bone viz a titanium vun. Zare are zum people I know, colleaguez, zey haff zome ideaz on how to zubzitute your muzzelz vit a hyper-rubberized alloy zat could, zeoretically, make you even ztronger zan you are now."

"Wait, we talking superhero stuff here?" Duane asked. "Make Sheldon into, what, Wolverine?"

"Not az zuch, no, but zee bazic idea iz zee zame. Sheldon, you haff a unique opportunity to completely revamp zee human body. Ve'd haff to keep zee digeztive zyztem intact, but ve've already zeen zat your body can take a lot of punishment. Theoretically, ve could *eventually* replaze your entire body viz zat of a zyborg."

"So, this is possible?" I asked. "I could become a, a supersoldier?" I looked closer at the rough plans; I was certain I was looking at some sort of gun lodged in the chest cavity.

"Superzombie," Duane said. "Shel, you could fight crime. That is so *awesome*." I shushed him with a finger.

Rhodes nodded. "Zeez are, az I zaid, hypozeticalz. But Sheldon, you are vazting avay. Vizout major reconztruction I cannot do much more zan vat I haff already done."

"And what would be the purpose?" I asked. "I'm not saying no. But we've already kept me. Running for this long. Why should we go longer?"

"I von't lie to you," Rhodes said. "You couldn't be an actor anymore, not looking like ziz. I am zinking, maybe military? If ziz vold vorked, you vould be more machine zan man. Ve could uze you in combat." His accent got thicker as he became more animated at the thought. "Ve could get government contractz, jah? Build you into zee ultimate mobile veapon. Zink of zee money, Sheldon. Zink of zee glory."

"Captain America," Duane whispered.

"Captain Canuck," I corrected.

"Take on the Taliban, one on one. You'd be Robocop, Shel."

"Come on!" I said, angry. "This is beyond stupid. I am not going to wander into a war zone. And become a tool of the military. I'd be blown up in a day. I'd rather just rot away in a corner."

"No, don't you get it?" Duane said. "They'd keep you safe, they can't touch you, you're a celebrity. These wars aren't popular, even I know that. They'll do whatever they can do for some good press. I mean, fuck those phony action stars, visiting a few soldiers for photo ops. You'll really go in there, in the shit. Holy god, you could be a hero. Think of the people you could save."

I almost let myself think about it. I had killed a number of people, could this work as absolution? I shook my head, sure I could feel my vertebrae loosen. "Absolutely not. This is idiotic. We can't work with the government. I start down this road? I completely lose all rights. I am not willing to become a. Fucking machine in a stupid war. Just to keep up morale." Duane looked crushed, almost betrayed. "Duane, I know you mean well. But this is not an option."

Rowan popped her head back in, still cradling the cell phone next to her ear. "Doc, I need you outside. Now."

He patted my knee as he stood up. "Vell, you zink about it, jah? I von't make you do anyzing you don't vant, but ziz iz alvayz an option." He made to the door, then paused and turned back. "Unt time iz running out. Right now, if ve do nozzing, I giff you four monz. Zen, you fall apart completely."

As the door shut behind Rhodes, Duane made as if to speak. "Don't," I said. "Don't say a thing."

"I don't want you to die," Duane said.

"Die more, you mean."

"Don't make jokes." He picked up Sofa and squeezed her to his chest. "I want you to stay. I don't care if you're a zombie or a robot or a cyborg or a head in a jar."

"I don't get a say? Aren't I entitled to the right to die? Again?"

"Aren't I entitled to ask you to stay? If there's a choice?"

"As a head in a jar? You'd be happy with that?" I tried a joke. "This is the weirdest conversation I've ever had." The wit fell flat to the thin carpet beneath our feet. "Duane, I don't want you worry. I'll leave you everything. You'll be fine."

"Gosh, thanks, *Dad*," he hissed. "That's not what I'm worried about. Can't you see beyond yourself for a second?"

"Sorry to make my death all about me." Duane began to cry. "Duane, stop. Your makeup." I stood up and went to him, started to dab at his wet cheeks with a napkin. "You'll have raccoon eyes if you're not careful."

"Oh fuck you." But he smiled over his sniffling, which was something.

We both sat on the bench. "Duane, I am no good. At being noble. But I think this is for the best." Duane's mouth opened to protest. I held up a hand. "Duane, I've never told you this. I was never going to. But I will now. Because you need to understand what I am. What I've done. You've stuck by me. You deserve the truth."

And for the second time, I told someone the complete story of my death.

I scarfed down the remainder of my shmeat plate while Duane mutely used the silence to think. He mulled over my killings while I refilled my mug from the fridge with the contents of another blood bag, squeezing out every drop. Duane reflected over the fate of my mother while I shut the washroom door behind me and evacuated my rotting bowels, taking care to light every one of the candles I had placed about the tiny space to spare others as much as possible the stench of flaming excremental Hell pits.

When I finished, turning on the exhaust fan and lighting a handful of matches to wage aromatic war against my sundry indigestibles, I returned to the table, Duane still deep in contemplation.

"I'm sorry I didn't tell you sooner," I said. His hands lay flat on the tabletop, but I made no move to touch them.

"Why didn't you trust me with this?"

I shrugged helplessly. "Rowan told me not to, at first. Then, it was . . . I don't know, you looked up to me. I let it lie, and now? This is the longest. Relationship. I've ever had. We couldn't ever do anything. But you stuck around. Why?"

"Because I love you, don't I." We let that hang above the table between us.

"And maybe I love you too. But how do you tell someone you love. That you've killed a dozen people?"

"I knew you were a zombie."

"You knew, but you didn't. It's my fault; I let you. Believe I had it under control. We let ourselves believe this was normal. But I'm a walking contagion. You're not in a relationship with a man. You're in a relationship with a disease."

"My choice, though."

"No, *my* choice." I took hold of his shoulders and looked him in the eyes. "I am not ending things now. You are the best thing in my death. We still have some time together. Let's make the best of it."

He sniffed, wiped at his nose with his costume handkerchief. "Can I . . . be there?" I frowned. "When it's time?"

"Duane."

"I just don't think this is something you should go though alone. I mean, again."

I shook my head and smiled. "You. You astonish me. If it can be arranged. I'd be honored."

I took to the platform in the center square, running my lines over in my head while extras in period dress were corralled into the area beneath me. The scene was my entrance into the film, and while it would be a passing-by POV from Johnny's carriage, it was important my character's absolute command over his constituents be apparent from the start. It would help explain the ease with which I raised riotous mobs to chase Johnny around the town late in the second act. My gratuitous power over the townsfolk was to be immediately identifiable.

There was a sheer Plexiglas sheet six feet in front of me, invisible to the camera under the right lighting. One extra took it upon himself to be brave and rap on its surface, waving up at me when he caught my eye. Look at the monkey. He pulled a small digital camera from his pocket and held it up to his eye. Before he could snap a picture, Iris was beside him, his neck cocooned within the musculature of her inner elbow. She had passed through the throng like a shark through chum and taken the would-be photographer down in a crushing chokehold, forcing him to the ground and dragging him off set for a summary beatdown/firing. They were all warned ahead of time, do not approach the glass, do not taunt the monster, so I didn't feel too bad.

Shaken, the rest of the extras looked up at me now, more afraid for their jobs than of me. I gave them a conciliatory smile and wink. All part of the show.

Funny. They didn't relax at my good humor.

"Extras," Samantha mused, walking up and taking her place at my side. "There's one in every crowd. Once, in *Minority Report*, an extra ran up in the middle of a scene, pushed Tommy out of the way, and proposed marriage to me."

"Aw, did it happen again?" asked Duane, taking his mark next to her. I nodded. The three of us looked over the crowd. Past them, I could see Iris dislocating the man's shoulder as she threw him against a trailer wall and patted him down. She crushed his camera underfoot, and did the same to his toes when he complained.

"Well, at least he'll have. A story to tell his friends." Iris launched a virtuoso haymaker up beneath his chin. Samantha and Duane winced involuntarily. "Once his jaw resets, that is."

Samantha giggled, primping at her hairpiece. "We haven't really had a chance to talk, Sheldon. Johnny and I are meeting up later, just for drinks, you and Duane want in? No lines, no acting, just staying sane, right?"

I mulled it over, thinking about the freezer of meat I had in the trailer. It should be safe, if I glutted myself first. I looked over at Duane. He smiled. "If you're sure you're all right with it."

"Oh, psh." She waved a hand in affected nonchalance. "I've watched you, and you don't strike me as a danger. I once met Queen Elizabeth, now *that* was frightening." She trembled at the memory. "Couldn't remember which foot to curtsey with, almost fell on her."

"Well, you should have. No problem with me, then." She smiled and punched me lightly on the arm. Duane breathed in an obscenity. *Brie and tomatoes*, I thought. That's what she would taste like. I gave Duane a low-key wave of my fingers, *I'm fine*.

"All in place then?" Tim yelled out. I pulled myself up to my full height, straightening my collar while Samantha fluffed her hands over her dress and Duane ran a hand lightly over his slicked-back coiffure. To my far left, past Tim's crew, I could see Johnny climbing aboard a horse-drawn carriage, joining a small film crew that would get his reaction shots. As the script had it, Doctor Thompson was to drive slowly through the square, sticking his head out the window and watching as I orated to the massed citizenry, my faithful progeny at my side. Samantha and Johnny would exchange innocent glances while I ranted about the evils that would beset our humble burg should Satan get his talons into us. The people would hang on my every word, attentive and obedient, little realizing that in Act Three I was to be unmasked as a cult leader of the undead, who raised the bodies of the recently deceased back to semi-life through black voodoo magic. The role called for a serious amount of wicked chortling on my part, and I intended to throw myself into it whole ham. If the doc was right, if this was to be my swan song, I was going to go out in a blaze of acting that would stand the test of time.

Tim pointed to our trio, arching his eyebrows, *you ready?*

We nodded.

"And . . . action!"

The driver snapped at the reins and the horses moved calmly forward. I could see Johnny preparing to poke his head out.

I took in a breath and began to sermonize.

"Good citizens, we are at a crossroads." I let my voice play with the tones, putting in a deep tremor that caused every face before me to whiten. Beside me, Samantha gasped, putting a hand up to her chest in shock. Duane, better prepped for it, fought a grin even as his intestines twisted. "Today, another head of cattle was found. Dead in this square, its head removed, its innards. Draped over this very podium." I played the pauses, feeling the crowd follow me, waiting for my next words. Feeding off their attention. The carriage pulled slowly around them. Johnny stared at me, transfixed. "My friends, I fear the dark one is in our midst. In this community. Lurking. He is afraid, you see. He is afraid of *us*, of what we represent. Goodness. Purity." I gazed heavenward. "God-fearing. And because of this, we must be vigilant in our watch. Both over our neighbors and ourselves. We must amputate this corruption from our township as we. Would lop off a gangrenous limb. Painful, yes. But necessary."

The carriage was halfway across its arcing path. Johnny had now opened the door and leaned himself out, standing straight, noble, and proud in his character's bemusement of the scene before him.

Past the carriage, out of camera range, a wardrobe mistress collapsed in a heap, tossing an armful of shirts into the air as her hands jerked up and backward. Two techies watched her fall, took steps toward her, and folded quickly into the dirt, one, two.

It was so goddamned quick.

There was a *sput* sound, the noise of a moist spitball hitting a wall, followed by a crystalline tinkle.

The aroma of copper hit my nostrils. My teeth began to ache.

Samantha inhaled a quick gasp. Sudden scarlet freckling dotted the bare ivory of her forearm. A small hole had appeared in the Plexiglas, cracks webbing outward from the center.

A blossom grew in the middle of Samantha's white blouse. She wavered, mouth agape. Her breath whistled thinly as she began to teeter, her hands clawing at Duane's shoulder for support.

"What?" Duane asked. I looked at her, then him. He gave me a grin as he propped her up, a weirded-out smile, not understanding what had occurred, are you kidding me, what's the joke here? A small dot of red jigged over his face. "You okay, Sam? Tim, can we get a cut here, Sam has—"

A commotion from behind the extras, Iris charging, shoving people to the earth, reaching for her holster.

Another spit, tinkle, thump. A small moist rose bloomed prettily in the center of Duane's forehead. He shuddered casually at the intrusion. The dais beyond his head was abruptly painted with gore.

His left eye swiveled loosely in its socket. The right remained fixed on me. His lips still bore a smile of uncertainty. "I don—" he said, and the top half of skull exploded forward, drenching me in the substance of his soul, bullets shearing through the bones of his face and erasing his consciousness from the margins of life.

Iris was closer, just behind the screen, making to dive at me through the suddenly pierced divider. Her body jerked mid-stride as another hushed hail of bullets impacted her side, sliding through her thorax and embedding themselves in nearby extras. Iris collided with the Plexiglas, splitting her temple, spattering the retreating crowd with gore. She spat up a lump of blackish sludge and lay still.

I dropped to my knees and scrabbled at Duane's still-twitching remains, ignoring Samantha's dying whines, shutting out the screams of people caught unaware that a war had spontaneously erupted around us. The screen peppered red as more slugs found their marks, thrusting their merry ways through bone and brain and sinew. From my vantage point on the floor, trying to scoop Duane back into his head, I spied several jackbooted men stride to the middle of the set and begin pumping shotgun shells into the chests and faces of anyone moving.

My hands were gore-soaked, bits of Duane's brain sticking to the tips of my fingers. His blood smeared my face. My tongue twitched, stomach heaved.

I surrendered, and became lost in the red.

Without a thought I dove my face into Duane's neck and feasted, his heart beating its last, blood flow slowed to a trickle that languidly escaped his arteries and filled my mouth. All was fireworks. Galvanized, I rolled over and sunk my teeth into Samantha's shoulder, my teeth scraping against her clavicle. She moaned, a single lonely note, and breathed her last.

There was a scream behind me, more shots. Turning, more fully aware than I had been in months, I watched Tim's upper torso part from its lower as a pair of men dressed in black fired full clips into the camera crew. Tim somehow still stood despite holding his own intestines in his hands. He held them up, looking at me before he bisected completely, both halves thumping to the ground, his eyes wide with wonder, asking me, *How do you deal with this every day?*

I left the remains of my only friend on the ground and stood up. A brutally strong pair of arms wrapped themselves around my neck from behind. "I've got him!" their owner shouted, directly behind my ear. I reached up over my shoulder and clawed at him, pulling off the plastic guard that covered his face and sinking my fingers into his eye sockets, gripping his suddenly shrieking skull like a bowling ball. I swiveled around in his loosened grip and chewed into his face, the rush of life energizing me, pulling us both to the ground as I ripped his jaw free from its anchors and shoved my left hand up through the soft palate of the roof of his mouth and tore away at whatever I could grasp. The jawbone had snagged on my frills and danced from my arm as I dug into the man's wits, the world's grisliest charm bracelet. Another pair of gloved hands grabbed at me, two, three, pulling at me, not before my fingers immersed themselves in brain matter and wrenched the entire wad out of the open maw. The man's head flopped back, evacuated, and I bit and snarled into the damp sponge even while the hands lifted me from the floor and threw me back off the platform.

I climbed to my feet, my body ferocious, savoring the rush of hot bright blood as I gnawed at the brain stem. Teams of soldiers were making their way through the carnage, adding to it, slaying anyone still expecting that there might be a way out of this. This was a special effect gone wrong, this wasn't the movie they signed up for. A sharp whinny pierced through the shrieks as two soldiers laid waste to the carriage horses and then went to work on the riders. I saw Johnny scrambling upward, clawing to reach the top of the carriage before one of the men stepped forward and planted a bayonet blade in his backside, using gravity to increase the damage as Johnny curved his back and fell away, the blade slicing him up and through from hip to shoulder, his wetness pouring forth, his lifeline over before he hit the ground.

I turned away, facing a group of attackers as I finished my snack. Six men, all clad in black, rifles and machine guns aimed at me, laser lights glinting off smoke and red mist. One stepped closer and lifted his arm, displaying a strange boxy handtool. I rushed toward him, knocking the instrument away with my left arm, my right fist raised. I recalled a long-forgotten piece of boxing knowledge from years of movie watching; *don't hit the target, hit six inches behind it.* My hand shot forward, pushing from the shoulder, fingers curled and tight, and I thrust my fist into the surprised face, shattering the visor and going in deeper, exploding the nose, into the sinus cavity and beyond, his face caving in around my wrist as I pushed through to the other side, his helmet hanging loosely at the end of my arm, the whole of his head now enveloping my forearm, his body twitching as I raised my arm higher to show my attackers what they were dealing with.

The five men stood there, arms slack, weapons pointed to the ground. "Jesus," one whispered.

I inhaled, the carnage now a physical part of the atmosphere, tickling my lungs, and began to bellow, a sound to raise the dead from their slumber, to summon death gods and Valkyries and the hell hounds Cerberus and Garm and Syama from their depths and to my side, to start a battle that would make Ragnarök appear a slap-fight between first-graders — when I was cut off mid-screech, ending my primal rage with an embarrassing *ubpf!*

The taser was state-of-the-art; Iris' was a peashooter in comparison. My limbs clenched and seized inward upon themselves as the wires embedded themselves in my chest and voltage coursed through me. My body buckled and fell, curling into a fetal comma. My lungs were deflated balloons, refusing my commands. A large rubber ball was knowledgably inserted into my mouth, keeping my jaw forced open to its maximum size, and a belt wrapped around my head to keep it in place. A leather satchel was fitted snugly over my skull, but not before I caught a glimpse of one of my assaulters talking to Doctor Rhodes. My arms were handcuffed behind me and linked to thick chains that surrounded my legs and feet. Finally, as my muscles started to uncramp themselves, I was rolled up in what felt like vinyl sheeting, and then the whole of me was slid into what felt like a body bag and zipped up tight. I tried to scream over the ballgag but could only manage a loud hum.

I was lifted, carried, and thrown into a container. Men climbed in after me, jostling me with their steel toes as they took their seats and the truck started up.

Somewhere in the dark, I could hear Sofa howling in anger.

Depression

Blackness.

Again with the blackness.

But not eternity blackness, not this time; just good old-fashioned North American boredom blackness from having a sack tied around your head and then being left alone and ignored for hours. My hands were cuffed to the arms of my chair, my ankles chained to the floor. Never had I been so happy to have lost the ability to itch.

Although itching would have alleviated the tedium.

After a lengthy wait — I kept myself focused by replaying the reel of the last day's events over and over; the last exhalations of Samantha, the shrieks of the faceless extras, the sight of Johnny's innermost contents, the sloppy chunks of Duane's personality exiting through the back of his head and caroming off the background props, my involuntary salivation at the sight — there was the familiar sound of a lock clicking open, and a door opened a mile or so behind me. Then, footsteps, faint, gradually getting louder, honing in on my location. And a heavy buzzing, something mechanical, speeding closer. I remained slumped in my seat until the footsteps arrived and stopped, presumably to give me the once-over.

"Can he hear me?" The voice gouged into the quiet. The words were guttural, falling to the ground like beetles shaken from a log and scuttling away. It was a voice of advanced years, but there was an undercurrent of stress beyond the normal ravages age inflicted on the voicebox. A vigorous voice, but riddled with torture.

"I'm not sure, sir. He hasn't moved in hours." This speaker a woman, slightly unsure of herself, nervous but eager to impress the other voice's owner. Cowardice fringed her consonants.

Had I hackles to raise, they would have risen. I knew that voice. I would kill the owner of that voice. Puzzle pieces began to slide into place.

"He's so quiet, he doesn't even breathe."

"You didn't kill him, did you?"

"Well, um, he *is* a zombie, sir." A nervous laugh from the woman, forced out, flattened by the weight of tension floating about us. "I really don't think that's possible."

"You don't think," said the aged voice. "That's absolutely one hundred percent correct. You don't think. So let me do the thinking or you'll find yourself out and searching the gutters for loose change."

"Yes, sir. My apologies." So cowed. I grinned under my hood, enjoying her obsequiousness. I had always wondered what that would sound like.

"So, is he all right?" the older voice asked again.

"I thi— . . . I believe so, sir."

"So wake him up then."

"Me, sir?"

"This is your show, isn't it? Aren't you the expert here?"

"Well technically, *he* is."

"Ja, dat's correct, zir, I zuppoze I am zee true egzpert in zeeze matterz."

It figured.

"You suppose. Lord save us all. Do me a favor, son; grow a sack, fill it with something approaching balls, and let's get this over with."

A foot cautiously nudged my leg, then again, harder. "Sheldon?"

I chose to snub the query.

Another push, longer. "Sheldon? Time to get up."

I ignored him.

"Nothing, zir."

"Nothing." The woman's voice was soaked in contempt. "Fat load you are. Take his hood off."

Rhodes coughed nervously. "Ach. I . . . vell, I'm not . . ."

"Oh, for Christ's sake! Just rip it off him!"

A pause, then fingers at my neck, hastily fumbling at the knots. I gave it a few seconds, judged the distance in my mind, and snapped my jaws forward through the cloth, sinking my teeth deep into his fingermeat. He screamed, but it was a yelp of panic, not pain, and it soon stopped, even while I continued to crush his knuckles tight between my teeth.

"Are you all right?" the man asked.

"He iz biting me, zir! Sheldon, let go!"

"Hm. A zombie playing dead. Very clever."

I bit down deeper, grinding, straining to taste blood. My teeth severed the canvas threads of the hood and my tongue snaked out and tasted his skin. A metal mesh was my reward, pressing back against my tastebuds. Disgusted, I spat the steel out and struggled against my bindings, growling and thrashing and generally making an ass of myself. Getting nowhere, I relaxed and patiently waited while the bag was slipped off my head. All was still hazy; my contacts had not been moistened in ages and had dried directly to my lenses. I blinked wildly until they both popped out into my lap. Not much better; the light now flashed against the pockmarks on my corneas. Beyond the scratches I could discern three blurred figures, one tall and close, the other two at the edges of the light, lurking in the dim. "Could I have my goggles, please?" I croaked to the nearer blur with the bag in its hand.

"You have his goggles, Doctor?" the female blur asked the tallest haze.

"No, zey vere broken in zee attack . . ."

"Oh, damn it to . . . here, just put these on him."

A pair of sunglasses were slipped over my eyes, bringing my surroundings into slightly better focus. "Thank you, Doctor," I said as the fog solidified into forms.

"You're velcome." All pretense of the doctor's former composure was absent. His eyes were manic, darting everywhere, refusing to focus. A flop of hair hung loosely over his forehead, damp with fear.

"You're to thank for all this?"

"I . . ."

"Save it. Not interested. You're fucking dead if I. Ever get loose. I need you to know that." I yelled past him into the great wide dark. "You are all. Fucking! Dead!"

217

Rhodes wiped at his eyes. "I am zorry, Sheldon, truly I am. Zey made me do ziz." Random words tap-danced on his tongue, trying vainly to find a rhythm, a syntax. He clapped a hand over his mouth as if to stem the tide of nonsense. "Zey know zings, you zee. Zings I haff done." He whispered the last, and then, inaudible to everyone, just a silent plea for me alone, his lips moved. *Forgive me.* He dropped to his knees and placed his head on my foot, barking out a sob.

"That's not my job, Doc. You dug your own grave on this one."

"This is all very touching," the sour voice of the elder remarked. "Igör, get up now, you're embarrassing us both." Rhodes slid down further, pressing his face into the floor, still clasping my foot, beginning a mangled Anglo-Czech version of the Lord's prayer, bawling throughout. "Christ. Simon, would you?" A fourth figure moved into the light, a looming musk-ox of a man, leviathan, neck as wide as my chest, arms the consistency of oak, hair buzzed to a flattop of exacting specifications. So level you could calibrate instruments by it. He hoisted Rhodes to his feet with the nonchalance of a man picking up a napkin.

I took in the room. "Rowan," I said into the darkness.

"In the flesh," Rowan said. She stepped forward into the light, calm and in control. She had put aside her fear of the old man and was back into her persona of slicked composure. "Surprised?"

"Not really. You *are* an agent." The old voice laughed at that. Rowan blushed and played with her gloves. Shiny gloves.

"Chain mail?" I asked.

"Very good," said the older man, still blurred beyond the border of the light. "We felt that some precautions were in order given your . . . unique qualities. Hence the gloves. Simon, do show him." The giant released his hold on Rhodes (who fell prostrate to the floor, still blubbering) and put his hand up to my eyes. His gargantuan fingers twinkled daintily as he wiggled them, lit in the overhead beam, the only illumination in the room. "Divers wear such gloves in case of shark attack," the man continued. "They can withstand enormous pressure. We felt they would do the trick in your case."

"Handy."

"Make no mistake, however; despite the protocols we have initiated, we *will* gag you if you don't behave. The choice is yours."

I squinted, but the man remained an anonymous shape in the shadows. "Look, could I ask you to. Move closer? I'm getting tired of the whole. Evil supervillain vibe."

"Of course. Where are my manners?" He moved his right hand slightly. A whirring noise started up and the man trundled into sight, nudging Rowan to the side ("Move it, woman, goddammit," he said as she spat a complaint), the gears of his motorized wheelchair whining as they spun. He expertly guided the chair up close, centering himself directly in front of me, our knees almost touching. "How's that, Mr. Funk? Better?"

I took in the whole of him and winced. Having been kidnapped and now treated with the forced over-geniality of a James Bondian evildoer, I felt civility wasn't necessary. "Worse. Coming from the living dead. I hope that means something."

If his feelings were hurt, he didn't show it.

The man's entire head was a mass of aged tissue. *Burn victim*, I thought at first, but that wasn't quite right. I would have smelled the char. The skin looked as fragile as crêpe paper. What I was seeing was advanced age of a sort not seen since Methuselah up and croaked after nine centuries of lingering around the desert. The figure I could make out beneath the immaculate suit was emaciated. His skeleton was hunched from several lifetimes of weakening bone structure. His neck looked to be sliding into his chest, the top of his balding head only inches above the apex of his hunch. His pants draped loosely over the scrawniness of his legs, the creases fitting smartly over his thighbones. He was barely more than a collection of bones with delusions of flesh.

But who was I to judge?

The wheelchair was a mobile life-support system, cocooning him in an electronic cradle. He was contained within a score of medical devices silently keeping track of heart rate and blood flow. Intravenous tubing snaked down his thigh and calf and back up underneath the fabric of his pants. Settled snug within the contraption, the man looked like a wizened fetus, something that should not be, something aborted that refused to perish.

His voice, however, was improbably strong, and his eyes were hard and alert. "I am well aware of the monstrousness of my visage, Mr. Funk. You would not be near the first to recoil in disgust."

"I could be the last, you give me a chance," I said.

A smack on the back of my head, hard. "You do not talk to Mr. Dixon that way, Sheldon," Rowan hissed in my ear. She grabbed my head and held it steady. "This man deserves your respect, and you will give it to him." I waited for the standard *or else*, but none was forthcoming, only a squeezing of my skull presumably meant to imply a promise of pain. I wasn't worried; she hadn't nearly the upper body strength necessary for such a threat to be taken seriously.

"There is no call for that," the man snapped. "This man is our *guest*, here at our bequest, and you will treat him as such."

Her hands relaxed. "But sir, he's—"

He shushed her with a wave of his hand. "This is a stressful time, and I think calmer heads must prevail. Miss O'Shea, why don't you wait outside for me? I won't be a moment."

"But—"

"Simon will see you out. Simon, please? Take that Nazi crybaby with you. And bring back the package?" Simon scooped the doc off the floor, flopped the still-weeping heap over his shoulder, and escorted my agent out, one massive hand covering the whole of her elbow and quite a bit of her upper arm. Her protests quickly receded as they left, their footsteps echoing though the dim.

"And turn the goddamned lights on!" the old wheeled man yelled out after them. "I'm tired of squinting!"

The man and I sat quietly as Rowan continued insisting Simon let go of her arm, she was an agent to the stars, she'd have his goddamned *head* for a *keepsake*, until at last there was the *click* of a lock, hinges squealing under the weight of a heavy door, and then a thick metallic *slam* that cut short her objections. Then switches clicked, fluorescent bulbs flickered into consciousness, and the room lit up. We were dead center in a chamber the size of several football fields, the ceiling an easy hundred feet above. Surrounding us was a sundry of military automotives in varied states of disrepair: jeeps without engines, tanks lacking treads and cannons, something that looked to be a deflated hovercraft; even a helicopter, its rotors gone missing but a menacing set of machine guns still attached and aimed directly at the two of us. Heavy footsteps reverberated off the metal as Simon thudded his way back.

"Much thanks, Simon," Wheels croaked when Simon arrived.

"Don't mention it, sir." Simon held a large object in one hand, a plastic pet carrier. Sofa's enormous marble eyes stared out at me accusingly.

Somehow, this is your fault.

"You see, Sheldon? We're not so bad. We brought you your little pet." The man pushed the carrier forward with his chair. "Consider it a gesture of good faith. A sign that, despite all evidence to the contrary, I am not wholly without consideration for your feelings."

"Gosh, thanks. You've thought of everything."

Dixon waved Simon forward, and the giant coaxed the fifteen pounds of feline from her cage and plopped her into my lap. I stroked her ears with my fingertips, all I could do with my arms bound. "Hey, babe," I whispered. "They treating you okay?" She shrugged her entire back in a stretch, and then jumped down to explore the new territory, leading Simon on a chase among the abandoned wrecks. He nabbed her before she could squirm her way into some loose jet fuselage and plopped her back in her cage over her immensely unhappy objections.

"Can I let you in on a secret, Sheldon?" The geriatric leaned forward and theatrically cupped the edge of his mouth with his hand. "Between you, me, and Simon here, I can't stand that Rowan cunt. To me, she's nothing more than a slack-jawed hausfrau who just won't shut the fuck up. But she does have her uses." He spread his arms out toward me. "She brought me *you*, you see. Once word got out, I reached out through channels to make sure she'd follow my specific instructions concerning your movements. She kept you in line, never letting you off your leash. And I always reward success. She'll be quite happy, don't you worry about it."

"That's a load off my mind," I said.

"The secret to success, young man. Reward the achievers! As for the others—" He threw his thumb over his shoulder, sticking out his tongue and blowing a wet raspberry to accentuate the move, spackling my face with spittle. "*Pbbbf!* Trash heap. Life's too short for failure. Far too short. Most people cannot appreciate how little time we get. But then, look who I'm talking to!" He cackled until he began to choke, whereupon Simon slapped his back several times with well-practiced virtuosity. A sizable planetoid of phlegm was expelled from the man's mouth and arced over my left shoulder. Comets of sputum broke off and collided with my cheek, the main mass splattering against hollow metal outside my view.

"Ah, thank you, Simon," Wheels said when he had recovered. Simon expertly mopped up the spittle on the man's chin with a handkerchief, not bothering to award me the same courtesy. "I don't have much opportunity to laugh these days, so when it happens, I have a tendency to overindulge."

He leaned back in his chair and took me in, taking a few puffs from an air mask adjacent to his seat. We wordlessly stared at each other.

"If this is a staring contest," I said at last, "I'm going to win."

"I imagine, Sheldon, that you have some questions."

"Just one." I took a breath in, deep, and held it for a time, letting it collect strength in the rotting remnants of my lungs. Clenching my muscles, I threw the sound forward, up and out my mouth, as ripe and threatening and gruesome a scream of rage as I had ever attempted. I'd figure out a way of escape later, but at that moment I craved death. I imagined the walls out in the dark bulging and warping under the force. I wanted the man's eyes to liquefy and ooze down his cheeks, I wanted Simon's bowels to detonate as his spinal fluid boiled and leaked from his nostrils. For a full minute I stormed in my bindings, closing my eyes as I strained my arms to break their chains, pushing at the floor with my toes. I bellowed one final time, a demand for release that would lay waste to a city block, would kill civilizations, would crack the barrier between time and space, and then stopped, opening my eyes, preparing for the bloodbath.

I couldn't help but notice that the two of them were still conscious, observing me with clinical detachment, Simon stoic, even bored by my tirade. The man smiled at me, the smile never approaching his eyes. They were the eyes of someone long past true emotion. They were my eyes, glazed with death.

As the shriek echoed and died in the chamber, he turned his head and gave me a clear view of his ear. "Extraordinary things, these," he said. I glimpsed a glimmer of chrome lodged deep in his earwell. "We did study you beforehand. In addition to the armor, some of my more clever employees were smart enough to craft these little darlings. Noise dampeners, tuned specifically to block out certain decibels and frequencies. Marvelous. I take it, Sheldon, you haven't taken the time to consider just what, exactly, your voice does to people, and why?"

"Does a bird ask why it sings?"

"No, of course you haven't. Introspection is for the intelligent. You are many things, Sheldon, but *intelligent* is not a word I'd use. We do have some theories. Some of my advisors actually believe your croak might just be the voice of God himself. Or maybe the devil. Audio analysis shows that your lovely voice can actually be separated into seven individual voices overlapping each other. I've heard them.

I've heard and seen many things over a lifetime and a half, but I can honestly say, I've rarely been more scared than listening to the separate elements of your septuplet of voices." The man allowed a shiver to cross his spine, shaking his entire body in the process. "Damned spooky, in a way none of us can explain.

"But laying aside possible supernatural underpinnings, your voice has practical applications. Military applications. We're working on replicating it. A device for soldiers, worn about the throat. I don't pretend to understand the mechanics — it modulates their voices into alternate registers or some such nonsense. I admit the results thus far are not promising. We have the sound, but there's an ingredient missing from the recipe. We desire to cripple our enemies with shock and awe, as you do, but the most we've been able to achieve in our test subjects is a tolerable headache."

"Vulcan neck pinch," I said. "Can't be taught to humans."

"*Star Trek*, sir," said Simon in response to the man's furrowed brow. "The television show?"

"I am aware of *Star Trek*, Simon," said the gent with patient irritation. "I am old, not ignorant. Never cared for such tripe myself. A waste of valuable brain matter, fantasy. For me, hard work and the Bible is all that's necessary to get me through life."

"Yeah, the Bible," I said. "No fantasy in there. Nothing but facts and figures."

In a swift movement that belied his condition, the gentleman withdrew a small revolver from beneath the folds of his jacket and shot me twice in the left leg, the shin, the bullets sliding clean into the bone and out the other side, thrusting mingled shards of tibia and fibula out through the skin and onto the floor behind me. Bioformaldehyde oozed out and pooled beneath my feet, and a token charley horse radiated from the wounds. I looked down at the damage, then back to the infirm geezer calmly aiming the smoking weapon at my other leg. "Something I said?"

"I am your friend, but I will not be spoken to with such insolence," he said, voice crusted in anger. "It offends me. Now, play nice, Sheldon, or I will have Simon here poke your eyes out." Simon whipped out a butterfly knife and expertly danced it around his fingers before placing it underneath my sunglasses and laying its tip directly against the lens of my right eye. "I trust my point is understood. I do need you, Sheldon. Just not every part of you."

"Give me a reason, freak." Simon's threat rustled in my ear. "I need the practice."

I kept my head still. "Nice moves with the knife, Simon. You learn that in the seminary?"

"Nuns, man," he said, my vision distorting further as the blade depressed my cornea. "They will fuck you up."

"Eye for an eye, got it," I said. "You're reading the Bible. I get it. That turn the other cheek part. Probably comes later. Near the back. You should take notes." The blade skimmed the edges of my view, threatening imminent puncture. "Fine, call off your goon. I'll behave."

The knife withdrew. Simon sheathed the blade out of sight and stepped back, returning to taciturn mode.

"Why the hostility, Sheldon?" Wheels asked. "Surely you knew something like this was bound to happen eventually."

"You killed everyone," I said flatly. "You just came in. And slaughtered them."

"Unhappily, that was necessary."

"You killed the entire crew. The actors. The technicians. You killed Johnny Depp!"

"Hm?"

Simon leaned in. "*Pirates of the Caribbean*, sir."

"Oh. Well, that's a shame, I rather enjoyed that one."

"You killed Duane," I said.

"That would be Duane Linwood, sir," Simon said. "Caught in the raid."

"Hmm. Duane, Duane. Doesn't ring a bell, but . . . oh yes. Your *bum boy*." His lips narrowed into a slit of contempt. "With all your many faults, you had to be faggy as well." He looked up to Simon, grinning. His skin stretched tighter. I could see the muscles beneath, working his jaw. "You remember, Simon, how they all crowed to me, 'He's the messiah!'" He chortled again, laughing around the coughs. "Oh my boy, if only you had played your cards right." He drove his chair closer until we were side-by-side and placed a palsied hand on my knee. "You could be running this world right now. Every religion, Sheldon. The churches, the synagogues, the mosques — the Vatican itself would have fallen to your every whim. You could have changed the face of the planet. I said to them, 'This looks like the Second Coming to you? A fag atheist Canadian actor?' They let me alone after that. They would have twisted their beliefs to accommodate a Canadian, they would have found a way to justify worshipping an atheist. You could have been a *woman*, and they'd have reread their texts to allow for it. They would have swallowed you whole and asked for gravy. But a queer? A cockgobbler?" He patted my knee. "Not one of them could imagine pledging fealty to a son of God who enjoyed getting fisted. Imagine how the next Testament would read."

He wheeled back and repositioned himself in front of me. "But still, my apologies for the death of your friend. I had hoped that this could have been done without bloodshed. But it is a sad fact that, in war, innocents must be sacrificed to ensure triumph."

"We're at war?"

"I am. Of a sort. Ask away, ask your questions, Sheldon, I'm sure you're dying to know." He laughed weakly at his joke.

"Where am I?" I asked.

"Right. The beginning then. You, Sheldon, currently reside in the great state of Utah. More precisely, five hundred feet below it. I was born and raised hereabouts, and as such I have learned a great deal about the history of the area. This room you are in is part of an old government bunker complex, built beneath the Uinta Mountains in the fifties in the event of nuclear attack by the communists. Not many even remember its existence anymore. I pulled a few strings to purchase the whole structure from the military for a song. You'd be surprised how often a few dollars trumps national security, especially in a recession. You see, people have always lacked the ability to perceive the world on a long-term basis. Short-term results are the only thing people care about anymore. Not me, though." He pointed two fingers at his eyes, and then swung the fingers out, aiming them at the blackness beyond. "I am not interested in the short term. Most cannot grasp anything beyond the next twenty minutes, but me? I see through time. It comes with age. I see where this society is headed. And I do not like it. People need to be led, like cattle if need be, with spikes through their nostrils and chains linking them all together. Long-term plans, my boy. For me, it's all about the next twenty centuries, not the next twenty minutes."

"And who exactly are you?" I asked.

"Oh my heavens, I am sorry. I was so excited to meet you, I plum forgot about proper introductions." He pulled himself upright, fighting against gravity and age. Several noticeable pops emanated from his chest and back as he did so. He gasped, wincing. Simon calmly twisted a small dial on the side of one of his monitors. The man waited a few moments until the pain subsided. "My name . . . is Lambertus Dixon."

I frowned. "That means nothing to me."

He coughed out another laugh. "Well, that's a relief. I'd be mortified if it did. Sheldon, if I may be so humble as to boast, I am the *they* in *that's what they say*. I am behind near every political, social, and economic decision made in the civilized world. There is not one facet of this entire planet that I do not have a hand in — agriculture, chemistry, nuclear power, bio-warfare, daycare centers, shopping malls, newspapers, furniture repair, space travel, coffee shops, publishers, education, oil, entertainment, telecommunications."

"Quite a list. I still don't get it."

"Once, so long ago it barely registers as memory, I started a company, a modest little investment firm that I run to this day. And over the years, I have managed the not insignificant feat of becoming, with all due modesty, the wealthiest person on the planet."

"Why have I never heard of you?"

"A valid question. Perhaps you do have some wit about you after all. I have learned many things over my time, but the most valuable advice I've ever received was given to me by my father when I was barely out of short pants. He imparted to me this wisdom, the only intelligent thing he ever said. 'It's not the man in power, it's the man behind him.' My father was nowhere near astute enough to succeed on his own advice, but I was. What he never realized is, you cannot start at the top. That's why he died penniless. I built myself up, slowly at first, moving my firm to New York, working on a municipal level, keeping my eye always focused on the next move. I read the news. I became known as someone who could predict certain events. It only required some basic knowledge of human character, but I was soon consulted on larger and larger issues. I became respected for my opinions. I offered advice, for free at first, then for money, and then for favors. My business grew, but my fame did not. I made it a mission to keep my name beneath the public radar, a figure existing only in rumor. I never advertised my services. Those who needed me found me, and that was enough. And soon, I was more powerful than anyone could ever have anticipated. I wasn't lurking in the shadows of great men, I was the shadow itself. Had we time, Sheldon, we could go through the history books together. I assure you there is not one significant event in the twentieth century that I did not have a hand in."

I did a few math problems in my head. "Exactly how old are you?"

He preened in his chair. "I will turn one hundred and forty-seven years old next March."

"Bullshit."

"Look at me, Sheldon." He swirled his index finger in the air. "Look at all this technology I am beholden to. I have not left this chair under my own power in many years. Considering your own refusal of death, is it so hard to believe a man of my means might find alternative methods of cheating the Reaper? In a way, you and I are kin, brothers in our plight. You found one way to dig yourself out of the grave, I've found another."

"So why all this? Why didn't you just take me? Why did you let all this happen?"

"In due time. I do have a few things to show you, things that will help you keep all this in perspective. Believe it or not, I have always had your best interests at heart. In fact, I am your benefactor."

I pulled at my restraints. "I'm not feeling. Your beneficence at the moment."

"Well, your mere existence should be proof of that. Did you really think that someone in your state would actually be allowed out in public at all? How is it, do you think, that you've been allowed to roam relatively free all this time? My God, boy, you are death incarnate. You hold within you the power to utterly destroy all humankind with a single bite. Christ, are you *that* stupid you'd believe a few lawyers would be all it took to dissuade the CDC from declaring war on your person? No government in its right mind, not even the U.S. government, would simply stand by and let a monster so dangerous simply walk around, let alone become an object of fame.

"There is not one single reasonable explanation why you haven't been dissected and studied mercilessly.

"Except for me."

A look of well-earned smugness creased his face. "It has cost me a pretty penny to keep you free, Sheldon. Almost not worth it. I called in every favor, I crossed the palms of every person of resource with silver enough to buy their nonintervention. You have cost me billions. And I am not a man who parts with money gladly. There are whole swaths of this country now functioning with total autonomy from my

227

influence. I am not used to letting things go, but that's what I have given up to finally get you here."

"Why would you do this? Why not have just. Taken me months ago?"

He made a face of indifference. "Call it curiosity. I wanted to see just how people would accept you. Would accept an undead being into the population. I see now that the world can be duped far more easily than even I previously believed. I wasn't honestly sure it could be done, but Miss O'Shea assured me of her capabilities to make you a sensation. She and I, we decided to take you public. And when it appeared to work, through the judicious use of complementary stories in the media, we made you a star."

"Should I be flattered?"

"Most would. Most would get down on their knees and beg for the protection I've afforded you. Until this moment, you have legitimately been the most protected individual on the entire planet." He pushed up at the armrests, tottering atop the footrests. Every vein in his skull began to throb as what remained of his heart battled to increase its flow. Simon propped him up with one massive hand. Dixon's voice weakened as he roiled, began to whistle. His ancient lungs strained. "I protected you for months. I, *I* let you continue to exist, no one else. *I* swept every murder you committed off the front pages — you didn't think I knew that, did you, you murderous cannibal! You owe me everything! You owe me reverence, you son of a bitch! You owe me some awe!" The shout discharged from his throat another globule of black jelly, a wad of his dilapidated insides rattling loose and sent soaring into open space to plop onto my restrained hand. He wavered, and his eyes rolled up white. Simon eased him tenderly down into his cocoon. I waited (I had a choice?) while Simon attended to a gobbet of dribble sliding down Dixon' chin, dabbing with a handkerchief at the polished gleam of Dixon's translucence until it gleamed wetly in the light.

"And now, I have you here before me," Dixon said when he regained consciousness. "Trussed up like a Christmas goose."

"I was hoping you'd. Get to that."

"First things first. I need personal verification. You understand, I'm sure, that there is always going to be that slightest of belief that this has all been a big joke on somebody. You don't get to my age without earning a few hundred enemies. Rowan swears you're the real deal, oh hell, every doctor confirms it, but I just can't help myself. And I pride myself on always personally checking the authenticity of my acquisitions. Simon, if you would do the honors . . . ?" Dixon motioned to my shirt. Simon reached out and ripped the fabric of my costume open, sending buttons soaring out into the darkness and plinking against the concrete floor. My torso, so lovingly tended, was exposed to the air. Dixon drove his chair forward so that we sat astride one another and ran an excited gloved hand over Rhode's network of stitches and zippers.

"My, but that is impressive," Dixon said, fingering one of the tabs.

"Thank you."

"A shame to desecrate such a marvelous creation. That man of yours, Rhodes?" He tapped a finger against the side of his head; I imagined I heard the hollow echo of an overripe melon. "He did some repair work on me as well, once upon a time, but I have to say, I think I only got his B game. Just couldn't get the ears right, they never stopped drooping. No denying it, the Nazi is a maestro when he wants to be. But alas . . . Simon?"

Simon leaned in and grabbed at the edging of one of my flaps. I started to say, *Hey, there's a zipper, you can just slide it open*, but Simon was determined to make sure I knew the parameters of my new position. I was an object, an appliance, a conversation starter functioning solely for their amusement and, if they so wished, disposal.

Simon pulled at the tissue until it started to tear, getting one finger underneath, then two, then all ten. Putting a foot against the chair between my legs for leverage, he jerked and wrenched my skin-flaps away from their moorings, peeling me like a flesh banana. Rather than stop at that, Simon keep pulling, the teeth of the zippers clacking free. Giving one more mighty tug, Simon ripped free the entirety of my trunk and offhandedly threw the whole floppy muck behind him. I sat there, more exposed than any being in existence. The visible man.

Dixon gasped as the irregular placement of my innards popped forth like toy snakes in a prank can of peanuts, leaving behind a hollow torso lined with spongy polyurethane spray-foam insulation. My intestines slithered across the floor as they disentangled themselves and lapped up against the front wheels of Dixon's chair. He nervously twitched at his controls, and the chair jerked forward, rolling over my entrails and spinning its wheels in my ooze, the membrane bursting under the weight. He backed away and a spoke snagged a loose strand of tissue, pulling my guts forward and rapidly spooling them around the axel.

"Jesus Christmas," Dixon sputtered, banging at his joystick, reversing the chair's direction but tangling further into the mess. I smiled as the two of them worked at the controls, Simon's feet sliding in my offal. He lost his balance, grabbing instinctively at the ropes of my insides for support and pulling the muck of me out completely. There was a muted sensation of being tugged at from within the inner wall of my hips — peculiarly satisfying, like picking at a scab or working a tooth loose from its moorings — and then the fleshy tube plucked itself free from its connective tissues and the anus end of my colon flopped out and scooted toward the duo, each fluttering in panic as the wheel spun faster and my entrails enmeshed themselves in the mechanics of the chair. My colon was squeezed like a tube of toothpaste until it burst, splashing liquid gore and undigested soldier brain over Dixon's carefully tailored suit.

Simon got down on his knees into the guck and began hammering at the electric motor underneath the seat with his fists and then the butt of his gun, cursing a blue streak until a panel dislodged. He shoved his hand inside and pulled out every wire he could feel. The engine whined in annoyance and the wheels seized, flinging Dixon backward onto the floor as the chair flipped over by the force of the jolt. He landed full-on in my gore, writhing, yelling for Simon to *do something, goddammit*. The engine kicked back to life and the wheels spun, furling my guts into the axel, cranking through my large intestines and making quick work of the small until what was left of my digestive system stretched tautly across the empty space between us. I felt another steady tug, this one up under my uvula, and my stomach shoved my lungs aside and popped out into the air for a look, a water balloon held aloft by strings, jerking at my esophagus and threatening to pull whatever remained of me out the bottom of my throat. The wheelchair gave another mighty pull, tipped over, and started reeling itself in, making its way relentlessly toward me.

I closed my eyes, not wanting to witness the unusual sight of an electric wheelchair work its way through my body and out the top of my head. My throat pulled tighter as it stretched, then closed altogether.

With a gooey *snap!* the pressure loosened. I opened my eyes to the sight of Simon standing unsteadily before me, almost close enough to taste. In his right hand he held his knife; the other held the last few feet that remained of my intestines, the duodenum if I wasn't mistaken. The wheelchair, freed of its tether, grumbled about in the soup for a few moments. There was an impressive roar and its engine exploded in a shower of sparks and slivers. The chair shivered its death, then went inert.

"Goddamn bitch chair!" Dixon had righted himself on his elbows, his body bathed in discharge, and was pointing his gun at the machine, the muzzle fuming. "Always hated that thing. Never worked right. Never buy American." Hissing another curse, he fired two more bullets into the device and then motioned for Simon to help him up. Simon released my entrails, and my stomach flopped back into place as my alimentary canal relaxed, the open end of my leftover intestines limp between my knees.

Simon righted the chair and spent a few moments tearing intestinal tissue from its wheels. Simon gave the seat a wipe-down with the arm of his jacket and lifted Dixon from the floor. He seated him and vainly tried to neaten his appearance, blotting away the gore with his shirt cuffs. Dixon waved him away.

"Well, I think that definitely proves your claim," he said. A lump of me clung to his earlobe and shuddered like a glob of loose jelly as he spoke. Simon flicked the matter away as Dixon continued. "My goodness boy, but aren't you all kinds of surprises. What do they say, takes a licking and keeps on ticking? What was that?"

"Timex, sir," Simon said. He had removed his coat and was sponging himself off with the lining.

"That's the one. Remarkable. I apologize, Sheldon, but I simply had to see for myself, you understand."

"No worries here."

"And you aren't in any pain? None of this actually hurt you?"

"Only when I laugh."

"And it still has a sense of humor." Lambertus tapped Simon on the leg. "You could take a lesson from this one, Simon. Above all else, a sense of humor keeps you sane."

"If you say so, sir."

I took a look. Aside from my lungs and the few scant remains of my digestive system, I was entirely hollow. The force of the uncoiling had dislodged most of the contents of my lower abdominal cavity. Mustard curtains of pericardial fat shrouded the opening. The grayish remains of my liver lay at the base of my chair, lobes ruptured, leisurely leaking into the morass of innermost Sheldon in which my chair was now an island. A desiccated snot-green sac, my gall bladder, clung tenaciously to its roost, unaware that its purpose, always nebulous to me, was at an end. Loose threads of tributaries and veins dotted the interior wall, secreting fluid that dribbled down and pooled around my still-intact bladder. My pancreas and one kidney were lumpy stones at the bottom of a pelvic well, playing in the mud. I couldn't find my appendix, scanning the floor sludge for any sign, absurdly sad that I had held onto the useless organ for so long only to lose it like this, an innocent bystander, victim of the goriest Three Stooges sketch ever made.

". . . wondering about our purpose here?" Dixon was still yammering on, daintily dabbing away the spewage on his face and neck with a handkerchief.

"Hm?"

"I said, we should get to the meat of the matter, so to speak."

"Ha."

"Sheldon, you, to put it simply, you will be the vanguard of a whole new evolution in humanity."

I took that in, and then turned my good ear in his direction. "Come again?"

"You are death made flesh, Sheldon. An emissary from beyond, possible proof of God's dominion over life *and* death. Billions of people have waited the whole of their lives for just this possibility. You are the resurrection."

"I thought we were off the messiah kick."

"You must let me finish. You are the resurrection, yes, but not in the way most would have it.

"You are not for them. You are for *me*. You are *my* resurrection. I have sought my whole life for someone like you. I kept myself alive all these years, searching, directing the course of human events, all to have a chance for this exact moment to occur.

"You are the Second Coming, a triumph over death. You're a miracle. You are *my* miracle. I'm going to see what the hell is making you tick. I've got some of the most deranged medical thinkers of the century outside this room just drooling to get their probes into you."

He clapped his hands together excitedly. "Enough preamble! This isn't going to be easy, and I dare say it will not be pleasant for you, so sooner started, sooner completed. It's already been a very long day for me, so I'm going to leave Simon and you alone for a while. Simon was

CIA up until a short while ago. An ace interrogator at Gitmo, weren't you, my boy?" Simon allowed a miasma of pride to cross his face. "They actually let him go, if you can believe it, for being *too efficient*. That's code for ruthlessness, by the way."

"I gathered."

"More terrorists cracked under him than any three other agents combined."

"I hold the record," Simon added, "for the quickest successful interrogation. Seventeen seconds. Three fingernails, one pinky, and an ear."

"Ouch," I said. "How many actual plots did you uncover?" Simon's face blackened, and his knife returned for an encore dance.

"If you're going to waterboard me," I said, "I can hold my breath. For a very long time."

Dixon watched the blade pirouette around Simon's fingers, then placed a calming hand on the man-monster's arm. The knife retreated up his sleeve. "Simon's a little touchy."

"Hey, who can blame him?"

"But don't worry. He's only got a few questions, just baseline stuff. Nothing hard. He'll handle you with kid gloves. We just want background for now. Tomorrow, the fun starts. Samples, probings, vivisection — the works."

"I can't wait."

"And then, when we're all done with that, the *real* work starts. You are about to become a father, Sheldon. *My* father. You have a gift, Sheldon, which you are going to share with me.

"And when we are done, when you are scattered about our laboratory like so much litter, I shall be released from the confines of this miserable body, and take my rightful, well-earned place as the first true immortal."

"Oh Christ," I said.

"Truer words never spoken, my boy."

The beast and I spent a few hours together while he gathered data on the past few years of my pre-resurrection habits. Where had I traveled? What had I eaten? Who had I copulated with? Had I bitten or been bitten by them before or after said copulation? Etcetera.

Simon dragged a car seat from the back of a rusted-out jeep to make himself more comfortable during the interview. No concern for my comfort was shown; I was left exposed and leaking, my residual duodenum dotting the floor with what was left of my innards. Which was not much.

The questions were all public record stuff, innocuous, available in previous issues of *Scientific American* or online to anyone who cared to search *zombie Sheldon background*. True to Lambertus' word, Simon did his best to lay nary a finger on me. His engorged digits, hard as railway spikes, each capable of piercing a man's skull with one quick flick of the wrist, were kept busy manhandling a pad and pen. The instruments were farcically tiny in his mitts; he idly snapped more than a few pens as he jotted down my answers. By the time we were through, his writing hand was inked indigo. I thought to ask *isn't there a tape recorder you could use* but opted not to, determined to take what simple pleasure I could.

Simon was disillusioned; after a career's worth of finessing intel from unwilling suspects through subtle interrogation techniques interspersed with lengthy bouts of open torture, it must have been demoralizing to grill someone who was — as my entrails testified — obviously torture-resistant. Every now and then he would halt his scribbling and look me over with wonder, reflexively searching for pressure points to prod, joints to snap, wounds to desecrate, skin to puncture. He itched to inflict damage, but the worst he could do to me was to swipe my sunglasses and crush them into slag between his paws. I couldn't even summon the will to be irritated.

He couldn't keep me awake and disoriented. I was immune to pain. Duane and Mom both being dead, he didn't even have the leverage of loved ones to threaten with violence. He tried to threaten Sofa, poking his pen half-heartedly at her, shaking the carrier, getting a few yowls of protest, but Simon was a latent cat lover; abusing felines was that one line he couldn't bring himself to cross. Blushing fiercely and cursing at himself, he put the carrier down and whispered an apology.

"You old softy," I said.

That was all it took for him to snap. He thrust the nib of his pen up and under my right eye and flicked it forward, popping my eyeball out and leaving it to dangle at the end of its tether. From that point forward my left eye watched his every move; my right took in the terrain of my chin, chest, and lap. It was disorienting, my view now a broken stereoscope, but I wouldn't give him the satisfaction of complaint.

I *was* hungry, though. I'd become used to always having a calming wad of bogus phlesh nearby. *How long could I last?* I thought. I'd never actually tested myself. Would I eventually become like Mom, mindless, all shuffling appetite? Was she like me at first, conscious after death, confused as hell? Without access to what her body craved, did her mind devour itself?

Simon snapped his fingers under my nose, shocking me out of my reverie. My loose orb jiggled and swayed, spinning my world. I hadn't even noticed that he'd placed his bare fingers mere millimeters from my teeth. I snapped at the air, ashamed I couldn't control the impulse even as my teeth gnashed, but Simon's bulk contradicted his speed and he was sitting back smugly before my bite had finished its routine. He smirked, finally seeing leverage; the oaf was not nearly as dense mentally as he was physically.

After that, Simon would occasionally curb questioning to take stock of my reserves of willpower. He rolled up his sleeves to reveal mouth-watering forearms, the skin taut around the sinew. He walked around the room, waving his bare arms over my shoulders, brushing the back of my neck, so fucking close. He removed his shirt and did a quick ten-spot of pushups, forcing blood to the surface, veins erupting into blue mountain ranges, casting alpine shadows over the pink plains of his chest.

His mockery served no purpose; I answered all questions asked. He was just wasting time before I was collected, processed, and sieved into oblivion. Simon was making this personal.

I endured the boredom by poring over him as I would a butcher's wares on a visit to the grocery, the fresh cuts kept clean under the sneeze guard, pondering which haunch of meat would be most tender. Simon worked out, so his biceps were nice and lean beneath the skin. He had let himself go slightly to seed; this lassitude encased his musculature in thickening sleeves of succulent fat. I pictured the meat of his hindquarters, fresh on a clean white plate, the pink steak fresh and bloody and ribboned with white, and began to drool.

My stomach growled moistly in the open air, bouncing limply against the back wall of my hollow. Simon noted that, his mouth a curved knife-edge of malice. He put a glove back on and grabbed my mouth, holding it shut while he caressed the underside of my nose with the bare fingers of his other hand. Blood-heat soaked through my skin and massaged my brain. My jaw labored to open, fighting my orders, determined to bite. Simon moved his free hand down, and I felt an intestinal squeeze as he slid his hand up under my ribs and between my lungs, grasping my stomach. He brought it out and held it up to my stable eye, compressing it in his palm.

"Could you do without this?" he asked, sincerely curious. "Is a stomach even necessary? How long could you go without it?" He gave it a quick jerk and my trachea began to rend. "*I* don't think you need it. *I* think we'd all be better off if this were in a jar somewhere."

I tested the strength of my bindings at that, raising my right arm, letting the teeth of the cuffs bite down into my wrist as I steadily pulled up and reached at him. The metal chain began to complain at the tension.

I was rewarded with a sudden glaze of fear over his face. He let my stomach thump back hollowly against my lungs.

"You have no idea what's in store for you, freak," he promised, releasing my mouth. "What they're planning for you, you'll look back fondly on these moments."

"Should I be scared?"

"Most definitely."

"Terrified?"

"Oh yes."

"Well, you tell me. When the scary part comes. I wouldn't want to miss it."

Zing!

Such wit was a short-lived triumph. Simon filched a roll of duct tape from somewhere and bound my upper limbs good and tight to the armrests. He did my legs, too, for good measure, and then, since the audio portion of the interrogation was well and truly over, my mouth. He wasted a few more hours teasing, childish really, but it seemed to make him happy. It also tired him out, and he finally left to get some sleep. He lifted Sofa's carrier — his stare dared me to comment — and left the arena. He turned off the lights on his way out, leaving me bound and gagged in the dark.

When the lights clicked back on, I had spent a good forty-eight hours alone, working out various scenarios for revenge through the judicious application of my teeth. I would leap at Lambertus Dixon and segment his head from his shoulders with one fell swoop of my hand

and devour his brains by sucking up through the neck. I would take Simon down with a quick slice at the ligaments behind his knee and then gut him as he had me, slurping down his intestines like thick spaghetti while he watched. I would run amok through the complex and unleash the appetite of the devil on anyone foolish enough to try to take me on.

I would do all of this without somehow gaining release from my bindings.

Foolproof.

Between fantasies, I passed the time by playing ball-and-cup with my eye, jerking my head back to try and slip the peeper back into its orifice. Without the ball as cushioning, however, I could not command the lids to open, and the eye bounced off them like a child on a trampoline.

I could hear electric wheels trundling closer. I sat patiently — because I had no choice — and waited for Dixon's arrival.

"And how are you this morning?" he asked as circled to face me. The old man was outfitted in a new suit/wheelchair ensemble and looked rather fresh and alert for a man approaching his sesquicentennial. Behind him, Simon loomed, arms and chest clad in chainmail, alongside two soldiers at attention with semi-automatic handguns at the ready, sub-machine guns slung over their shoulders, and intensely painful-looking tasers at their waists.

"As you can see, I have recovered nicely from our escapades," Dixon continued as he put his chair into park, "and I . . . my goodness, what has happened to your eye?"

I tried to *mmm* a note of explanation for my loose orb beneath my mouth tape. Dixon waved me quiet. "Simon, this is your doing?"

Simon stepped forward. "He got a little lippy with me, sir. Couldn't be helped."

Dixon clucked his tongue in admonishment. "I did warn you, Sheldon, Simon does have a temper. But I do have something to show you today, so Simon?" Simon frowned. "Please pop it back in."

Simon winced. "Couldn't I just cut it off, sir? He'll still see with just one."

"Simon," Dixon said after a beat, "I have very little time to waste, particularly on explaining my orders. Be so kind as to relocate Mr. Funk's eye back into its socket. Now."

Simon sighed and approached me, motioning for the guards

to follow. Ordering them to hold my head steady and keep my jaw clamped tight — even with my mouth taped shut, I didn't blame Simon for not taking chances — he shucked his right glove off and delicately fondled my eye and stalk, looking for the best way to thread a thick noodle through a hole crunchy with gore. I closed my stable eye to combat the vertigo as my vision cavorted and his fingers slid over my lens. At his command, the soldiers craned my head back until I was theoretically looking at the ceiling. Removing his other glove for better flexibility, he carefully poked my optic nerve back into my skull with the index finger of his left hand while he guided the eyeball in with the right, then slid his inky finger around to make sure the eyelid enveloped the sphere securely. I blinked a few times and rolled the eye up and down. The muscles still worked, but were torn and weary after getting fingerbanged. My vision was slightly doubled, but I could make do.

Having the soldiers release me, Simon took a corner of the tape and slowly ripped the gag free. A biggish chunk of lip went with it. One of the soldiers muffled a gag and thickly swallowed back his breakfast.

"All better?" Dixon asked.

"Much," I managed. "Could I get another pair of sunglasses?" Simon grumbled, but slipped a new pair on me at Dixon's approval. I pulled at my restraints. "Any chance of letting me free as well? If I don't move about a bit. The muscles atrophy. I promise not to crawl away."

Dixon shook his head in mock apology. "I'm afraid this is as free as you get. We're at the end of a long path, and I want to make sure I get to the finish. Enjoy sitting up while you can; very shortly we'll have you strapped to a table, which should serve as base for the remainder of your death." He giggled and clapped his hands in anticipation. "Sheldon, we are so close now, can you feel it? Destiny has brought us together, at precisely the moment I need you most."

"I'm not yet clear on that," I admitted. "Why do you need me? I do get why. People want to study me. But why do you *need* me?"

Dixon began circling me as he talked, his version of pacing. "Sheldon, I have been searching for something as long as I can remember. A cure for death. I am not ashamed to admit it, what lies beyond has frightened me since I was a child. Can you imagine it; here I was, a little lad of six years old, already cognizant of my incipient greatness, and frustrated that no matter what I would ever do, death would take me in the end.

"Death should not be the great equalizer. I am meant to triumph, not perish. And so, from my first steps, I have been searching for a solution. Everything you see before you, this," he looked around at his electronic chassis, "all this, all these procedures, all the surgeries, the grafts, the implants. Stopgaps, performed to get me to just this moment. You think of that, Sheldon; everything I have done in this world over fourteen decades has been for this sole moment to occur. You lying there, me sitting here.

"These little chaps roaming your system, keeping you alive, if that's the correct term—"

"Close enough," I said.

"—*they* are what Ponce de Leon was seeking. The fountain of youth. I thought we just needed to figure out how to harvest them. If we can cure polio, surely this would be a breeze. Now, I told the others, this is plainly an earthly organism infecting our boy here. Mysterious, undiscovered up to now, yes, but surely still a *natural* occurrence. It may hold the appearance of a supernatural phenomenon, but that is only because we don't yet understand it. So let's do that. Understand the phenomenon, study it, and see if we can't filter out some of its" he waved his hands over my body as he glided by "less desirable qualities. But your bloodspawn in there, they don't want to give up their secrets. They don't correspond to any known tests. They don't correctly react to stimuli, they perish outside a human host, they're alternately too simple in structure to cause such a reaction in the human body and too complex to understand.

"Oh, it is only a matter of time, they assure me. The scientific method cannot be rushed, particularly when the stakes are so high. They just need better equipment, some high-powered electron microscopes, maybe a nuclear restabilizer or some such shit like that. We just need patience, and time.

"But patience is a game for the young. And I am out of time. The doctors tell me I have only weeks left. My pitiful little shell cannot withstand another transplant. The only reason I am alive is because of all these tubes flowing blood in and out.

"So we need to accelerate. At this point, I no longer care about how you are still here. I only care about results, and my doctors have assured me that their plan will work. Most likely."

He stopped wheeling about and parked next to my head. I had to crank my head as far as I could to the right to get him in view. "We're

239

going to have you bite me, Sheldon." He reached out and stroked my mouth. Damned gloves. His chain-linked finger probed between my lips, caressed my incisors and bicuspids. "Just once. Here, on my neck, at the external carotid artery, will allow for maximum infection in the least amount of time. It will hurt, they tell me, but not much. They have offered to numb the area, but I have refused. Like you, I don't have much sensation anymore, and if this is to be my last perception of true pain, I'd like to enjoy it." His finger stopped its examination. He withdrew it and patted my cheek, tenderly. "Think of me now as your last meal. Eat of my flesh."

I shook my head. "You're insane. It won't work. It can't."

"I assure it, it will."

"I assure *you*, it won't. You'll be like my mother. You'll be a monster, brainless, rotting. You'll be a corpse with delusions of life."

"Yes, your mother. About that." He leaned in, giving me a conspiratorial wink. "I rather liked her. For a ghoul, she had real spunk. It pained me to let her go; I thought we could use her to our advantage should you prove intransigent, but I understood." He patted my knee in sympathy. "We all need closure."

I didn't know how to take that. My face betrayed my confusion.

Dixon delighted in my befuddlement, waggling his bare eyebrows. "You didn't honestly think you were unique now, did you? Simon!" Dixon's beast-servant bounced forward to attention from where he was leaning against a deconstructed airplane. "Simon, prepare Sheldon for a trip, will you? It's time he visited the Chapel."

Simon's nose wrinkled up. "Should I get the masks as well, sir?"

"For yourself, if you feel it's necessary. I think I'll go in barefaced. I find myself wanting to experience everything as fully as I can." He looked at me. "Today, even the Chapel holds an allure." He took a deep breath through his nostrils and held it, smiling all the while.

I didn't know Lambertus Dixon long, but the time we spent together led to a belief that he was a man without a genuine sense of humor. The bleakest cynicism, yes, *that* he possessed, a fathomless pit of negativity locked in the coal-black recesses of what I, for lack of a better term, will call his soul. But as Simon whisked me into what Dixon labeled "the Chapel," I grew an appreciation of Dixon's wit.

"It's something, isn't it?" Dixon muttered. He appeared to be regretting his decision to enter *sans* mask. He stomach released a mighty *urp* that ballooned in his throat and forced everything it could up and out. Dixon no longer had the ability to consume solid food, but judging from the grimace, whatever was brought up didn't taste good.

Even *I* recoiled at the reek.

After Simon had sliced free the tape and released my arms, my revenge-fueled pipe dreams took root and I flexed my abdominal muscles to lunge forward and take down Simon for a quick nosh. With my body cupboard bare, it was all I could do to flop my upper half forward and let gravity carry me on. I succeeded only in shifting my weight enough to slide my mass ungracefully off the chair and plant my face onto the concrete. The rotten cartilage that kept my nose erect gave way and shoots of skeletal shrapnel plunged up into the great gray meat of my forebrain.

Simon laughed and let me flap about while the two soldiers pushed an un-ergonomic monstrosity of a chair out of the dark. Small wheels had been affixed to its legs for mobility. After unlocking my legs, the two gathered me off the floor and shoved me down into the seat, ignoring my wails and unperturbed as my teeth sought flaws in their body armor. They held me down while Simon unleashed his inner Bob Vila on my skeleton. My legs and waist were locked into place with steel cuffs. Simon kept me upright in the seat by fitting two metal clamps around my lower and upper spine and driving rivets directly through my skin and into the back of the chair. My torso trench was left open, my stomach drooping, the gaping end of my diminished intestines coiled in my lap. Satisfied, Simon took hold of the backrest and wheeled me out of the warehouse and down a lengthy hallway, the two soldiers taking point, Lambertus speeding his merry way along behind us.

We snaked our way through hallway after hallway, passing workers, soldiers, scientists, all halting their labors to take a gander at the galloping gay golem. After scraping our way through miles of corridors we arrived at a waiting freight elevator. Simon allowed Dixon to speed in ahead and then shoved me inside, mashing the top button with his massive index finger. The numbers descended down the ladder, from one to thirty-five, and we were all the way at the bottom.

It took fully five minutes for the lift to arrive at floor 1, during which we took turns not looking or speaking to one another.

The doors opened to a bustle of activity, people frittering about in what looked to be the emergency ward of a hospital. Gurneys lined the walls that stretched out before us, each makeshift bed holding a strapped-down inhabitant who plainly did not want to be there, each hooked through electrodes and tubes to the finest in computerized medical devices, each attended to by studious doctor types from central casting. *Boops*, *pings*, and *buzz*es filled the air, but from the patients themselves there emitted not a sound, their manic struggles against their bindings mute save for the clacking of teeth, muffled slightly by mouth gags.

Ghouls.

Twenty-five, maybe thirty. None smart enough to exercise their lungs. Each nothing but cannibalistic appetite clad in fetid flesh that sloughed off their bones.

"Confused yet?" Dixon spat in my good ear. "I can see it in your eyes, boy, even past all that damnable white. You're doing the math. You're asking yourself, how in blazes is this possible? Who are all these people?" I kept my face impassive, cursing his smug enjoyment of my bewilderment while figures churned in my head. Even if *all* my victims had somehow survived their mealtime encounters, it wouldn't account for even a quarter of what I was seeing.

"You are hardly an only child." Dixon clapped me on the arm, almost tenderly. "Your brothers and sisters, Sheldon. All of them. Siblings in death. I just thought you should know."

"This is the Chapel?" I ventured.

"Almost," Dixon replied, and guided his wheelchair between the beds, pointedly ignoring the kowtowing nods of doctors. Simon grunted and pulled me slowly along behind him, tugging me backward through the room, giving me ample opportunity to inspect the convalescents. Each was in a state of fleshly disrobing; epidermis peeled away in whole swatches, various limbs hacked off, crowns of skulls exposed, juicy segments of brain removed and placed jiggling in metal bowls. I saw Rhodes standing next to one bed, inserting thin rods of steel deep within the open cerebrum of his subject. He looked up as I rolled past, fear streaking over his face. He forced a weak, quivering smile and gave me an apologetic wave. I roared loudly and Rhodes explosively vomited over the head of his patient, who didn't seem to mind. The entire room was promptly saturated with sick. Quite a few medicos fainted, drooping over open orifices and slimy muscle. I giggled and guffawed as Simon pulled me quickly the rest of the way, hearing Lambertus curse his staff for forgetting to wear their mandatory hearing guards. As he heaved me into the hallway beyond, I saw those doctors smart enough to wear aural protection rushing to help the unconscious, pulling them away from piranhic jaws.

Dixon whispered an order to Simon. He re-entered the room, emerging moments later with the good doctor in tow, dabbing at the vomit that coated his chin. Complaining, Rhodes fished around in his pockets until he found his plugs and shoved them deep into his ears.

"We need you, Doctor," said Dixon. "I want you along for this part." We continued on, Rhodes bringing up the rear, well out of biting range. I bared my teeth at him anyway.

The next doorway led to an open hangar bay, vacant except for a few jeeps and cars, a small jet, and two technicians looking it over. They both saluted as Dixon trundled past. The hangar entrance was open; beyond, blurred even with the glasses, I glimpsed sunlight, azure skies, a mountain range of majestic heights. From down the paved road (a runway, I realized), a breeze wafted in and caressed my ravaged body, my few near-exhausted nerve endings perking up at the chill, and I allowed myself pleasure in the sensation, conceivably the last such I'd ever experience.

"Here we are!" Dixon announced, wheeling up to a nondescript set of double doors and thumping the automatic door opener with his fist.

"The Chapel!"

The aroma smacked into me, ruffling my few remaining hairs, and I knew what it was, but I couldn't comprehend the how of it. It was redolent of fast-food restaurant dumpsters, of happy maggots full to bursting, of overflowing diapers and cheese gone sickly-sweet. Simon and the others hastily fumbled for gasmasks hanging next to the doors, holding their breath until each had slipped one over his head and secured the rubber seal about his face. Behind us, I heard the plane techs gagging, complaining about the lack of warning. Dixon sped inside, sniffing, coughing with mirth. Simon rushed me in the few remaining feet, swearing at the exertion but plainly considering haste a virtue. He planted me next to a waist-high barrier, giving me an unobstructed view of my family tree.

Dixon belched as he leered, a gastrointestinal rebellion against the aroma of living dead, thick yellow drool escaping through the gaps in his grin, holding his own for several moments until he capitulated to the noxious miasma that filled his lungs and motioned for a gasmask. Simon speedily grabbed another and fit it snugly about Dixon's head, overwhelming his tiny skull, transforming him into a rubberized aardvark.

"Behold, Sheldon," Dixon's voice echoed through the exhalation valve. "Your heritage."

It was a living death pit. An animated charnel house.

We sat on a walkway suspended a few meters above a sunken rectangular storage chamber fully 200 feet long and half as wide. Access to the floor was only possible through open lifts controlled from the walkway. Down in the bay, beneath the squirming, I discerned workout equipment, weight bars, a leg press. Doubtless the room was once a recreation and exercise area for the many soldiers who would inhabit the structure should the end times approach.

The current dwellers had no such need for physical fitness.

I estimated five hundred, likely more, of every subset of humanity, a true melting pot, a multi-cultural glory of undead savagery. Males, females, whites, blacks, Arabs, Asians. All were clad in whatever garb they had died in; business suits mixed with turbans, yarmulkes and dashikis wandered beside boxer shorts and bikinis. Their flesh was black with putrescence, gray with mold. They shuffled and bumped into each other, turning around and performing the same action with another, and then back again, caught in an eternal loop.

Goldfish in a bowl, always forgetting where they'd been.

They trod over the bodies of fallen comrades, elder ghouls that had surrendered to rot and fallen to pieces. Beneath their feet I watched limbless torsos flop, brains still toiling, driven by perpetual starvation to seek sustenance. The ones nearest us diverted themselves from their routines, raising arms toward us and groaning, actually groaning. Some had figured out the rudimentary task of oxygen exchange, rewarded for their genius with the gift of song. They clambered at the wall beneath our feet, eyes scored pale, some altogether absent, with gaping hollows stringed with mucus, drawn to our voices, or Dixon's scent. The concrete walls were crusted with gore, inches thick. One of the guards fired a few rounds into the horde, chortling as bullets sliced through skulls. Simon cuffed him on the back of the head.

"We've been kept very busy," Dixon's voice echoed through his mask. "No lack of subjects for the good sawbones here. We keep the room ventilated, which helps reduce the fly population, but as you can plainly tell, it's impossible to dampen the smell."

"How . . ." I could not finish the thought. It was beyond comprehension.

"You vere hardly zee firzt zombie vee've found, Sheldon." Doctor Rhodes took a position beside me. "Vee haff been working on ziz for much longer zan you realize."

Dixon looked out over his undead preserve. "I have been scanning the whole of this planet for the better part of a century, looking for the key. I would hear tales, stories of friends thought dead walking through backyards. Buried fathers digging themselves free. Cancer-riddled children rising from deathbeds. All reported as myths, or foolish superstitions, or paranoid delusions, but I followed every lead. It was simply a question of having the money and the willpower to go beyond the story and find the truth. And I had so much money, and so much will.

"I traveled the length and breadth of this world a hundred times. I bribed officials in every country. I walked through swamps, I hiked up mountains, I slept in teepees and igloos. When I grew too old, I paid men to do it for me. It got so that I didn't even need the stories, I could simply *sense* when one of you was about. Something in the air, you could say.

"And in many cases — not all, but more than I ever anticipated — I found what I sought. And very soon, I had myself a menagerie."

He spread his arms out. "This is my life's work, Sheldon. Where some collect stamps, I collect zombies. We have studied every one you see here, and thousands more besides, trying to find the key. There is no single element in common with any of these resurrections, except that they exist. Some are survivors of attacks, but others just rise of their own accord. There is no religious factor common to them all, no physical commonalities, no environmental, no viral, fungal, bacteriological, ecological, geographical, socio-economical, or other. My scientists assure me that their existence is rooted in the physical, my roster of theologians insist only the supernatural explains them.

"I could have them destroyed, of course, but I find myself with little desire to. I come here to contemplate mortality. Seeing them gives me hope. They cheated death, so can I, but on my terms." He started pointing out individuals. "Why should Sally there, the one in the polka-dot dress, why should she, mother of four that she was, unhappily wasting her life away in an Alabama suburb, why should *she* receive this gift?" He swung his finger farther left, singling out a dark-skinned ghoul, the remains of a turban still clinging to its skull. "Why should a raghead Taliban be bestowed an eternity of existence and not me? Or next to him, that marine, why him? Why that African tribesman over there? That Eskimo? That Hassidic Jew, that Amish daughter, that Polish waitress?"

"I guess death isn't fair," I managed.

"Well put. But I mean to fix that." Dixon lifted his mask slightly and took a sniff. "Do you smell that, Sheldon? That's the smell of eternity."

"And my mother?" I asked.

"Oh, she was here. As soon as I discovered you through Miss O'Shea, I had a team extract her. I was truly excited to see her; we so rarely get one so fresh. It's a miracle she hadn't bitten anyone, even without her teeth, but then the care she was receiving was hardly first-rate. You couldn't have put her in a better establishment, the woman who birthed you? Shameful. Alas, she was like the others, useless, so we threw her in here until I got word that you wanted to see her. We dug her out, flew her to Phoenix, made up some nonsense that you bought wholeheartedly, and let you kill your own mother."

"Cold," Simon muttered behind you. "Stone cold killer, that's what you are."

"Fuck you," I shot back weakly.

My mother, part of that throng of appetite. I thought I had spared her some indignity.

"But for as long as I have been searching," Dixon continued, "I have never found one like you. The one who talks. There were always rumors. Men who walked and talked with full awareness after being crated up and buried six feet under. I believe most if not all of our religious ideologies evolved from such examples. Was Jesus a zombie? Was Odin, or Shiva, or Wawalag? I believe so. And so I knew, if it happened before, it can happen again. All I needed was to live long enough to find one of you and crack open your secret.

"I didn't think I'd make it. But then, there you were, walking around, drawing attention to yourself. *Working*. I have to tell you, I have cheated death many many times, but when I discovered that *you*, the Grim Reaper, you were actually hitting the pavement looking for *work*? I almost laughed myself to death." He chortled briefly and began to cough, pulling his mask up and horking a loogie into the horde where it splattered against the forehead of a desiccated Japanese businesszombie and crawled down into the folds of its expertly knotted tie.

"Death is not without a sense of irony," I said. I watched the ebb and flow of the crowd as the doctor gently thumped Dixon on the back to dislodge more sputum.

I could hear them, faintly, as I had Mom. I had no connection to any of them, but still a dim clamor tickled my thoughts, an imbecilic moaning that shook my brain in its container.

Across the zombie depository a door opened and a pair of soldiers strode in, each wielding a length of thick pipe. At the far end of each rod a set of thick pinchers extended forth, each clamped tight over the throat of an unhappy zombie held just outside of reach.

"Ah," said Dixon. "Good timing. Our newest acquisitions. Simon, move us closer."

The soldiers expertly maneuvered their captures onto a small platform that extended out from the track over the mob below. On a three count, they released the neck clamps and stepped back, where one attended to a set of controls attached to the railing. The platform began to slowly descend into the pit, its riders slowly turning to try and attack their handlers, already ten feet above them.

I couldn't quite make the arrivals out yet. But I could smell them. Simon moved me down the walkway to a better vantage point. The hazy picture came into focus. I clenched the armrests, imprinting my fingertips into the metal. The animated corpses of Duane and Samantha joined their siblings.

Samantha looked to be little worse for wear, with only a few bullet holes and a mouth-sized gash on her throat as visual proof of death. Duane's body was relatively untouched, but only the bottom two-thirds of his skull was intact; everything above his eyebrows had been jaggedly excised, including most of his brain. But the residue of matter he retained still flickered, and I could hear Duane's pleas for food join the mental sea of appetite.

"You bastards," I said, gritting my teeth. I felt my gums give at the pressure, surrendering finally to the rot, and two of my incisors bent outward.

"I though you'd be pleased!" Dixon said. "Look, there's your lover, in most of his glory. You can thank Simon for the surprise, he thought you might be more amenable if you saw a friendly face."

"Half of one, anyway," Simon said.

"Quite. If you like, Sheldon, I can arrange a conjugal visit."

I held my tongue, picturing myself snacking on Dixon's kidneys, as Duane and Sam mixed themselves into the mob, falling into the same mindless swaying.

There was an eddy in the shuffling current below me, distracting me from thoughts of revenge. I saw a white lab coat, its wearer fighting against the aimless flow of the mob. It raised its face to me and moaned, a plaintive keening I heard in my mind rather than my ears. I knew that face intimately.

You never forget your first, do you? Even now I can recall the taste of those few precious drops of coppery wine gamboling about on my taste buds as I made short work of his limbs.

Craig motioned toward me. His left arm was still contained in a filthy plaster cast, but his right was free; the bone had never completed setting, and the forearm now had an extra joint. The wrist and hand hung loosely at the end of the superfluous elbow, but his fingers still twitched wildly. Unlike his brothers and sisters who had, I could now discern, focused directly on the humans who surrounded me, the nearest source of food, Craig gawked at me alone. His teeth shuttered open and shut excitedly as our eyes met, catching his tongue and severing the bulk of it. He paid it no heed as it tumbled to the gruesome carpet. In my head, I could hear his tireless mantra.

You. You. You.

"Well, would you look at that," Dixon said excitedly through the carbon filters. "I think he recognizes you." He motioned down to Craig. "Doctor, what is that?"

"How—" I stopped myself, knowing the answer.

"How did we find him? As soon as he was on television talking about the attack I had a team put on him. We couldn't find you, you were too ridiculously minor a person to even exist, so we staked out his apartment. They waited for a few weeks to be sure. Depending on the bite, full infection can take anywhere from a few minutes to several months. Once they observed that he had turned over, they took him."

"I was there," I said. Dixon tilted his head, suddenly more attentive. "I was looking for him. I walked in, I saw everything. Your men must have just missed me." Behind me, Simon snorted a laugh.

"His child," I pressed on. "His wife. He killed them. Your men could have saved them."

A shrug of eyebrows underneath the mask, a sigh escaped the filter. "You understand, we had to be certain. There are limits to power, even mine, and I cannot afford to draw undue attention to this operation.

Every action I authorize must be a surgical strike to remove the infection, particularly in a highly urban environment. Until rebirth, the symptoms are almost identical to that of the flu. My men have strict orders not to undertake containment and capture until the birthing process is confirmed."

"They didn't have to die."

"You would have killed them anyway," he said, waving a hand dismissively. "Do not blame me for the actions of your firstborn." He turned his attention back to Craig, the zombie now audibly groaning his anguish at me as he struggled forward. "Your thoughts, Doctor?"

"I am unzertain," Rhodes spoke. He had walked forward on my other side at the commotion and was now leaning out slightly over the edge of the railing to get a better look. "I haff never zeen ziz zort of behafior before." Below us, Craig scrabbled against his partners in death, pushing them to the floor and standing atop their uncomplaining bodies to get a better look at me. As we watched, the ghoul to Craig's right, a long-dead refugee from the Jersey Shore, looked up at me as well. Then another, a man clad in a flannel shirt and hip waders. Then a small child, a boy scout. Then an elegantly dressed socialite. Then another. Then another. Soon there were dozens of zombies, all unmoving, staring at me, silently shrieking. It was purely impossible, but my temple began to throb.

Rhodes' eyes widened. "Zat iz fazinating! I zink ziz iz actual comprehension!"

Dixon lifted his mask for a clearer view. "Doctor, what does this mean?" he asked. "Why are they following him?"

"It muzt be zomezing in the viruz, a rezidual memory zomehow tranzferred whole." Rhodes frowned. "Zomehow, zere iz a telepathic connection between Sheldon unt zem." Forgetting himself, he grabbed my arm and pulled it against the chain, laughing as my acolytes followed it like bored spectators at a tennis match. He looked back over his shoulder to Dixon. "I zink zey may zee Sheldon az a fazzer, perhaps, jah? Or pozzibly a mezziah figure. Jah, ziz may haff major zeological ramificationz." He moved his hand up to my wrist and gaily waved it at the crush of ghouls, pulling me forward as he leaned out over the railing. "Zir, ziz behafior muzt be rezearched further. Zee implicationz are—"

My fingers grabbed his and pressed in, pulping his digits into mush. Beyond pain, he gasped at the mangling. Before Simon could react I pushed my weight against my shackles, wheeling the chair forward slightly, enough to knock Rhodes' balance off-center. His arms pin-wheeled and I rocked the chair again, the merest of extra nudges.

Rhodes slipped out into the air, swiveled his body in midair as an involuntary objection to gravity's rules, and was enveloped in claws and teeth before he hit the floor. His one scream was short-lived, as was the rest of him. Chunks of jellied red flew upward as my siblings macerated their lunch. I sensed thoughts of gratitude as they feasted on him; I fancied I could taste the metallic piquancy of Rhodes' flesh on my tongue.

The whole process took five seconds. Neither Simon nor Dixon had moved. I sat back in my chair. Craig ignored the meal, staring up at me.

"I'd like to go now," I said. For a change, Dixon had nothing to say, and together we silently contemplated the future.

The men in the white coats came soon after.

I'll say this for them; unlike with Simon, I was never bored.

A white room. Glaring spotlights. Stainless steel cabinets and instruments. Men in lab coats, faces hidden behind surgical masks, concealed mouths mumbling arcane medical lingo.

I was back where I started.

Full circle.

Morgue to morgue.

Ashes to ashes, dust to dust, sunrise, sunset.

Rebirth to redeath.

They can take away my organs, I thought, *but they can never take away my sense of irony.*

As they sliced their way into my skull, soft gray tendrils of smoke rising as the saw blade whirled through my braincase, spraying marrow over an inattentive attendant, I began to laugh.

"How are you, my boy?"

"All things considering?"

"Good, good. Like I always say, a sense of humor—"

"—keeps you sane. I remember."

Lambertus visited me in the vivisectorium every day, engaging me in conversation between scrutinizations of my depleting inner geography. I was a work in progress, splayed out and bound so that any medico could simply come in and examine whatever portion he desired at his whim. My torso was left open, its contents scooped out like a pumpkin on Hallowe'en. The lungs and remaining major digestive organs were left intact, but everything else was up for grabs. My head was propped up on a block of wood and a temporary plastic cap had been snugly fitted over the top to protect the now-exposed brain and still allow for ease of access.

Simon would be alongside Lambertus, scoping me out for new physical mortifications, taking notes. Sometimes anonymous others would join the duo, men and women in suits, men in holy vestments. They never spoke, but the presence of a slop bucket to catch their inevitable spewage spoke volumes on my appearance. Senator Kud passed through once to bless my condition with a sneer.

"How are you today?" Lambertus would always begin, to which I'd rejoinder with something pithy about being akin to a fetal pig awaiting a classroom of eager sixth graders armed with plastic scalpels. Frankly, I began to enjoy the company; our conversations were at least a brief respite from the usual medical pillaging.

They wouldn't even give me a magazine to read, or a television, or iPod. They at least allowed me Sofa for companionship, constructing an ad-hoc cat tree out of discarded engine parts. She watched my daily disembowelings safe and high from her roost, and came down occasionally to feast on whatever Simon had brought that day. The doctors and nurses spooked her, however, and she rarely came close enough to visit.

Beyond the cat, Lambertus was my only link to anything beyond the reinforced steel walls that contained me. So I had to take him at his word when he assured me that no one was looking for me.

My disappearance was news, of course, it was all anyone had talked about for weeks. You couldn't kill a few dozen people and hope no one would notice. No, my exit from the public stage had to be manufactured, edited to completely remove all doubt.

Simon laid a board roughly across my thorax and dropped an open laptop on it. Lambertus jabbered as I watched the footage, released to news organizations *only because* what occurred was so monstrous an event it deserved to be seen by the widest possible audience. The chaos was edited down to a thirty-second news nugget; the footage was hectic, blurred with action, but it was clear that the zombie once beloved by all had finally snapped. Despite the heroic actions of security guards kept on constant standby by the production company for just such an eventuality, Sheldon Funk had slain the entirety of his castmates in a frenzy of blood-spattering savagery. The camera never lies; there I was, blood reddening my teeth, lurching toward Duane as he fell to the ground, his head marinated in his own brains. In the background, Samantha screaming as she bled out. A brief cut to Tim, intestines slipping through his fingers. Johnny slit open like an envelope. A close-up of me pulling one guard's spinal column out through the front of his chest (I didn't recall doing that at all). And at the end, a head, mine, exploding in a burst of bone and brain as bullets were pumped into it, the body slumping against a wall, loose arteries decorating the air with red.

Had I been consulted, I would have told them that my blood didn't spurt. No heartbeat, no circulation.

Had I been consulted.

The sham-zombie *did* look like me, an impressive likeness. A homeless person plucked from the streets of New Orleans, Dixon confided; no family who cared enough to come searching, no friends to wonder *whatever happened to that guy?* Thought he had won the lottery, picked up by good Samaritans and assured that his troubles in this life were soon to end. Conspiracy theorists already claimed the erupting head was not mine, that a frame-by-frame analysis clearly indicated a person with a more pronounced jawline, and a different eye color besides.

"So, no smoke, no fire," Lambertus said as Simon packed up the computer. "As far as the world cares, you're in a box somewhere awaiting cremation. The point is, no one is looking for you save a few whackjobs with too much time on their hands."

"You can't keep this secret," I said. "Not this. Someone will talk eventually."

"Key word there, *eventually*." He swiveled his chair around and headed to the door. "Eventually, everything comes out," he shouted over his shoulder as he left. "But sooner than eventually, that's not going to matter."

I lay on the tabletop for weeks while scientists busied themselves with my genetic makeup. Any remaining liquids had been extracted, replaced with untainted blood (a surprising rush), studied, extracted, replaced, studied, extracted, replaced. If you've never withstood the sensation of having well nigh every cherished corpuscle of crimson fluid sucked from your body, I can't say I recommend it.

I once read that a giant squid injects its prey with an acidic solution, liquefying the innards until the victim is nothing but a sack of juice. The squid then drinks the body dry.

So, like that, repeated every few days.

Nasty stuff.

The arguments and hypotheses filled the room as they worked me over, figuring out what precisely they could and couldn't remove so that I remained "alive." It was a virus, plain as day, tests all but proved it. But how could a virus not only kill its host but also serve a secondary function as oxygen proxy, surely the only thing that explains my post-death mobility? It thereby couldn't be properly classified as a virus and must be categorized as a higher level of organism. But if it was a higher organism, it wouldn't transmit itself through the blood and saliva to others, would it? It multiplied as a virus, it infected others along virus parameters, therefore, a virus. Maybe it's a parasite, living off its host while somehow synthesizing oxygen supplies to keep the body mobile after clinical death. Is this even clinical death? The heart is inert, yes, but the brain? Could this be a new form of prions? Possibly, but the brain has actually been enhanced, not decimated. But . . .

But.

But but but but but but but.

But where did it come from? But why this guy? But couldn't it be . . . ? But haven't you considered . . . ? But isn't it impossible that . . . ?

At this point in the analytical reasoning circle jerk, someone of the more religious bent would invariably pipe up with a poorly received insight on how we could not predict nor understand the will of God, I was a miracle whose existence should not be questioned and these experiments were a waste of everyone's time.

Questions, no answers.

Vainly trying all avenues of diagnosis, they even showed me a vastly magnified picture of the wee beastie, I assume to somehow trigger my memory. *That's it, officer!* I yelled when the thing popped up on the screen, squirming happily about in its bath of me. *That's the one who stole my wallet! I'd know those beady little cilia anywhere!*

They didn't talk to me much after that, not beyond the occasional *This doesn't hurt? Really? Wow.*

All the while, my body was whittled away slice by slice. A thin wafer of upper arm here, a hunk of ass-flesh there. My thorax was deboned and my foamy new interior lining scooped out, deflating me on the table and spilling the rest of me out. My loose organs were gathered up, separated into jars and spirited away for necropsy. I bemoaned the thought of all my entrails suddenly apart, brothers no more.

My heart was pried loose from Rhodes' expert gluing, the entirety of the local scientific community gathered around for the operation. There was no reason; the heart was plainly there only for show and sentimental value, but just to witness a human body continue to function perfectly fine without it was an event. My stomach was left alone, and I was fed according to schedule to ensure my deterioration was slowed. The meat was definitely human; I presumed I was eating convicts, or illegal immigrants, but I never asked. The stomach would bounce in my chest chamber like a rock in a tumbler as it digested the mystery manmeat, and anything left would sluice through the short tubelet of intestines I had left and spatter into an awaiting plastic baggie. It was then spirited away for a fecal freak to study, and I'd await the next meal.

After a time, the novelty of me wore off, and I became another daily chore for everyone to complain about. Poke, prod, slice. Poke, prod, slice. Every day, going down the checklist. Still here? Check. Still sensate? Check. Still bored? Check. Poke, prod, slice.

I had become unwanted topiary.

My brain was swabbed, greased, fondled, mopped clean, and gently impaled with metal spikes. Subdural reactions to images of frolicking puppies and pastoral farmlands were interspersed with variations along the theme of *let's see what happens when we poke him here.* Once in a while, to alleviate their tedium, they would switch the flow, and I would feel a pulse deep within my cranium. My legs would then spasm, or my hand would twitch, or my eyes would blink, or the smell of burning hair would inundate my world. Every few days I was wheeled out into the next room — *Whoo! Change of scenery! New cabinets!* — where I was slid headfirst into an enormous (and antique, by the looks of the rust) CAT scan for a distressing few minutes while

X-rays pierced my skull and body, everyone cowering behind a large lead screen in an adjoining room.

And every day, aside from basic indignities no sentient body should ever suffer — I was often referred to as Mary Kay, if that gives you any indication of the level of discomfort I withstood — a little bit more of my brain was slivered away. Never much at one time, just a gossamer shaving off the top, an insubstantial sanding from the side. I couldn't see the results — unlike the front row seat I had to the rest of the procedures, they wouldn't supply a mirror so that I could watch my personality get julienned to bits, a subject watching its own brain vivisection apparently too disturbing to contemplate — but with every trim, I imagined the generous lumps of my cerebrum eroding away, eventually leaving me with a perfectly spherical lump of gray matter, a bowling ball of brain.

Then a softball.

A baseball.

Squash ball.

Olive.

Pimento.

One day, the probings stopped. The monitors and machines were unceremoniously unplugged and rolled away, tubes hurriedly ripped from their perches in my limbs, needles left dangling from my skin. Electrodes were rudely wrenched from the underpinnings of my parietal and occipital lobes, wires monitoring my speech center and body coordination nodes disconnected and left to scrape against my bones. A disinterested doctor — #5, I think, I had never bothered to learn the names of any of the anonymous, surgical mask-clad neurosurgeons who had defiled my anatomy without so much as a how-do-you-do — slapped some cellophane over my open brainpan and kept it snugly in place with a large rubber band that grooved itself into the wrinkles of my forehead. "Keep you fresh," he quipped as he gave whatever remained of my frontal lobe a quick caress to smooth out the air bubbles. "Nothing but leftovers up there now, you know." He chuckled, gave the wrap a friendly slap with his fingers that jiggled my memory bank.

"I'm going to miss carving you up, Mr. Funk. It has been a real pleasure."

He checked on Sofa's food and water and affectionately chucked her under the chin as she lounged on her carpet tree. *Traitor!* I thought.

"Good luck tomorrow," the doctor said as he reached for the door.

"What's tomorrow?" I asked, but he was already gone, turning out the lights behind him. The lock clicked in, and his footfalls diminished as he walked down the hall. I heard the *whoosh* of elevator doors opening and closing, an infinitesimal hum as the winch lifted him off to a world that no longer existed for me.

I lay on my slab, feeling like the family schnauzer left alone while my masters went off to a late-night movie. At least the dog could have leapt on the couch for a nap, or looked out a window, or nadgnawed for a few hours to pass the boredom. My bindings were still as solid as ever, and my body so atrophied I couldn't have fought off an aggrieved kitten with any chance of success. Sofa bounded over in the dark, bumping up my legs and torso as she deigned to visit me for a few precious moments. She paused at my fumbling fingers for a stroking, traversed the hollow to bequeath me a friendly lick on the chin, then returned to my useless legs for the day's umpteenth siesta.

I strained to hear something, anything. No snatches of murmured conversation from nearby rooms. No footsteps above reverberating through the concrete. Not so much as a creak of the walls settling. If it weren't for the inimitable feline vibrating on my thighs, I would have assumed my death had finally taken hold. But I was certain there wouldn't be purring in Hell.

Once again, in blackness.

Somewhere above me, the members of my blood sect silently stood at attention, swaying in a breeze only they could sense, awaiting . . . something. Seeing them as a herd, I thought I finally understood the virtue inherent in their mindlessness. I had feared them as a reflection of my worst self, but now I envied them their tenaciousness of purpose.

They would never question their instincts.

There was no room for insight or compromise in their world view. It was consume, and wait to consume again.

Ideological purity.

I suddenly understood the appeal of the Republican Party.

The wraiths were patient when left alone to their devices, content to linger until time itself ceased its flow. Ignorant of deterioration, their limbs gradually lengthening as ligaments stretched and snapped, their genitalia shriveling like grapes on the vine. Eventually their flesh would putrefy, exposed muscles would crisp and split in the open air, and they would collapse in heaps of dehydrated gore. In the end the room would be a sepulcher of bones; unmoving, noiseless, completely harmless except for the hunks of brain peeking out through blind eye sockets, cradled like fetuses within parched calcium wombs. The brains would continue on until man had either killed himself off or evolved to the next level and left the planet for better climes. They would wait until the sun winked out and the Earth's crust became ice, and still the brains would bide their time in freeze-dried hibernation until distant astronomical explorers happened upon our once-mighty civilization and exhumed the contents of the tomb; they'd wait until some clumsy intergalactic intern dropped a vial of mysteriously still-sparking matter and cut itself on the glass, flecking alien bloodmass over the only functioning remnants of humanity and starting the whole thing up again.

That would be our legacy to the galaxy.

One final fuck to you and the horse you rode in on.

Alien zombies.

And who was I to rebut this future? There had to be some reason for all this. Walking and talking after death, living off the blood of others, a voice gone spectral with the sounds of the grave, the mind-bond between myself and Craig, myself and Eileen; these couldn't be written off as mere side-effects of a contagion. I couldn't fathom the purpose for it all, but perhaps that was not my role.

Whether it was mere happenstance of unforeseeable circumstances or a supernatural extension of the evolutionary process, I had been denying the truth of the matter.

I was a zombie.

It was high time I embraced my pop culture heritage and started acting like one.

That said, I was strapped in tighter than a child in a car seat. Hard to behave like a ghoul when you're obviously not goin' nowheres.

So I lay there, angry and impotent. And after a time, I heard him through the silence.

Duane.

It was a feather touch tickling the base of my ganglia.

A sense of overwhelming appetite. Agony.

He was so very hungry.

I closed my eyes — ridiculous in the dark, but it helped in concentration — and stretched my mind up and out, visualizing my consciousness slipping through the crack beneath the door and down the hallways until I came to the elevator. I wasn't sure of the direction, but his hunger pangs guided me, as clear as the peals of an alarm clock. I passed effortlessly through the metal doors and rose up the shaft, the cries gaining strength in number. Nonsense vowels but the meaning was clear.

My children needed food. There was no anger in this, no malice to others, no philosophy of hatred dictating their actions. It was what it was, and they would strike the first chance they got.

A few more sets of doors and I emerged into the room, hovering above the pit. Duane's face shone like a beacon, glowing with inexpressible pain. His eyes met mine, despite my non-corporealness. I watched as the connection spread, geometrically, until the room was silent and still, the entire occupancy staring upward at nothing. Even those with sockets of dark where eyes used to be craned their faces up, sensing their leader.

Awaiting a command.

I pushed out a thought at them.

Move to the left.

The sea of undead shuffled one step to their left.

Lift your right leg.

Knees were brought up in synchronized precision. A few zombies lifted the only leg they still had and crashed to the floor, their gaze locked on the ceiling.

Inhale.

The room wheezed as lungs long empty fought to inflate.

Scream.

As one, the demons wailed.

"Sheldon?"

My connection shattered. I opened my eyes to painful fluorescence.

"Big day today," Simon said. He had lifted Sofa from my legs and hoisted her onto his immense shoulders where she sat and looked at me.

"So they tell me," I croaked.

He snapped his fingers and two soldiers from the interchangeable dozen or so I had seen around stepped out from behind his massive back. One pushed a gurney alongside me and together they loosened my bindings and tried to slide me over to the new surface. There was friction, and my back flesh began to peel as they shoved. Simon flicked open his knife and slid it underneath me, cutting at the dermis that had permanently adhered itself to the metal until I slid free with a squirmy *splort*. As they bound my hands to the gurney with plastic straps, I looked over at the table I had spent the past weeks in medical rape on. A sizable amount of my hide remained behind.

Another snap of Simon's fingers and I was wheeled out to the elevator, beginning the unscenic trek up to level two. The soldiers pushed me through another dozen hallways until we finally arrived at a pneumatic door. The men took up positions on either side, standing at attention, while Simon affixed a surgical mask over his nose and mouth and pushed the entry button. The door hissed and slowly swung open. A stream of sterile air washed over me as Simon guided me inside, last guest to the party.

A plethora of medical devices greeted me, all blinking lights and overpriced *bleeps* and *blinks*. A few doctors and nurses were briskly checking them over, confirming that the *pings* and *blorks* were accurate. I was sidled up next to a luxuriously appointed four-poster bed that brought the whole room together, Victorian décor meets Lucasfilm futurism. There lay the man of the hour, his eyes alert and searching as Simon brought me to a halt alongside him. Practically every piece of him was linked to one machine or another. He looked trapped in a multi-colored web.

"Nd tho id nds," Dixon said. The clarity of his voice was dampened by the breathing apparatus enclosing his lower face, and muffled further by the strange apparatus that sheathed the entirety of his head. I couldn't put my finger on its medical label, but it resembled nothing less than a clear plastic fish bowl. Black rubber tubing was attached to its apex, just atop his skull, and pure oxygen was being pumped in. The few remaining wisps of hair flattened under the force.

His words were unintelligible, but I got the gist. *And so it ends.*

A masked face loomed over me. Doctor #3, I remembered, the one with curly auburn hair and eyebrows like bristling caterpillars. He would taste of back bacon and crushed black pepper.

"How are we today?" he asked me.

"It's a good day to die," I said. "Again, I mean." That earned a laugh from the doctor, a smirk from Simon.

"And why are you here?" I asked the figure lounging in the far corner of the room, the shape in a sharply pressed business ensemble of tasteful greens and yellows. The person I had sniffed from three floors down. The woman who would taste of beef and onions.

"I asked if I could attend," Rowan said, removing her surgical mask. "Mr. Dixon saw fit to fill me in on his plans, and I felt, after all we've been through, you deserved a friendly face at the end."

"But you came instead," I said. "Thoughtful."

Rowan walked over and laid an armored hand on my arm. "I do feel bad, you know, for this. From a professional standpoint, there was no limit to where we could have taken you. It would have been fun."

"But all good things."

She smiled, the grin never nearing her eyes. Her face was a slack plane of emotional numbness that exposed the Botox treatments she had undergone. "Sheldon, when the most powerful person in the universe orders you to do something, you do it. It's only good business. I've already been rewarded; you'll be happy to know you are looking at the new CEO of Masters Talent and all its subsidiaries. I am now one of the reigning queens of entertainment."

"At least it hasn't. Gone to your head."

"I *could* have retired of course, but I love my work. And as one added bonus, for all my efforts at controlling you" she mimed a gun with her finger "he is letting me put the final bullet to your brain."

"Metaphorically speaking," the doctor piped up. "There is still much to learn, so we're not *actually* going to shoot you." He held up a disagreeable-looking electric rotary handsaw. "Miss O'Shea is going to sever your brain stem with this. You'll then be portioned out to several laboratories across the country, along with various other sections of your anatomy." He handed the saw to Rowan with ersatz solemnity. "I'll let you know when it's time."

"Thank you, Doctor." She smiled again; this time it brightened her entire face. The moment passed, and a fog of contempt descended over her features as she looked back at me. "You really should have treated me better at the end, Sheldon."

"Would it help if I apologized?"

"No, but I might have felt worse about all this. As it is . . ." She let the sentence trail off and tossed me a jaunty salute with the blade.

At a gesture from the doctor, Rowan stepped back and replaced her mask. The nurses tinkered with my gurney, swiveling the bed up on its axis until I was almost fully standing, the bindings around my chest and throat the only things keeping me from sliding to the floor in a puddle of bones. The doctor pointed to my lips, and I opened my mouth obediently to allow his metal-linked fingers access. He prodded my teeth, poked at the tongue, stroked the salivary glands at the back. "Teeth are a little loose, two missing, but still serviceable." Satisfied, he withdrew and turned to Dixon's withered near-corpse.

"How is this supposed to work?" I asked.

"It's very simple," the doctor explained as he checked over the headgear. "It's all *theory*, of course, but we have had extensive time and opportunity to examine exactly what is the difference between the unblemished human brain, we'll call it Brain A, your brain, Brain B, slightly abnormal, yet fully functioning, and the garden-variety zombie brain, Brain C. Aside from some slight irregularities such as the overacting ventromedial hypothalamus, which explains the constant hunger, there is very little overt difference between Brain B and Brain A. But Brain B, you, has actually evolved, for lack of a better word, to more fully employ those various recesses we humans theoretically never use. This accounts for how we have been able to carve away such enormous portions of your matter with no significant loss of either motor control or intellect.

"Here, you may find this interesting." Doctor #3 pointed to something behind me and a nurse handed him two mirrors, one of which he propped up behind my head. He had the nurse hold the other up high in my eyeline. What I could see was my yawning brainpan, its lone resident a disfigured lump of putty left in an open sewage gutter. The doctor ripped the plastic wrap off; the rubber band *sproinged* away. "You can see here," he continued, his reflected finger tracing the remains, "we have removed exceptional amounts of your frontal lobe, as well as," he pried up the corner of the organ and poked a finger underneath, "your cerebellum, here. We've also scraped away much of the cerebral cortex to get at the thalamus, the amygdala, the pituitary gland, etcetera." He slipped his finger out and let the mass plop back into place with a nauseating squelch. "All told, we have removed more than half of its total weight.

"Yet here you remain, conscious and alert. A complete enigma." He held up a clear glass jar. Inside, a dull gray nugget morosely soaked in a pool of goo. "This is you. Your, um," he checked the handwritten label, "pons. This little conglomeration of nerves and fibers connects the two hemispheres of your cerebellum. Plainly put, you should be spasmodic

261

without it, the two halves of your brain fighting it out without a bridge to connect them. Yet, you function normally. And, as an added bonus," he waggled the jar, bouncing the lump against the glass, "this little piece of you is still working. The neurons are still firing, even now, sitting in a beaker, unattached to anything. If I hooked electrodes to this, scanned it in an MRI, you'd see that it is still alive, that what we perceive as thoughts are still being generated. This little sample of dura is, right now, beyond all limits of rational science, contemplating something." He held the container up to his eyes and peered at its contents. "What do you think is going on in there?" He tapped the glass with his finger. "Sheldon? Are you in there, Sheldon? Hello?" He chuckled, and tossed the jar to a nurse. "Fascinating stuff. I'll write a book when all this is done, now that Rhodes is out of the picture. And thank you for that, by the way. I didn't want to get merely a contribution credit."

"Anything for science," I croaked.

"Ain't that the truth?" The doc moved back to Dixon and checked the sealing around the dome. From where I lay, I could see a rough circle had been inked over the old man's neck wattle. "How are you feeling, sir?"

"*Llls gt nwt it,*" the mucho-geriatric skeleton mumbled. *Let's get on with it.* His chest rose and fell with the pumping of the air. I suspected that was all that was keeping him alive at this point.

"As you wish." The doctor turned back to me and motioned to the nurses, who began loosening my straps. "You see, after much comparative examination of your brain with that of your compatriots, we've determined that somehow you sidestepped around a state of anoxia."

"English, please."

He sighed the sigh of university professors saddled with dim-witted first-years. "Your brain has remained oxygenated. All death can be traced back to the ultimate final step, the removal of oxygen to the brain. Without it, the brain simply starves. The heart ceases its blood flow, the brain doesn't get what it needs, and thus is rendered kaput. We feel that may be the main reason why your friends on level one are so, well, stupid. No offence."

I coughed a cackle. "*Now* you take my feelings into account?"

"Without oxygen, their brains, while still somehow functioning at the most primal level of existence, have ceased their work at memories, personality, empathy, what have you. In effect, they've suffered monumental brain damage."

"Retards," Simon spoke up. "You've got a pit of retards. Hey, maybe they're not trying to eat us. Maybe they just want hugs." A few of the nurses tittered, egging Simon on. "What about it, Doc? Think a plate of sugar cookies and a few 'Great jobs!' would keep them in line?"

The doctor pursed his lips in distaste and continued. "As I was saying, we suspect anoxia is the crux of your unique development. We're going to continue the flow of oxygen to Mr. Dixon's brain as he dies, while your whatevers do their work. If the flow continues, we feel that his brain can bypass the damage you inflict on others while his body dies." He looked over his shoulder at Dixon. "You see that circle? You're going to bite him, right there. We thought about extracting some of your matter, surgically injecting him with this virus rather than have you get one last meal, but all our experiments thus far have failed. There are quite a few" he air-quoted with his fingers "'volunteers' in our pit because of our failures thus far. We feel that a fresh dose from your mouth is the only option left."

"And if it doesn't work?" I asked. "If he's one of Simon's retards?"

Simon pulled out a massive semi-automatic pistol equipped with a high capacity magazine and cocked the trigger. "Then I put him down. One to the brain, one to the heart. As per Mr. Dixon's written instructions." He looked to his employer and snapped a sincere salute. "It has been an honor working with you, sir."

The doctor clapped his hands. "To work, everyone! Positions, please!" The nurses freed my hands and took a firm hold of my arms. Simon placed his massive gloved paws on the sides of my head.

"Feel free to dig in and enjoy yourself, buddy," he whispered in my good ear. "This is the last meal of the condemned. Confidentially, this is a crapshoot anyway. Fifty-fifty chance. But the old man is dead anyway. Without this, he won't make sundown. I fully expect to be unemployed in less than an hour. Either way, I retire a very rich man."

I felt the last of my muscles quiver and weaken. I had no more reserves of energy. My barrels of willpower had been tapped of every last drop.

I gave up. If the wealthy sociopath wanted this, he could have it. I failed at life, might as well fail at death.

The doctor took one last quick survey over the machines, and then gave a nod to Simon. The nurses freed my bonds. On a count of three, a separate nurse taking each arm and leg, another tending to my torso, I was lifted, head held straight and true by Simon, and hefted across the space to Dixon's side. The medicos rotated me until my chest was aimed floorward, lifted me slightly, and then aimed my mouth at the bull's-eye on Dixon's neck.

I did not struggle. I could not have had I wanted to; I was the only thing in the room more debilitated than the emaciated supercentenarian.

My stomach, dragging on the ground beneath me, whimpered in anticipation.

I looked up into Dixon's eye while Simon pressed my mouth to the sweet spot. The old man was still awake, still hellishly aware. The area hadn't even been numbed with a local; blood pushed furiously through his veins, throbbing against the skin of my lips. Saliva exploded in my mouth, and I drooled over his flesh. I let out a mute sob of shame and threw wide my maw. My teeth pressed against his meat, my tongue lapped up his sweat.

Dixon threw me a wink.

In that one blink of a lid, I saw all his condescension, all his ego, all his madness.

Fuck this.

If there was any way to stop this, I would.

This was *my* gift, not his.

All of a sudden, I didn't feel like sharing.

I slipped my teeth across the hairs of his neck and clamped my mouth shut. Dixon's eye widened, and I heard a few of the background *beeps* speed up their rhythms. Smothered curses escaped the corners of his respirator.

I thought, hysterically, if Dixon would only die in the next ten seconds or so, all this would be for naught.

I ground my teeth together, cracking my canines, and I felt my molars begin to pulp into mush.

No teeth, no bite.

It was the only plan I could come up with.

The doctor leaned in for a look, then motioned to Simon for assistance. Simon stuck his chain-linked fingers between my lips and jammed the blade of his knife into the gaps between my teeth. As expert as an oyster shucker, he pried my jaws open and forced my incisors and canines into Dixon's insubstantial epidermis. My tongue retreated as his skin folded over the embankment of my teeth. Instructing the nurses to hold my head secure, Simon then slipped the palm of his hand beneath my jawline, and slammed my mandibles closed.

Dixon squawked beneath his mask as I tore in. The background sonar pings accelerated in pace, matching the alarming rate of his heart.

My body shuddered orgasmically as plasma spurted out over my taste buds, the severed meat already hurtling toward my stomach as my trachea convulsed in joy. The blood was rich, thick and wholesome, plainly not his own, and I had time to wonder at the high quality of his transfusion pool. If blood was cocaine, this was pure uncut Peruvian flake.

I gulped.

I chugged.

I guzzled.

I quaffed.

As Lambertus Dixon screamed and twitched I slurped back the entirety of his essence and gnawed at his throat. Simon held my head fast, refusing to let me crane forward and get a good toothy clamp on Dixon's tender pharynx. I made do with the musculature, and nibbled and sucked at whatever tendrils of raw fiber I could reach.

It had been so, so long.

After several lifetimes, the machines began to quiet, one by one, their cheery bells altering into long stretches of sustained tonal monotony until they silenced themselves. And still I fed, the wet clamor of my final repast filling the spaces until only chewing and swallowing echoed through the arena, accompanied by the occasional retch of a nurse.

"That should do," the doctor said finally. Simon retracted my head and heaved me back gracelessly onto my gurney. I landed face first, the collision popping out my loose eye, the force of the throw swinging the bed back into a horizontal position. My leftovers of brain rattled about, and I could feel my good eye pull inward as my jouncing memory bank tugged at the optic nerve. The nurses quickly swung the bed away into a corner, abutting one of Dixon's wheelchairs. My feet brushed against Rowan's hip and she shuddered in revulsion.

I lay there, abandoned, already forgotten, my head dangling over the edge, my lips still smacking, tongue prodding every oral crevice for one last drop of life.

I had never felt so alive.

"What now, Doc?" Simon asked. I lifted my head for a peek and managed to slide my arm around to cover my free-floating eyeball and cut out its view of the floor. They had gathered around Dixon's body, the doctor inspecting the fishbowl to make sure the oxygen still flowed. Rowan and the nurses hung back while the doctor attended to the wires that had detached during Dixon's death throes. Simon's cannon hung from his hand, ready for the first quiver of post-death.

There was very little blood around the wound, I noticed; I had been quite efficient in my appetite.

Barely even needed a bib.

The doctor completed his checklist and took a position at the foot of the bed. "I'm calling it." He checked his watch. "The death of Lambertus Dixon officially occurred at 11:27 a.m."

He ordered the nurses to leave the room. They didn't need to be asked twice. As they quickly filed out, the two soldiers entered and stood at attention at the door, weapons at the ready.

"Now," the doctor said to the room, "we wait."

They stood back and waited. Every two minutes, the doctor would once again check over the machines and then intone, "Two minutes, no signs of reanimation . . . Four minutes, no signs of reanimation."

At the fourteen count, Simon uncocked his pistol and blew out a lengthy puff of annoyed air. "How long is this supposed to take, anyway?" he asked, checking his watch.

"There have been variations in the viral response time," the doctor said. "Some volunteers, if pricked in an area relatively distant to the brainstem, have taken weeks to succumb. But all test subjects, if bitten at approximately the same spot on the neck, adjacent to the brain, have died and experienced complete reanimation within an hour. Considering the severity of the bite, if all goes accordingly we should have twitching soon."

"Do I have time for a smoke?" asked Rowan.

A light blipped on a computer screen.

Dixon's left foot trembled.

"Here we go," the doctor said. "Fifteen minutes, signs of animation in the left leg. This is textbook; for some reason, the left side always revives first."

The left leg jerked slightly, the muscles of the thigh convulsing. Then the muscles of the right constricted, raising the ankle off the bed.

Simon cocked the hammer of his gun and readied his stance, aiming at the skull. The soldiers hoisted their weapons.

Dixon's eyelids flipped open.

One of the soldiers barked in alarm.

The doc snapped a penlight on and pushed in close to the eyes. "Sixteen minutes, eyes open. Pupils are dilated and nonresponsive." He cupped his hand to the fishbowl near Dixon's ear and yelled in. "Sir? Sir, can you hear me?"

The mouth cracked open beneath the mask. Viscous bog water ran down his chin. A whiff of the fecal escaped the fishbowl and graced our noses.

"Jesus, that's ripe," Rowan said.

The doctor continued to address Dixon as the body started to shake. Rowan moved back, resting her rump against the lip of my gurney.

"Can you hear me, sir?"

The corpse looked the doctor in the eyes.

"Eighteen minutes, possible eye responsiveness to aural commands. Sir, can you hear me? Are you in there? Blink once for yes, twice for no."

A wait, then one blink.

"Was that a yes?" Simon asked.

One blink.

The doctor touched Dixon's right arm. "Can you feel this?"

Blink.

"Try to raise it, please."

The arm quaked at the effort, then lifted a few inches off the sheet.

"Nineteen minutes, definite signs of intelligence." He looked up, ecstatic. "This is astonishing! We have never achieved any result remotely this successful, actual comprehension! Response to verbal queries!" The immensity of the moment overcame him, and he sat heavily on the bedspread, cupping his head in his hands. "Do you realize what we've done?" He looked up, delighted in himself. "I'm going to be famous!" he whispered. "The man who cracked immortality!"

"Not good enough." Simon moved in and placed the barrel of his gun to the fishbowl, just above Dixon's temple. "I have my orders," he said over the doctor's protests. "The boss speaks, or it ends here." He looked into Dixon's eyes. "Sir, your orders were very specific. I will stand down when I have been issued the verbal password we agreed upon. Do you remember it?"

Dixon's eyes widened. He blinked, then nodded.

"It's not that simple, you oaf," the doctor complained. "It took Funk hours to learn to talk, you cannot expect him to master it here!"

"Orders are orders. Mr. Dixon did not want there to be any doubt. He talks, or he never leaves this room."

The doctor cursed, motioning Simon to stand down while he briskly removed the gadgetry from Dixon's head. The respirator released its grip on Dixon's mouth with a clammy sucking sound.

"Once again, sir," Simon said, this time placing his gun directly between Dixon's eyes. "Password."

Dixon's mouth opened, his lips pursed, forming soundless consonants.

The doctor placed his hands on the old man's chest. "Sir, you have to remember to breathe. Here, feel my hands. Breathe in, sir. Swell your lungs."

The eyelids blinked once, *yes*, and then closed as Dixon concentrated. His mouth opened wide.

After a minute, his chest rose.

"That's it, sir. Now let it out, try to make a sound."

The lips pursed themselves into an oval. The lungs deflated, and a draft of air from the filthiest outhouse in existence spewed forth. Simon gagged, but kept his weapon pressed between Dixon's eyes.

The lungs inhaled again, a little stronger, and then a lengthier exhalation.

"*. . . whiskers . . .*"

It was the first time I had heard the full bloodcurdling effect of utterances from beyond the grave from the point of view of a spectator. It was a multi-layered sound, its various aural strata proficiently assaulting the eardrums, intestines, and diaphragm. My chunks of rich elderly trillionaire struggled to stay put. Both soldiers whitened at the sound and began patting themselves down for their earplugs. One rushed to a corner and ejected his breakfast.

"I told you idiots to keep those in at all times," Simon cursed. He leaned closer to his employer. "Once again, sir?"

Inhale, exhale. "*. . . whiskers . . .*" Inhale, exhale, inhale, exhale. "The. Password. Is. Whiskers."

"Correct." Simon stood up and holstered his gun. "Mr. Dixon has confirmed the password, Doctor. You are good to continue."

"Whiskers?" Rowan asked.

Simon blushed. "The name of my first cat."

Rowan sniggered. "That's adorable," I said.

Simon swung a murderous look my way as the doctor helped Dixon into a sitting position. "You still with us? You'll get yours soon enough," he promised, and began propping pillows behind Dixon's back.

Dixon took a few more cautious breaths and then began to speak, his phrasing a halting mix of pauses and words that sounded barely human. "It seems. Your theory. Was correct, Doctor. My thanks." He looked about the room. "Extraordinary. I feel so. So strange."

The doctor was walking past the computer screens and penciling marks on a clipboard, reading out his checklist. "Heart rate, nil. Blood flow, nil. Body temperature cooling rapidly." He drew a stethoscope from his pocket and held the bell to Dixon's bare chest. "Confirmed, heart has ceased to function." He clicked on his penlight and shone the beam into Dixon's eyes. "Please follow the beam, sir, as best you can."

Dixon grabbed the doctor's hand. His mouth shaped a few keen words.

"Breathe in, sir. Remember."

The old man focused, swelling his torso with air, the first time in decades his lungs had worked under his own power. "Get. That light. Out of my eyes. You idiot." He shoved the hand away and motioned to Simon. "Help me. To my. Feet."

The doctor protested. "Sir, we must take this slow. You haven't walked in over forty years. We have to be cautious." He looked to Simon for assistance. "We need to get him upstairs. This is a significant achievement, we must document it thoroughly."

Simon considered his options, looked to the living corpse, and shrugged. "He's the boss, Doc," he said. "He wants to stand, we're going to let him stand. Move aside." He moved his bulk to the bedside and slipped an arm beneath Dixon's legs. Placing a large hand protectively behind his head, Simon hefted the old man up and carefully lowered his feet to the floor. Wires and cables remained embedded in his skin, some detaching from the machinery, lending him a kaleidoscopic fringe.

Dixon wobbled on legs thin as reeds. Simon braced Dixon's shoulders, allowing him to find his balance.

Dixon lifted his right leg slightly and shifted it forward a few precious inches. "I haven't. Walked. Since. Nineteen. Seventy. One." He shifted his weight to the right, swinging his left leg forward. Haltingly, in spurts and stops, Lambertus crossed the room and back. His frill of electric filaments jingled lightheartedly as he walked.

"Astonishing," he said. He looked at me and arched a hairless eyebrow. "Sheldon, you. Were holding. Back. You never. Said how this. Felt. I feel. Wonderful."

"Sir, we need to get you upstairs," the doctor said, placing a stabilizing hand on Dixon's arm. "I really must insist. We have so many tests to run."

Dixon stood still, resisting the doctor's efforts. His eyes blanked, taking on a sheen of disconnectedness, the pupils focusing past the walls. He looked to be in a trance.

Threads of drool slipped out from bloodless lips.

The doctor pushed a little harder, motioned for Simon to take Dixon's other arm. Behind them, a computer began to blare a warning as Dixon's brain activity shot into overdrive.

I could have stopped them. The doctor could not sense the thunderbolts shooting up Dixon's arm from the heat of the doctor's hand, thoughtlessly bare of protection. He could not feel the rush of blood through the fingers that caressed the old man's skin. Simon could not see Dixon's eyes bulge with anticipation; he could not hear the sudden roiling erupt from the doddering zombie's hyperactive stomach. Neither could see the world from Dixon's point of view, suddenly painted cherry.

I could have told them, had they asked. Step one was animation. Step two: lunch.

Simon wrapped a paw around Dixon's upper arm and made to turn him, walk him back to the bed. Dixon's jaw opened near to dislocation and the frail old man bounded onto Simon's chest, straddling the vast torso with his thighs. Before Simon could raise an armored hand as protection, the elderly ghoul sank his few remaining teeth into Simon's neck, tearing through the epidermis and ripping free the trachea. He tugged, and the windpipe came free, tearing loose from the lungs and hanging from his gorestained grin like a tube of raw rigatoni.

Simon panicked as his life bled away, knocking the doctor down and carrying Dixon back, crushing Rowan against my gurney as Lambertus wrapped his limbs spider-like around the giant's body and continued to feast, the two of them bouncing off the walls in an obscene waltz. Wires whipped the air as they spun, opening trenches of the red wet across Rowan's face. The soldiers fought for handholds on the writhing corpse, but Simon's wound was firehosing over the two of them, lubricating them with blood. Finally, Simon worked one hand between the snapping jowls and another beneath the zombie's ribcage and pushed. Even intoxicated and refreshed with raw meat, his muscles stronger than they'd ever been, Dixon weighed barely north of eighty pounds; he flew across the room and crashed into the bank of computers, falling directly atop the still-floorbound body of the doctor.

Dixon may have retained his intelligence, but he was blood-drunk, and gave himself willingly over to the dictates of appetite. The doctor's frenzied screams were short-lived, his wet moans only slightly longer.

Simon's will to live was merciless. He stumbled around the room as his heart evacuated itself of its last beads of blood. His eyes widened as his brain quit on him. His legs weakened, his bowels loosened, and he collapsed atop me, snapping a few of my vertebrae. He slid off to the floor, where my arm draped loosely over his trunk. Our eyes met, and I watched his consciousness expunge itself from its prison.

There was screaming. I lifted my head to see with one eye the singular image of a naked geriatric piggyback-riding a heavily muscled mercenary, tearing off the gunman's ear and ecstatically tonguing the hole. My other eye swung free, spinning, seeing Rowan sitting up against the wall, her face lacerated. The eye swung back, getting a glimpse of a large black object protruding near Simon's waist. I fought to reconcile the dual images, gave up, and pulled at the loose orb until it tore loose, automatically halving my visual spectrum. *Goodbye, depth perception.* The ball and nerve plopped to the floor as I took a clearer look at the carnage.

The second gunman had gathered his wits and was aiming his weapon, the red light of the laser sighting playing across the tussling duo, trying to get a bead on Dixon's forehead. The frenetic assault made a clean shot impossible, and the soldier began to fire rounds into anything moving. Bullets tore through Dixon's back as the dying blue plate special he straddled pirouetted, trying to throw the old man off. They punched through Dixon's body and embedded in the merc's chest and neck, ceasing the screams. Dixon rode his prey to the floor and then leapt at the other, clearing a six-foot gap with ease and wrenching the surprised soldier's jaw clean off. As the chinless man gargled a howl, the old man brought him down and proceeded to shuck the remainder of his face.

Could I have jumped like that? I thought, amazed. *Jesus, could I ever have moved that quickly?*

As the soldier's dying breaths bubbled forth from his lungs, Dixon stood up and took stock of his massacre. The ichor smeared over his skin, his body looked healthier, fuller; if anything, he seemed to have put on mass. His skin was tighter, his musculature more defined. The bullet wounds that peppered his chest and back were small, smaller than they should have been.

Is he healing?

He turned to me, his red grin enormous, his eyes blazing, transformed. I was a monster, but he was *the* monster; Lambertus Dixon was the apogee of our species. Compared to him, I was little better than the brain-numbed walking dead that even now I could sense screaming for release from their prison. If I was a poor man's idea of Jesus Christ, then this was Our Father Who Art in Heaven in all His terrible glory.

His chest bulged as he forced a breath in. "Well," he exhaled. "That was. Unexpected." A silent giggle shook him. "Is it always. That intense?" he asked me. "The thirst?"

"Always," I said.

"It was so. Unstoppable." He shivered as he licked his fingers. "I couldn't help myself."

"You'll need to work on that."

"Oh, Sheldon. If I had only known. I never would have waited." He stretched out his limbs, examining muscles that had not moved with such grace in generations. "Glorious. Absolutely. Glorious. I have never felt. This good." He walked over to me, his stride smooth and unwavering, and crouched down to look me in the eye.

"This isn't right, is it? You could never. Move like this. With such. Fluidity?"

"Can't say so," I wheezed. "Always preferred the. Lumbering look myself."

"Fascinating." He looked himself over again. "It seems I. Have changed a bit. From your template. I'd say we were. Able to refine the process. Filtered out the impurities." He raised his hands to the sides of his head and closed his eyes. "Sparks. Such. Such colors! Sheldon, I can *see* my brain evolving. To a higher level of consciousness. Already I can feel myself. Getting stronger."

He looked back at me, thoughtful. "How long did it take you. To learn to speak?"

"Hours."

"And here I've mastered. It in minutes. I'm not a zombie, Sheldon. Not entirely. I am something new. A step in evolution. What a gift you've given me." He cocked his head, looking up. "And what is that noise? No, not noise. But in my head. Do you hear that? The screaming?" I nodded glumly, my scraps of brain bouncing about. His eyes brightened. "It's them, isn't it? Your children. No. *My* children." He clapped his hands in joy, and his still-withered manboobs quivered. "What wonderment. They're just waiting for their orders. A whole species, mine to control. Much like humans."

"At least it hasn't. Gone to your head."

He shot me an expression of pity. "And there you were. With all this power. This potential. Wasting it. Hiding from your true self. You don't deserve this."

"Never thought I did."

He stood, stretched his limbs, becoming aware of his newfound death. "Imagine what I'll be like. Once I get my full strength! Once we start the alterations. That Doctor Rhodes had planned. I'll be unstoppable."

"Not if you keep eating your doctors."

"Details. I'll become invincible."

"A king among men," I said.

He nodded to himself. "To start. I think—" His eyes widened, then bulged, an impossibility with no blood flow. "Oh my," he whispered. "Can you see them?"

I glanced around.

"There, Sheldon." He pointed past the machinery, to the wall. "In the cracks. Between the atoms." I looked, seeing nothing but painted concrete. His face slackened in astonishment. "Oh, Sheldon. If you only knew. I understand. I see it all now. I see *them.*" He looked back to me, unnervingly peaceful. "You never knew about them, did you? Somehow, you never knew."

A whimper rose from the corner of the room, distracting Dixon from the invisible spectacle. He looked over his shoulder at Rowan, huddled against the wall, watching us, knees curled to her chest, her fingers dabbing at her wounds.

Lambertus slid his eyes over her, and I watched the appetite return. Blood oozed from her injuries, alive with copper, the scent already distinct from the dead plasma that filled the room.

He gave me a slow wink, not yet a mastered skill. "What do you think. Sheldon? Should I let her live?" He took a deep breath. "*Shall I let you go?*" he bellowed. "*Shall I be merciful?*" His voice ripped through the boundaries of time and space. The gouged remnants of my brain shriveled at the sonic assault. Rowan's electronic plugs sparked in her ears, singing her hair. She vomited over her blouse.

He laughed, taking a breath beforehand, the intake of air already a natural process. His cackle was a crime against humanity. "What fun. Sheldon, you truly missed out. And to think. I thought *you* could be a messiah. You are a worm compared to me. You couldn't even be. A proper zombie. You had to be *conflicted*. How pathetic."

He reached down and tore off a mercenary's arm, biting off the index finger and swallowing it whole, bones and all. "You disgust me, Sheldon," he said as he nibbled on the thumb. "That I ever thought I should. Be like you. I see now, there is. No limit to what I can achieve."

He smiled, his grin broad, his teeth red. "Perhaps I'll keep you around. As a pet. A reminder to myself. Of what could have been. I will feed you scraps. Just enough to keep you aware. And you can watch as I fulfill your potential."

I wish I could have thought of a witty rejoinder. Something pithy and devastating. Something a hero would have said. Something a movie star could have spat out before the climactic turnaround.

Even a non sequitur would have done.

But my mind was blank to all but purpose.

I was no hero. I never was. You can't be a hero *and* a cannibal.

I wasn't even human. I was a zombie who dreamed of humanity.

It was time to wake up. But not before one final gasp of compassion for what I once was.

I raised my arm, my hand gripping the gun Simon had tucked away into his holster, and fired.

The slug pierced Dixon's throat, pureeing the Adam's apple, puncturing the trachea, and splintering the cervical vertebrae. The shards gladly joined the bullet in its destruction and rampaged through the spinal cord, punching nerve cells through the back wall of Dixon's neck.

Dixon gaped. His arms twitched as he tried to raise them up, to plug the hole. His legs gave way and the old man fell forward to his knees, next to Simon's body, closer to me. Dixon tried to speak; his new orifice whistled.

I took aim and fired three more times, almost completing what I started.

Dixon's head flipped back, the vertebrae useless, the discs punctured, the spinal cord almost completely demolished. His body went into spasms as he tried to order his limbs to fight back, to attack. The movements ruined whatever balance he had, and he fell back, knees bending at unfamiliar angles. He squirmed as his appendages protested their orders, confused.

I couldn't finish the job from where I lay. Dixon was twitching his way across the floor, out of my line of fire, and I didn't know how many shots I had left. I swung the gun Rowan's way. "Rowan, would you be a dear. And toss me that saw?" She looked at the tool in her hand, her face slack, responses sluggish. She was going into shock. I fired a shot over her head to get her attention focused on the here and now. She squeaked and threw the saw across the floor, sliding it through the fluids that drenched the tiles. It came to a rest next to Simon's groin.

I heaved myself off the gurney and fell heavily onto the dead giant's chest, forcing a glut of black matter to eject from his mouth. A small chunklet of me wrested free from my open brainpan (*How much is even left?* I worried) and landed next to Simon's nose, jiggling as I rolled off his torso.

Holding the gun in one hand, grabbing the saw in the other, I crawled toward the zombie that was convulsing itself away from me. My digestive tubing snagged behind me, leashing me to Simon's belt. Cursing, I switched on the saw and sliced away at my intestinal rope until I was free, leaving me with an esophagus, trachea, stomach, and not much else.

Wouldn't have needed it much longer anyway.

I arm-walked through the sludge until I reached Dixon's side. He was flopping away, still angrily commanding compliance from his rebelling physique. His neck had twisted around; his face banged against the floor. I slid in next to him and used my gun hand to right his skull. The two of us stared up at the ceiling, his twitches slowing.

"Can you hear me?" I asked. "Dixon, can you hear me in there?"

His frame calmed its thrashings.

I turned his head so that he could see me. His eyes shook in their housing.

Yes. The word filled my mind. *Yes, I can hear you still, cocksucker.*

"Nice. That makes this easier."

With the saw, I carved through the last shreds of his spinal column. Dixon's body instantly deactivated itself.

His eyes blinked at me. I *had* always wondered whether that was possible.

I took him by the nose and slipped the two of us forward, feeling his curses swarm over my neurons, tossing him across the doctor's body and having him wait for me as I lugged myself over. I brought myself to a sitting position against the wall and picked the head up to face me.

"So," I said. "Here we are."

What do you want, Sheldon? There wasn't much movement in the face, the musculature too vandalized, but his eyes still shone with fury.

"What do I want?"

I can help us both, Sheldon. We can *be rebuilt. You know this is possible.*

"You trying to bargain with me?"

You and I, Sheldon. We could rule this world. You just need a little guidance.

"You know, I'm sick of guidance. It feels like I haven't been myself in. Forever."

We can be gods. I can feel the power out there, in a way you never could. I am so much more than you. I can sense the powers beyond our world. Given time, we can harness them! Reshape the planet with our minds!

"Wow, *magic* zombies. Where were you when. I was looking for scripts?"

Don't be a fool, Sheldon. There has to be a reason why you were chosen. I believe this is it! You were meant to be so that I could be! Sacrifice for the greater good! I see this now. They tell me this. We are their emissaries. It was fate that brought us together, to become avatars for beings long absent from this reality!

I mulled that over. Rowan started to slide herself over to the door as I pondered; I fired another shot over her head to keep her still, raining plaster dust over her hairdo.

Fate. If there had to be a reason . . . maybe the gods did choose me as a vessel. Who was I to say they didn't exist, or that there wasn't *some* force beyond my comprehension moving me across a hyperdimensional chessboard? Nothing about me made sense anyway. Wasn't it just so much fucking easier to say I never had a choice at all? That I was just a pawn, a character in a poorly conceived pulp novel of gore, tragedy, and painful metaphors?

I thought of Fisher, watching myself gut him with my fingers.

I thought of setting fire to Mom's body.

I thought of Duane, above me, brain all but gone, his lovely soul scrambled like eggs in an omelet. I thought of what could have been with him, had I still been alive and not a coward to my own insecurities.

I thought of my stomach, open in my lap, somehow still gurgling.

"I never put much stock in gods," I said. "As you said. I've never been the contemplative type."

This is a chance for immortality! We'll become vessels for beings of unimaginable energies. Can you not see them? Can you not hear them, bellowing from the void? They are ordering us to proceed, Sheldon! The plan is almost complete. They are willing to forgive; they understand that they didn't get the formula right with you.

"You know," I said, bouncing Dixon's head back and forth between my hands like a basketball, "there are schools of thought. That say when you eat someone. You gain their knowledge. I saw some movies like that. Until now, I knew that wasn't true.

"But in your case" I raised his head and stared him in the eyes "I wonder."

I placed him on my lap, face down, and sawed through the top half of his skull, spinning him slowly in my lap as the blade spun through the bone and freed his pulsing cerebrum to the air. I plunged my fingers in and ripped loose a McNugget of Lambertus and popped it into my mouth, hearing his screams of anger and somehow tasting his rage as my molars made quick work of whatever embers of personality abided within its tissue.

I tore out handfuls of his personality and squished them in my fists before licking his cogitations off my fingers. Around me, I fancied

I could hear the walls scream as I denied vast gods/monsters from hidden realms their exit strategy.

As I devoured him, I began to see. Random clouds of his consciousness crept through my system while I chewed, jolting my neurons, pushing the rods and cones of my one eye to the edges of their capacities and then beyond.

I began to see. The walls were tissue, reality a thin veneer that masked untold wonders and horrors. Light filled the infinitesimal interstices between atoms, and silhouettes the size of mountains wriggled and pushed against the fabric of existence. Colossal tentacles wrapped around the room and squeezed. Teeth the size of galaxies gnawed at the walls.

Do you see them? the morsels asked as they were impaled upon my incisors.

"Yes," I answered truthfully. "I see them."

Do you understand?

"Oh yes."

They were nameless, and leviathan. What peeked through the fractures were the original old ones, the progenitors of every religious movement that had existed since man had shrugged off the last drops of primordial ooze and decided to wonder what else there could be to life. I was to be their vessel. They had been waiting eons for their chance to break through and claim their birthrights as rulers of time itself. Past efforts had been futile; our brains were too simple, our technologies unprepared, and the best messiahs they could summon were deceased humans with thought, and even that success they achieved only a few times among untold numbers of braindead corpses hungering for flesh. But deathlessness had taught them patience; they continued to experiment, reaching though the ruptures between worlds, molding our minds, raising us to do their bidding. Now humanity had split the atom, finally advancing to the point where we could conceivably open gateways between dimensions; all they needed was a patsy. It had been me, but as Dixon said, they had once again fucked up the recipe, and it was only through happenstance that the old man had lucked into the proper procedure.

A creature as old as the universe pressed its scaled digits into reality and pleaded for release.

I lifted Dixon back into my eyeline. Only a few tablespoons of thought remained in his skull. The old man's eyes were still bright and focused, and he pleaded with me to stop, that it wasn't too late. My stomach burbled in my lap, digesting a god.

"Can they hear you?" I asked the severed head in my hands. "Are you in contact with them?"

Yes, Sheldon. They understand your confusion. They are willing to forgive. This can still work; I can still open the doorway. I see how, it is so simple.

I bore the tips of my fingers into his remnants and took a firm grip.

"Tell them something for me."

Anything, Sheldon.

My fingers tightened.

"Tell them that this is all your fault."

His memories imploded.

"You should never have killed Duane."

I wrested the last of Dixon free. His eyeballs sucked back and out of his sockets and jiggled between my fingers.

I crammed Lambertus Dixon into my mouth and swallowed him up.

The walls blinked back to normality.

I let the empty head tumble from my fingers. It rolled into my chest cavity, and I was too tired to care.

I looked over at Rowan, still sitting, watching me warily.

"Do you know what I just saw?" I asked her.

She shook her head.

"Neither do I. And I am too tired. To think about it."

We regarded each other.

"So, what happens now?" she asked uncertainly.

"What do you think. Should happen?"

"Could I go?"

"That's one option. Or I could eat you. Option two."

"I always had your best interests at heart, Sheldon."

"That's true. Until the end, of course."

"Well, I *am* an agent, after all."

We shared a chuckle over that.

"I don't know what I am anymore, Rowan. I thought I was an actor. Then I thought I was a zombie. Just now, I could have become a god. Where do you go from that?"

"We could still make some money together. Go on an international tour. Tell people what you've seen. You could donate the profits, if you want. You're still functioning, more or less."

I lifted up my stomach, dancing happily as Dixon's eyeballs dissolved. "Definitely less."

She smiled. "We'd have to clean you up a bit, of course."

"I think that would be. Like putting lipstick. On a pig at this point."

"You'd be surprised what a touch of rouge can do."

"I'm sure I would be. Catch." I tossed the saw over to her. She picked it up hesitantly.

"Do you . . . do you want me to . . . kill you?"

I waggled the gun at her. "Don't get any ideas, Rowan. No, I still blame you for Duane. And all this, of course. You could have told me at any time. But you used me. Like a good agent should. Sold me out for thirty pieces of silver. I don't think I can forgive you."

She hung her head. "I *am* sorry, Shel."

"Too little, too late."

"Then why—"

"Why the saw?" I pointed at the bulk of Simon. "Don't you see him twitching there?"

Rowan looked. Simon's fingers were beginning to spasm.

"I don't think. I'll have much time left here. But since I'm going to go. I'm going to go as what I am.

"I am a zombie. It's time to monster up. But I figure I do owe you. A fighting chance. You *did* stay with me. When others doubtless would have dropped me. I haven't forgotten that. And I am grateful. So we're going to wait here. Until my new disciple Simon. Is good and ready."

Simon started to shake. Rowan rose unsteadily to her feet.

"And then, we will see. If you deserve to leave this place. Alive."

She took a step toward Simon, raising the saw.

I cocked the gun, stopping her.

"Not before he's up. Let's keep this fair."

She gave as good as she got. Have to give her that.

After Simon finished deboning his meal, I had him scoop out Rowan's braincase and wolf down the matter; I didn't want her returning.

By that time, both soldiers and the doctor had reanimated. I let them get a few noshes down their gullets, and then had them stand at attention. They obediently lined up by the door, swaying in an invisible breeze. I considered letting them run free through the complex, have some fun, but I had a few things left to do, and I'd need a little help.

At my command, in fits and starts, Simon ineptly bundled me up in his arms and hefted me over to Dixon's mechanized wheelchair. Strings of red meat hung from the crevices in his teeth, drool poured out of his mouth and filled the cavity where I once had a circulatory system. I then had him gather as many lengths of wire as he could and wrap them around me, binding me into a sitting position. This was arduous for the mammoth ghoul; lacking the basic faculties to understand the difference between *wire* and *intestines*, he more than once scooped up handfuls of my past agent's colon and handed them to me. I had to mentally order him to *walk forward two steps, bend down*, and *pick up those things directly in front of you*. In this manner, I had enough cord to wrap around me fully, supporting my useless torso and neck. It was an ugly job, but then again, I was the wholly disemboweled remains of an up-and-coming Hollywood star; I was as ugly as it got.

Successfully trussed in my vehicle, I maneuvered the chair to the door and pushed the door lock button, releasing the five of us into the clean white hallway outside. Simon led the way, and I kept the others wandering behind me as spares. I collected all their weapons on my lap, thankful I had had one day's worth of arms training when I played Cop #7 on the set of *X-Men*. I couldn't have told you what kind of guns they were, but I knew which end would spit lead should it need to.

We unhurriedly shuffled to the elevator and waited while it rose to our level. A male nurse stepped out as the doors opened, saw us before him, and found himself gutted and decapitated before he realized that this wasn't his floor.

I couldn't swing the chair close enough to reach the buttons, and ordered the doctor to press level thirty-six. The good doctor had lost a lot of accuracy in his aim, and I had to have him mash his palm over every button, praising him with a *good job!* after every successful depression. We stopped at every floor on the way down. I kept a gun leveled at the door for the entire trip, but the complex was hardly fully manned, and we saw not a soul as we descended.

Sofa, as much as it is possible for a cat, looked pleased to see me.

She jumped into my lap and purred mightily as I scratched her behind the ears and on the sweet spot between her eyes. She wasn't as pleased as I loaded her into her carrier, but I threw a few treats inside to keep her content. I directed Simon to carry the cage, and had the soldiers take point for our trip to the surface.

The doctor was more effective this time; we stopped at only five extra floors. I had to shoot a mercenary taking a cigarette break on level seventeen, and I allowed my soldiers to make short work of an unlucky trio of scientists on level five. Unbidden by me, one soldier ceased his munchings long enough to offer me a chunk of thigh.

Level one. The doors opened to the medical bay, each bed still occupied by one of my cousins in various states of disrepair. Doctors and nurses tended to the corpses, hacking at bone, withdrawing fluids, carving abstract sculptures from brains, not bothering to look up, not willing to admit that they weren't learning anything new, just going through the motions, another day at the bloody office, unaware that each of their charges had ceased its struggle and had swiveled its head in my direction.

I had the doctor walk calmly forward between the beds toward the far doors where two gunmen lounged, bored, on either side. They quietly mumbled to each other across the doorway, seeing only another doctor come to check on his patients, barely noting the slight stumble in his stride, the abnormal crook of his neck. *Nothing out of the ordinary here,* I thought, *just keep doing your jobs, please ignore the enormous wound decorating my throat.*

Simon remained at my rear, shielding Sofa with his body. I waited until the doctor was a few yards away from the men and then reached out, sensing the filaments of my mental energy float through the room until they each fastened to an awaiting ghoul.

Attack, I pushed out at them. *Rise up, kiddies. By God, let's give them what for.*

And the room was anarchy.

The doc was the first to strike, pulling down the gunman on the left before he could offer more than an *erk!* of surprise. As the other yelled a curse, fumbling at his holster, I fired, one gun in each hand, emptying the clips, missing far more than I hit, but enough bullets finding their marks to bring him down with two belly punctures.

Meanwhile, each bed-ridden zombie had grabbed onto anything moving nearby. As the medicos found themselves suddenly snagged onto their invalids, a few caught by articles of clothing, a few already in the process of dying, my two soldiers swarmed forward and began snapping at anything with a pulse they could latch their teeth onto. I let Simon put Sofa down and join in the fray while I watched my relatives do what they did best, a happy parent watching his children jump around the jungle gym.

When the red dust settled and the only sound was of mastication, I wheeled my way to the nearest upright table and picked up a scalpel. I rode about the room, slicing at the bonds of my rotting brethren. As I freed each corpse, a crazy impulse took me and I yelled, "I am Spartacus!" at the top of my lungs, mentally asking each unfettered hostage to do the same as I giggled, the tethers of my sanity stretched near to snapping. They each moved their lips, but only Simon managed to inflate his lungs, gurgling *Aw em Splartkus!* over and over in a voice like dead leaves scuttling across pavement.

Finally, I had a platoon of twenty-seven volunteers (with more soon to rise), each pledging allegiance to the cause. I sent them on ahead to the hangar to raise some well-deserved havoc while Simon and I stayed behind. *Eat hearty*, I thought, as confused screams and sporadic gunfire filtered in through the doorway.

Simon held Sofa's cage up in front of me while I opened it to let Sofa slink out into my lap, slightly put out but no worse for wear. I held her collar, and as the echoes of warfare died down I drove us forward, pushing Simon forward in case there were still pockets of resistance.

I needn't have worried. My troops had made short work of anything that breathed, as the lake of blood that filled the room attested. Simon picked up a few heaping handfuls of entrails to nibble at while he led us on. I steered around the bulk of the slaughter to avoid getting my wheels caught up in any intestinal mud puddles.

Beyond the open hangar doors lay freedom. Outside, the sun was beginning to set, and the sky past the mountains foretold a night of purple beauty.

"One more thing," I promised Sofa. "Then we go."

We pushed into the Chapel.

Save for the zombies, the room was uninhabited, its guards having fled deeper into the complex or outside, becoming part of the buffet. It was silent, all eyes on me.

I looked out for the only pair I cared about.

Time enough for one last act of mercy.

I piloted my chair down the track to the controls and sent the lift down into the crowd. Ordering the zombies to stay clear, I asked Duane to step on, and elevated his salivating remains until he was standing next to me. It looked as if he had not eaten since reanimation. His skin was beginning to spoil. Patches had loosened and fallen off, and one eye had rolled back completely in his head. The other, milky with scratches, looked around the room, never settling, searching for food. But the gobbets of mind lodged in the crater of his skull still performed their tasks, covered with grime yet fresh and new as that of newborn children. His foggy appeals for food scratched at the walls of my consciousness.

Below me, I sought out Craig and Samantha, finding them wandering the far end of the pit, looking for anything to gnaw on. I threw them out my deepest apologies as they each looked up from their searches and watched me with uncomprehending eyes. I couldn't free them, and there was no way I was a good enough shot to even try to give them release through a well-placed bullet.

Then, the only person I had ever truly cared about in death and I slowly meandered from the Chapel and toward the setting sun, joined in my lap by the being I had the longest relationship with outside of my parents. Simon stalked his way behind us.

"This is it, Duane," I said, nudging him past the slavering hordes of fellow zombies and out into the open air. His response was a hushed groan, his mind vacant of any thoughts save food. I ignored the request. I was selfish to the end, and didn't want my last few moments with Duane to consist of his feasting on human flesh.

"This is the end. For real this time. You wanted to be with me when the time came."

We worked our way over the paved road and into the brush. I turned us about to look at the sun as it clocked out for the evening, its final rays peeking out over the range, burning away the last of the day with detonations of color I could barely discern.

I took his hand and kissed it.

"I never thanked you for your kindness, Duane. When I first met you. I thought you were an idiot. I never told you that." I smiled, holding on to his fingers as he swayed. "I was so stupid. Don't get me wrong. You weren't much of an actor. But you were a good friend."

I asked him to kneel. Simon took up a position behind him.

"This is the best I can do, Duane. If you are in there, somewhere. Please know that I pray this will release you."

I looked away from his vacant eye and stared at the sun, its rim barely visible over the horizon. Dots of starlight began to poke through the darkening sky.

"I love you," I said, and gave Simon the command. As I forced myself to stare at the last few glints of light, Simon efficiently scraped out the last scraps of Duane and swallowed them. A few meager surges of leftover consciousness escaped Simon's belly, wondering when food would ever come, dissipating into a low hum, and then silence as digestive juices eroded them into nothingness.

Duane's shell crumpled to the dirt.

I willed myself to cry. Just one solitary tear. Anything to mark the occasion.

Nothing.

I picked up Sofa and hugged her as best I could to my chest. I had done what I could, but this was as good as it was going to get. At least she wouldn't die alone in a room. This gave her a chance.

"No cat daycamp for you, babe," I whispered in her ear. "Go on. Do what cats do best."

I placed her on the ground. She looked at me, confused at the sweeping panorama spread out before her after years of being an indoor cat. Then, yards away, a lone gopher popped its head out from its burrow for a peek. Using instincts she didn't know she had, Sofa lowered herself to the ground, flattened back her ears, and slunk off to feast on the freshest dinner she'd had in ages.

Behind me in the hangar, I heard the unfocused shamblings of my relatives, now finished their frenzy and already desiring new prey. I wondered at the prudence of letting them go on. There wasn't a soul around for them to bite; if the planet was lucky, they'd likely scuffle off into the desert where the Utah sun would bake them into jerky. But perhaps an unlucky nomad would stumble onto one, and the bloodline would continue. There was always going to be a chance of survival.

Doubtless there were larger armaments hidden within the compound; given enough time, I could rummage around the levels until I found a stash of explosives, a bazooka, say, and wipe the whole family from existence.

But I was at the end. I'd let them be, and leave it to fate.

I wondered if I'd wake up on the other side of reality.

I wondered if the leviathans were disappointed in me.

I hoped they didn't hold grudges.

I gave Simon the order, ending my command.

Up in the brush, Sofa bounded onto a gopher hole, her rear waggling fiercely in the air as she groped her paws into the ground.

My cat's ass.

Please let that be the image I go out on.

Simon ripped me from my husk, squeezed me between his fingers, and tossed me out into the desert.

Acceptance

Fuck.

Aw fuck, I'm still here.

Can't even get my death right. Not even the second one.

Simon threw me into the desert all right. He also left my eyestalk attached.

My fault, I suppose.

I lay there for a few days, watching whatever happened to amble on past my unblinking eye.

A few gophers, a snake.

A few sets of feet, aimless in direction.

Sofa, once, looking trimmer. Going feral was definitely her thing.

After a great time, a coyote came by and mercifully gnawed my sight away.

I am not afraid now.

I miss Duane.
   I miss Mom, weirdly.

Whatever this infection is, it's pitiless.

Not until all the pieces of my brain are ground into dust and fed to the four winds will I find release.

Should have found another way.

I just didn't want to be eaten.

Was that wrong?

I never did see the gods. If they're out there, they're ignoring me. Serves me right.

Right now, I'm a gray lump on a dusty cement road, covered in dirt.

Or I'm in a jar. Or many jars. Or a baggie. Shoveled up and tagged for later examination. Someone *must* have come by eventually.

Maybe I'm in a belly right now. A desert rattlesnake slithered up and gulped me down. Or that coyote snagged me in her teeth and brought me to her den, a delicious delicacy for her cubs. I mean, how often would they be treated to Mennonite food?

I have no conception beyond that which is me. I thought I had a perception of movement, I had a brief bout of excitement that I was being picked up and tossed about, but I may have been kidding myself.

Like Dixon told me, I never was one for introspection, but it looks like that's all I have left to do. That and rerun movies I've watched over and over again in my mind. I've already replayed *The Godfather* twice. Good stuff. Pacino was so cool.

I wonder if I learned anything from all this.

How long is this going to last?

How long is eternity?

I think I'm going to find out.

COREY REDEKOP has held down many careers in his short time on this planet: actor, waiter, tree planter, disc jockey, cameraman, editor, lawyer (almost), and now the odd employment triangle of publicist/librarian/author. Any day now, he's sure he'll figure out what he wants to do with his life. Probably optometry. His debut novel, *Shelf Monkey*, is either a work of insane genius or an intolerable left-wing screed, depending on which review you read. You've likely never heard of it. That's okay. A self-deprecating individual blessed with rugged good looks and naturally infused with the scent of mountain pine, Corey abides in Fredericton, New Brunswick, where he spends a lot of time making himself look good on paper. Find him online at CoreyRedekop.ca and on Twitter @CoreyRedekop. Or he'll find you.

At ECW Press, we want you to enjoy this book in whatever format you like, whenever you like. Leave your print book at home and take the eBook to go! Purchase the print edition and receive the eBook free. Just send an email to ebook@ecwpress.com and include:

- the book title
- the name of the store where you purchased it
- your receipt number
- your preference of file type: PDF or ePub?

A real person will respond to your email with your eBook attached. And thanks for supporting an independently owned Canadian publisher with your purchase!